Benjamin Renn

The Big Bad FOX

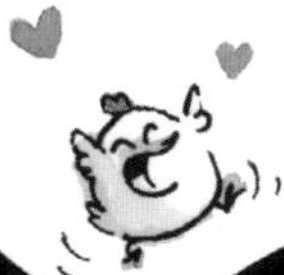

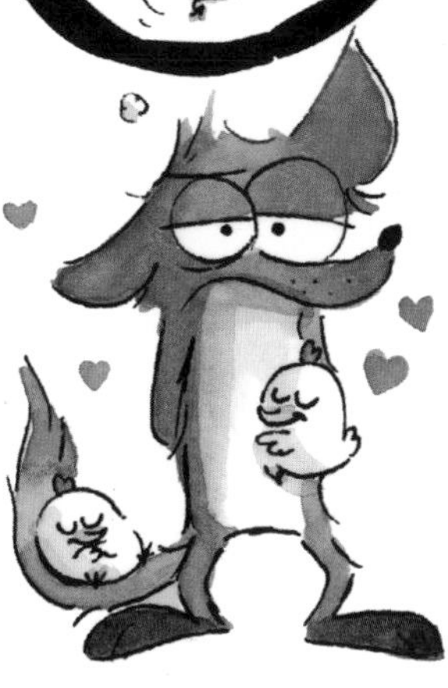

First Second
New York

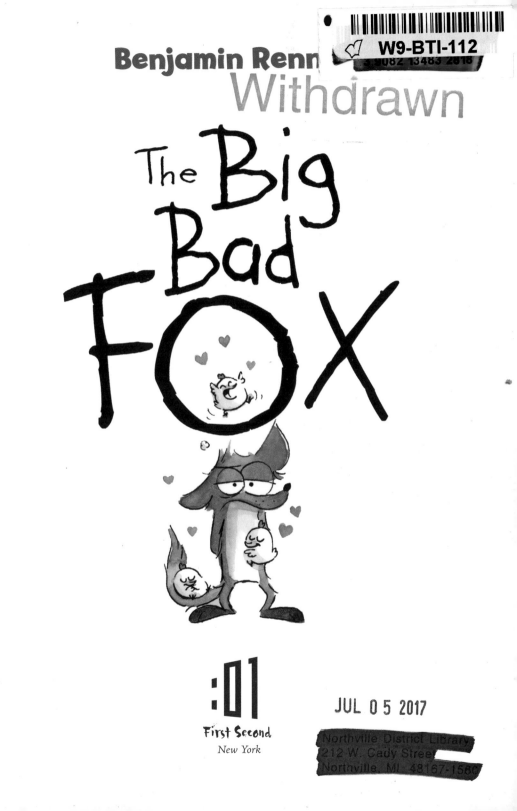

First Second

English translation by Joe Johnson
English translation © 2017 by Roaring Brook Press,
a division of Holtzbrinck Publishing Holdings Limited Partnership

Published by First Second
First Second is an imprint of Roaring Brook Press,
a division of Holtzbrinck Publishing Holdings Limited Partnership
175 Fifth Avenue, New York, New York 10010
All rights reserved

Library of Congress Control Number: 2016945555

ISBN: 978-1-62672-331-3

Our books may be purchased in bulk for promotional, educational, or business use.
Please contact your local bookseller or the Macmillan Corporate and Premium Sales Department
at (800) 221-7945 ext. 5442 or by e-mail at MacmillanSpecialMarkets@macmillan.com.

FIRST

EDITION

Originally published in 2015 by Éditions Delcourt as *Le grand méchant renard*
French edition © 2015 Éditions Delcourt
First American edition 2017
Book design by Chris Dickey
Printed in China by Toppan Leefung Printing Ltd., Dongguan City, Guangdong Province

10 9 8 7 6 5 4 3 2 1

To Pauline, Alex, and Evan,
the three little chicks who inspired this story

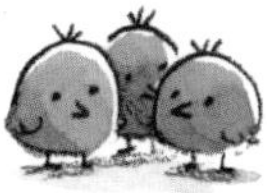

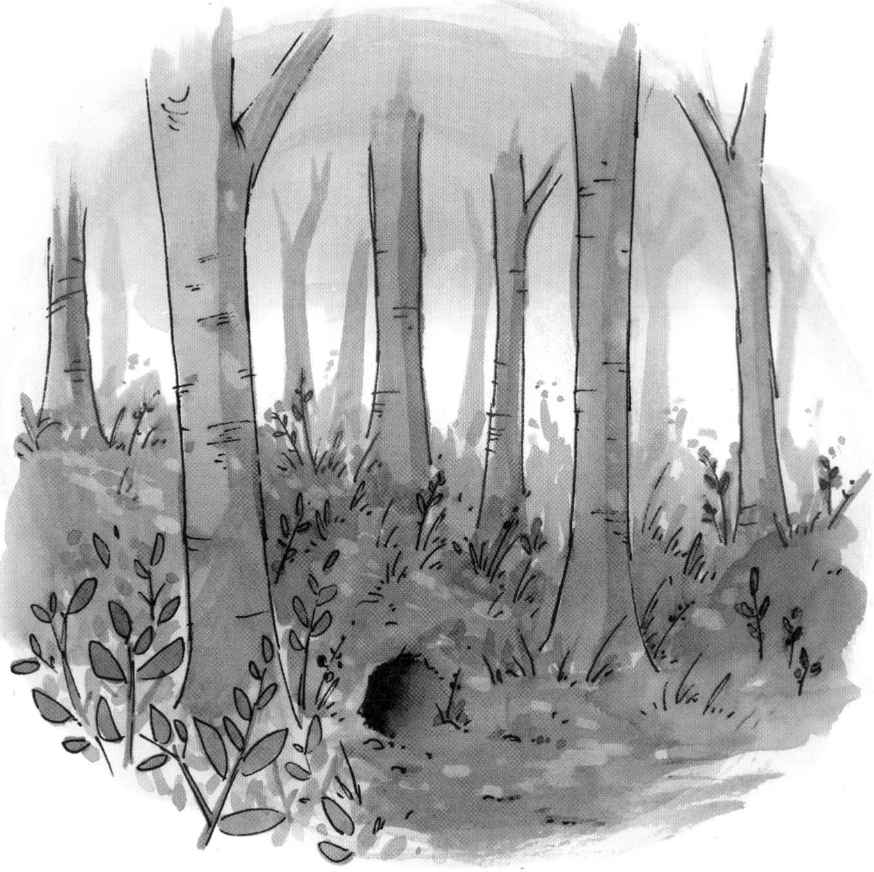

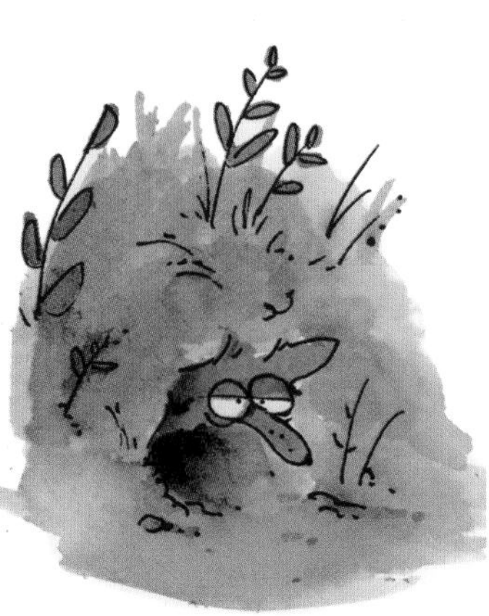

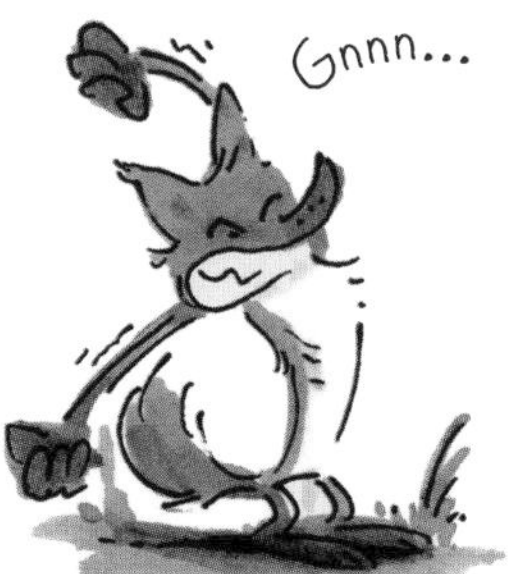
Gnnn...

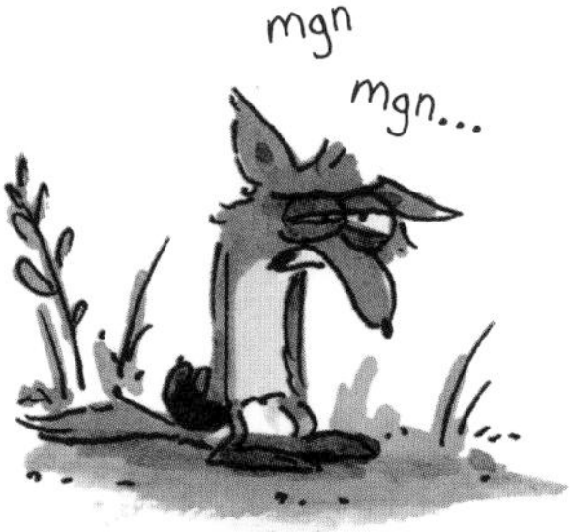
mgn
mgn...

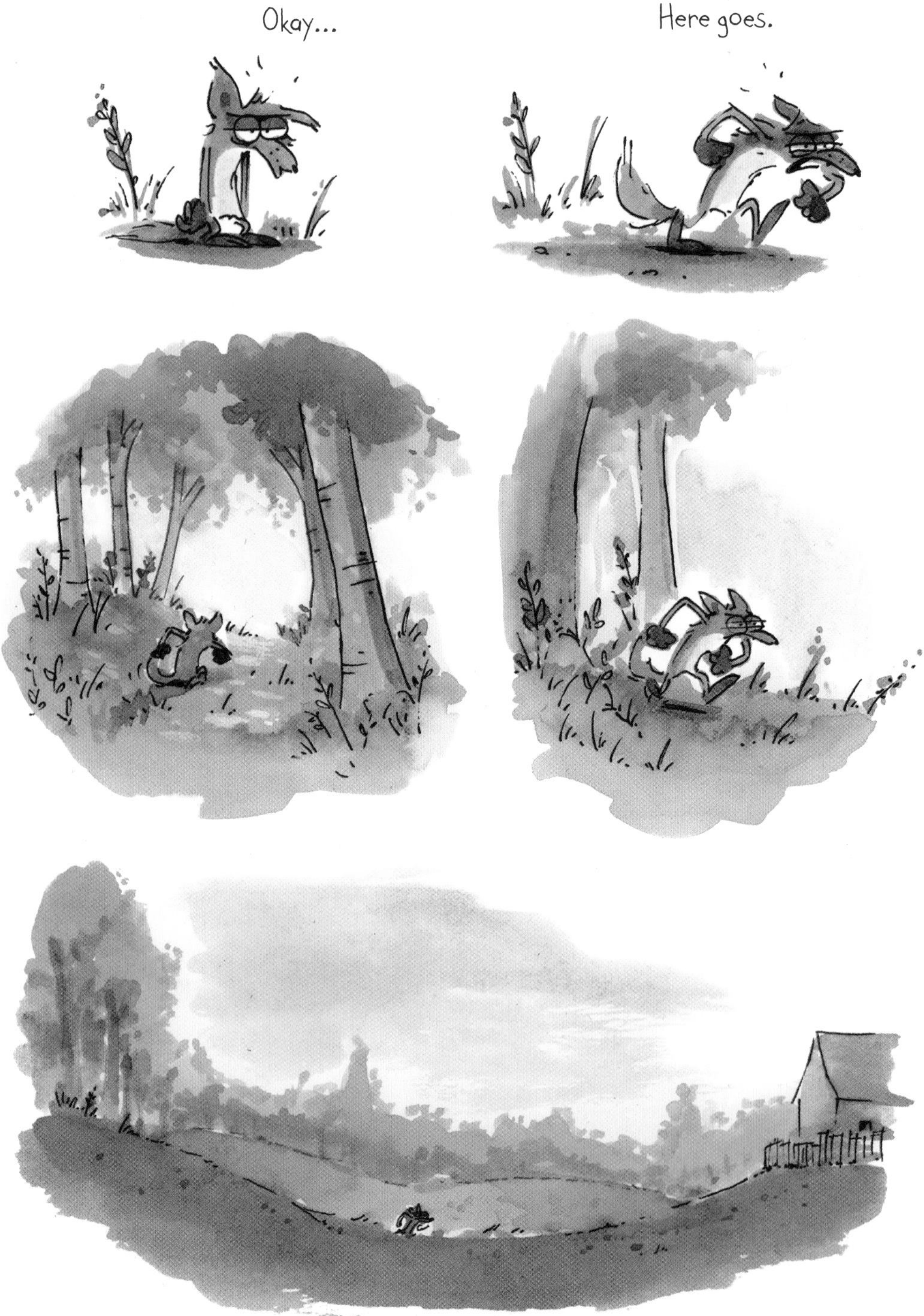
Okay...
Here goes.

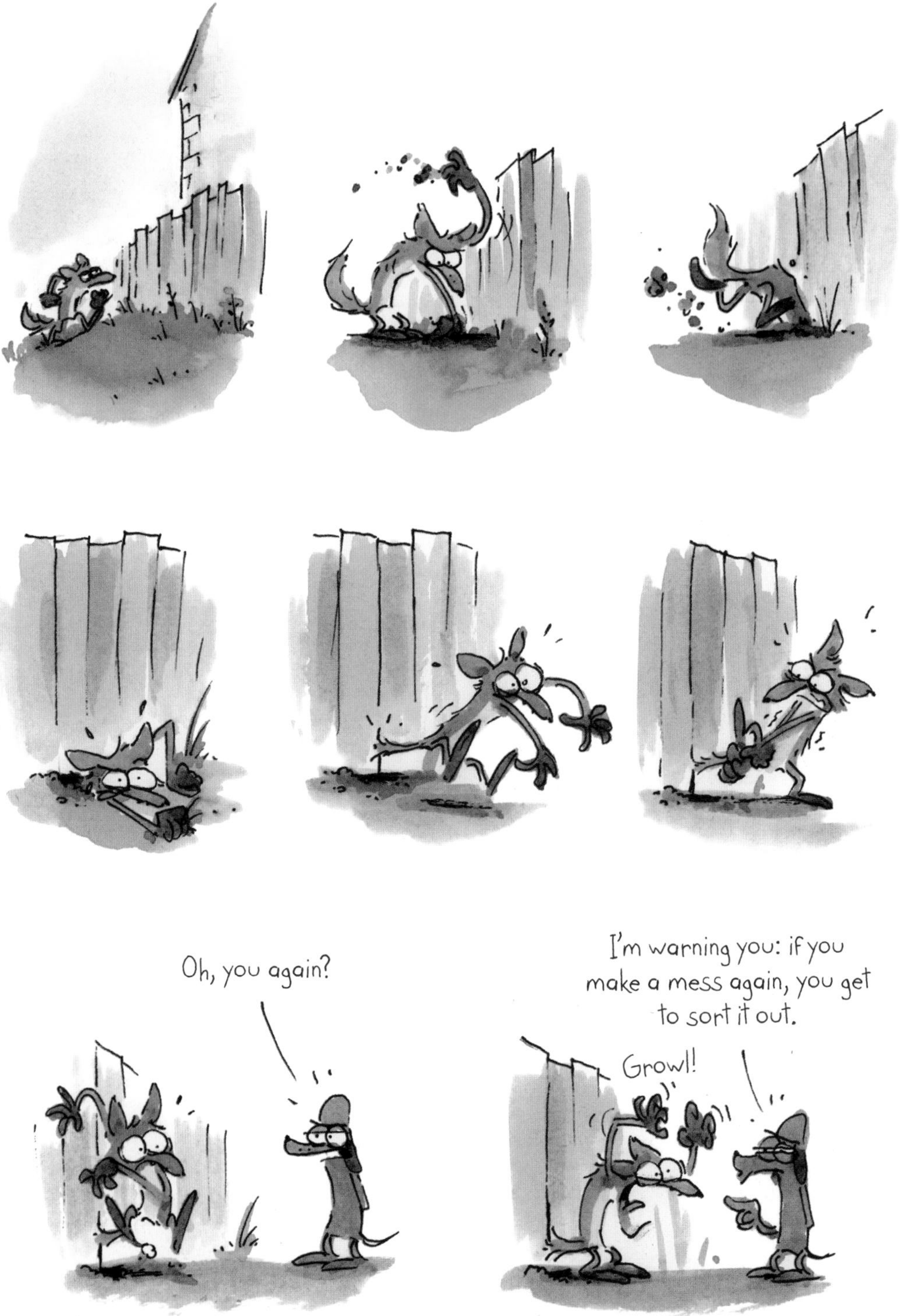
Oh, you again?
I'm warning you: if you make a mess again, you get to sort it out.
Growl!

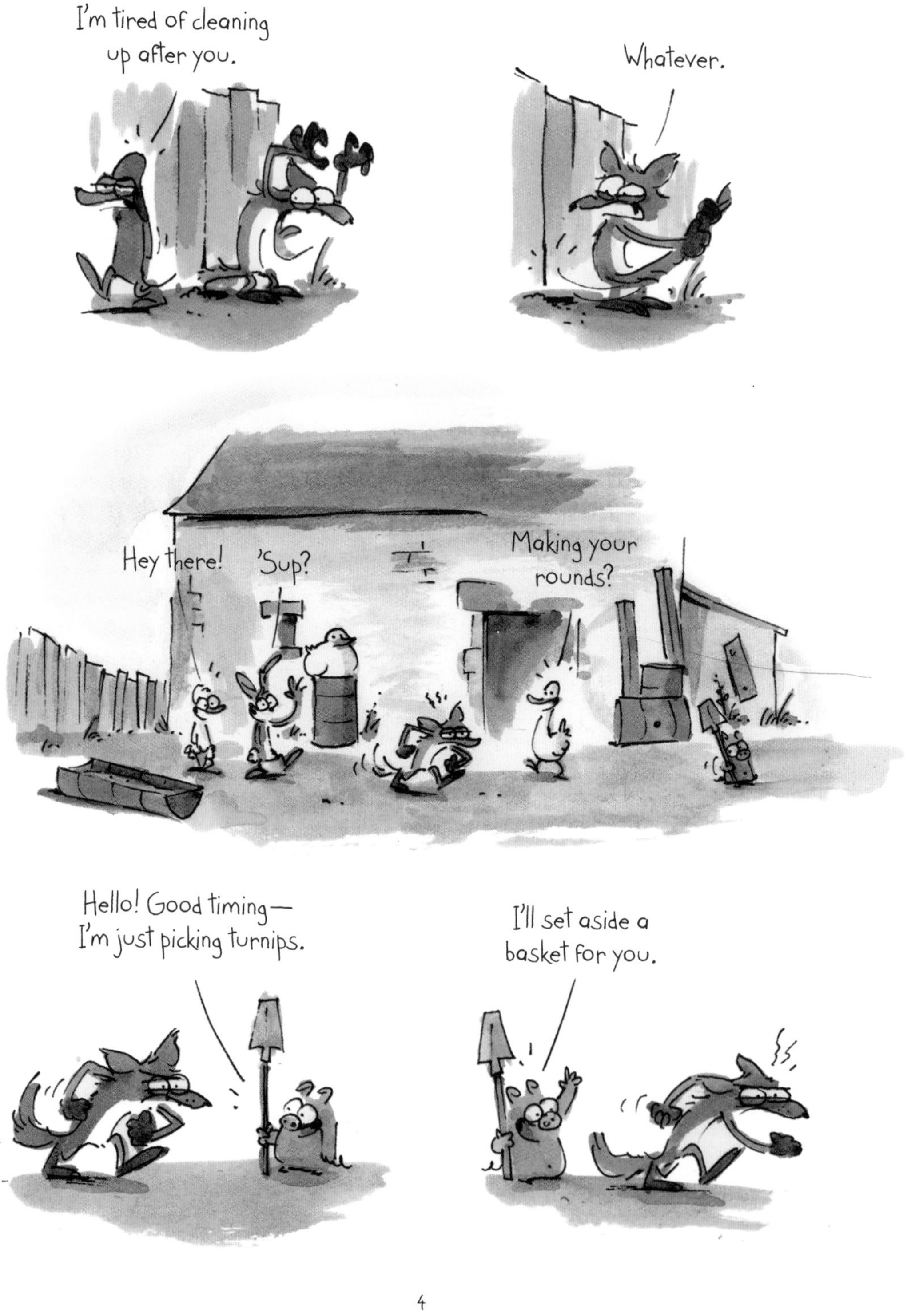

I'm tired of cleaning up after you.
Whatever.
Hey there!
'Sup?
Making your rounds?
Hello! Good timing—I'm just picking turnips.
I'll set aside a basket for you.

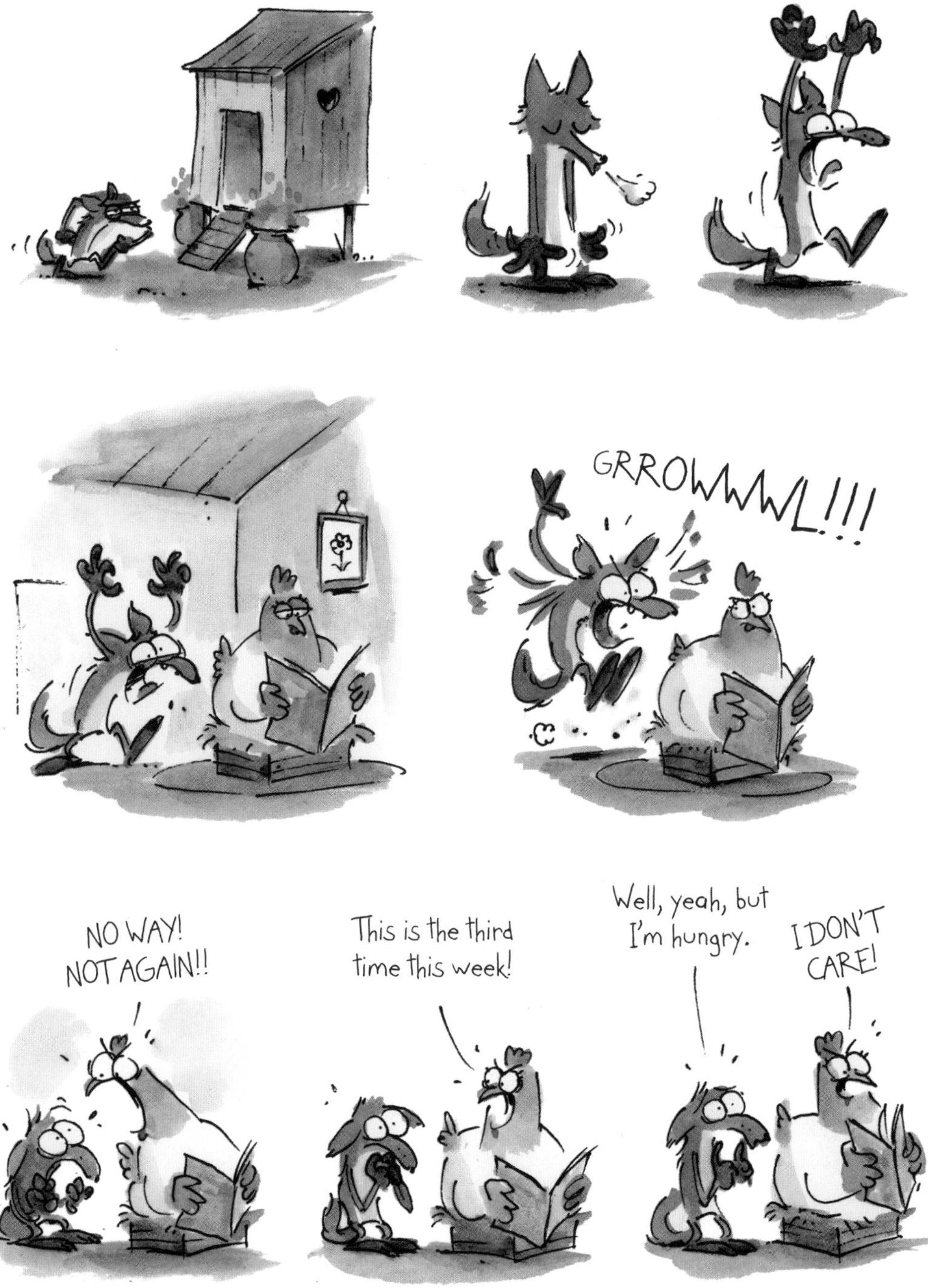
GRROWWWL!!!
NO WAY! NOTAGAIN!!
This is the third time this week!
Well, yeah, but I'm hungry.
I DON'T CARE!

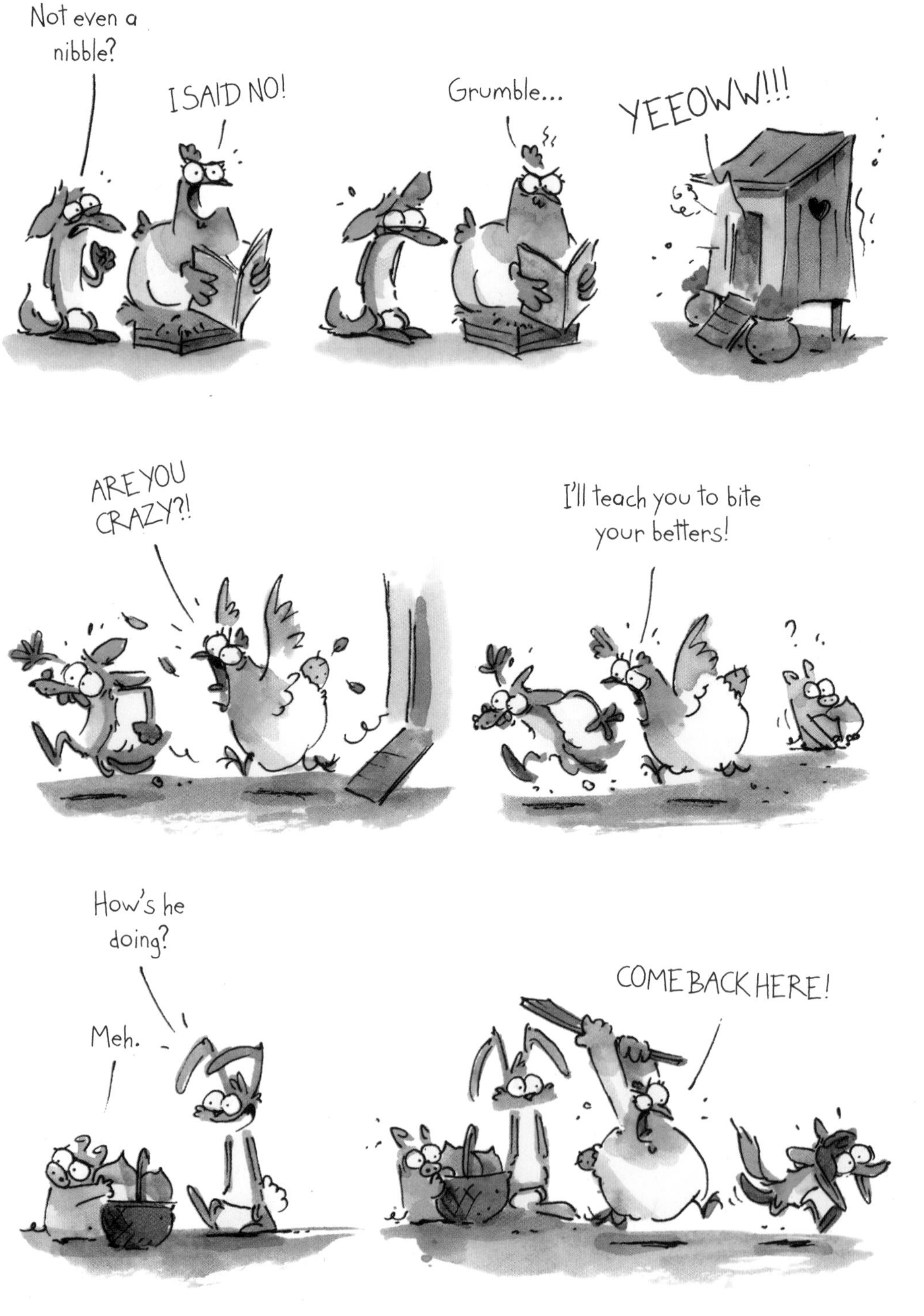

Not even a nibble?
I SAID NO!
Grumble...
YEEOWW!!!
ARE YOU CRAZY?!
I'll teach you to bite your betters!
How's he doing?
Meh.
COME BACK HERE!

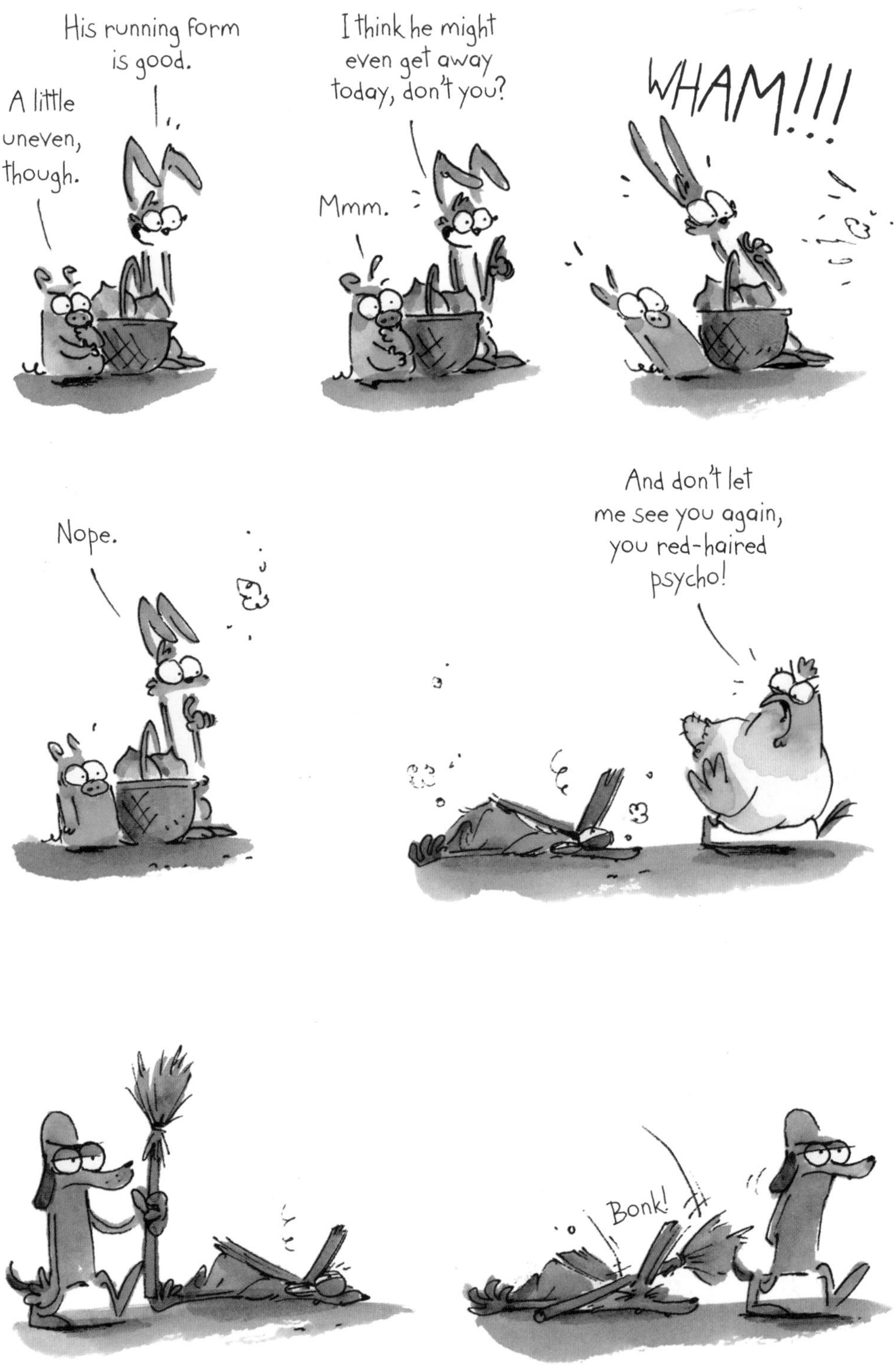
His running form is good.
A little uneven, though.
I think he might even get away today, don't you?
Mmm.
WHAM!!!
Nope.
And don't let me see you again, you red-haired psycho!
Bonk!

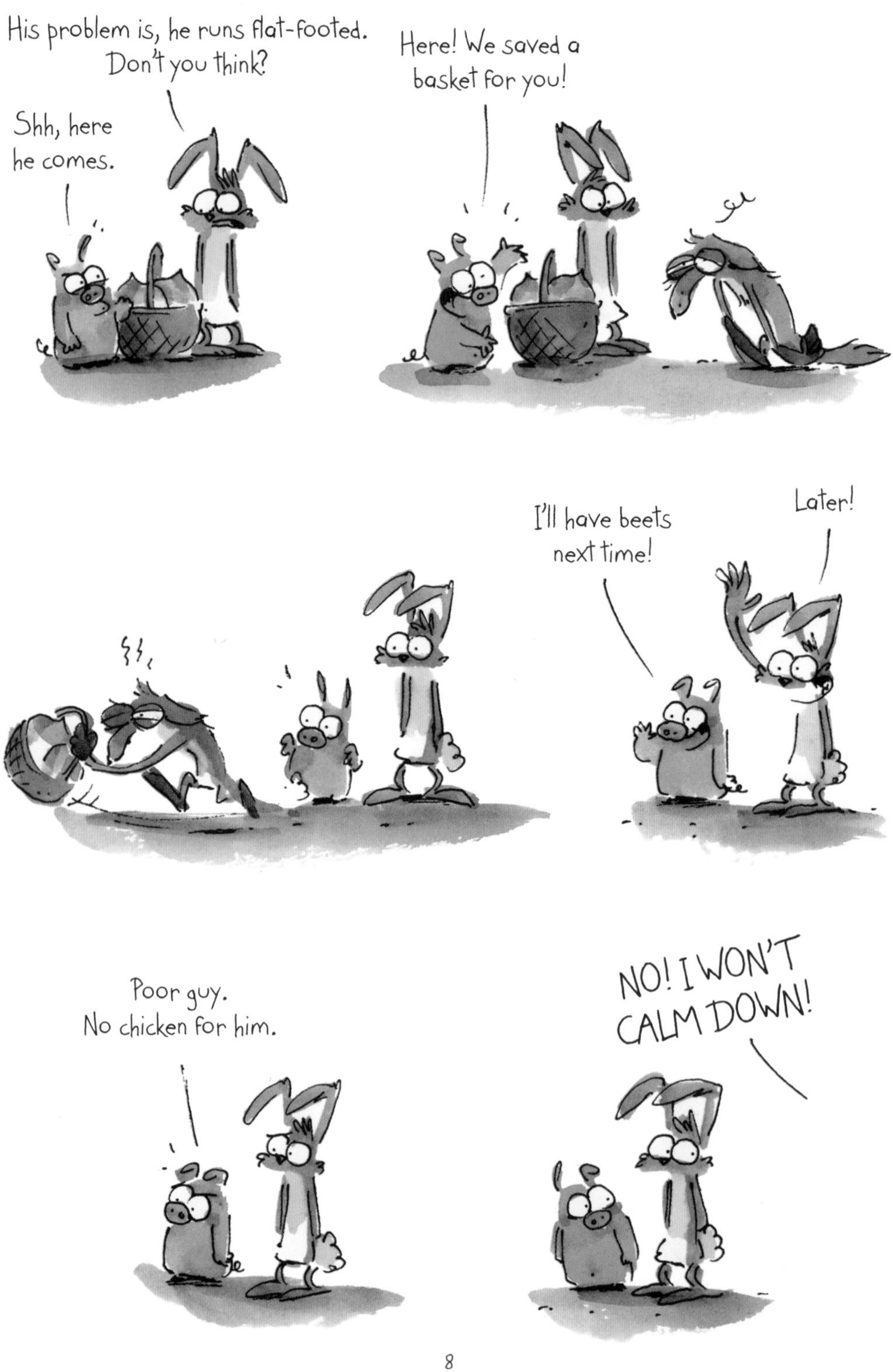
His problem is, he runs flat-footed. Don't you think?
Shh, here he comes.
Here! We saved a basket for you!
I'll have beets next time!
Later!
Poor guy. No chicken for him.
NO! I WON'T CALM DOWN!

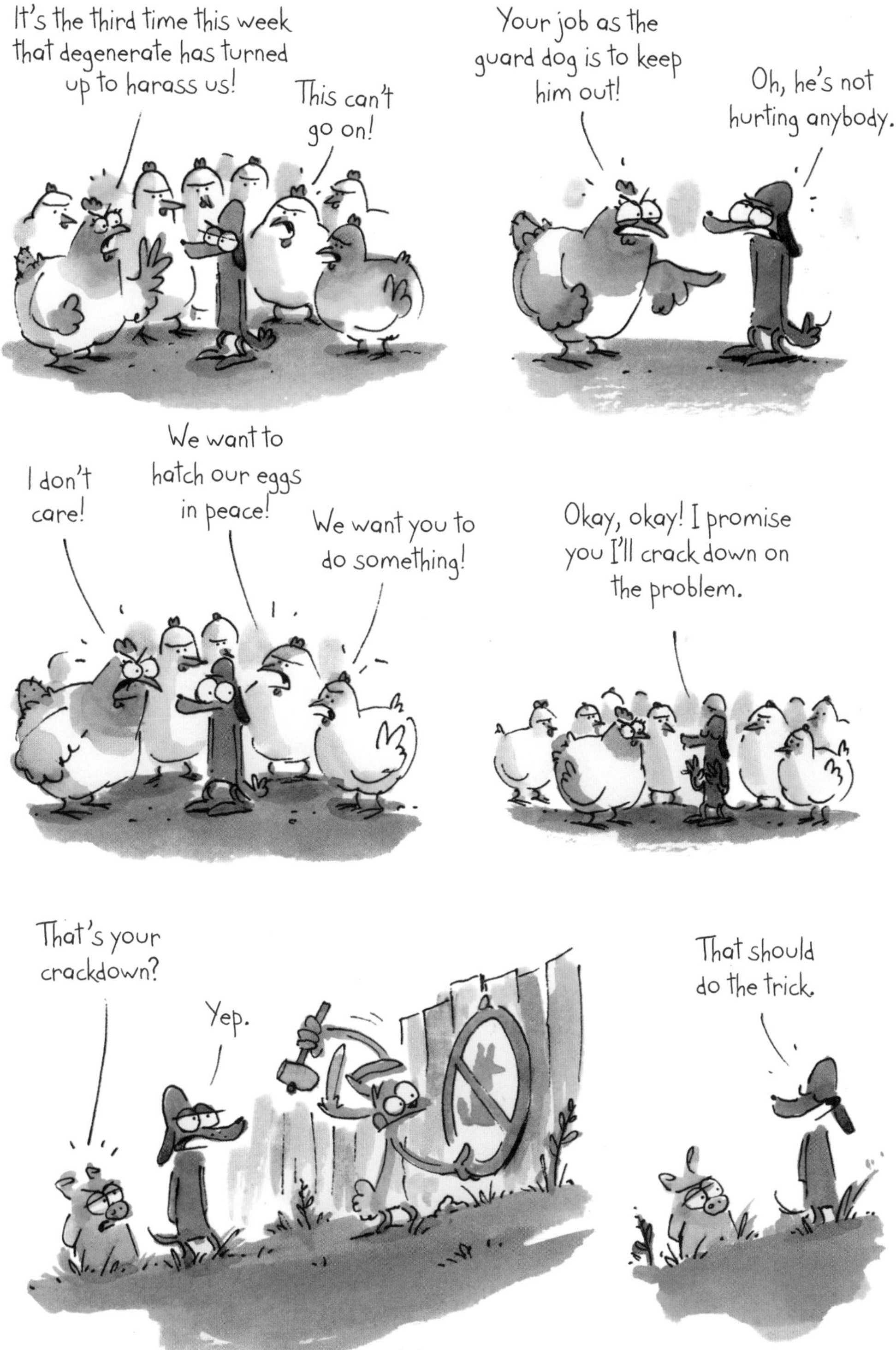
It's the third time this week that degenerate has turned up to harass us!
This can't go on!
Your job as the guard dog is to keep him out!
Oh, he's not hurting anybody.
I don't care!
We want to hatch our eggs in peace!
We want you to do something!
Okay, okay! I promise you I'll crack down on the problem.
That's your crackdown?
Yep.
That should do the trick.

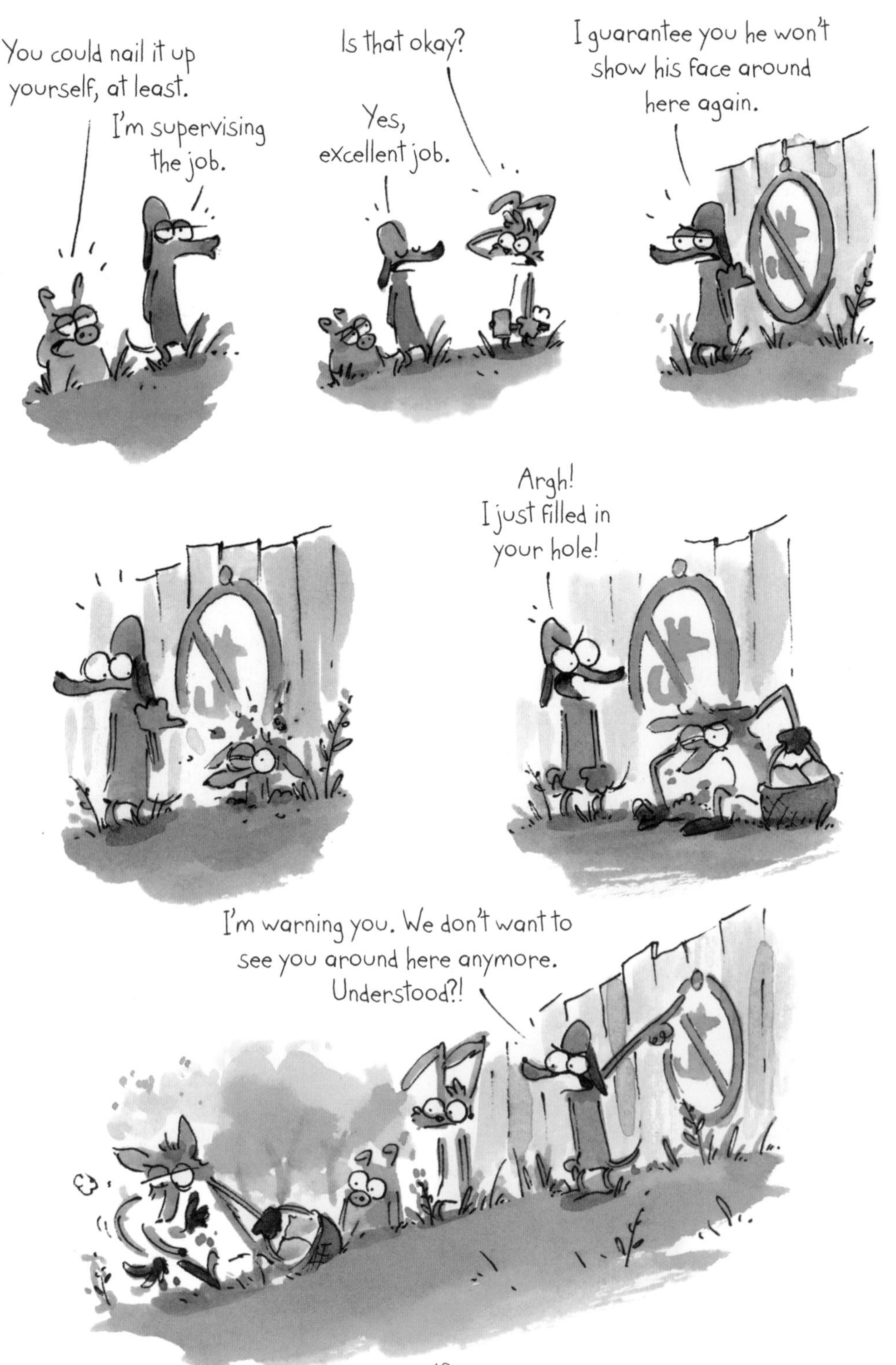
You could nail it up yourself, at least.
I'm supervising the job.
Yes, excellent job.
Is that okay?
I guarantee you he won't show his face around here again.
Argh! I just filled in your hole!
I'm warning you. We don't want to see you around here anymore. Understood?!

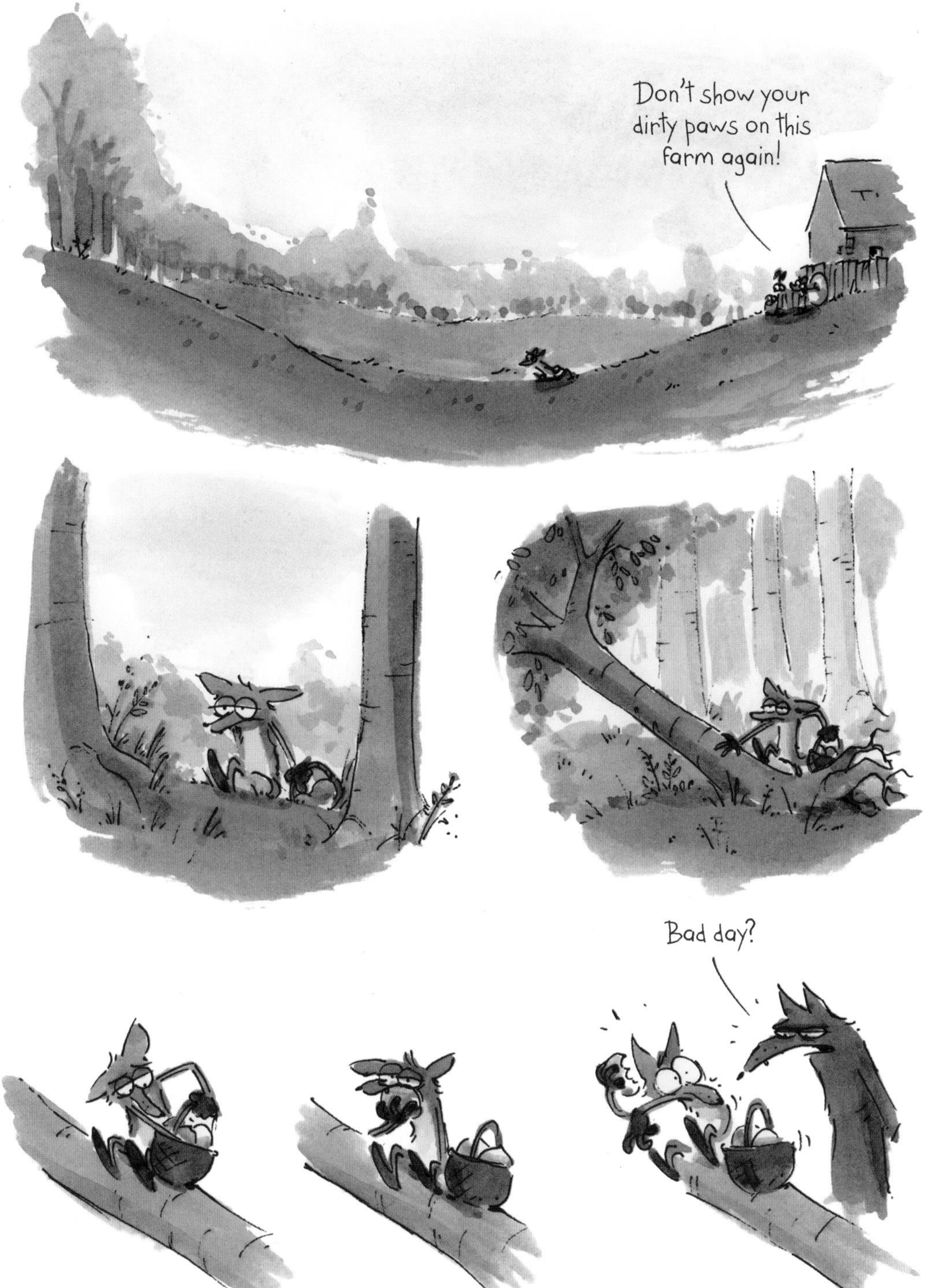
Don't show your dirty paws on this farm again!
Bad day?

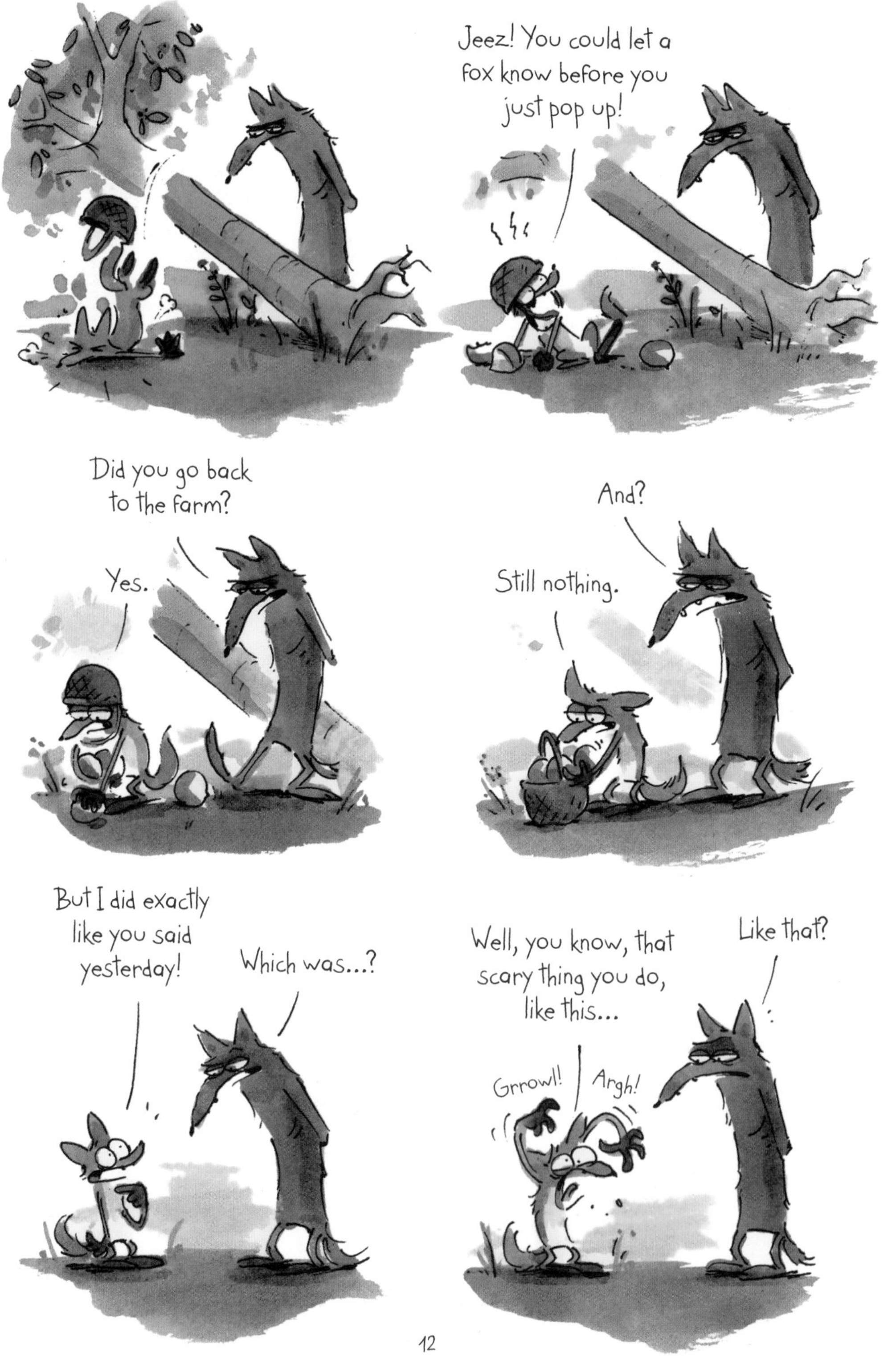
Jeez! You could let a fox know before you just pop up!
Did you go back to the farm?
Yes.
And?
Still nothing.
But I did exactly like you said yesterday!
Which was...?
Well, you know, that scary thing you do, like this...
Grrowl!
Argh!
Like that?

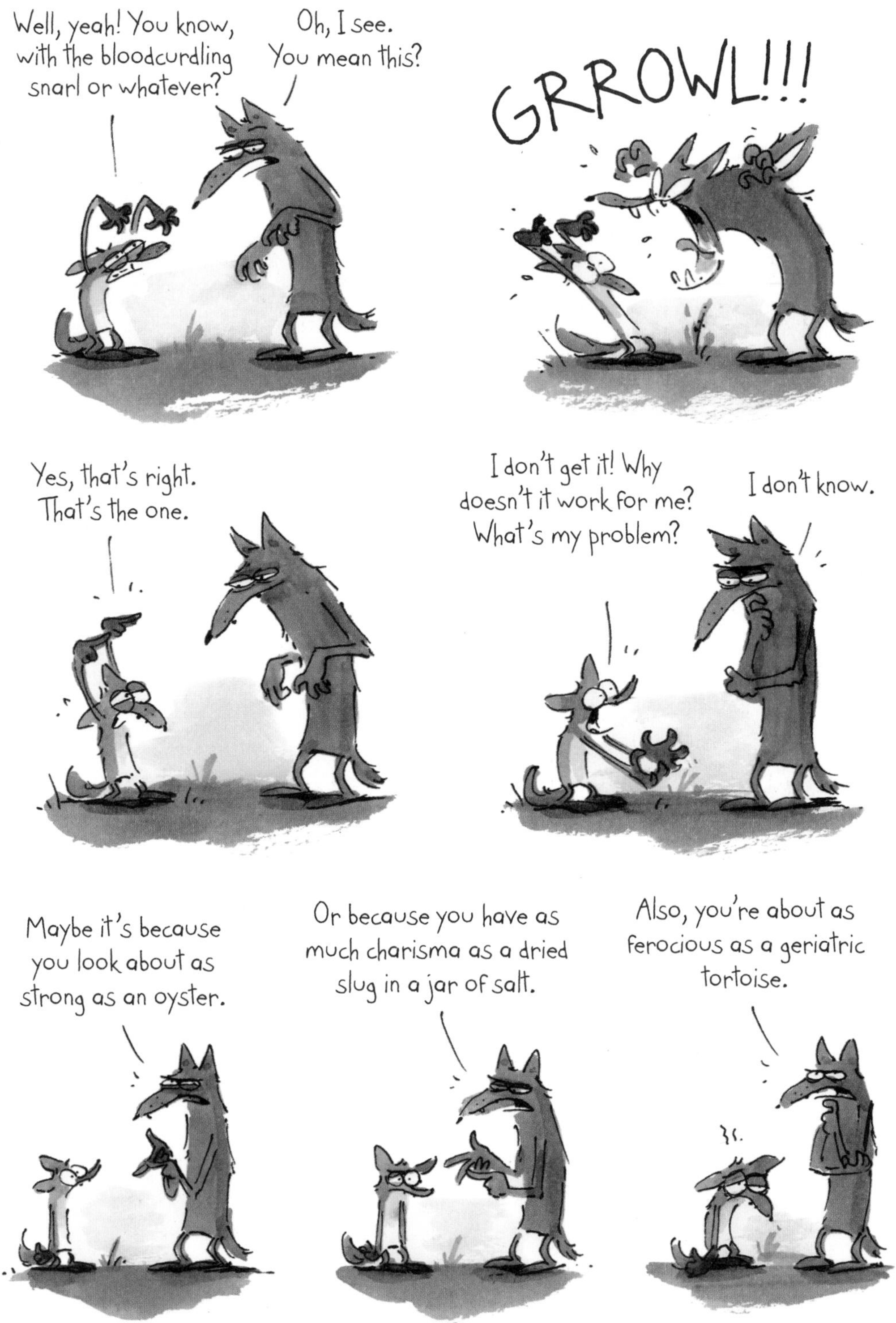
Well, yeah! You know, with the bloodcurdling snarl or whatever?
Oh, I see. You mean this?
GRROWL!!!
Yes, that's right. That's the one.
I don't get it! Why doesn't it work for me? What's my problem?
I don't know.
Maybe it's because you look about as strong as an oyster.
Or because you have as much charisma as a dried slug in a jar of salt.
Also, you're about as ferocious as a geriatric tortoise.

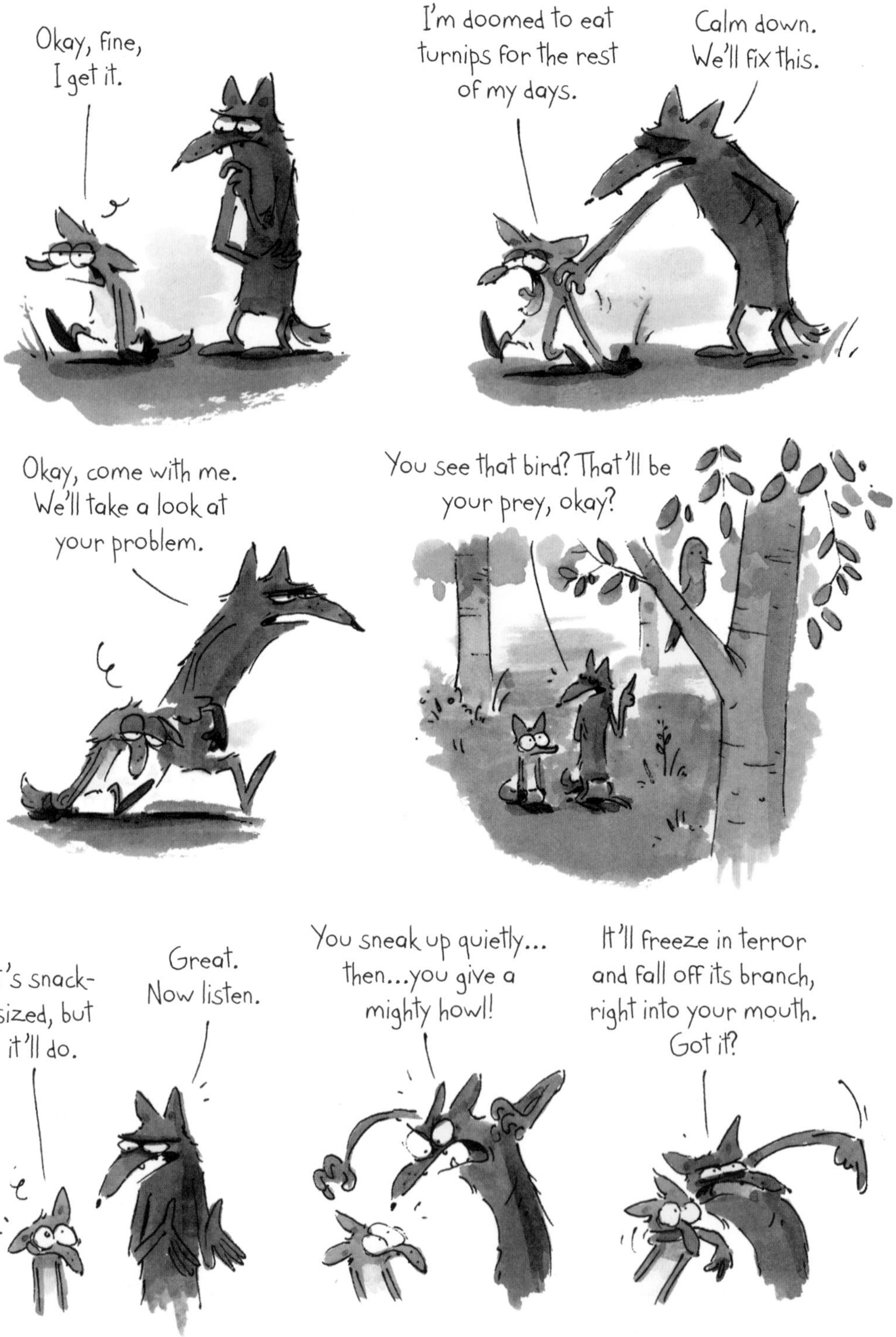
Okay, fine, I get it.
I'm doomed to eat turnips for the rest of my days.
Calm down. We'll fix this.
Okay, come with me. We'll take a look at your problem.
You see that bird? That'll be your prey, okay?
It's snack-sized, but it'll do.
Great. Now listen.
You sneak up quietly... then...you give a mighty howl!
It'll freeze in terror and fall off its branch, right into your mouth. Got it?

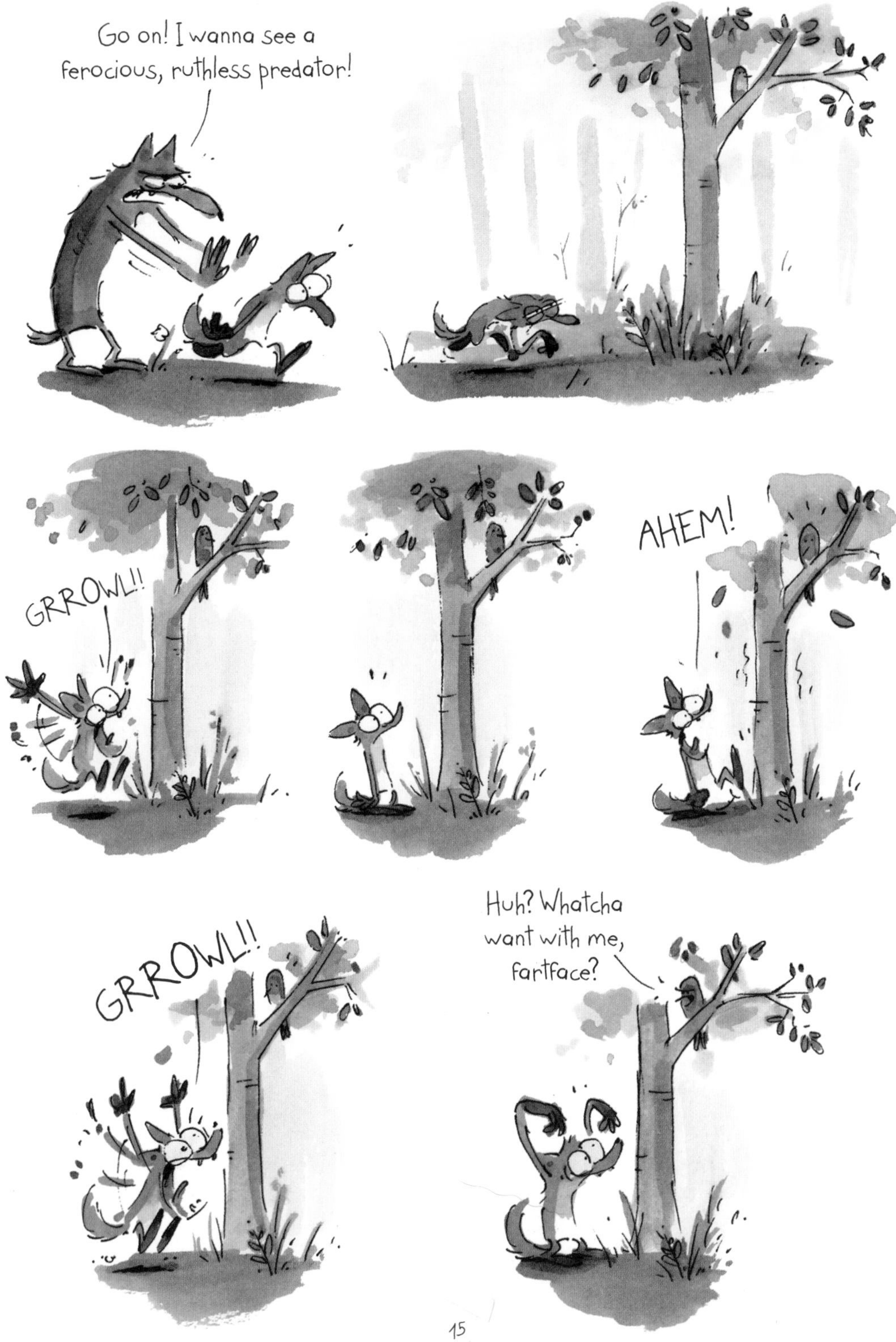
Go on! I wanna see a ferocious, ruthless predator!
GRROWL!!
AHEM!
GRROWL!!
Huh? Whatcha want with me, fartface?

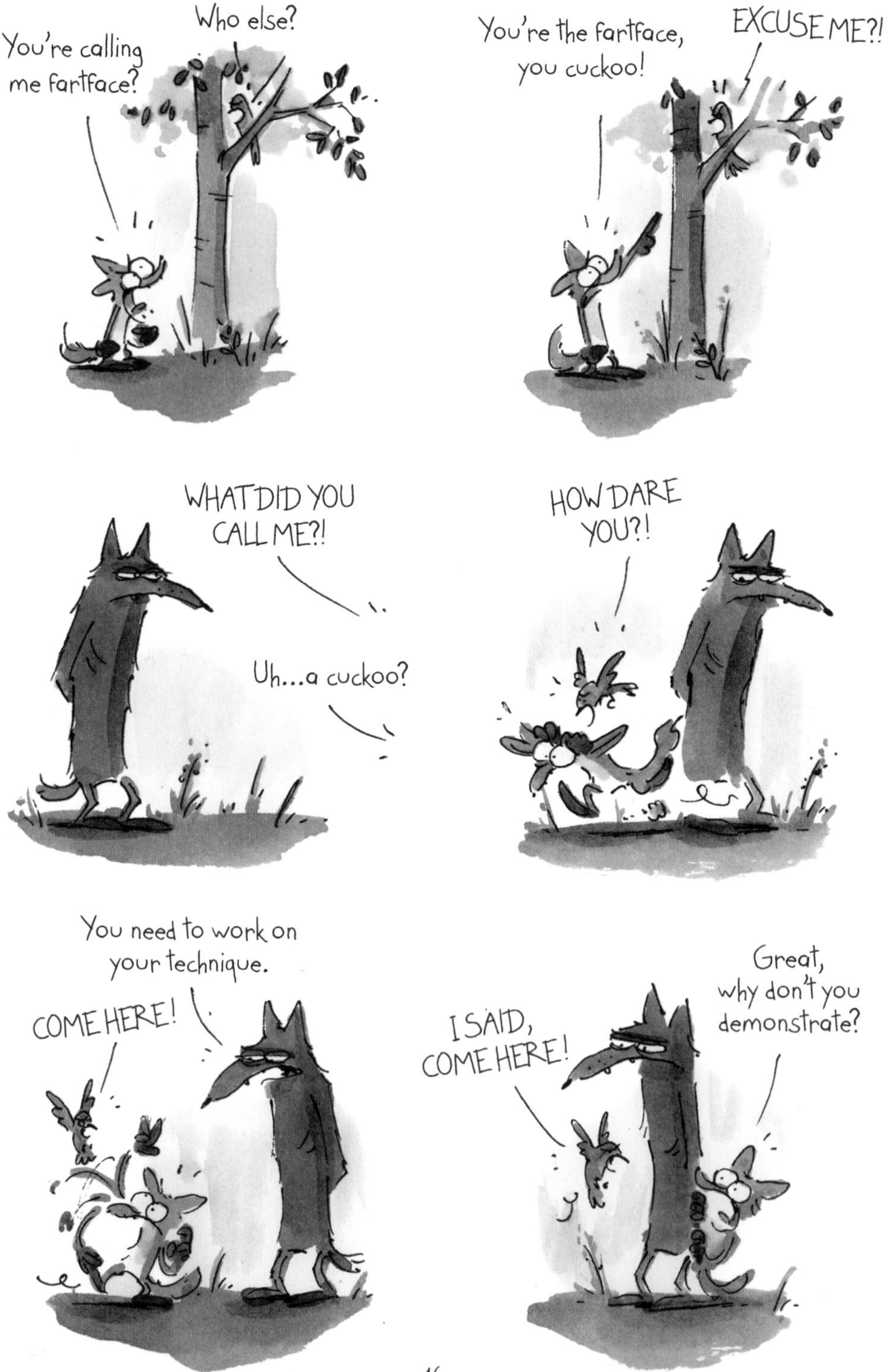
You're calling me fartface?
Who else?
You're the fartface, you cuckoo!
EXCUSE ME?!
WHAT DID YOU CALL ME?!
Uh...a cuckoo?
HOW DARE YOU?!
You need to work on your technique.
COME HERE!
I SAID, COME HERE!
Great, why don't you demonstrate?

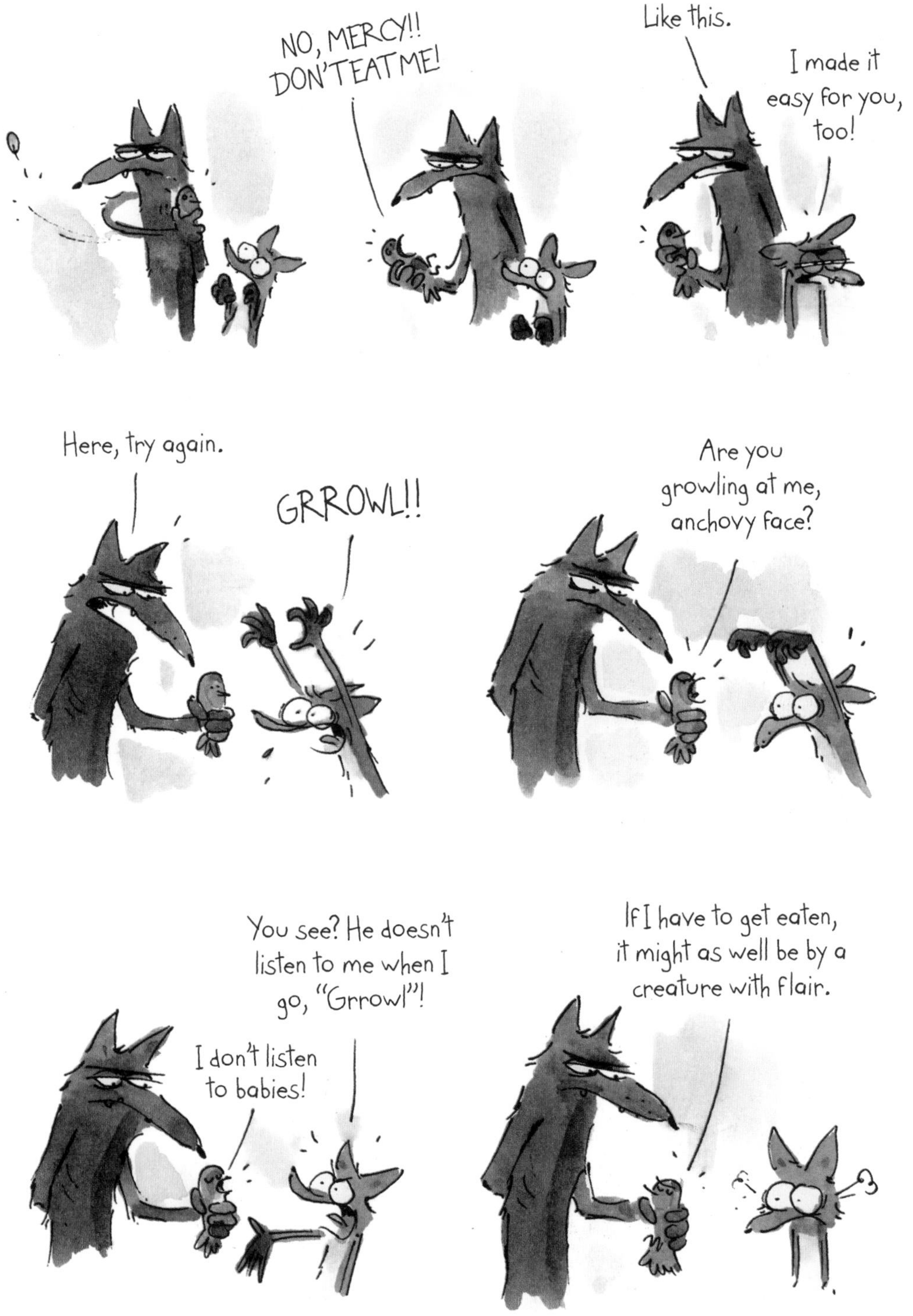
NO, MERCY!! DON'T EAT ME!
Like this.
I made it easy for you, too!
Here, try again.
GRROWL!!
Are you growling at me, anchovy face?
You see? He doesn't listen to me when I go, "Grrowl"!
I don't listen to babies!
If I have to get eaten, it might as well be by a creature with flair.

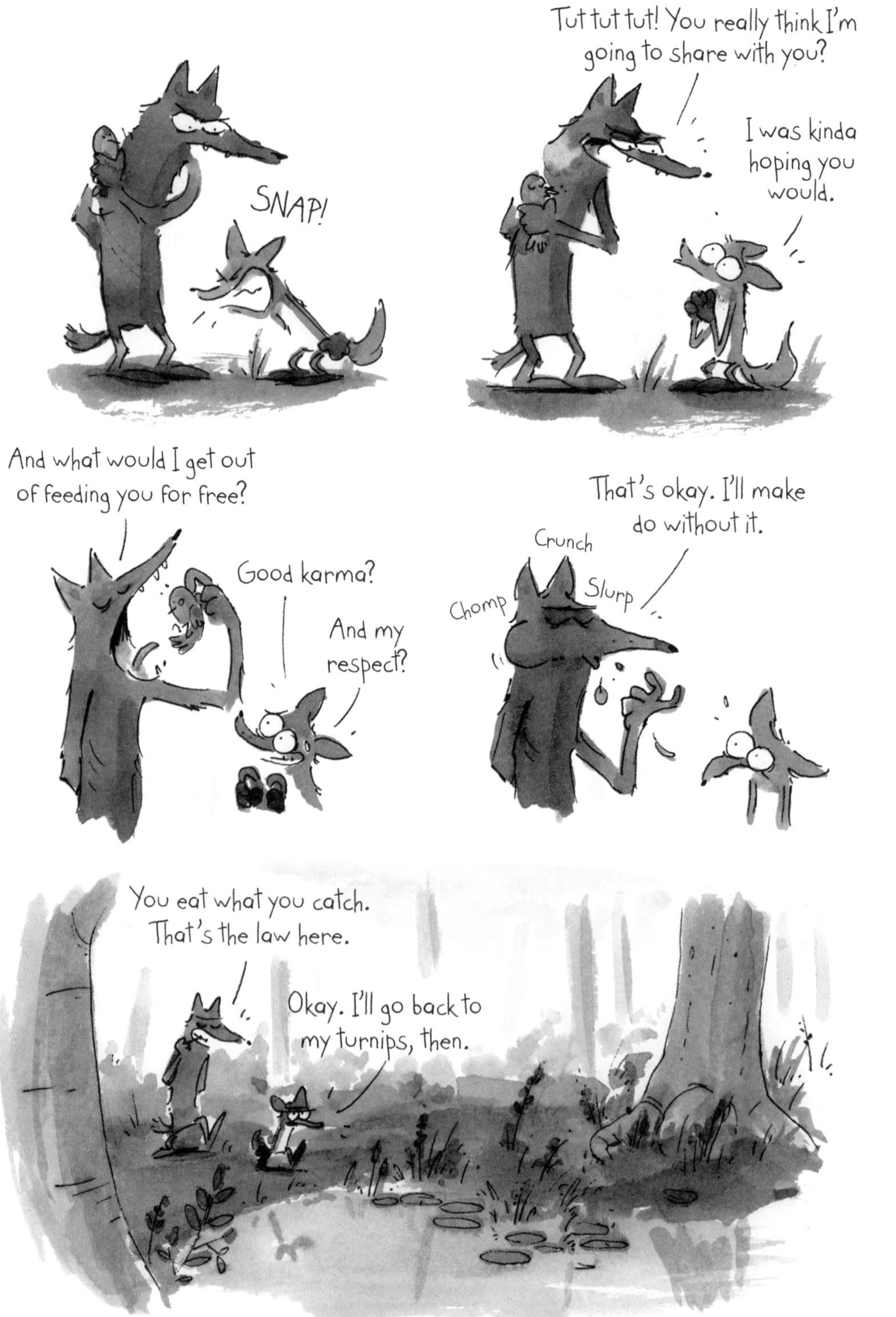
SNAP!
Tut tut tut! You really think I'm going to share with you?
I was kinda hoping you would.
And what would I get out of feeding you for free?
Good karma?
And my respect?
Crunch
Chomp
Slurp
That's okay. I'll make do without it.
You eat what you catch. That's the law here.
Okay. I'll go back to my turnips, then.

I can't even scare a sparrow.

The only dinner I could actually catch would be a chick barely out of the egg.

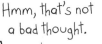

Hmm, that's not a bad thought.

What?

I have an idea that's going to pay off for both of us.

When you go to the farm, nobody's scared of you, right?

No, they pretty much just feel sorry for me.

But I can't approach the farm without raising the alarm.

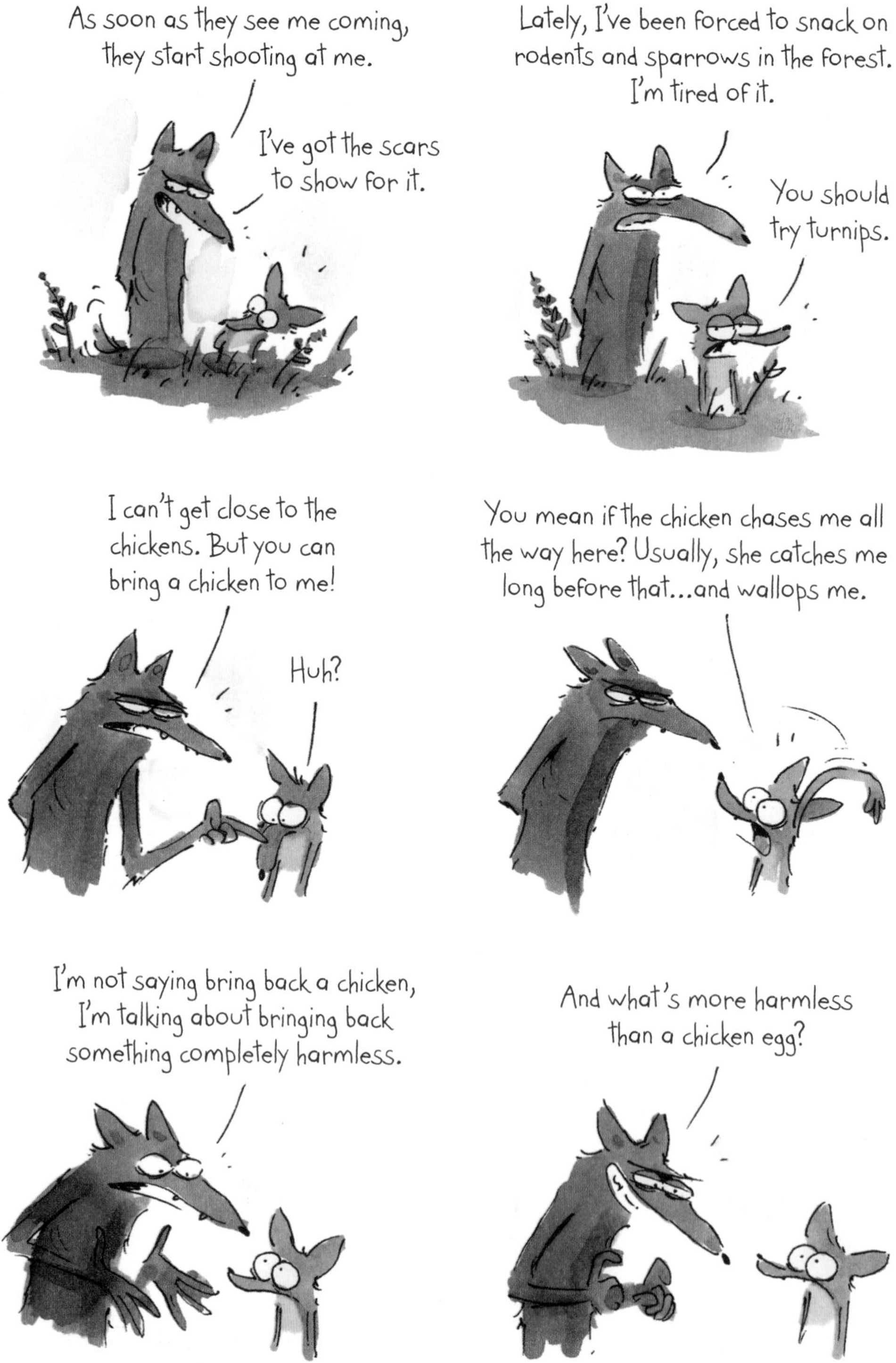
As soon as they see me coming, they start shooting at me.
I've got the scars to show for it.
Lately, I've been forced to snack on rodents and sparrows in the forest. I'm tired of it.
You should try turnips.
I can't get close to the chickens. But you can bring a chicken to me!
Huh?
You mean if the chicken chases me all the way here? Usually, she catches me long before that...and wallops me.
I'm not saying bring back a chicken, I'm talking about bringing back something completely harmless.
And what's more harmless than a chicken egg?

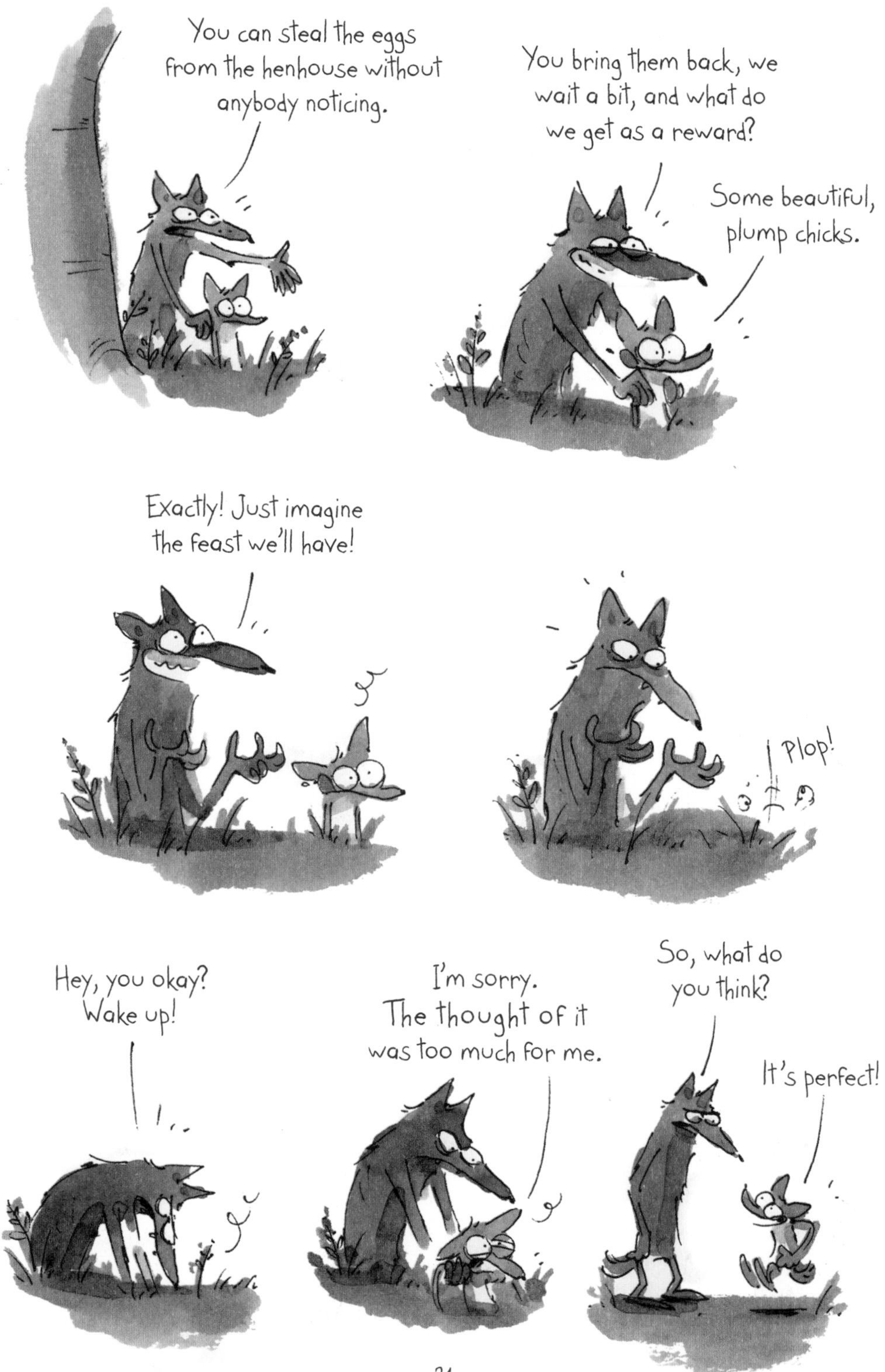
You can steal the eggs from the henhouse without anybody noticing.
You bring them back, we wait a bit, and what do we get as a reward?
Some beautiful, plump chicks.
Exactly! Just imagine the feast we'll have!
Plop!
Hey, you okay? Wake up!
I'm sorry. The thought of it was too much for me.
So, what do you think?
It's perfect!

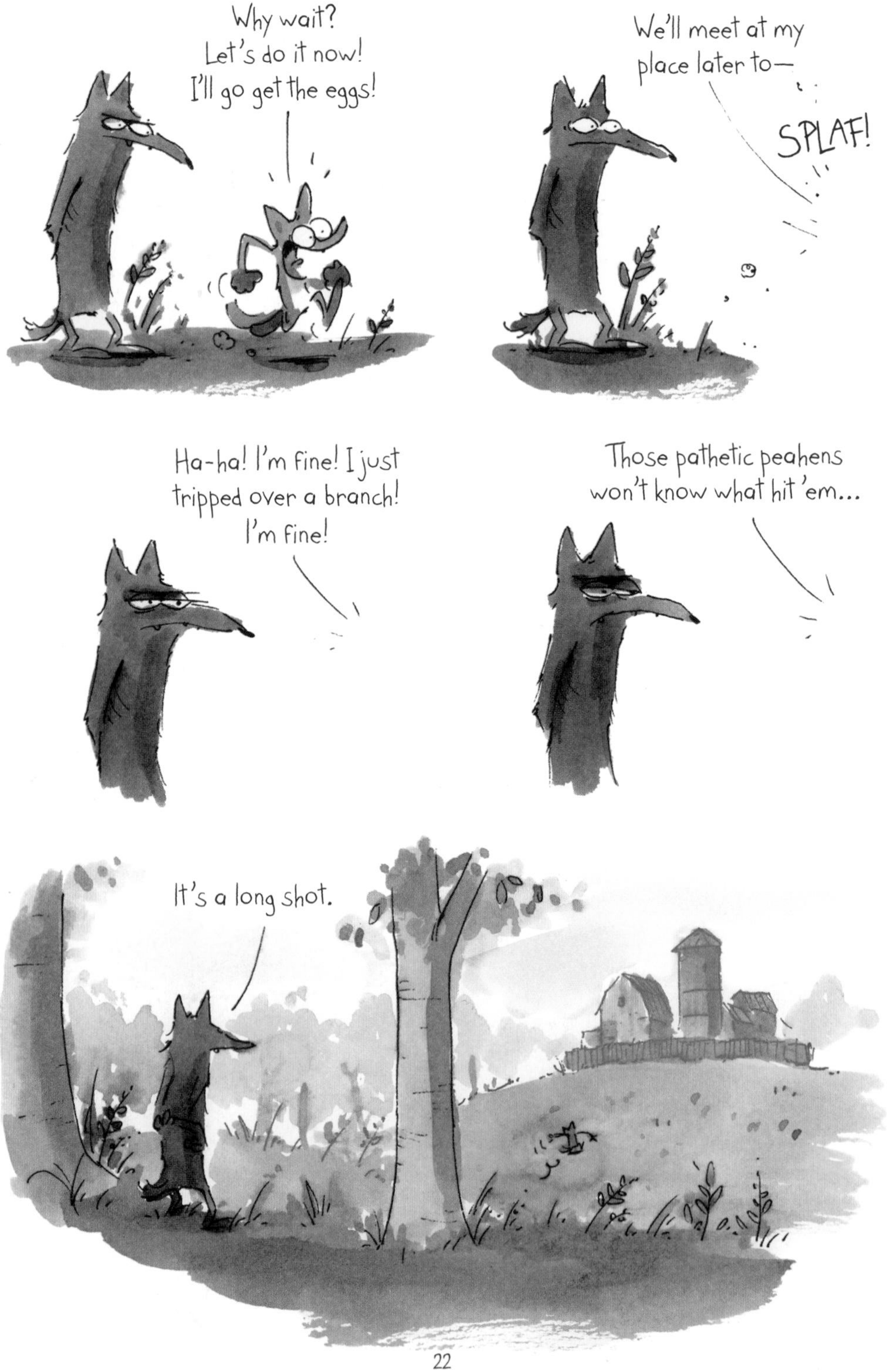
Why wait?
Let's do it now!
I'll go get the eggs!
We'll meet at my place later to—
SPLAF!
Ha-ha! I'm fine! I just tripped over a branch! I'm fine!
Those pathetic peahens won't know what hit 'em...
It's a long shot.

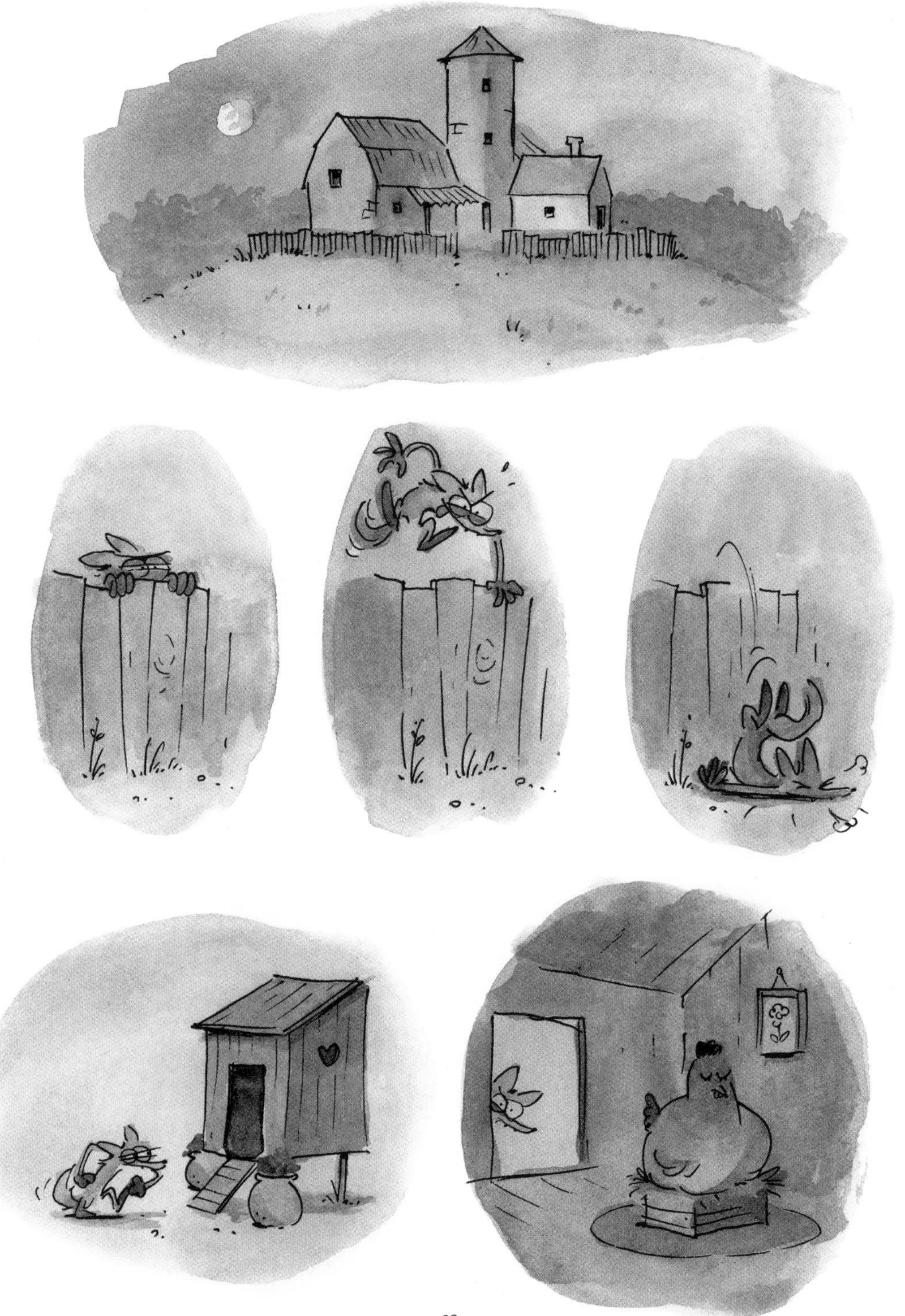

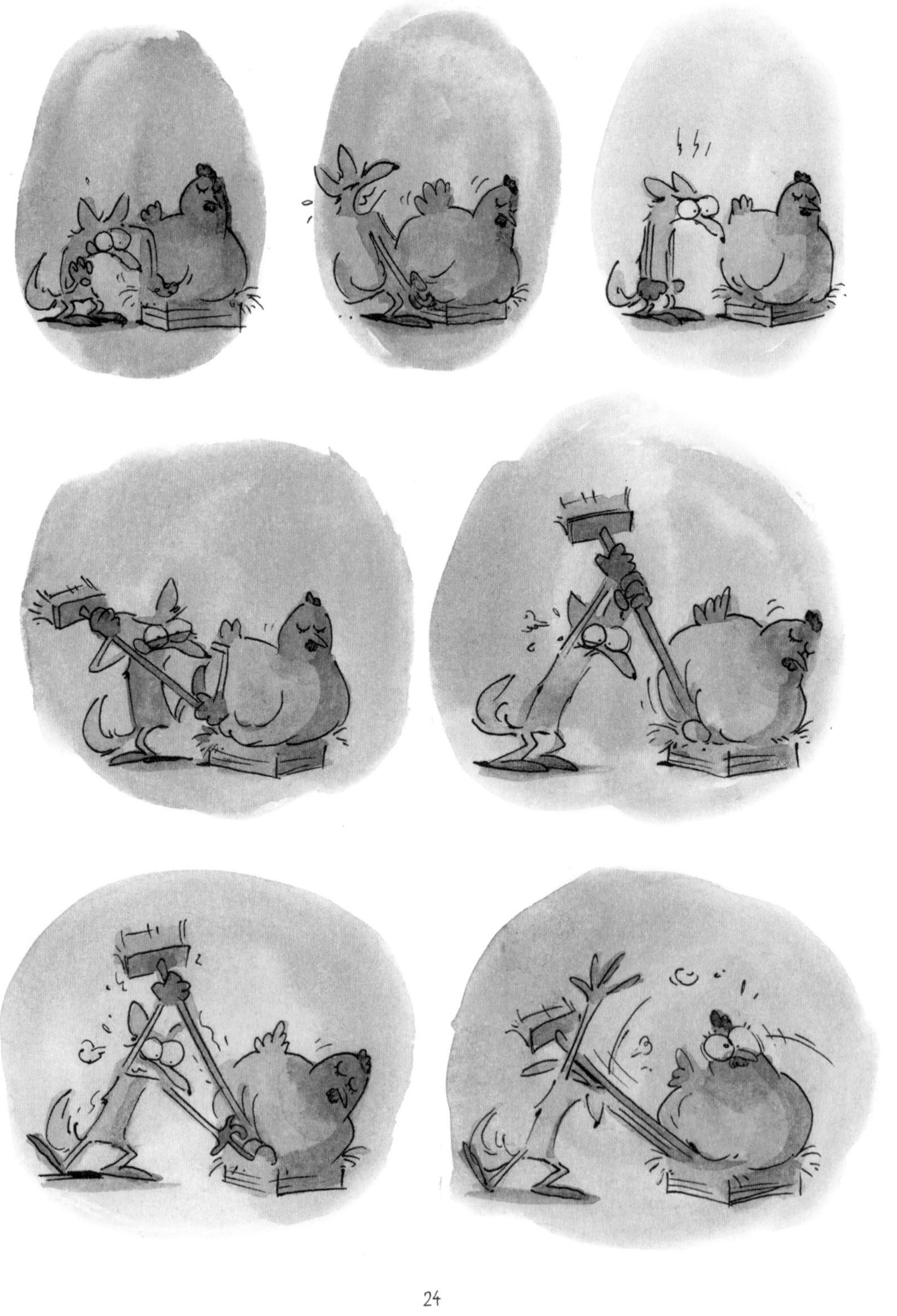

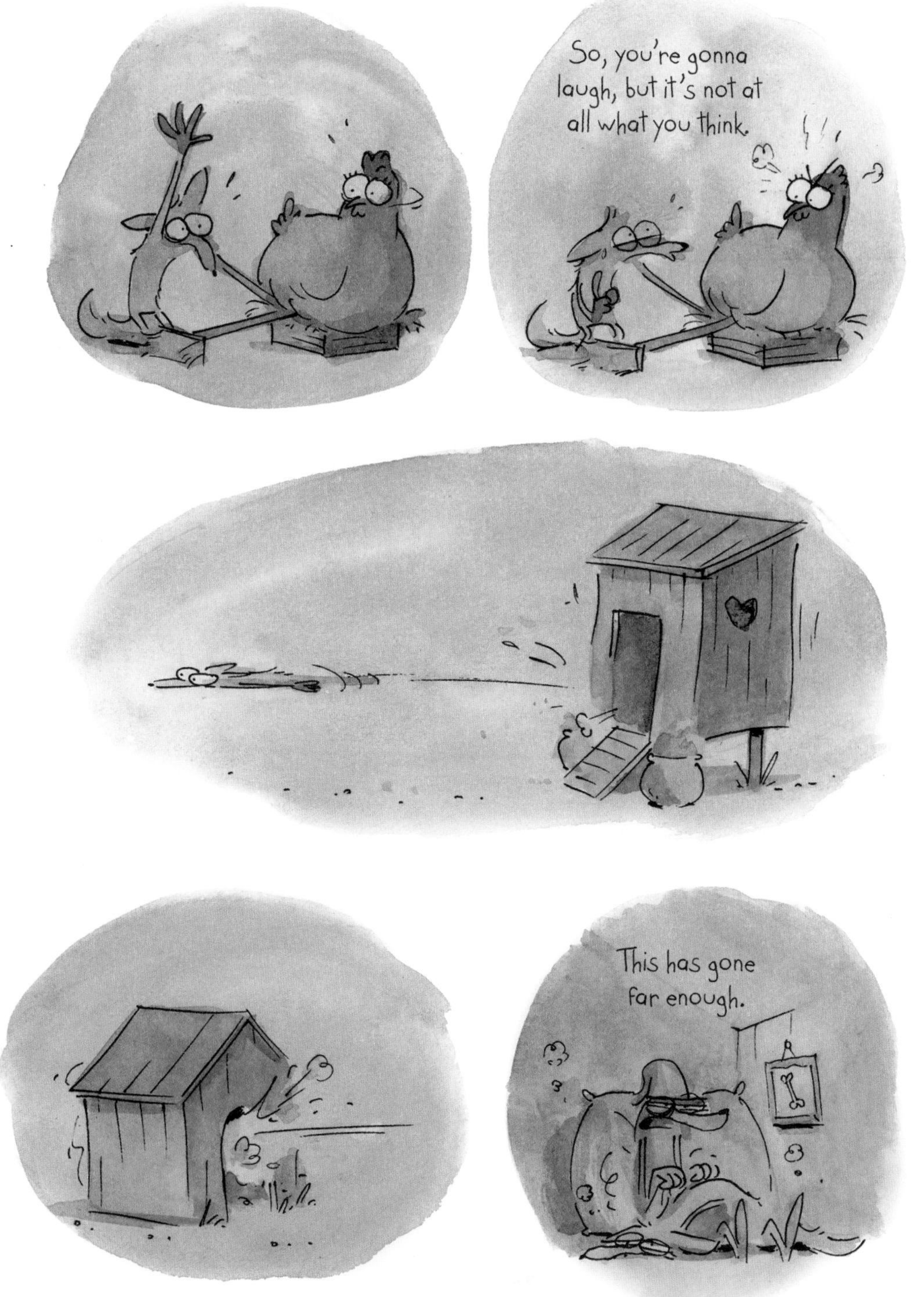
So, you're gonna laugh, but it's not at all what you think.
This has gone far enough.

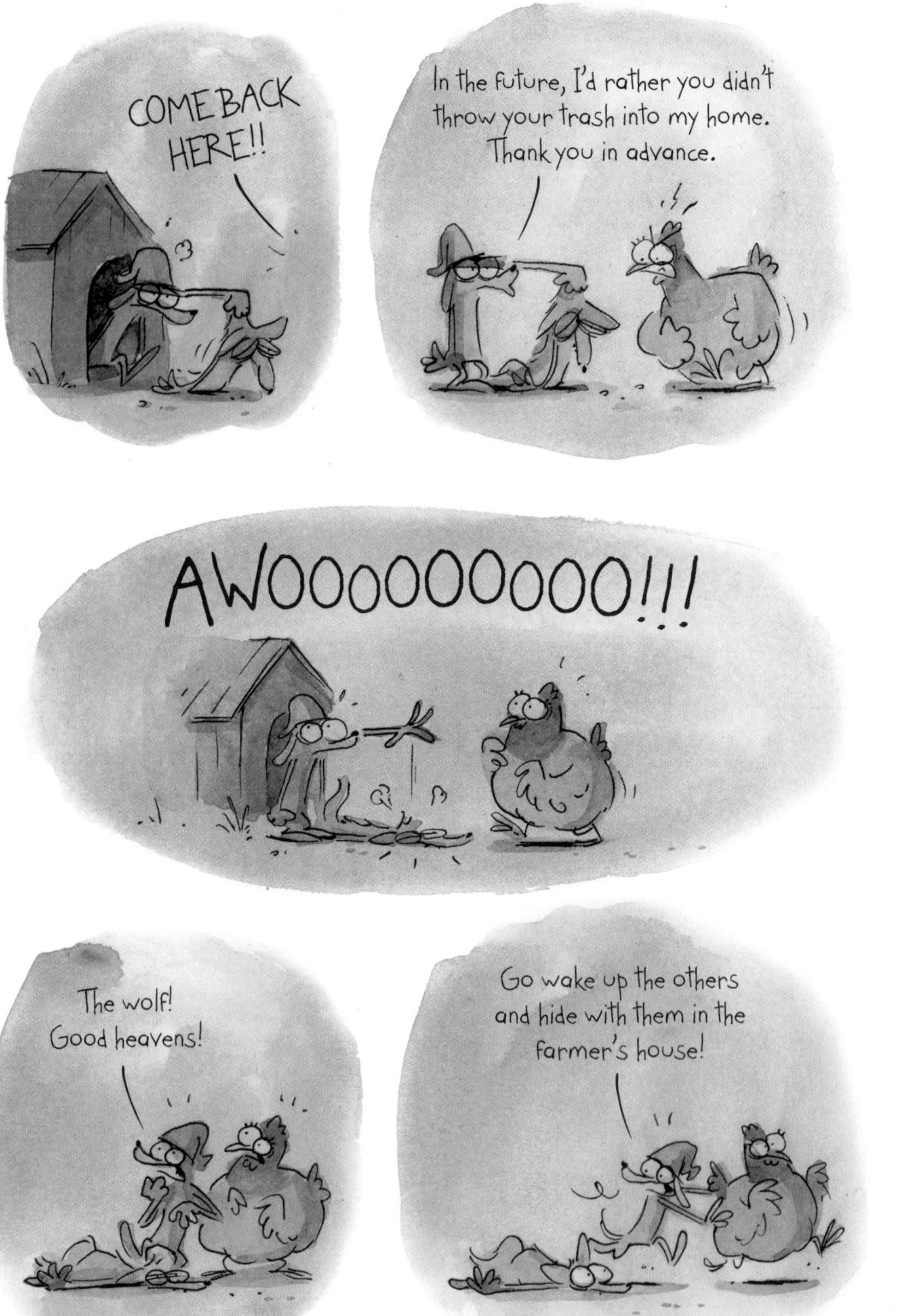
COME BACK HERE!!
In the future, I'd rather you didn't throw your trash into my home. Thank you in advance.
AWOOOOOOOOO!!!
The wolf! Good heavens!
Go wake up the others and hide with them in the farmer's house!

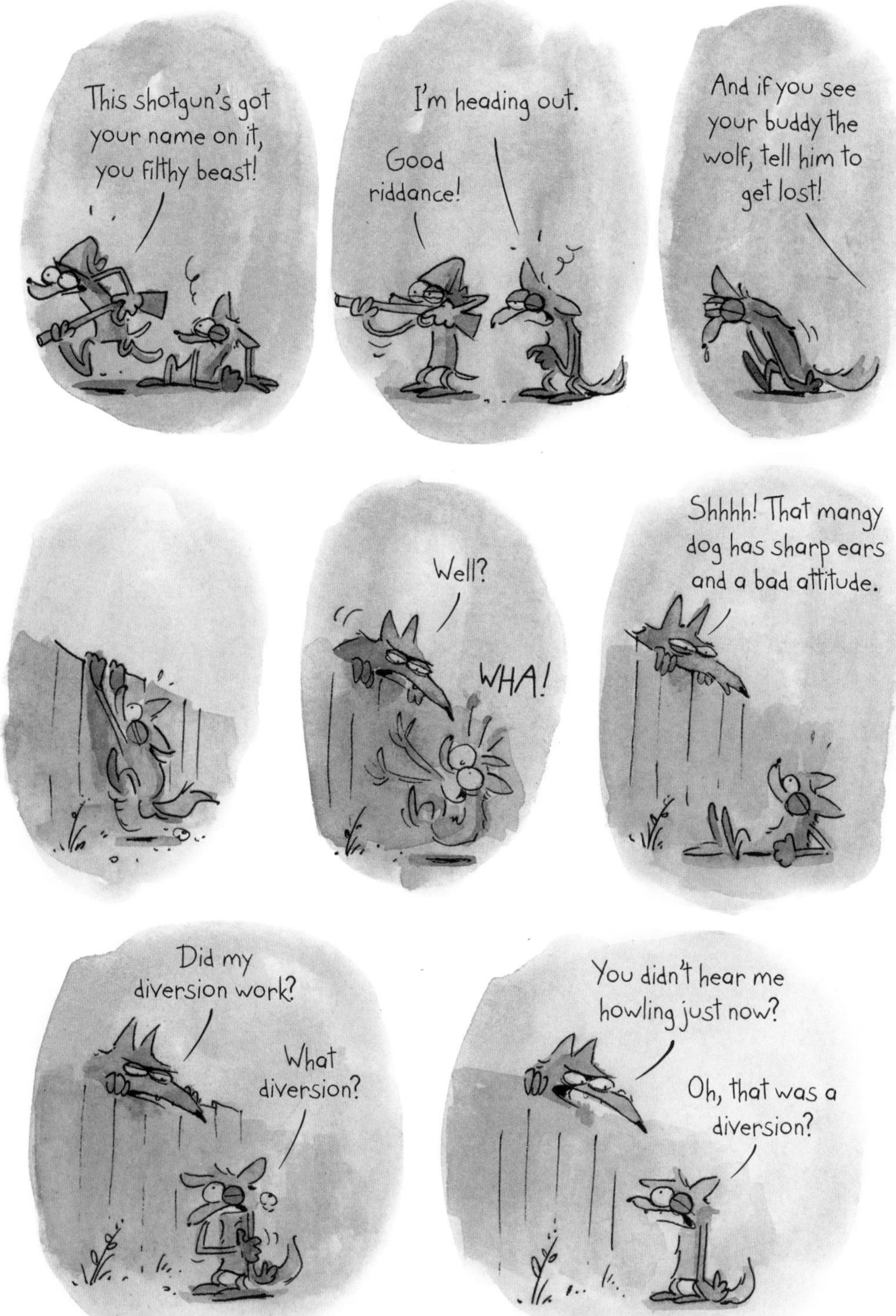
This shotgun's got your name on it, you filthy beast!
I'm heading out.
Good riddance!
And if you see your buddy the wolf, tell him to get lost!
Well?
WHA!
Shhhh! That mangy dog has sharp ears and a bad attitude.
Did my diversion work?
What diversion?
You didn't hear me howling just now?
Oh, that was a diversion?

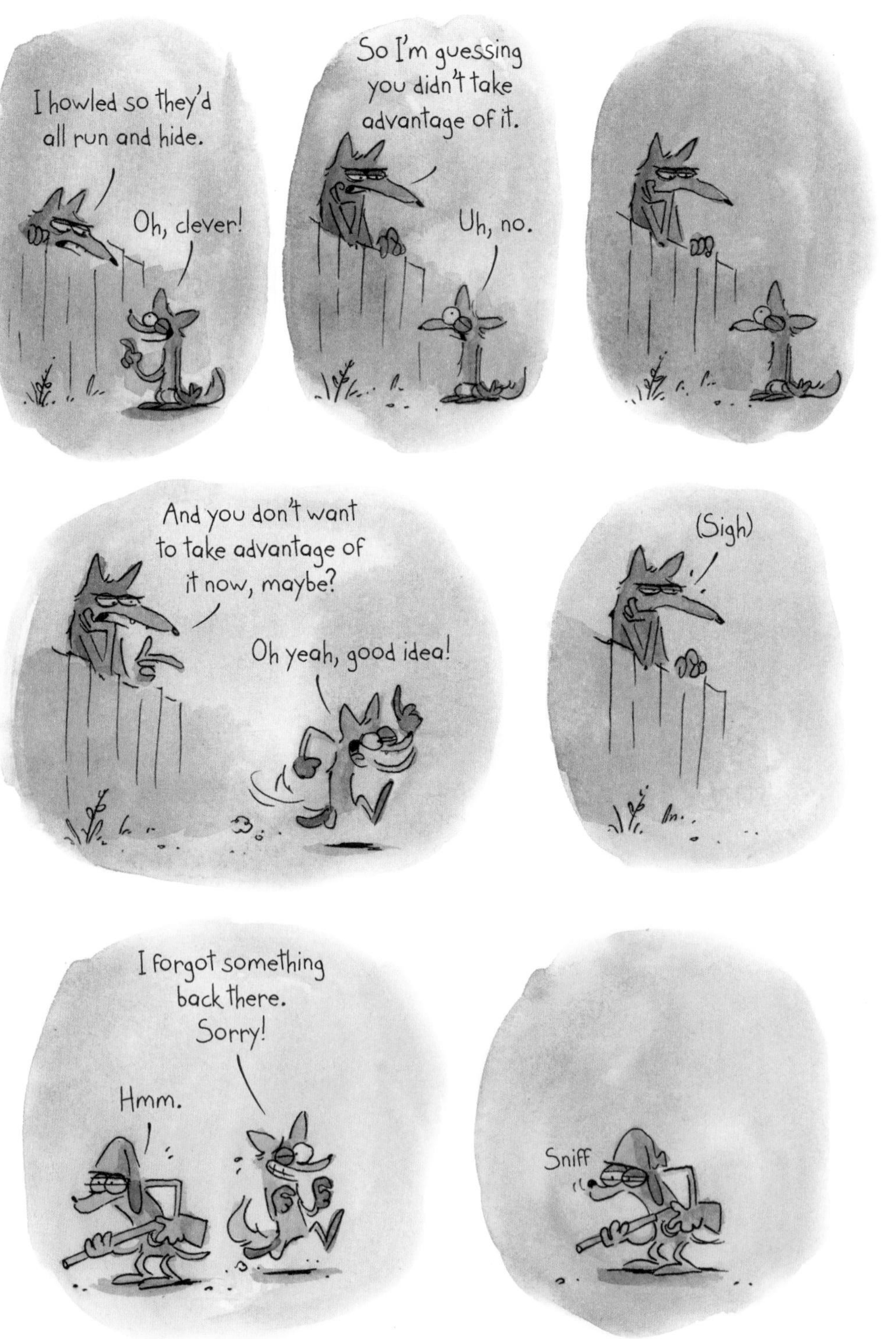
I howled so they'd all run and hide.
Oh, clever!
So I'm guessing you didn't take advantage of it.
Uh, no.
And you don't want to take advantage of it now, maybe?
Oh yeah, good idea!
(Sigh)
I forgot something back there. Sorry!
Hmm.
Sniff

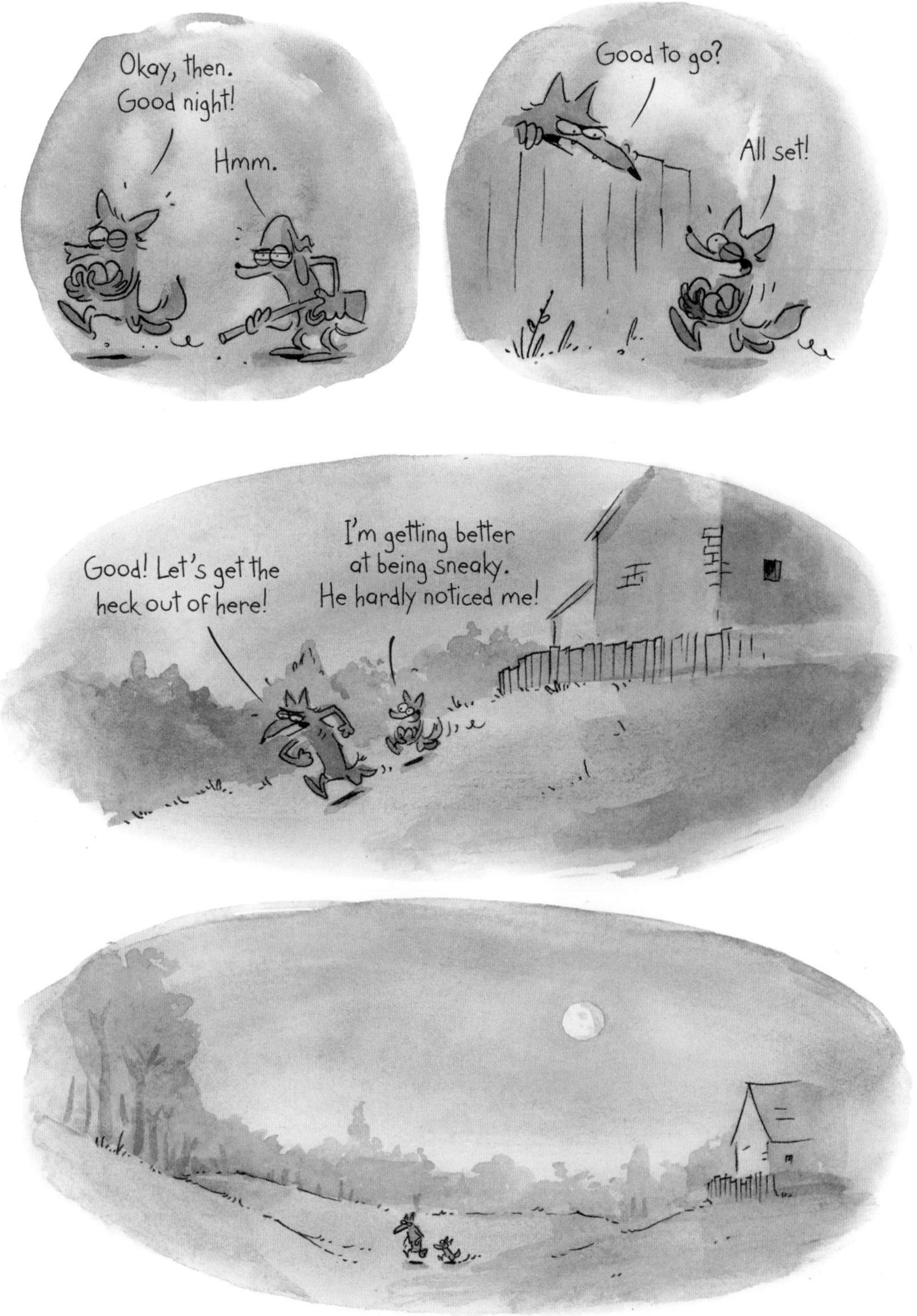
Okay, then.
Good night!
Hmm.
Good to go?
All set!
Good! Let's get the heck out of here!
I'm getting better at being sneaky. He hardly noticed me!

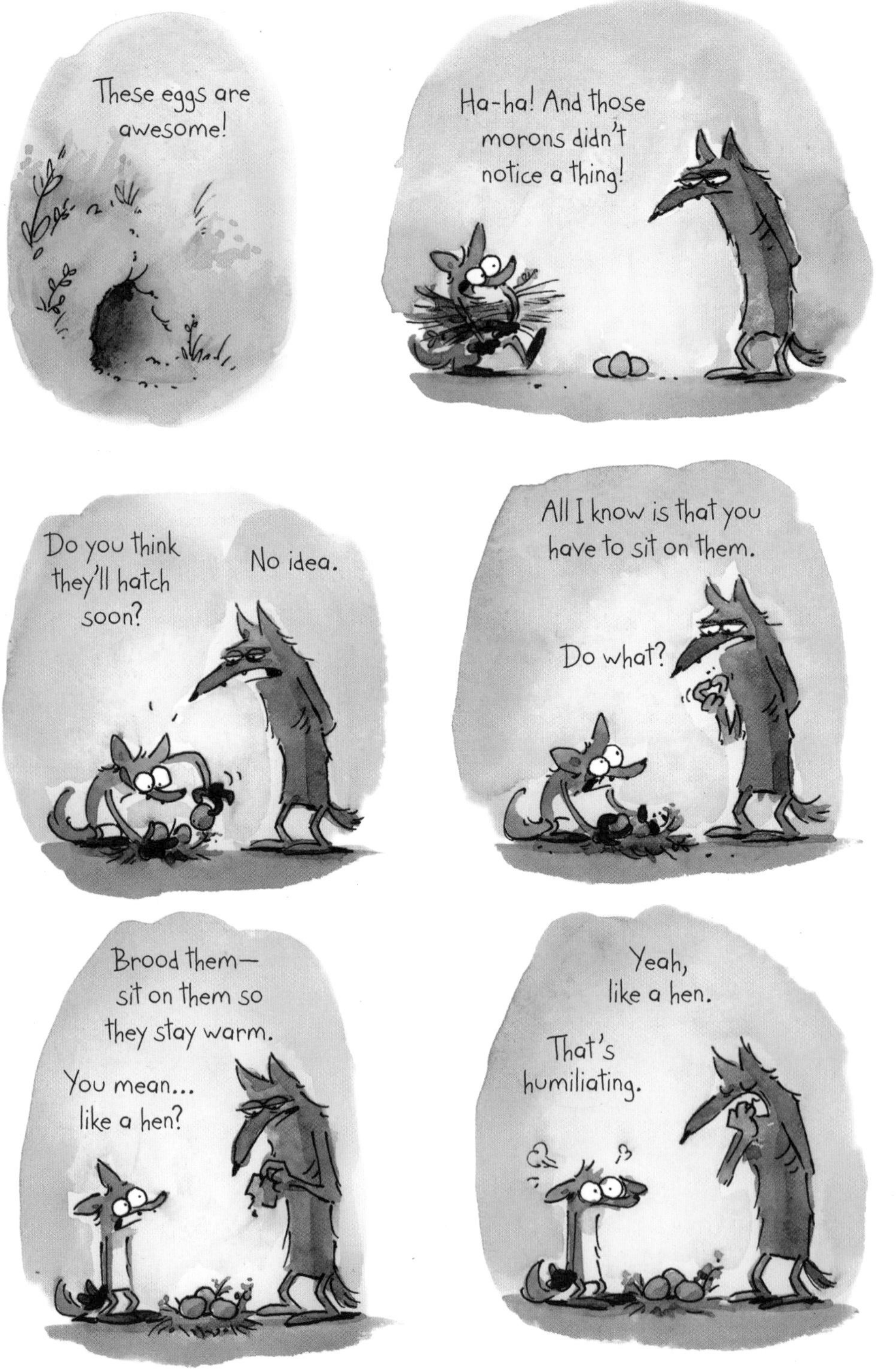
These eggs are awesome!
Ha-ha! And those morons didn't notice a thing!
Do you think they'll hatch soon?
No idea.
All I know is that you have to sit on them.
Do what?
Brood them— sit on them so they stay warm.
You mean... like a hen?
Yeah, like a hen.
That's humiliating.

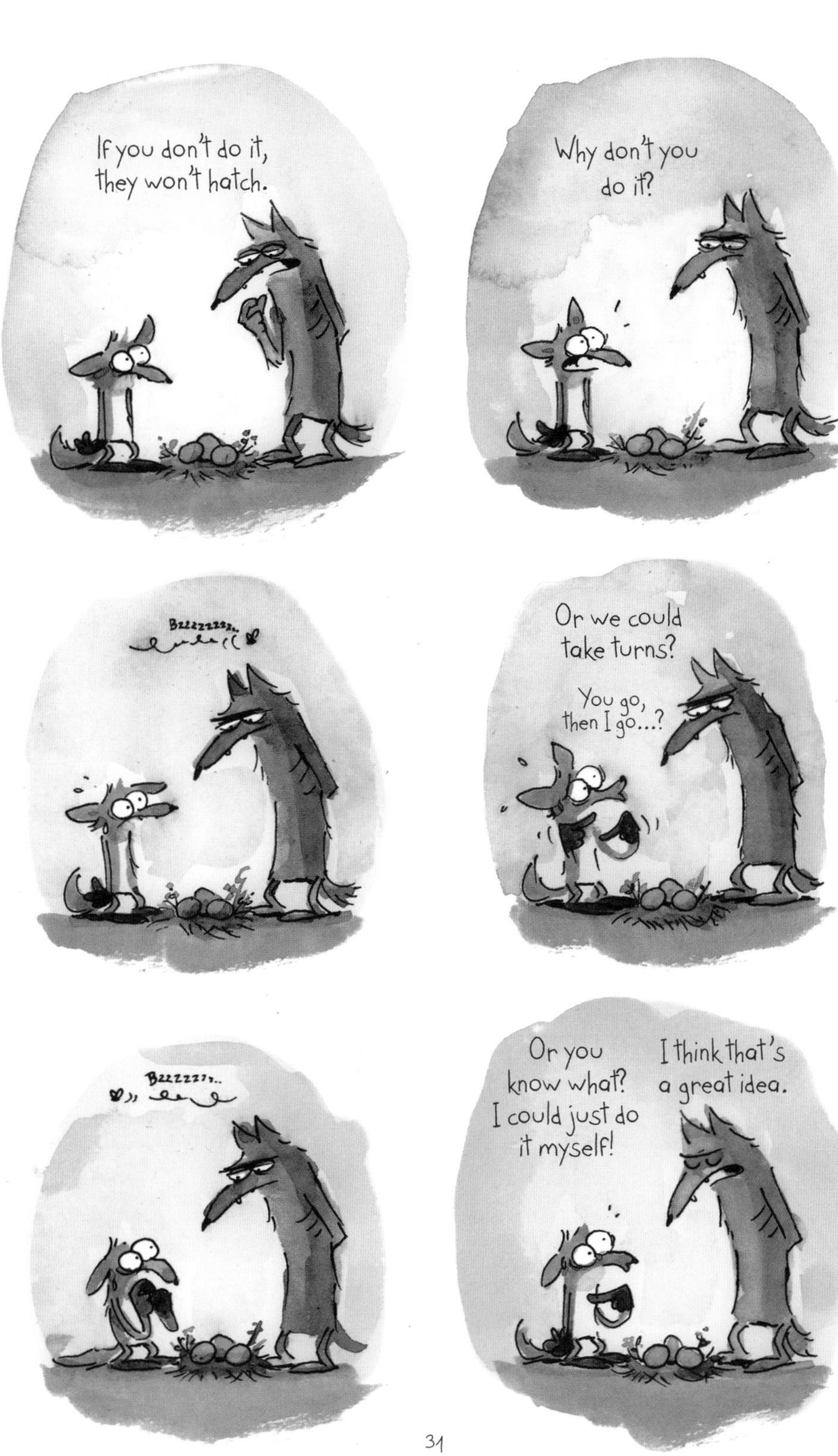
If you don't do it, they won't hatch.
Why don't you do it?
Bzzzzzzzz..
Or we could take turns?
You go, then I go...?
Bzzzzzz..
Or you know what? I could just do it myself!
I think that's a great idea.

Okay, then...
here goes.

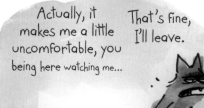

Actually, it
makes me a little
uncomfortable, you
being here watching me...

That's fine,
I'll leave.

It's not about
you!

Bye.

Come on!

Hmmpf!

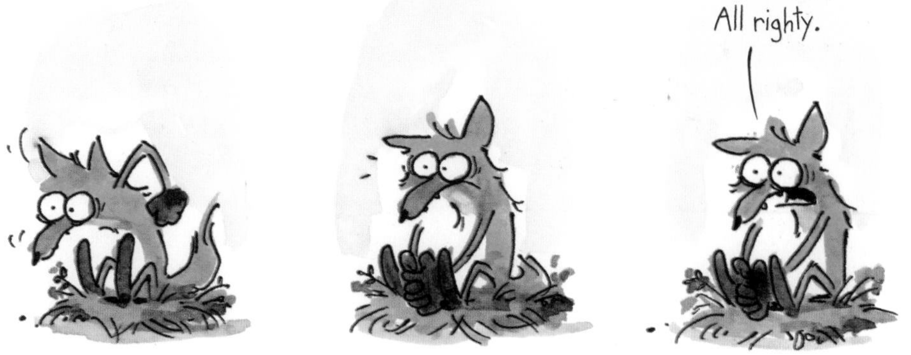
All righty.

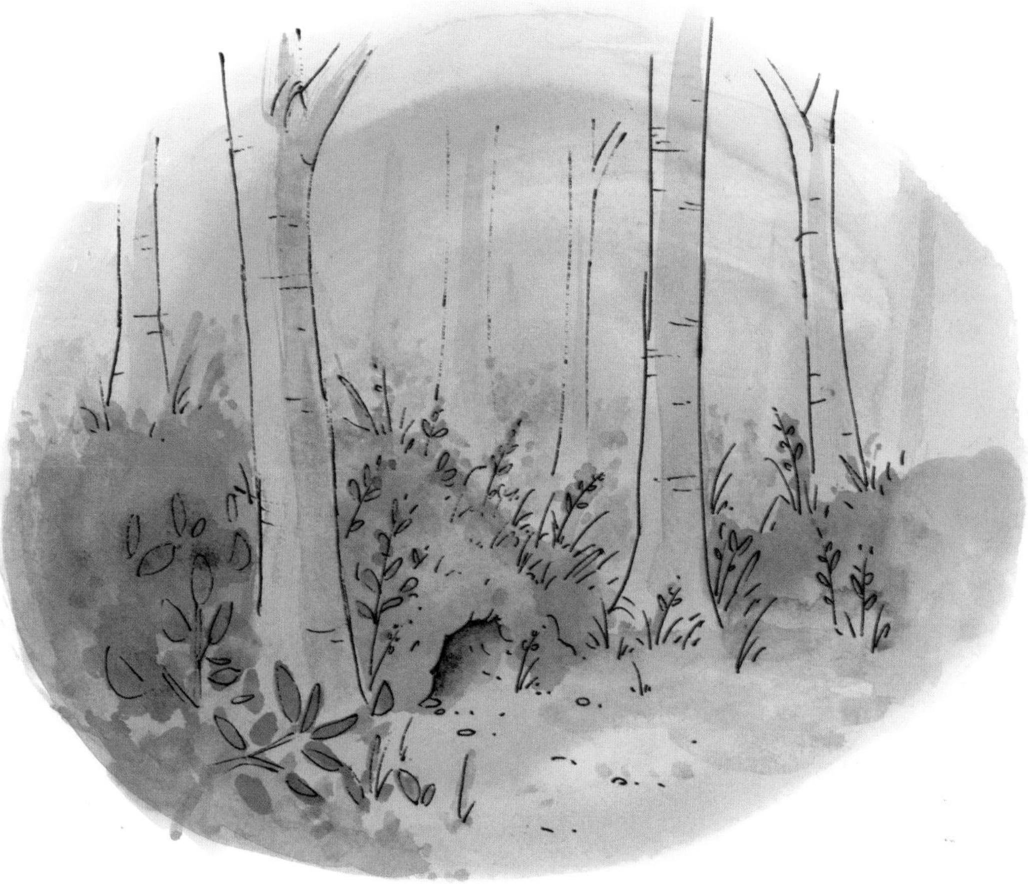

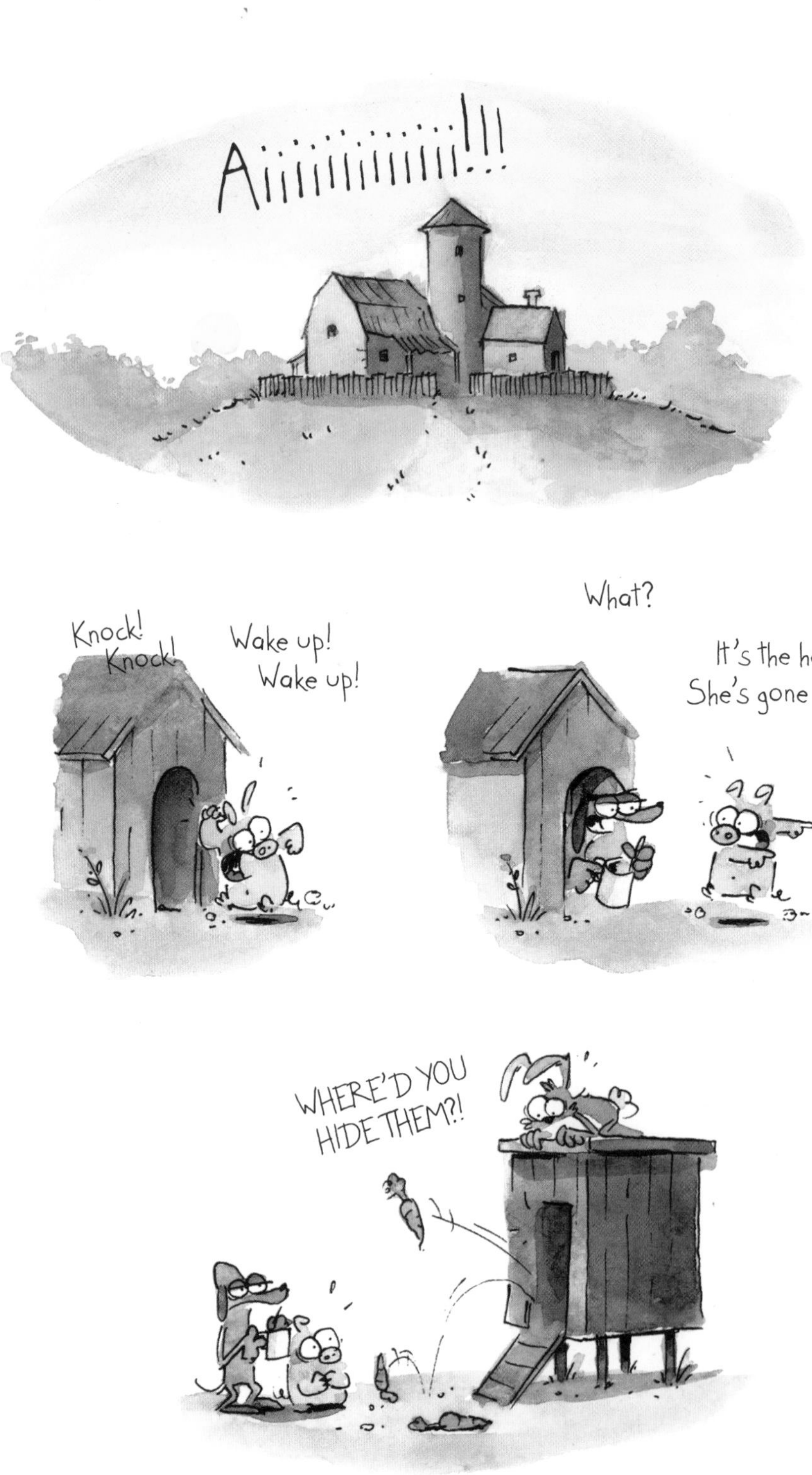
Aiiiiiiiiiiii!!!
Knock! Knock!
Wake up! Wake up!
What?
It's the hen! She's gone nuts!
WHERE'D YOU HIDE THEM?!

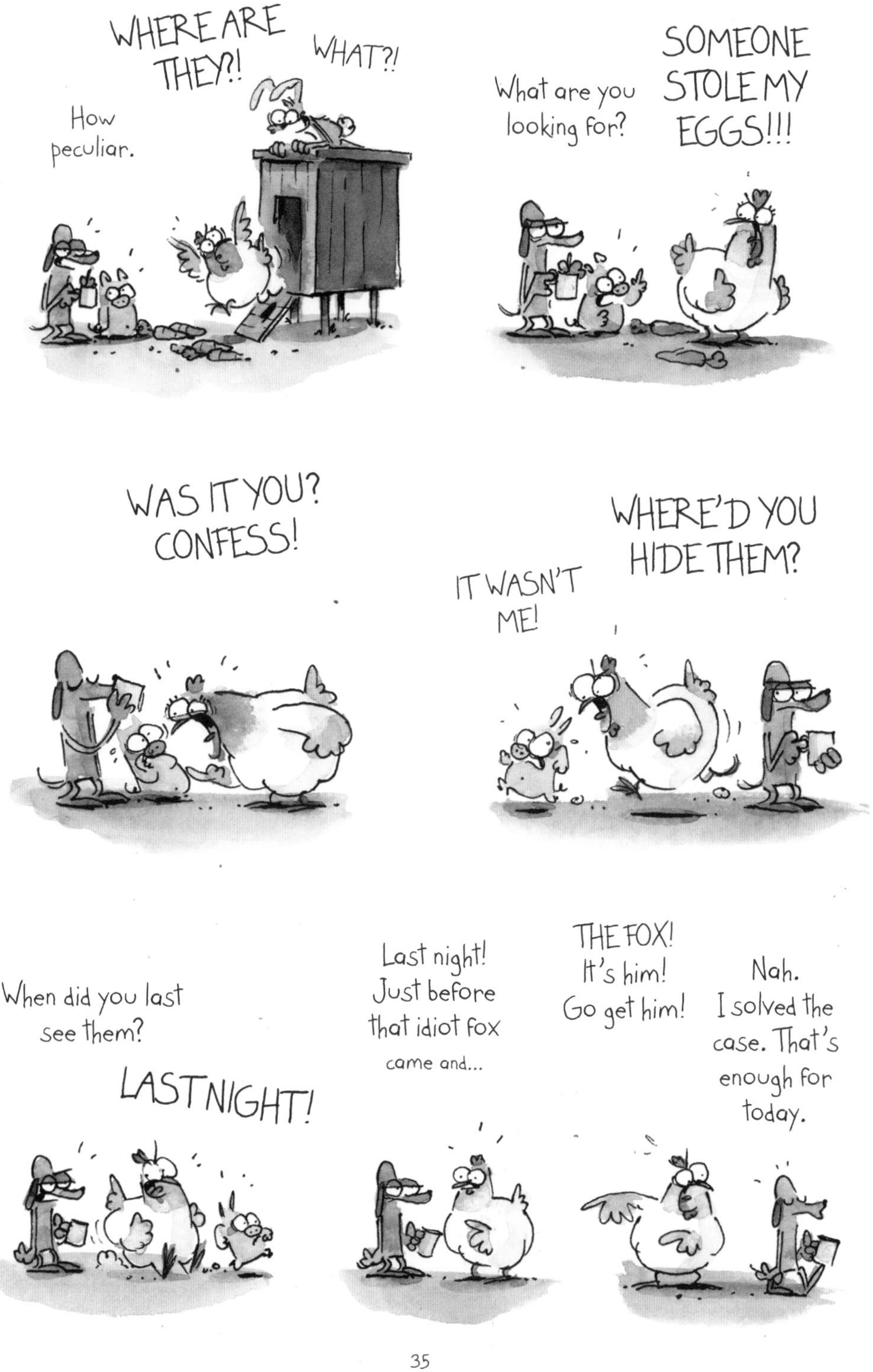
WHERE ARE THEY?!
WHAT?!
How peculiar.
What are you looking for?
SOMEONE STOLE MY EGGS!!!
WAS IT YOU? CONFESS!
IT WASN'T ME!
WHERE'D YOU HIDE THEM?
When did you last see them?
LAST NIGHT!
Last night! Just before that idiot fox came and...
THE FOX! It's him! Go get him!
Nah. I solved the case. That's enough for today.

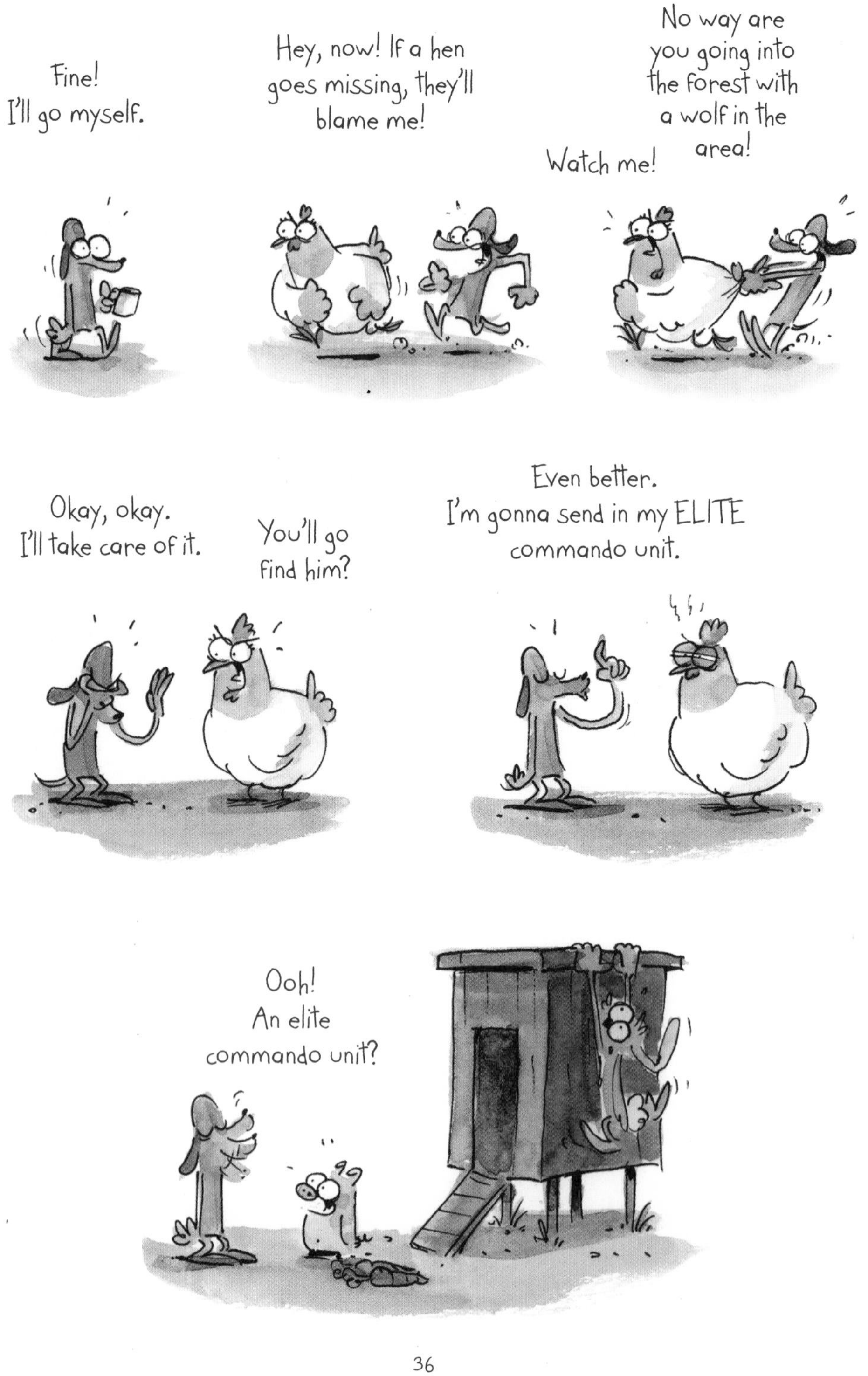
Fine! I'll go myself.
Hey, now! If a hen goes missing, they'll blame me!
Watch me!
No way are you going into the forest with a wolf in the area!
Okay, okay. I'll take care of it.
You'll go find him?
Even better. I'm gonna send in my ELITE commando unit.
Ooh! An elite commando unit?

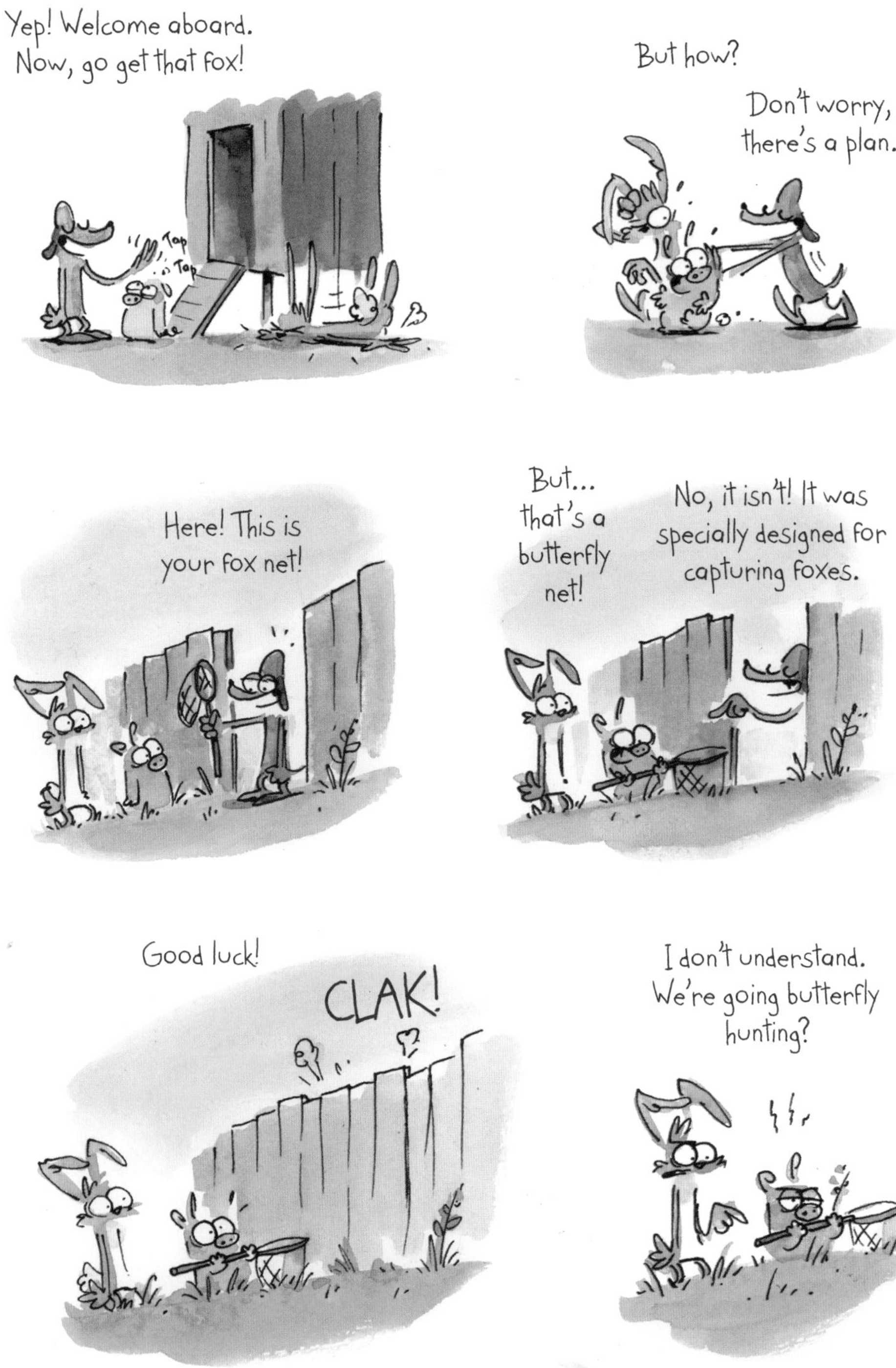
Yep! Welcome aboard.
Now, go get that fox!
Tap
Tap
But how?
Don't worry, there's a plan.
Here! This is your fox net!
But... that's a butterfly net!
No, it isn't! It was specially designed for capturing foxes.
Good luck!
CLAK!
I don't understand. We're going butterfly hunting?

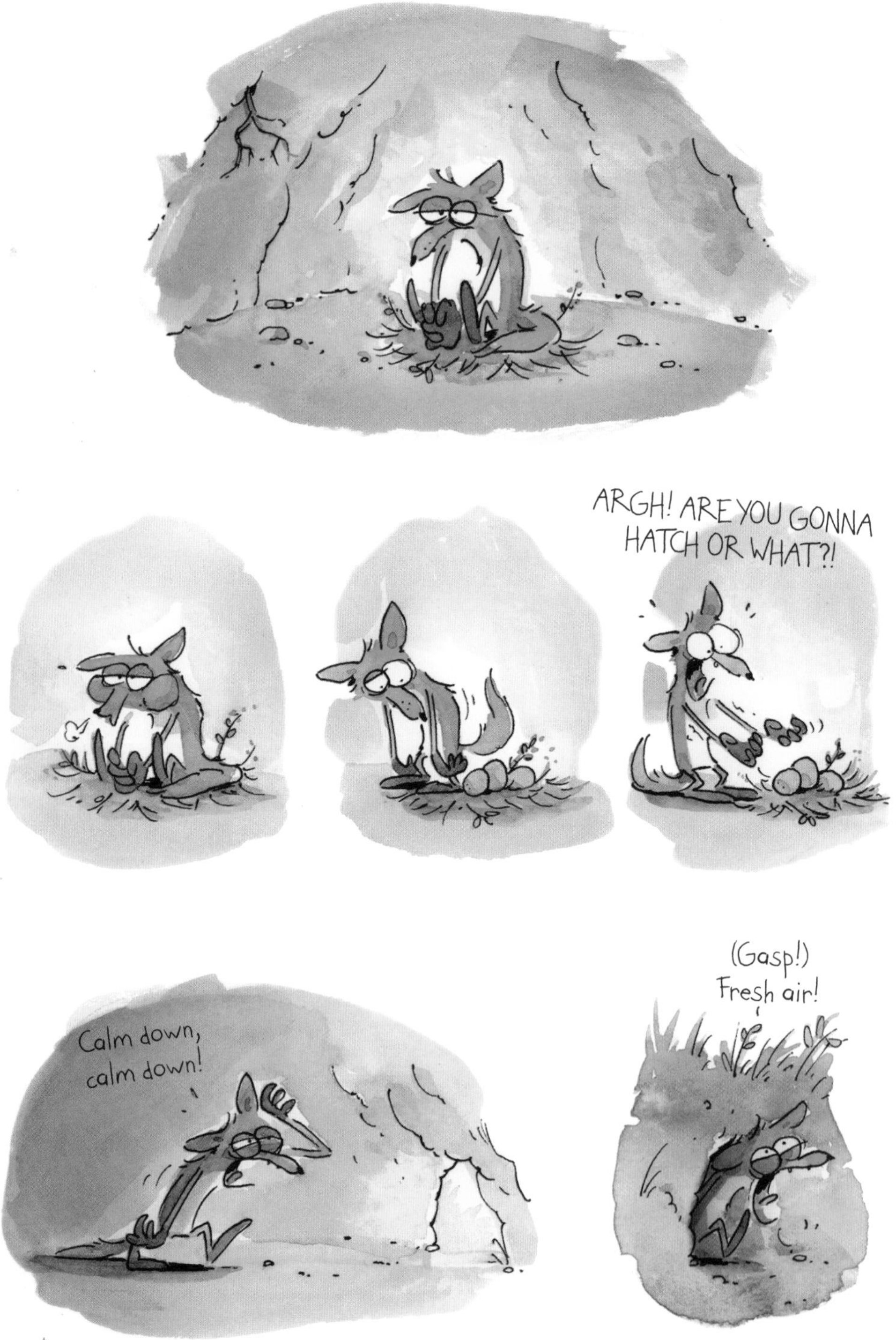
ARGH! ARE YOU GONNA HATCH OR WHAT?!
Calm down, calm down!
(Gasp!) Fresh air!

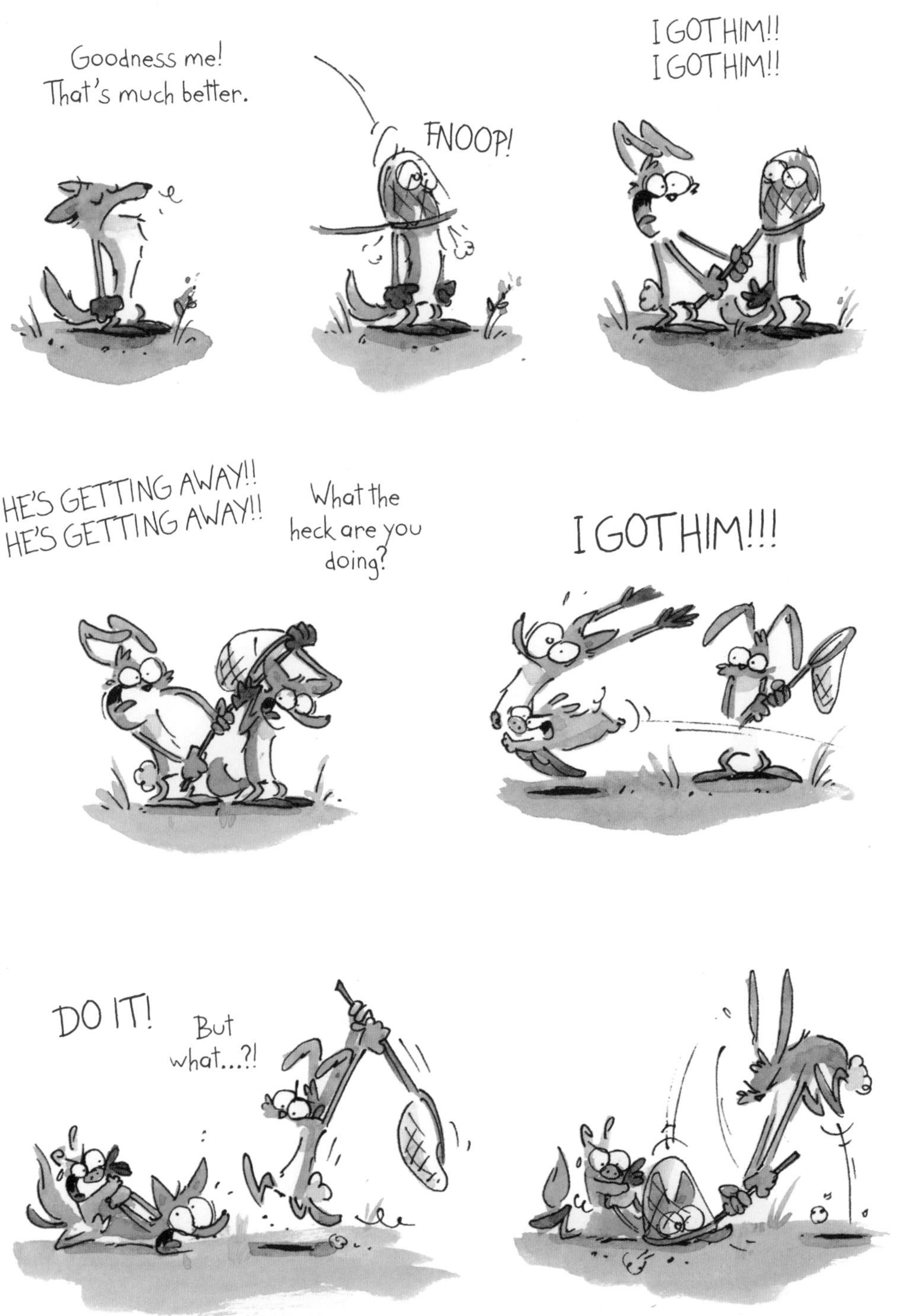

Goodness me! That's much better.
FNOOP!
I GOT HIM!! I GOT HIM!!
HE'S GETTING AWAY!! HE'S GETTING AWAY!!
What the heck are you doing?
I GOT HIM!!!
DO IT!
But what...?!

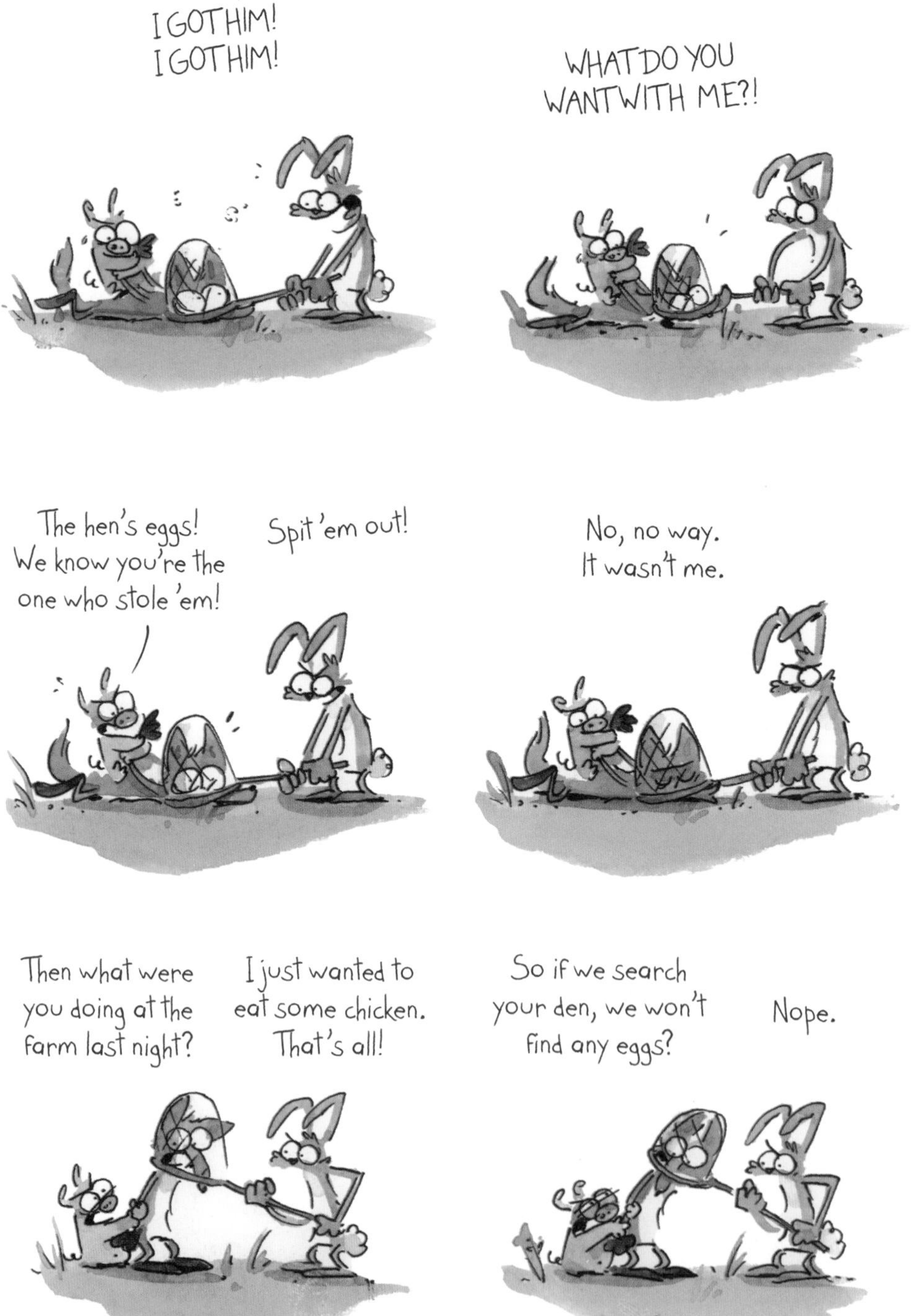

I GOT HIM!
I GOT HIM!
WHAT DO YOU WANT WITH ME?!
The hen's eggs! We know you're the one who stole 'em!
Spit 'em out!
No, no way. It wasn't me.
Then what were you doing at the farm last night?
I just wanted to eat some chicken. That's all!
So if we search your den, we won't find any eggs?
Nope.

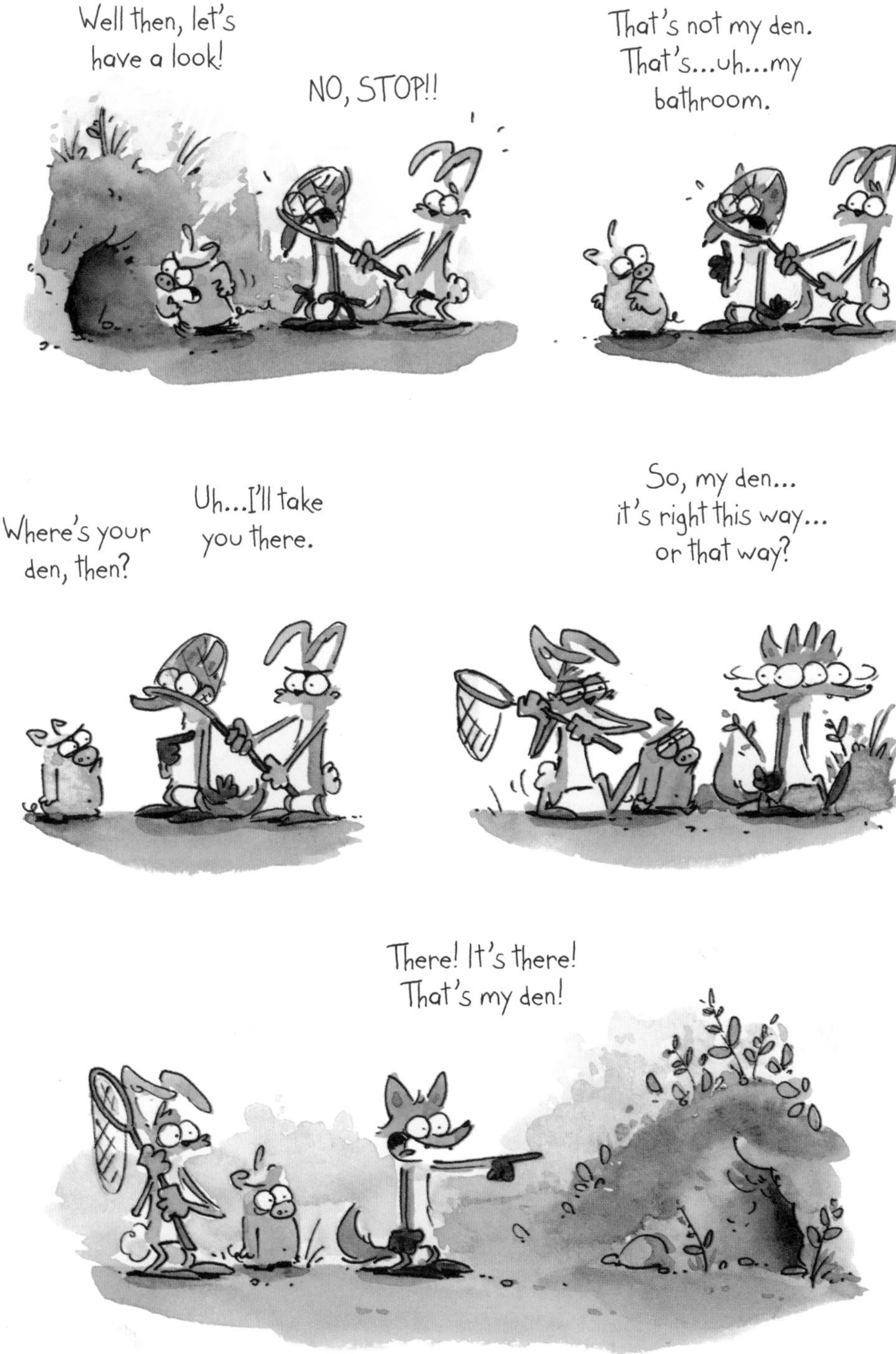
Well then, let's have a look!
NO, STOP!!
That's not my den. That's...uh...my bathroom.
Where's your den, then?
Uh...I'll take you there.
So, my den... it's right this way... or that way?
There! It's there! That's my den!

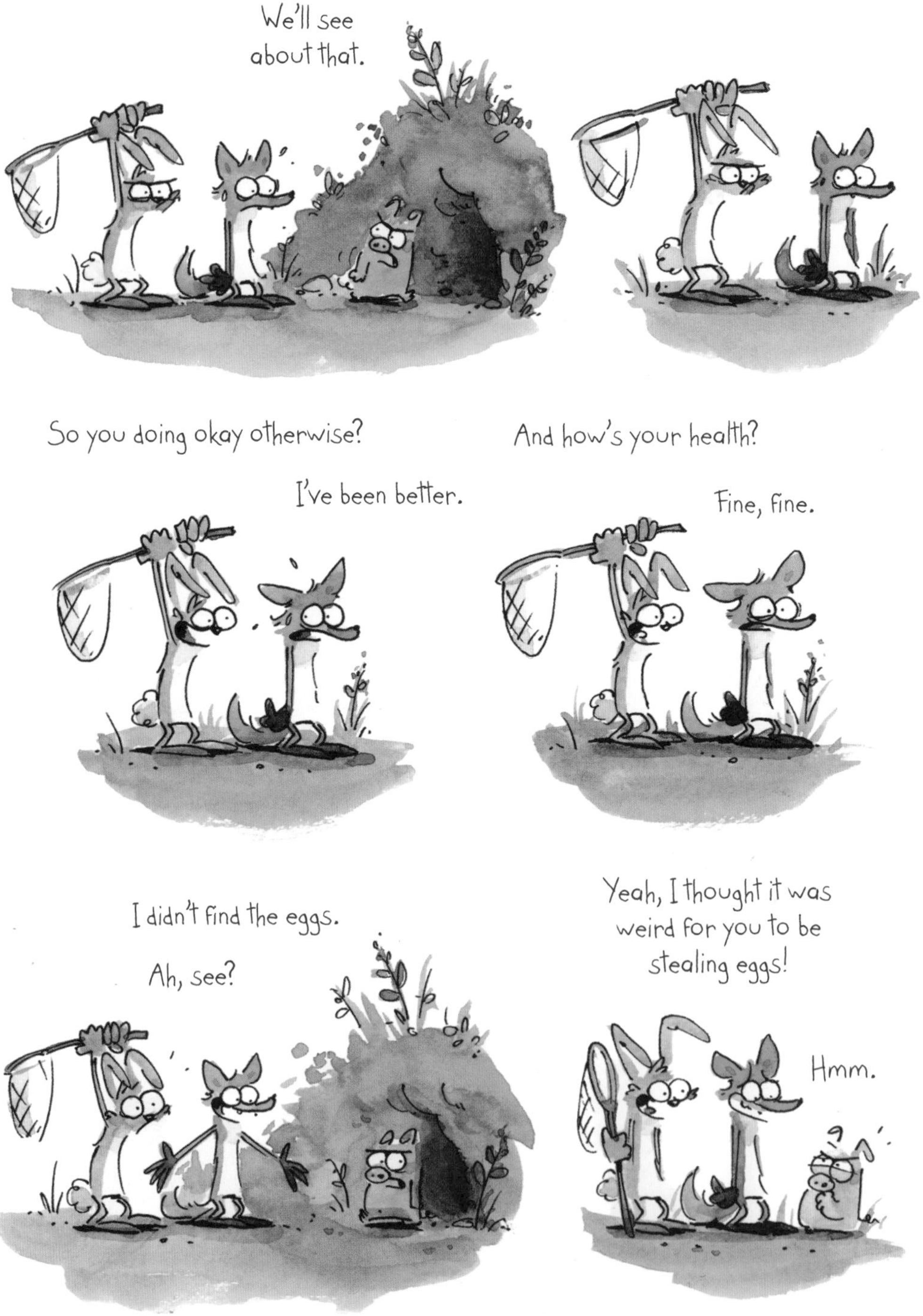
We'll see about that.
So you doing okay otherwise?
I've been better.
And how's your health?
Fine, fine.
I didn't find the eggs.
Ah, see?
Yeah, I thought it was weird for you to be stealing eggs!
Hmm.

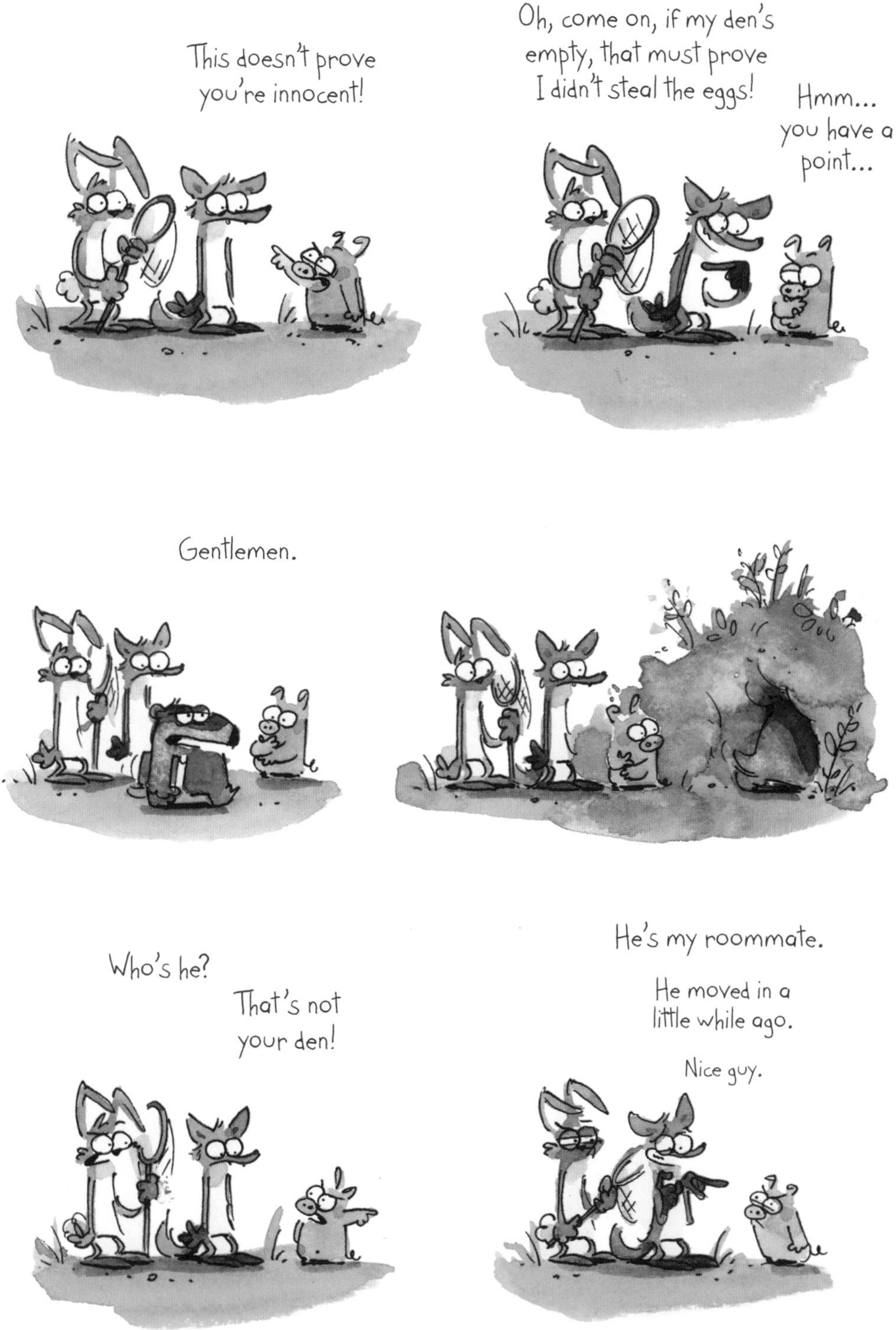
This doesn't prove you're innocent!
Oh, come on, if my den's empty, that must prove I didn't steal the eggs!
Hmm... you have a point...
Gentlemen.
Who's he?
That's not your den!
He's my roommate.
He moved in a little while ago.
Nice guy.

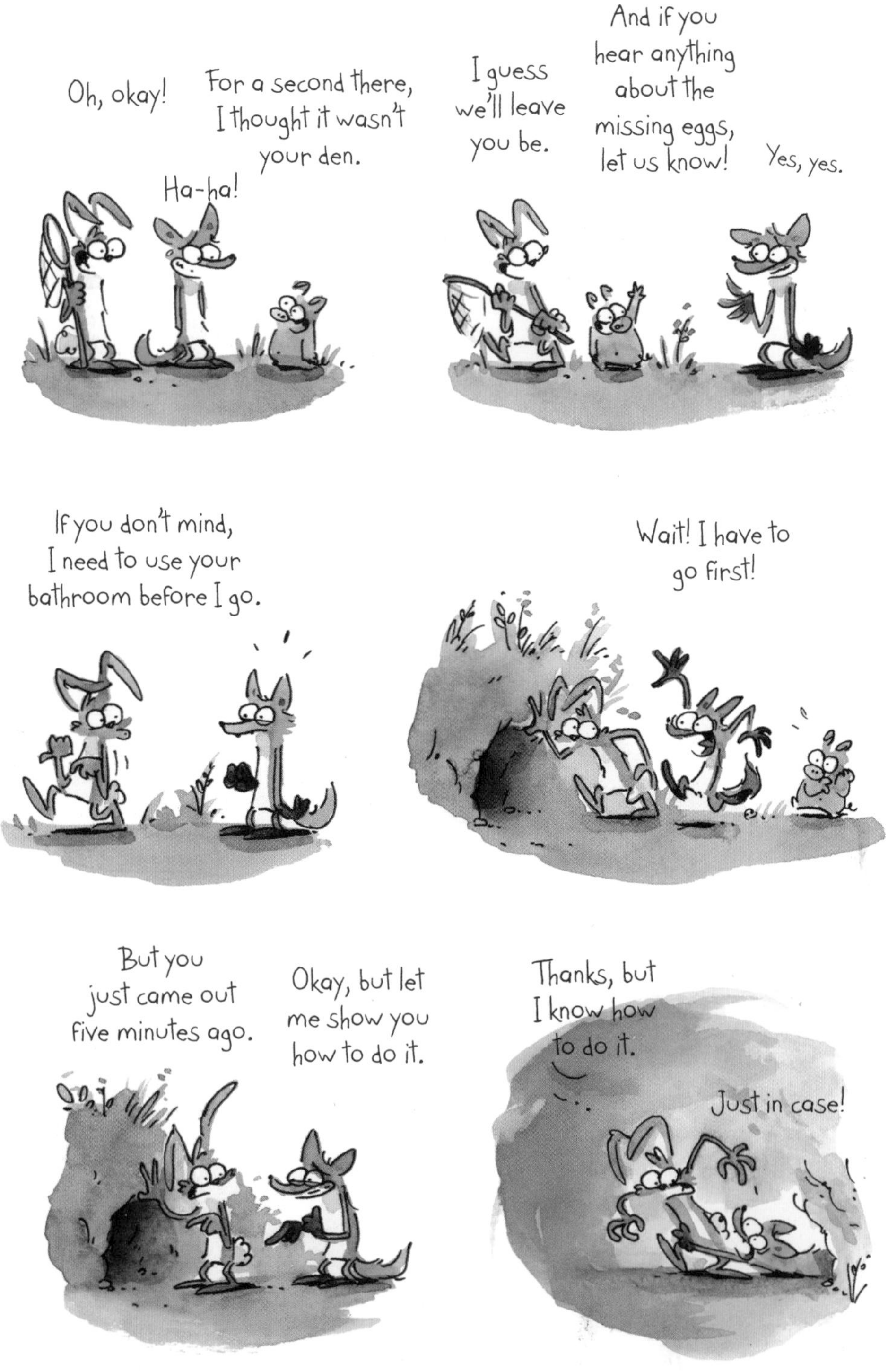
Oh, okay!
For a second there, I thought it wasn't your den.
Ha-ha!
I guess we'll leave you be.
And if you hear anything about the missing eggs, let us know!
Yes, yes.
If you don't mind, I need to use your bathroom before I go.
Wait! I have to go first!
But you just came out five minutes ago.
Okay, but let me show you how to do it.
Thanks, but I know how to do it.
Just in case!

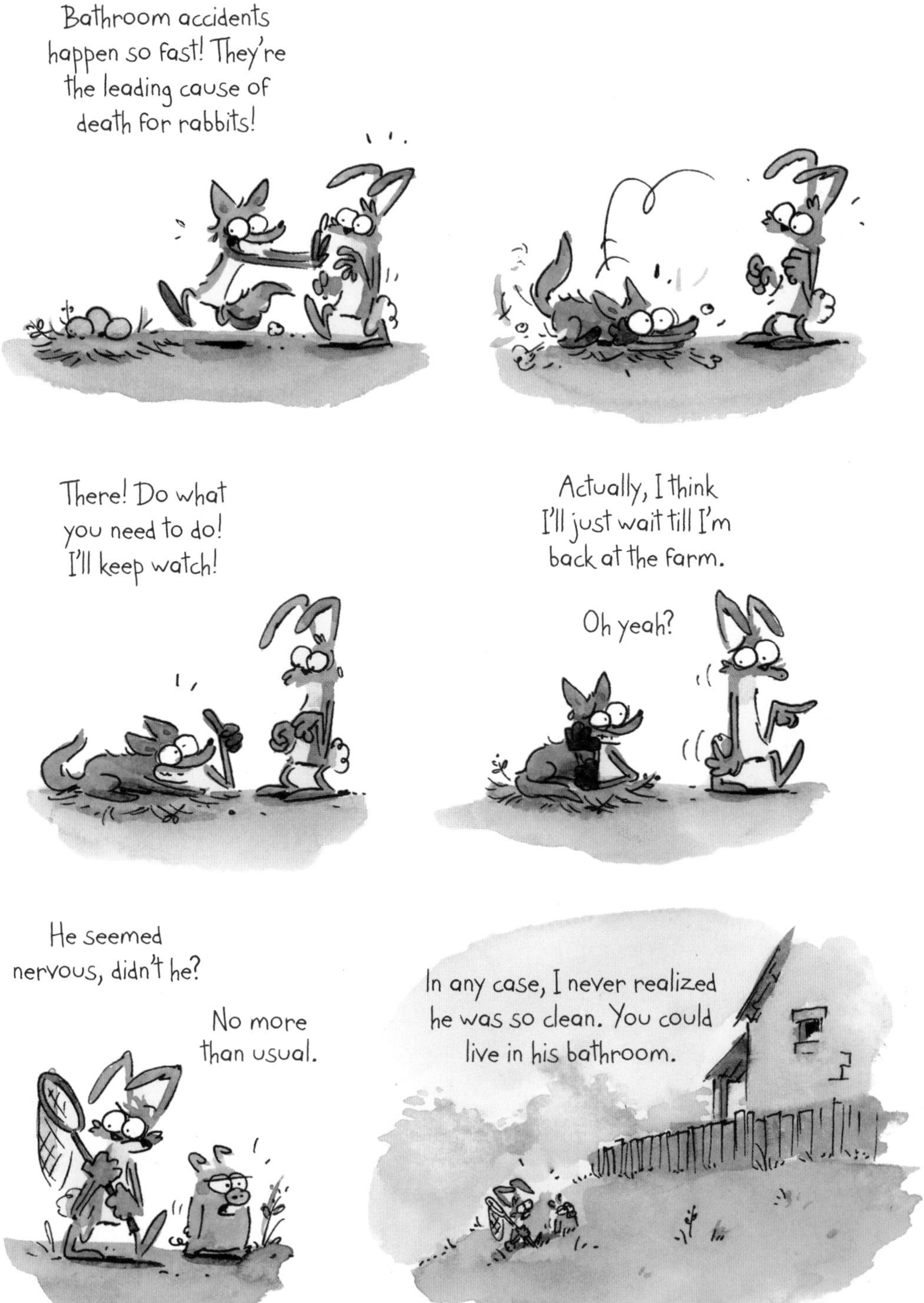
Bathroom accidents happen so fast! They're the leading cause of death for rabbits!
There! Do what you need to do! I'll keep watch!
Actually, I think I'll just wait till I'm back at the farm.
Oh yeah?
He seemed nervous, didn't he?
No more than usual.
In any case, I never realized he was so clean. You could live in his bathroom.

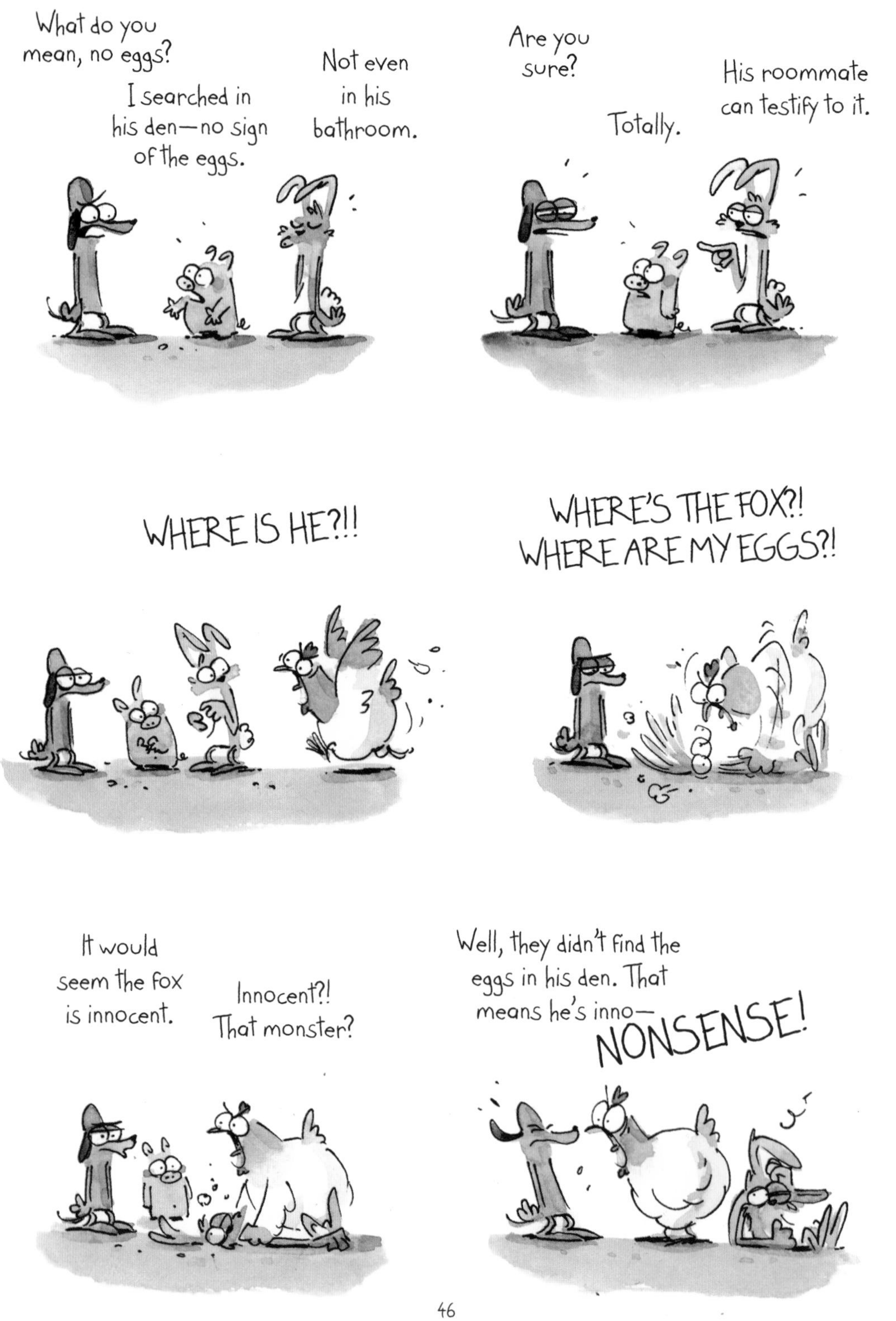
What do you mean, no eggs?
I searched in his den—no sign of the eggs.
Not even in his bathroom.
Are you sure?
Totally.
His roommate can testify to it.
WHERE IS HE?!!
WHERE'S THE FOX?! WHERE ARE MY EGGS?!
It would seem the fox is innocent.
Innocent?! That monster?
Well, they didn't find the eggs in his den. That means he's inno—
NONSENSE!

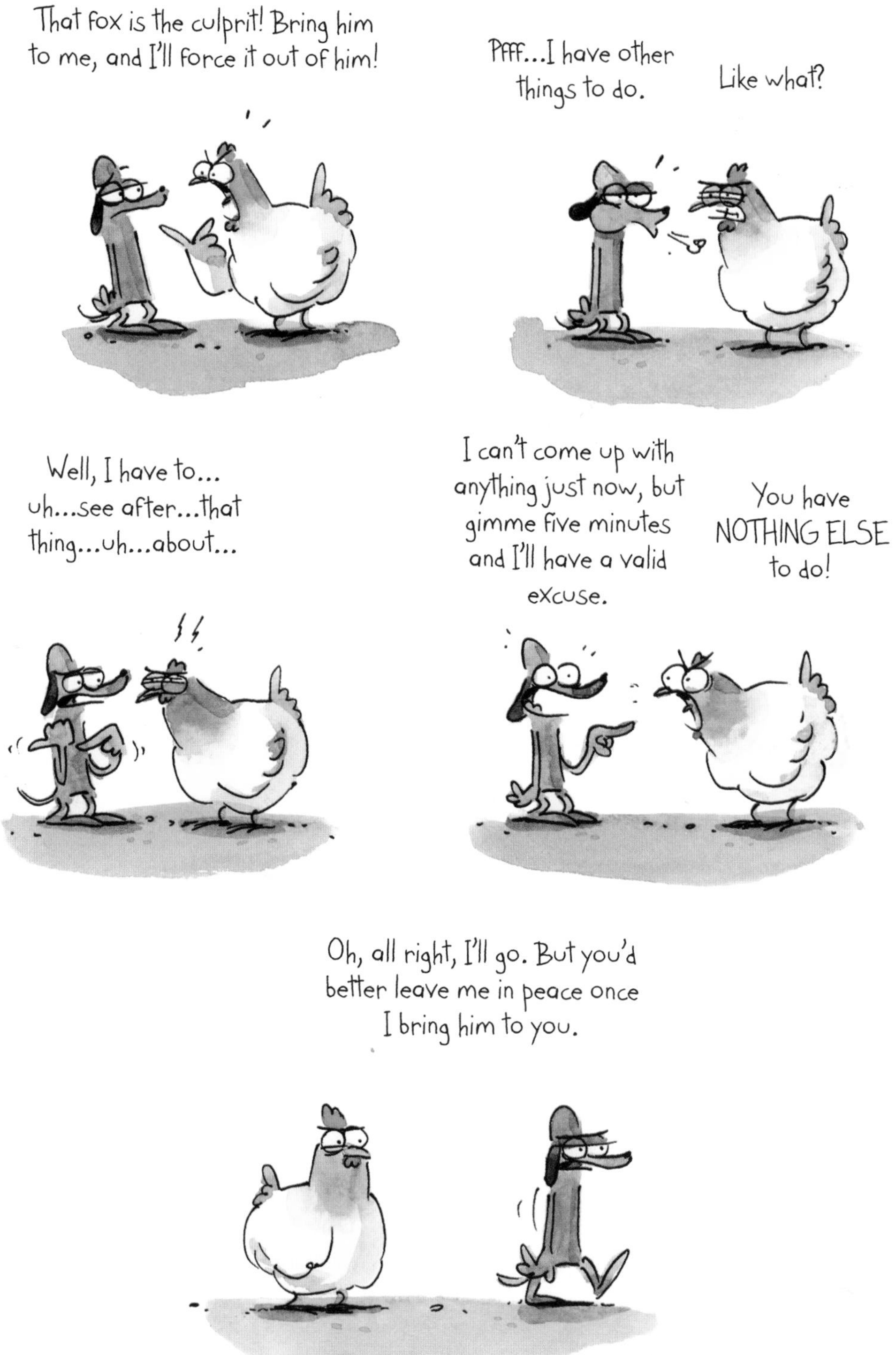
That fox is the culprit! Bring him to me, and I'll force it out of him!
Pfff...I have other things to do.
Like what?
Well, I have to... uh...see after...that thing...uh...about...
I can't come up with anything just now, but gimme five minutes and I'll have a valid excuse.
You have NOTHING ELSE to do!
Oh, all right, I'll go. But you'd better leave me in peace once I bring him to you.

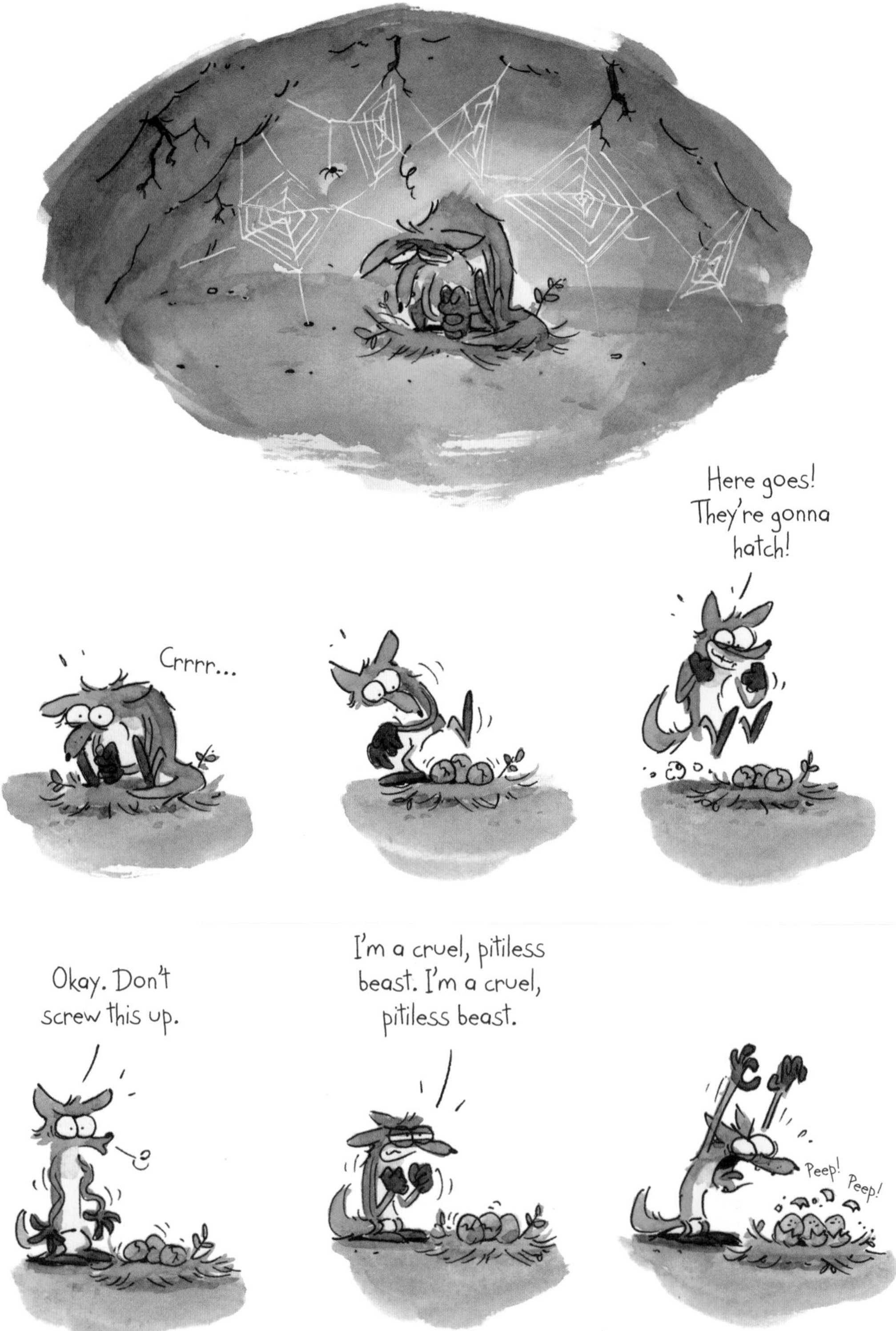
Crrrr...
Here goes! They're gonna hatch!
Okay. Don't screw this up.
I'm a cruel, pitiless beast. I'm a cruel, pitiless beast.
Peep!
Peep!

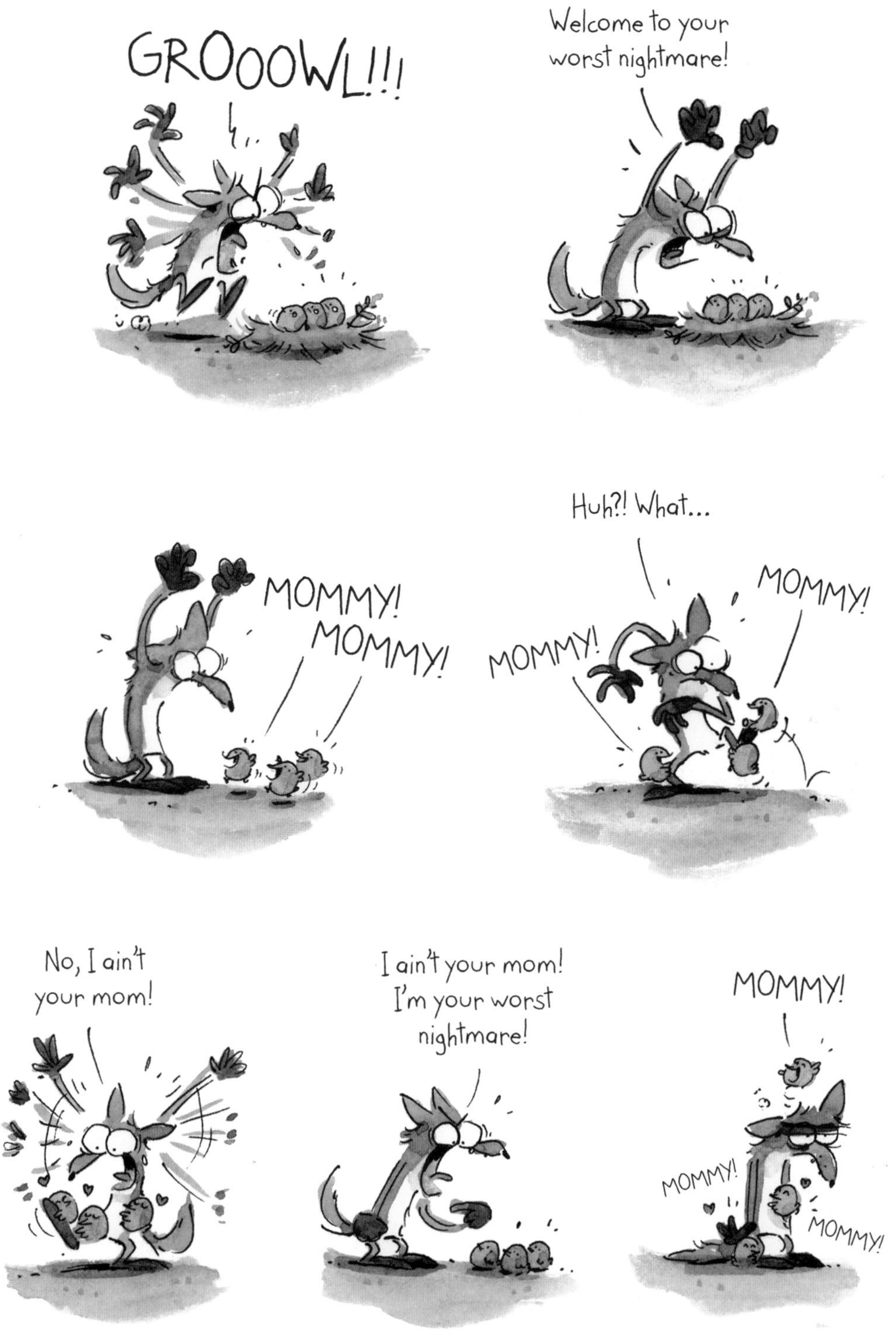
GROOOWL!!!
Welcome to your worst nightmare!
MOMMY!
MOMMY!
Huh?! What...
MOMMY!
MOMMY!
No, I ain't your mom!
I ain't your mom! I'm your worst nightmare!
MOMMY!
MOMMY!
MOMMY!

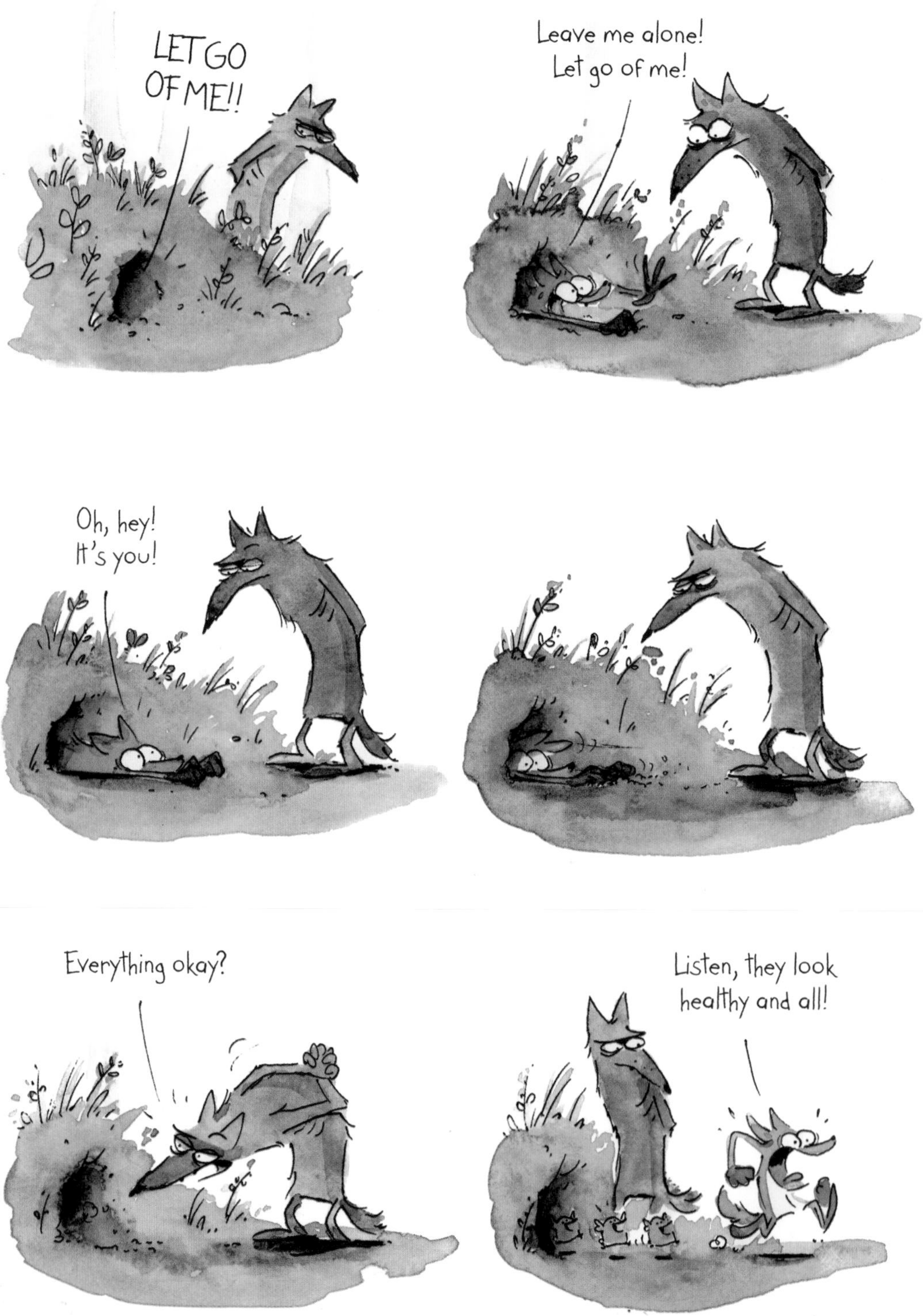
LET GO OF ME!!
Leave me alone! Let go of me!
Oh, hey! It's you!
Everything okay?
Listen, they look healthy and all!

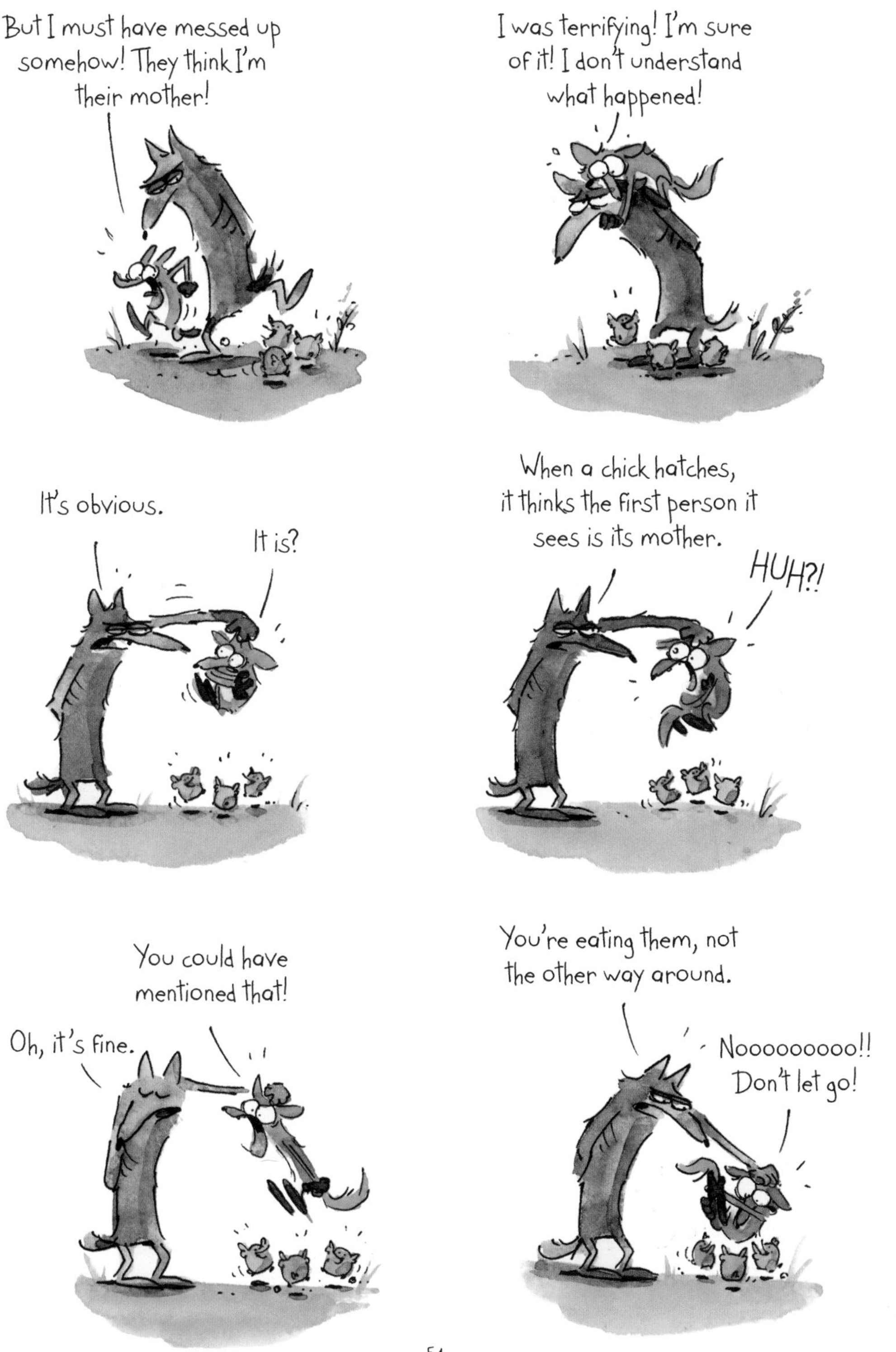

But I must have messed up somehow! They think I'm their mother!
I was terrifying! I'm sure of it! I don't understand what happened!
It's obvious.
It is?
When a chick hatches, it thinks the first person it sees is its mother.
HUH?!
You could have mentioned that!
Oh, it's fine.
You're eating them, not the other way around.
Nooooooooo!! Don't let go!

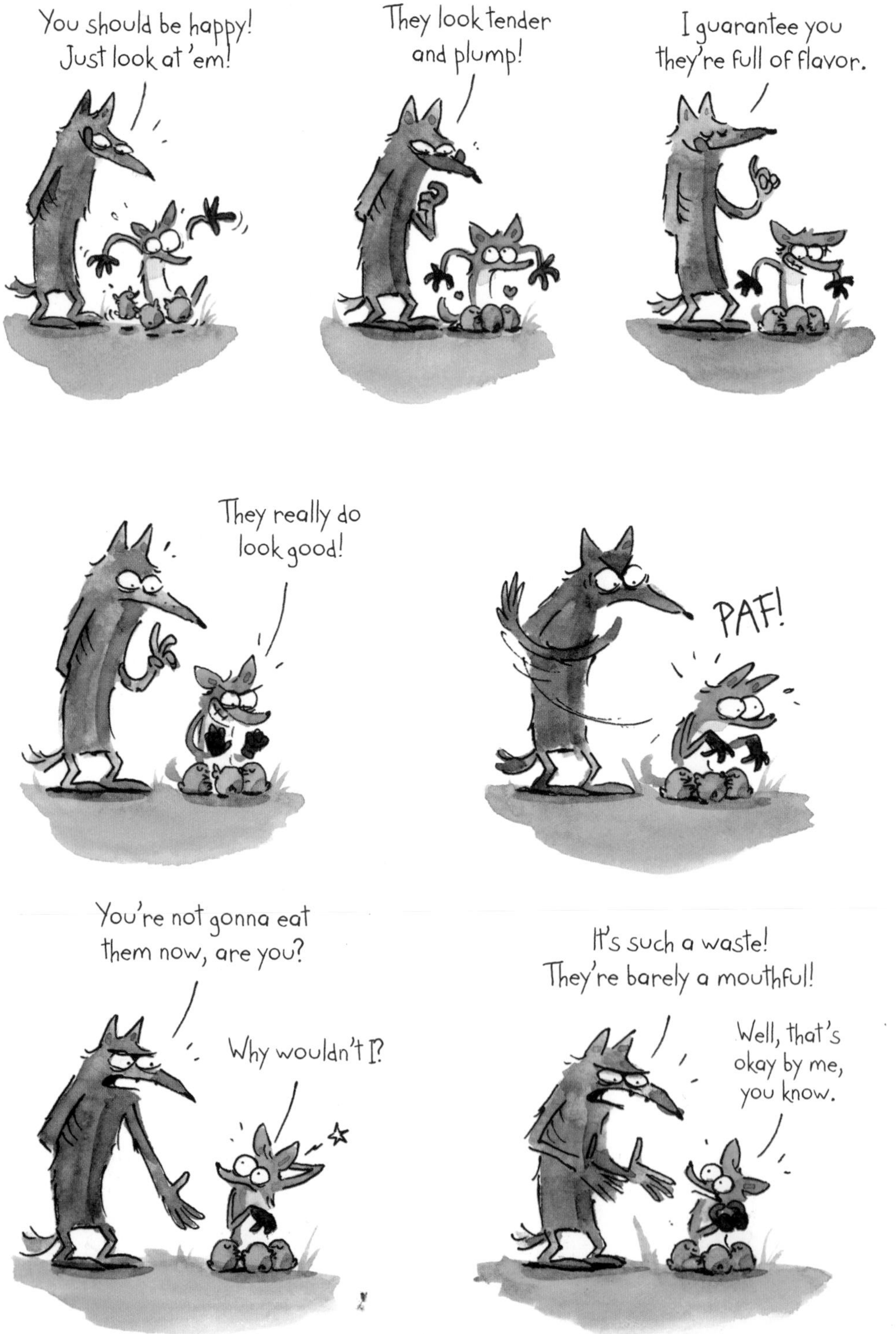
You should be happy! Just look at 'em!
They look tender and plump!
I guarantee you they're full of flavor.
They really do look good!
PAF!
You're not gonna eat them now, are you?
Why wouldn't I?
It's such a waste! They're barely a mouthful!
Well, that's okay by me, you know.

Let's wait a few months for them to gain a little weight.

A FEW MONTHS??

I'm hungry NOW! You're telling me I have to put up with these little fuzzballs for the next few MONTHS?

Yep.

Peep! Peep! Peep!

PEEEEEEEEP!!!

Make them stop!

How?

PEEEEEEEP!!!

I don't know! Rock them to calm them down!

Rock them?

PEEEEEEEP!!!

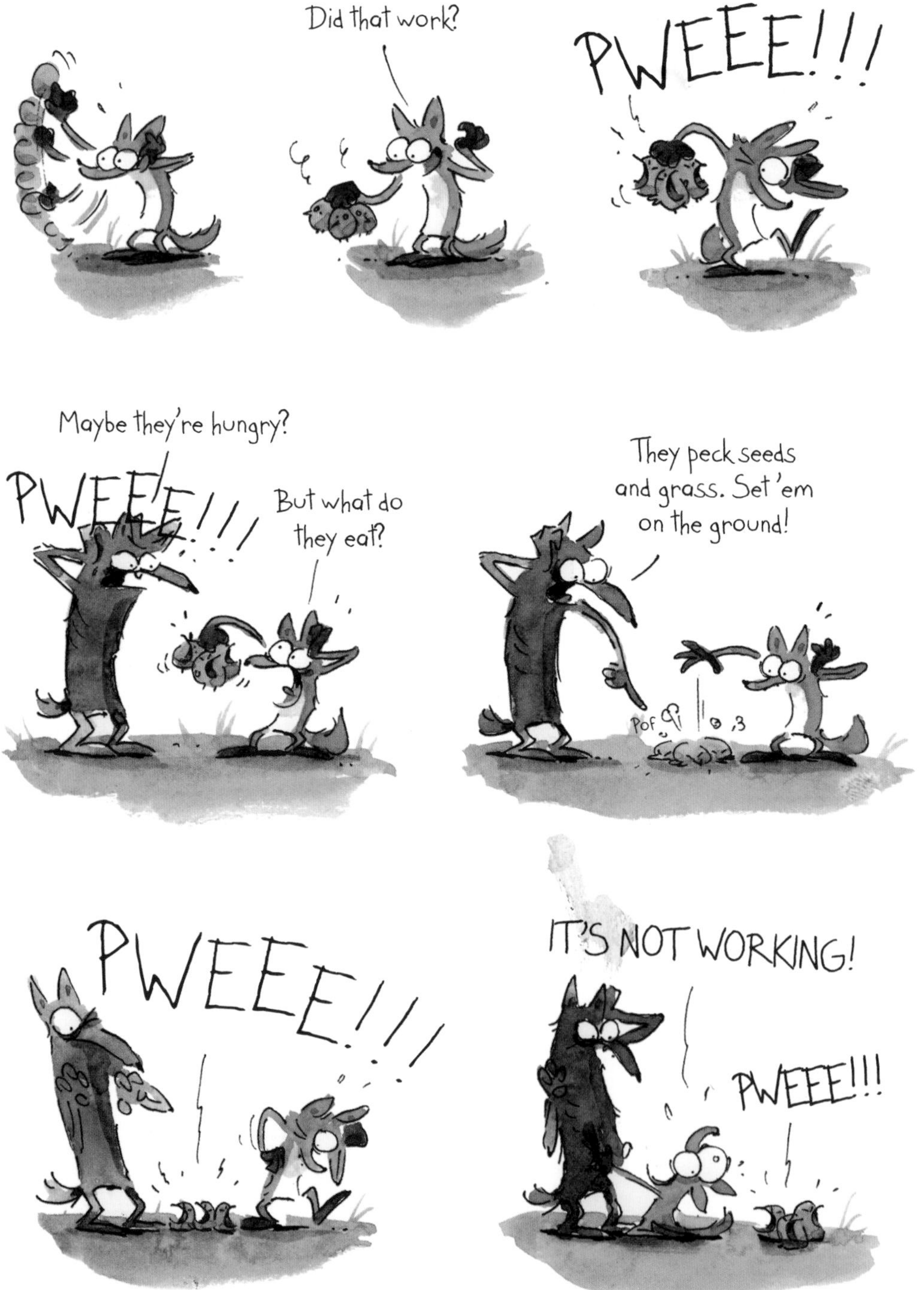
Did that work?
PWEEE!!!
Maybe they're hungry?
PWEEE!!!
But what do they eat?
They peck seeds and grass. Set 'em on the ground!
Pof
PWEEE!!!
IT'S NOT WORKING!
PWEEE!!!

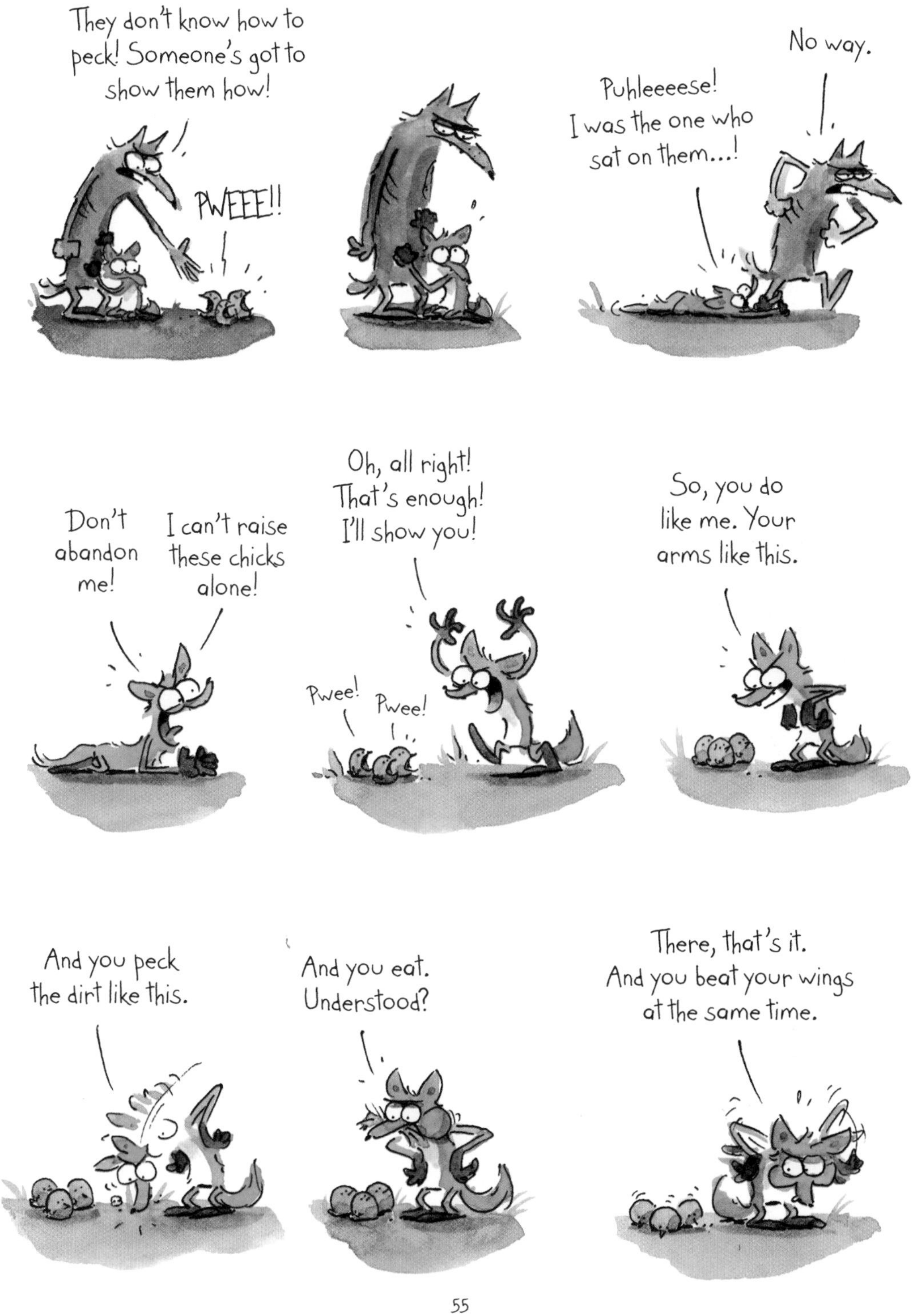
They don't know how to peck! Someone's got to show them how!
PWEEE!!
Puhleeeese! I was the one who sat on them...!
No way.
Don't abandon me!
I can't raise these chicks alone!
Oh, all right! That's enough! I'll show you!
Pwee!
Pwee!
So, you do like me. Your arms like this.
And you peck the dirt like this.
And you eat. Understood?
There, that's it. And you beat your wings at the same time.

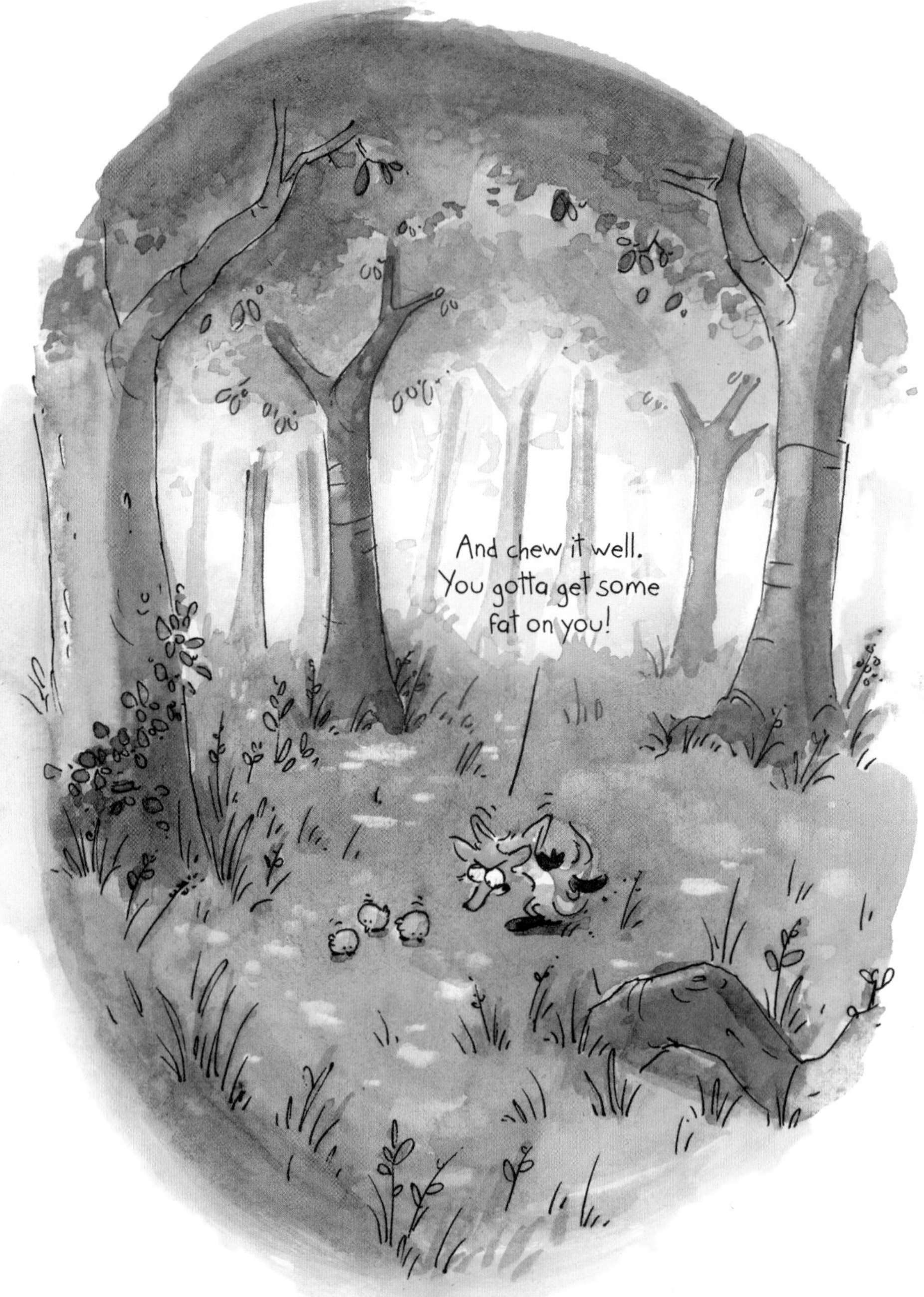
And chew it well. You gotta get some fat on you!

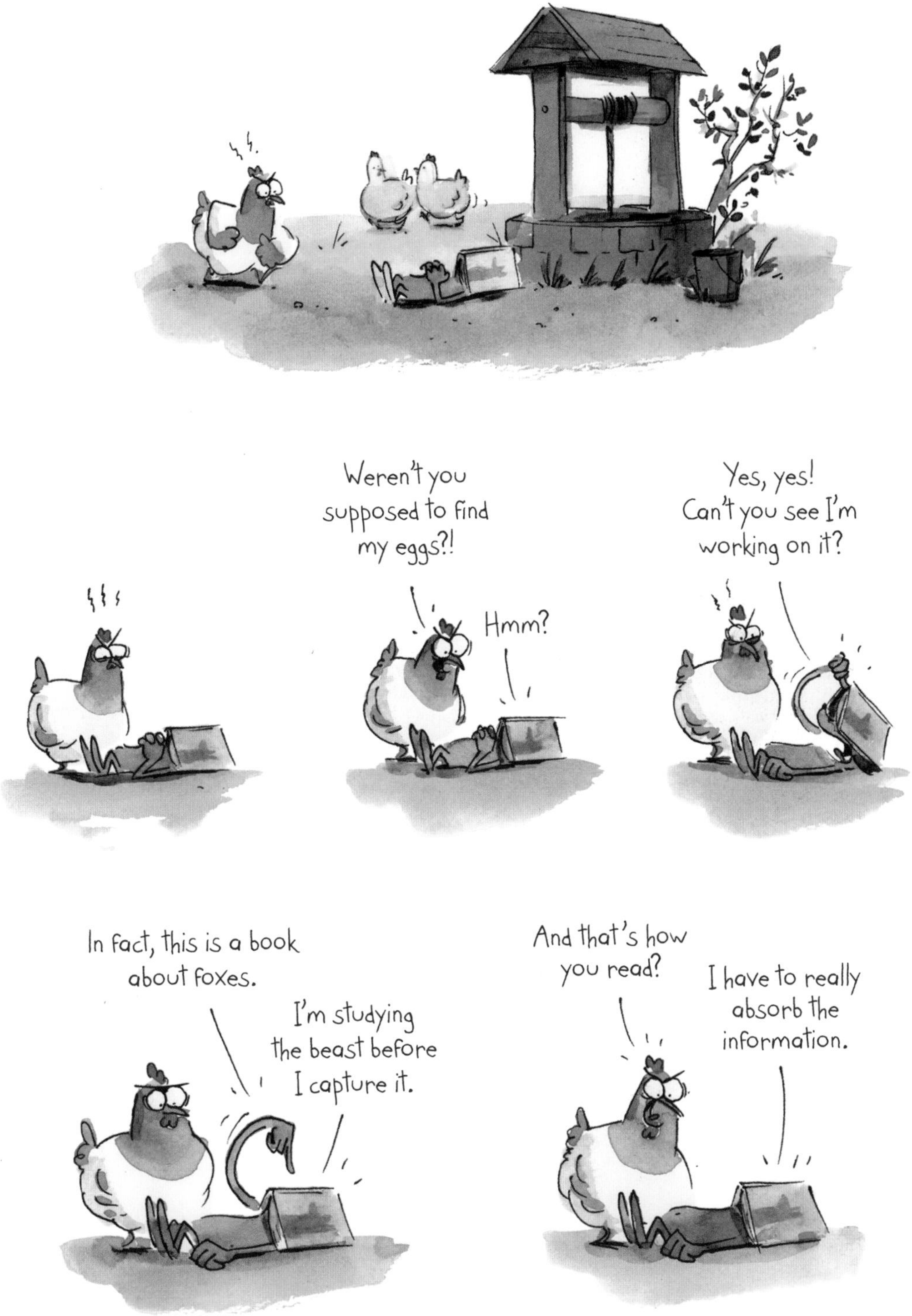

Weren't you supposed to find my eggs?!
Hmm?
Yes, yes! Can't you see I'm working on it?
In fact, this is a book about foxes.
I'm studying the beast before I capture it.
And that's how you read?
I have to really absorb the information.

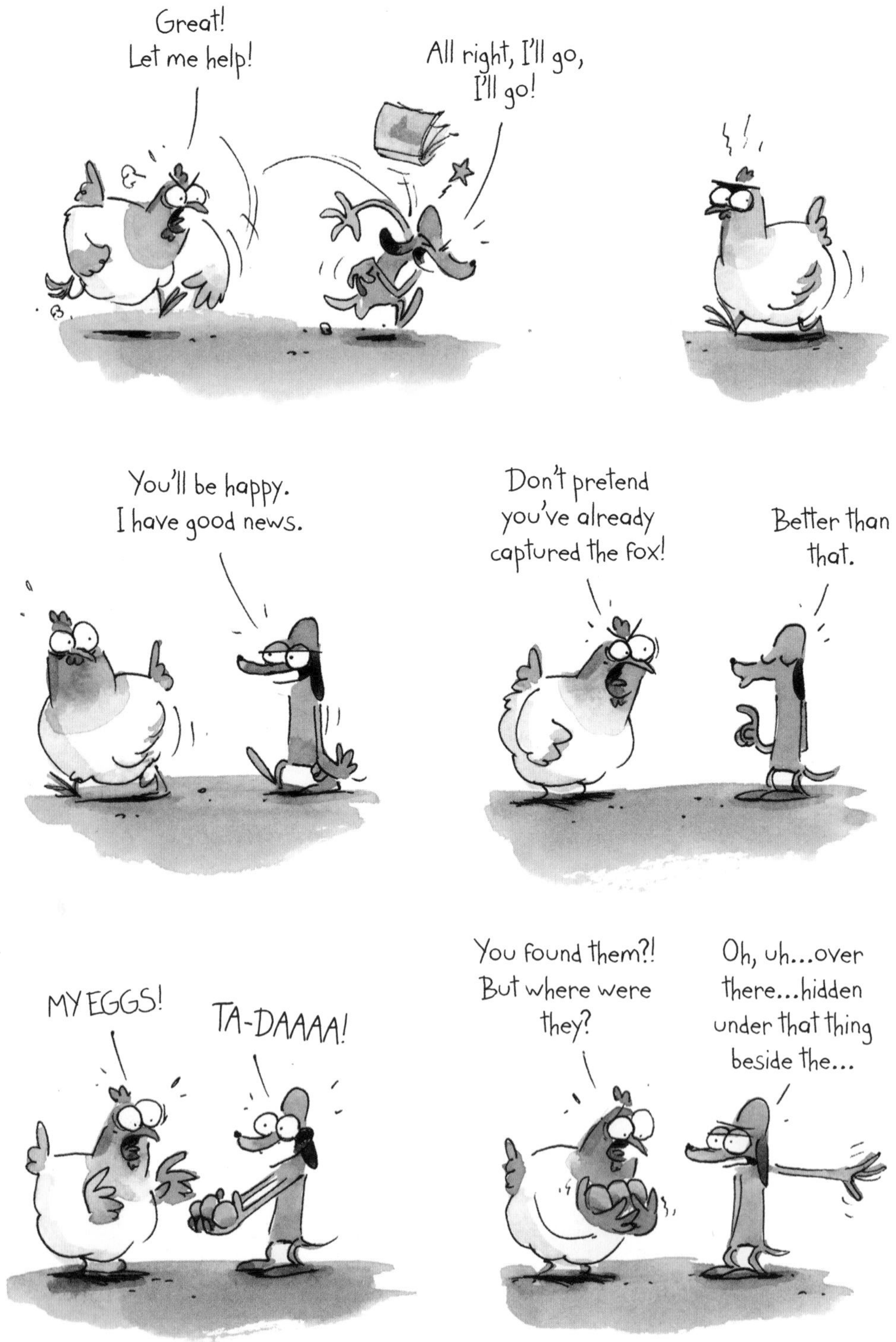
Great!
Let me help!
All right, I'll go,
I'll go!
You'll be happy.
I have good news.
Don't pretend
you've already
captured the fox!
Better than
that.
MY EGGS!
TA-DAAAA!
You found them?!
But where were
they?
Oh, uh...over
there...hidden
under that thing
beside the...

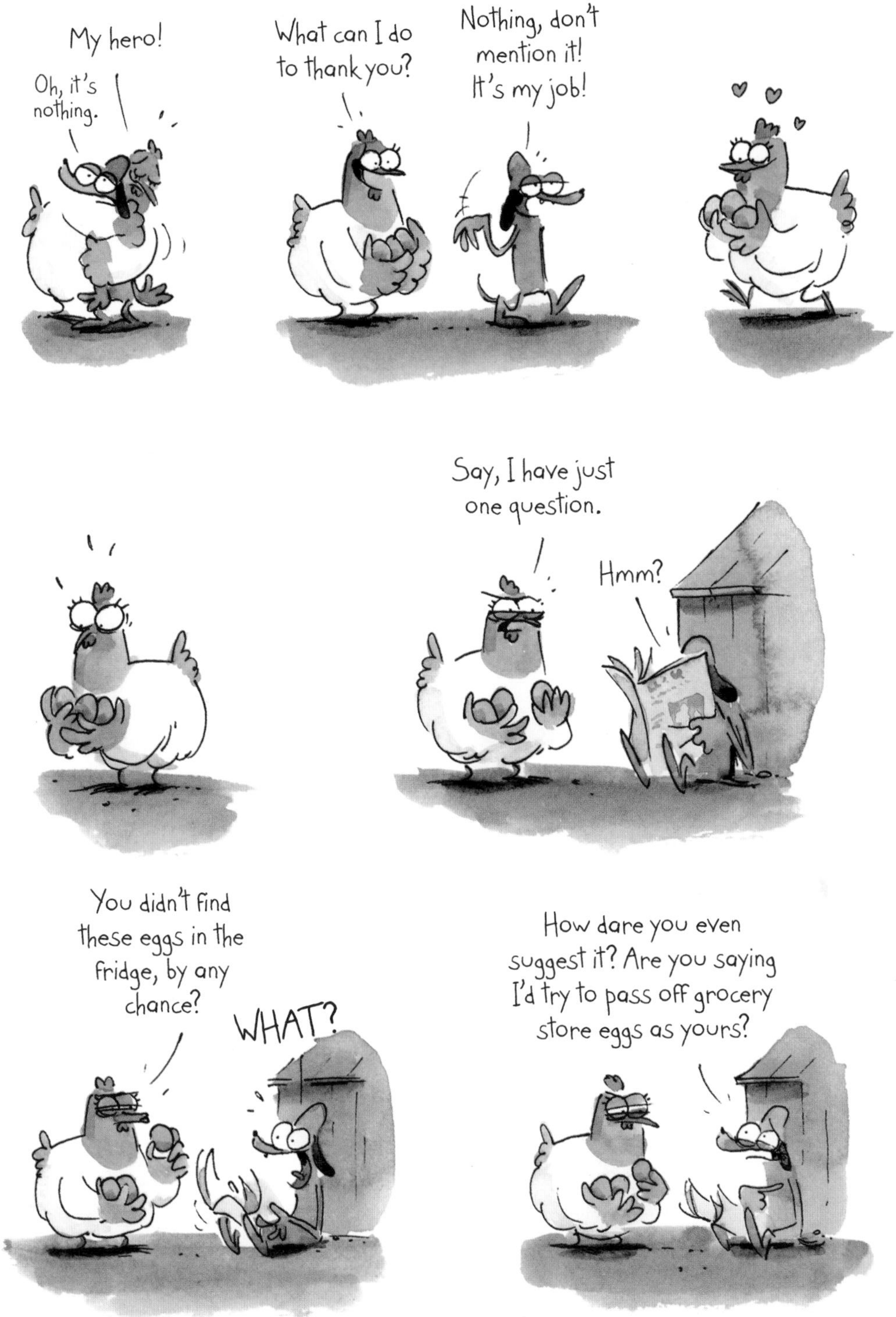
My hero!
Oh, it's nothing.
What can I do to thank you?
Nothing, don't mention it! It's my job!
Say, I have just one question.
Hmm?
You didn't find these eggs in the fridge, by any chance?
WHAT?
How dare you even suggest it? Are you saying I'd try to pass off grocery store eggs as yours?

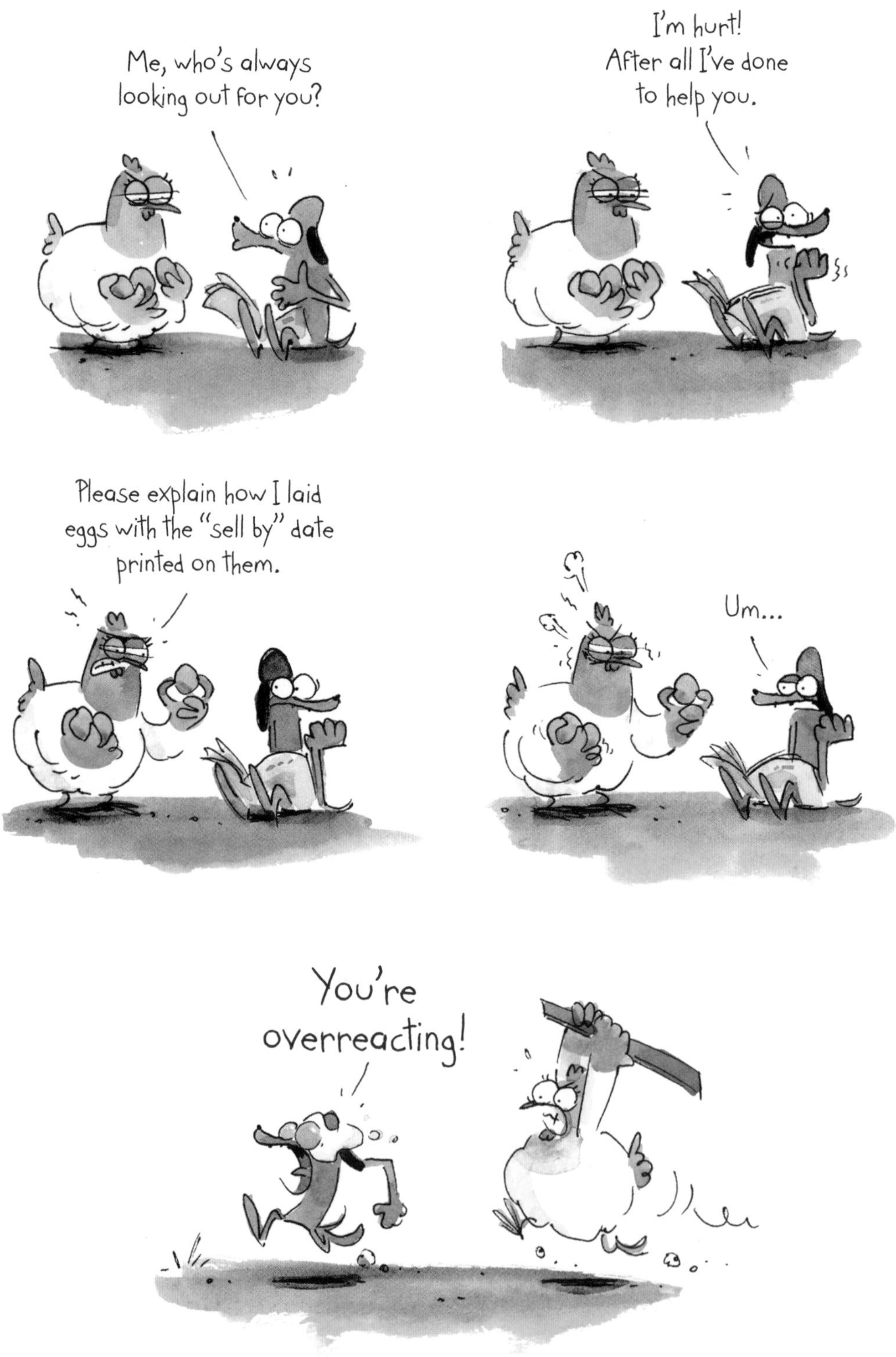
Me, who's always looking out for you?
I'm hurt! After all I've done to help you.
Please explain how I laid eggs with the "sell by" date printed on them.
Um...
You're overreacting!

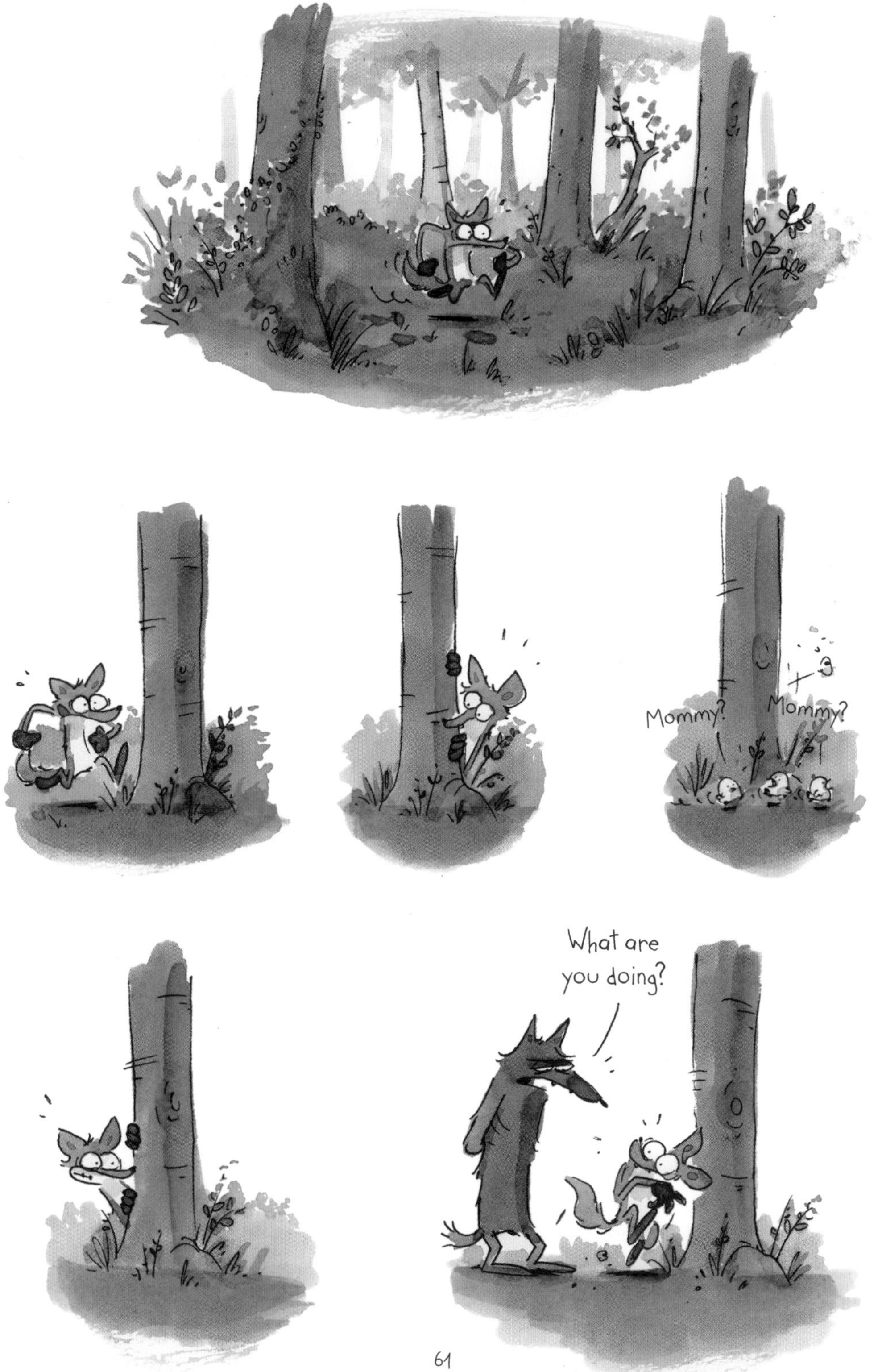
Mommy?
Mommy?
What are you doing?

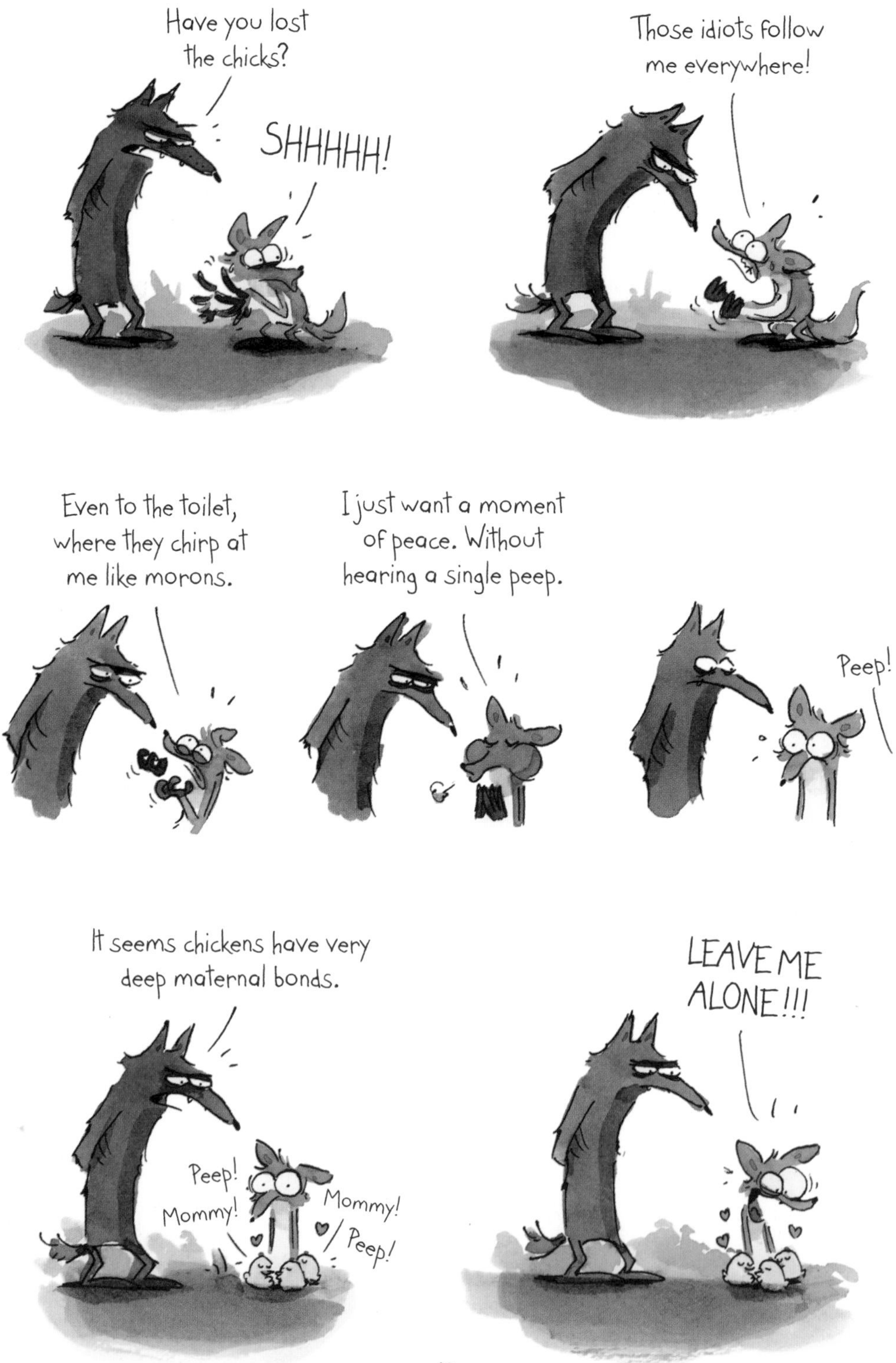
Have you lost the chicks?
SHHHHH!
Those idiots follow me everywhere!
Even to the toilet, where they chirp at me like morons.
I just want a moment of peace. Without hearing a single peep.
Peep!
It seems chickens have very deep maternal bonds.
Peep!
Mommy!
Mommy!
Peep!
LEAVE ME ALONE!!!

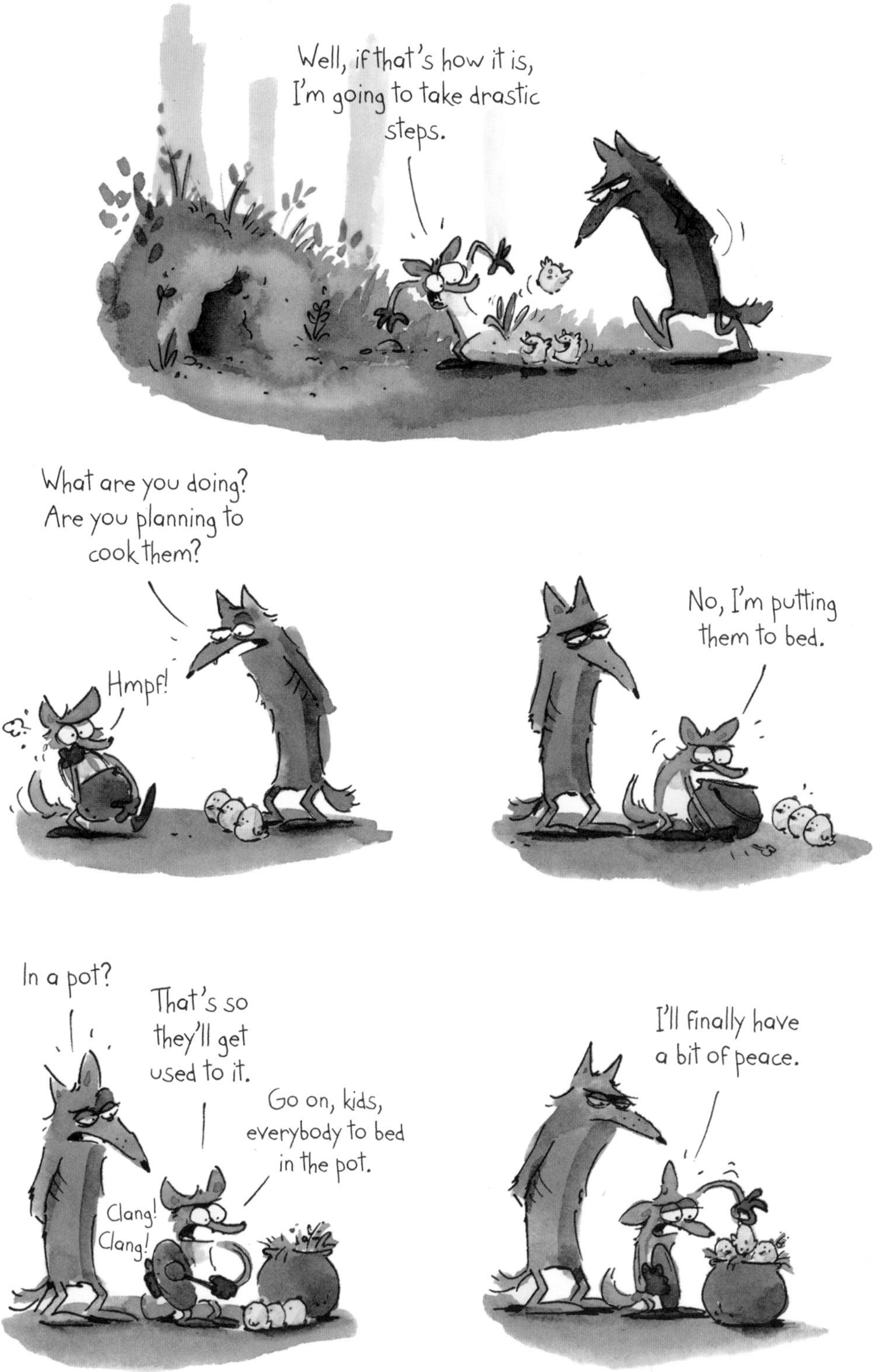

Well, if that's how it is, I'm going to take drastic steps.
What are you doing? Are you planning to cook them?
Hmpf!
No, I'm putting them to bed.
In a pot?
That's so they'll get used to it.
Go on, kids, everybody to bed in the pot.
Clang! Clang!
I'll finally have a bit of peace.

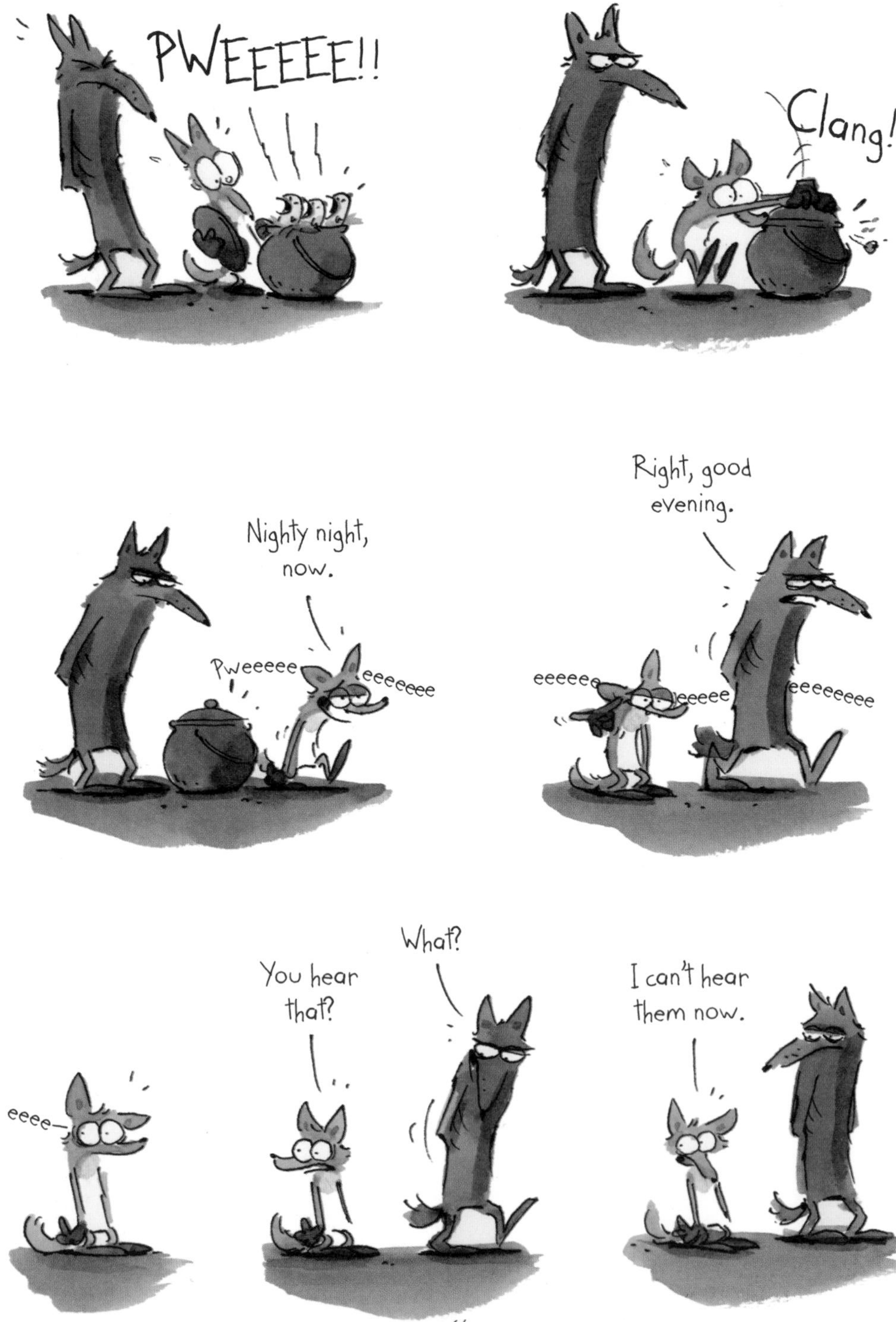
PWEEEEE!!
Clang!
Pweeeee
Nighty night, now.
eeeeeee
Right, good evening.
eeeeee
eeeee
eeeeeeee
eeee—
You hear that?
What?
I can't hear them now.

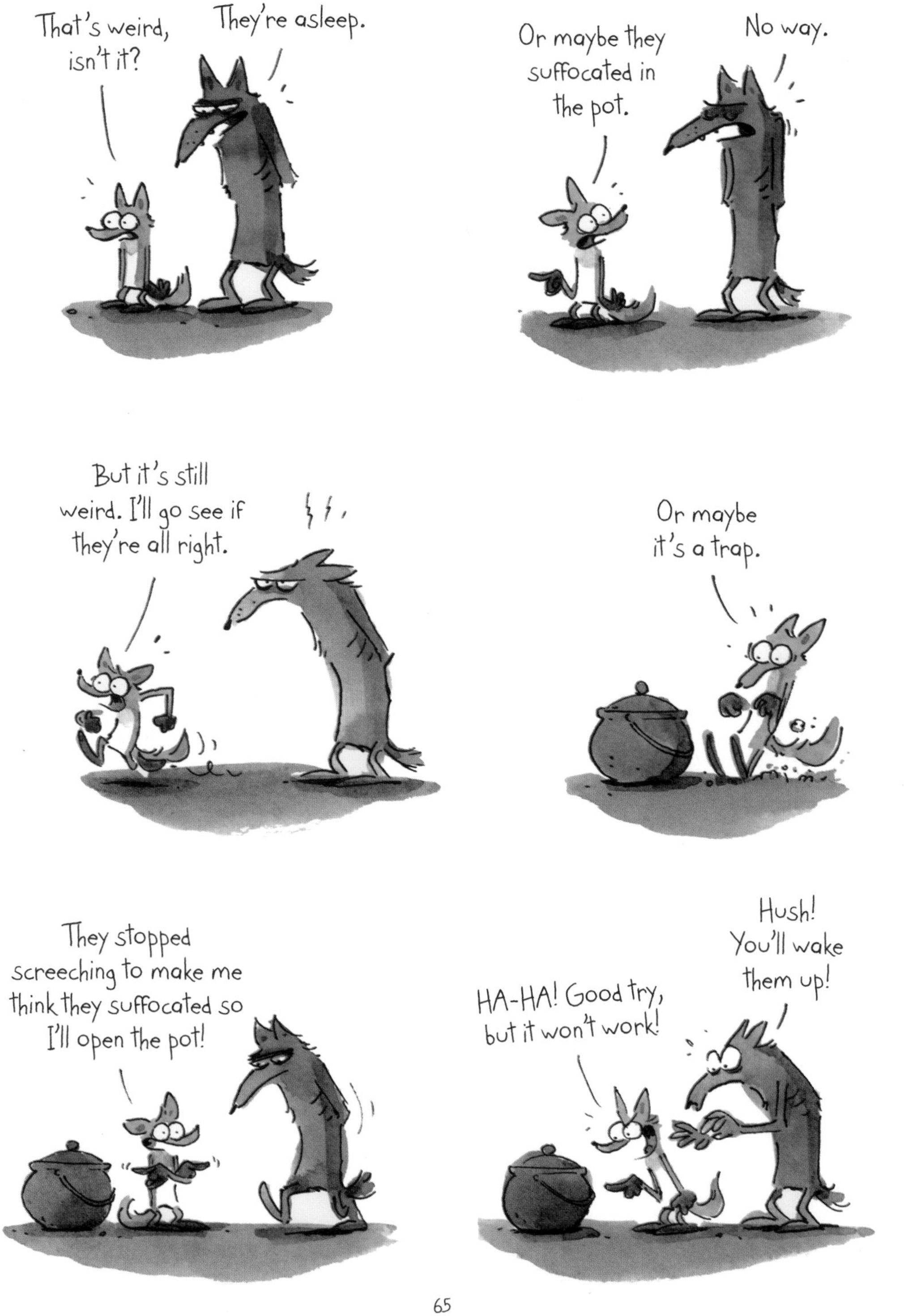

That's weird, isn't it?
They're asleep.
Or maybe they suffocated in the pot.
No way.
But it's still weird. I'll go see if they're all right.
Or maybe it's a trap.
They stopped screeching to make me think they suffocated so I'll open the pot!
HA-HA! Good try, but it won't work!
Hush! You'll wake them up!

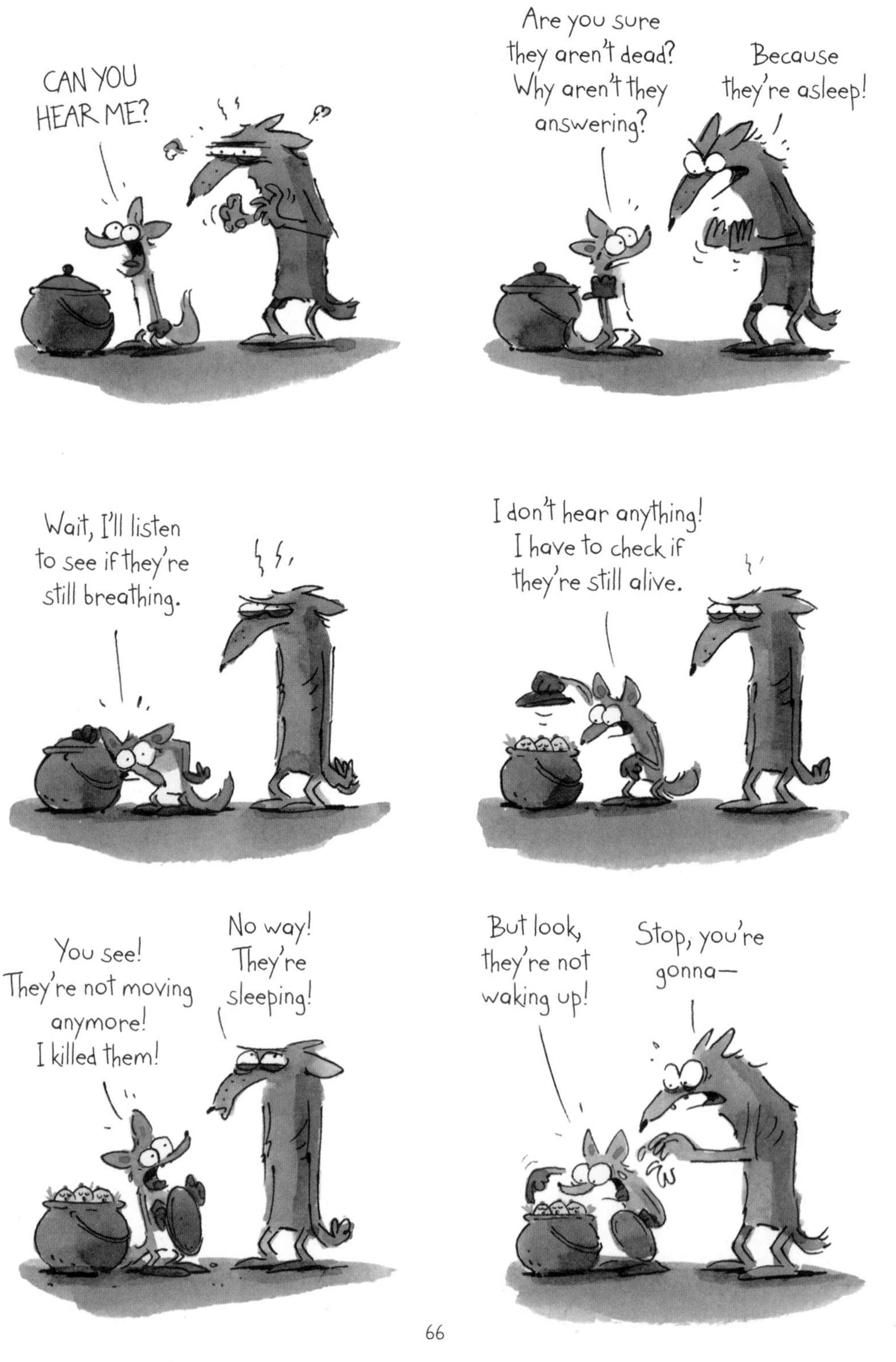
CAN YOU HEAR ME?
Are you sure they aren't dead? Why aren't they answering?
Because they're asleep!
Wait, I'll listen to see if they're still breathing.
I don't hear anything! I have to check if they're still alive.
You see! They're not moving anymore! I killed them!
No way! They're sleeping!
But look, they're not waking up!
Stop, you're gonna—

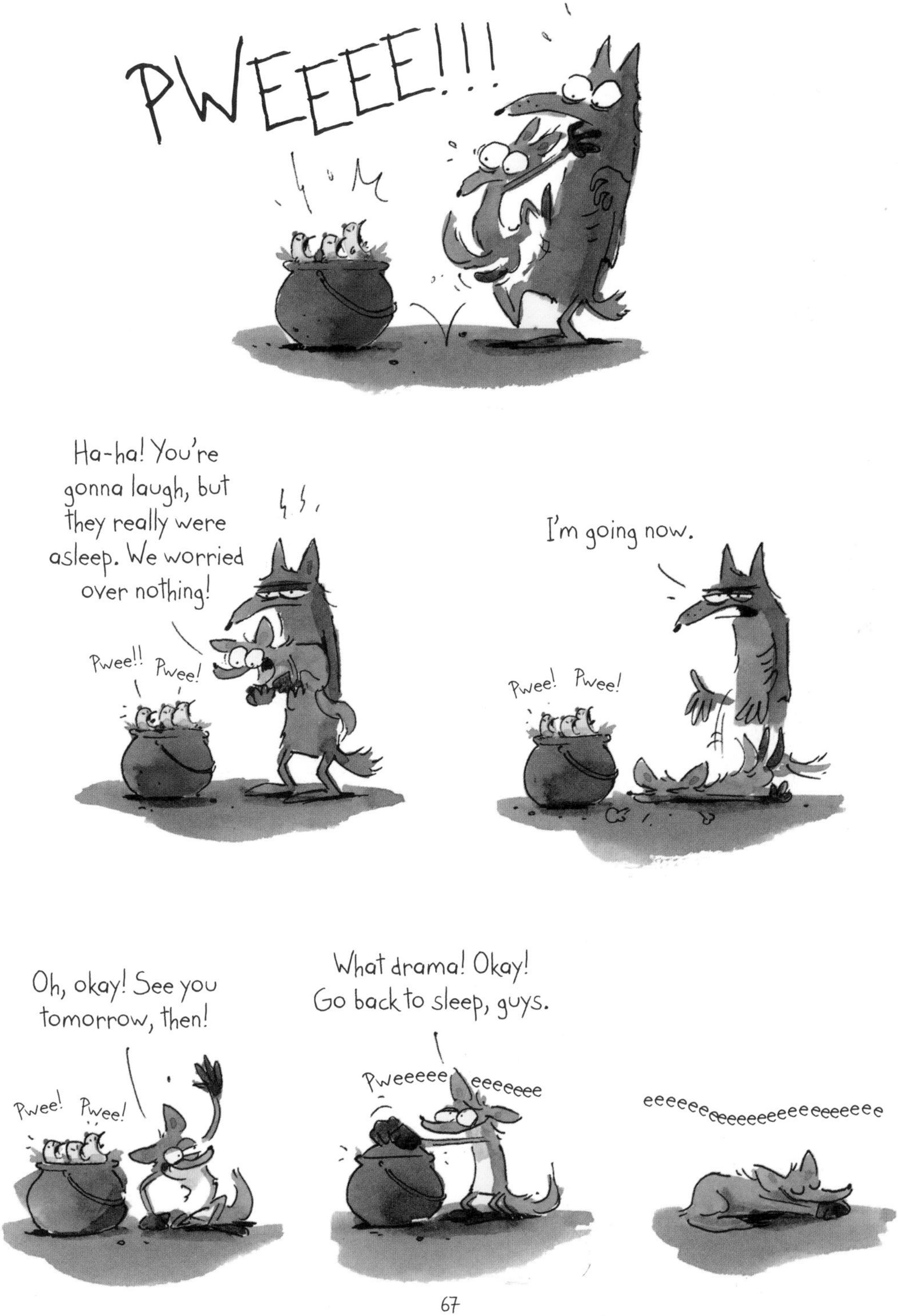
PWEEEE!!!
Ha-ha! You're gonna laugh, but they really were asleep. We worried over nothing!
Pwee!!
Pwee!
I'm going now.
Pwee!
Pwee!
Oh, okay! See you tomorrow, then!
Pwee!
Pwee!
What drama! Okay! Go back to sleep, guys.
Pweeeeeeeeeeee
eeeeeeeeeeeeeeeeeeeeeee

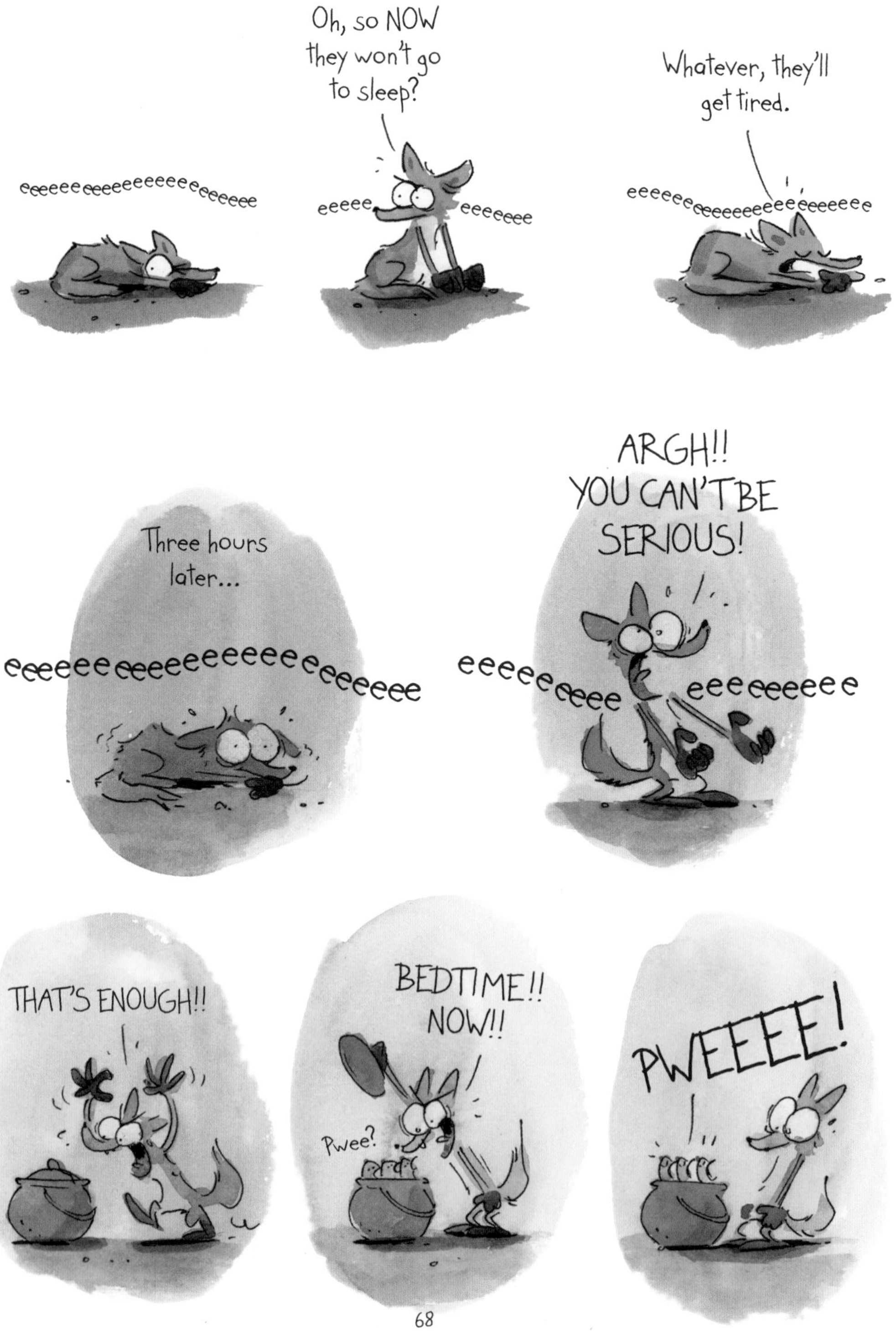
eeeeeeeeeeeeeeeeeeeeeeeeee
Oh, so NOW they won't go to sleep?
eeeee
eeeeeee
Whatever, they'll get tired.
eeeeeeeeeeeeeeeeeeeeeeeeee
Three hours later...
eeeeeeeeeeeeeeeeeeeeeeeeeeee
ARGH!! YOU CAN'T BE SERIOUS!
eeeeeeeee
eeeeeeeee
THAT'S ENOUGH!!
BEDTIME!! NOW!!
Pwee?
PWEEEE!

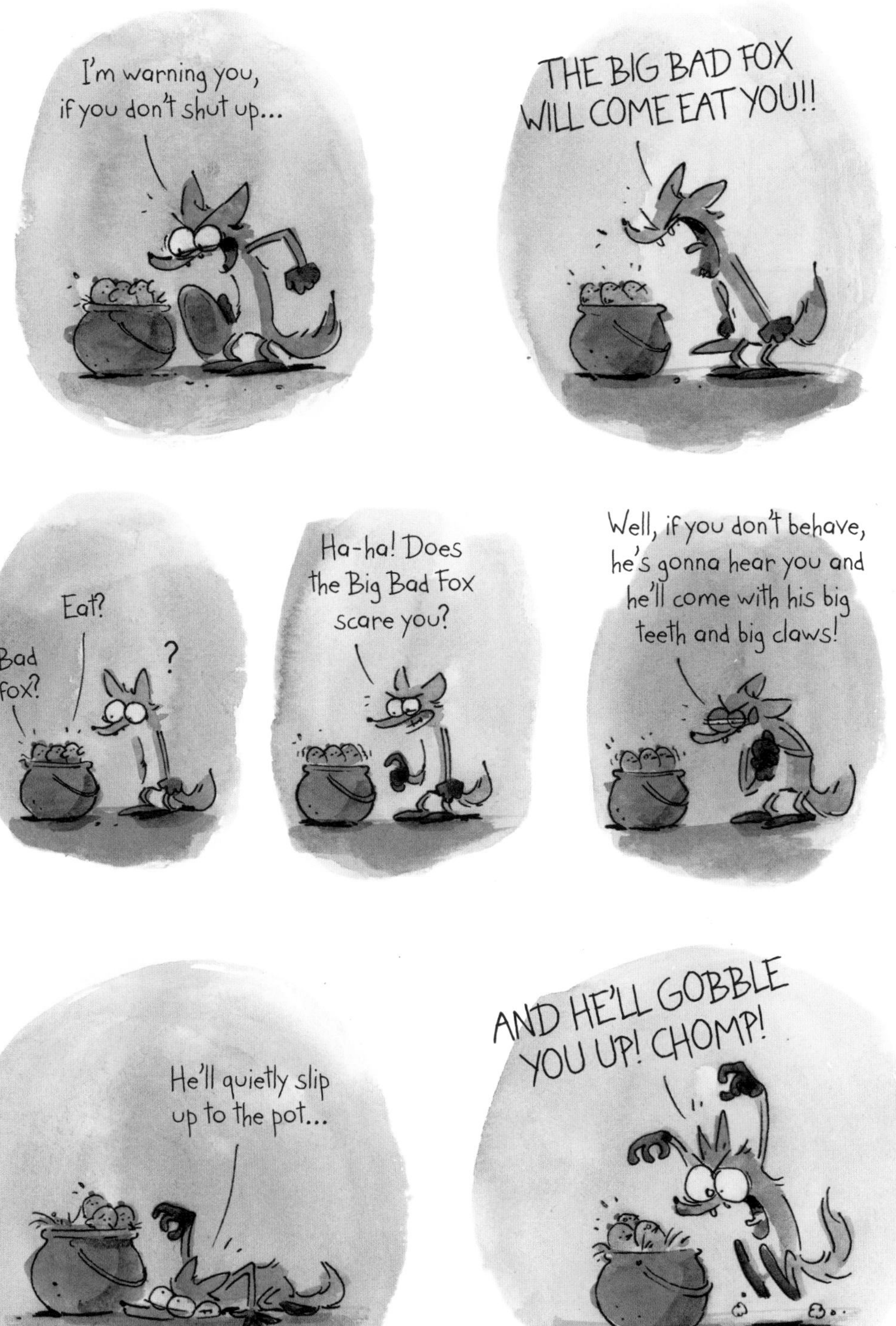
I'm warning you, if you don't shut up...
THE BIG BAD FOX WILL COME EAT YOU!!
Bad fox?
Eat?
?
Ha-ha! Does the Big Bad Fox scare you?
Well, if you don't behave, he's gonna hear you and he'll come with his big teeth and big claws!
He'll quietly slip up to the pot...
AND HE'LL GOBBLE YOU UP! CHOMP!

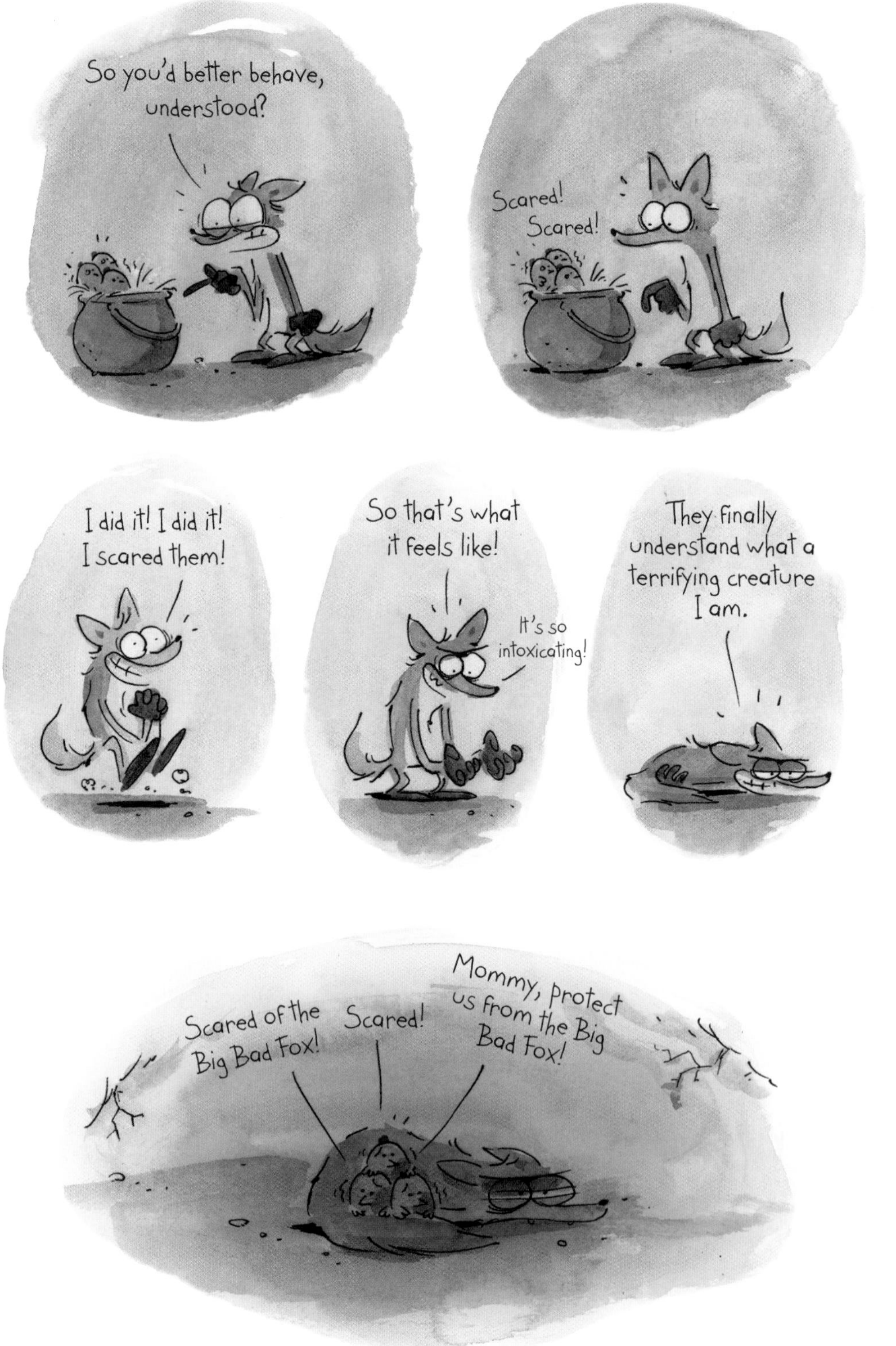
So you'd better behave, understood?
Scared!
Scared!
I did it! I did it! I scared them!
So that's what it feels like!
It's so intoxicating!
They finally understand what a terrifying creature I am.
Scared of the Big Bad Fox!
Scared!
Mommy, protect us from the Big Bad Fox!

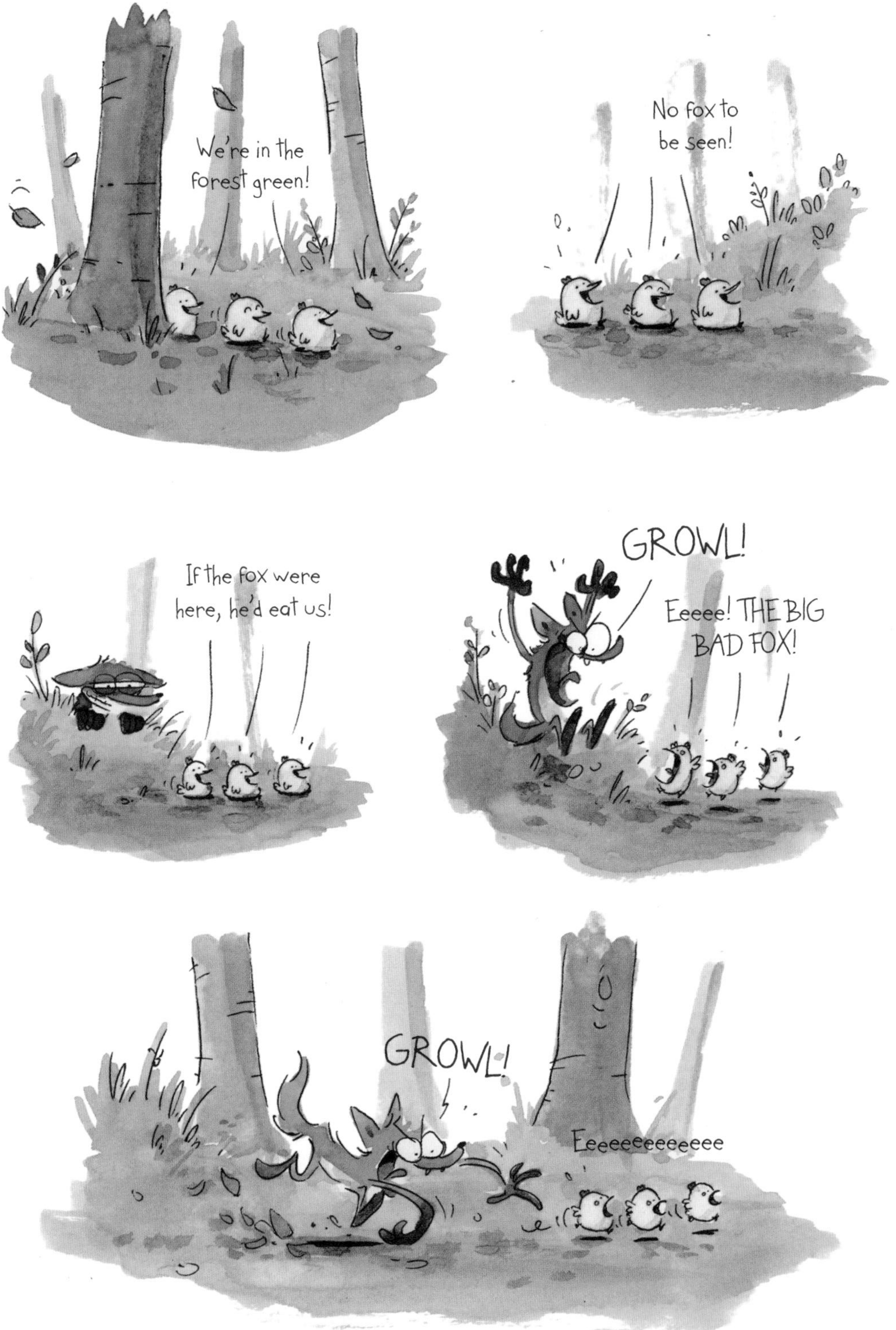
We're in the forest green!
No fox to be seen!
If the fox were here, he'd eat us!
GROWL!
Eeeee! THE BIG BAD FOX!
GROWL!
Eeeeeeeeeeee

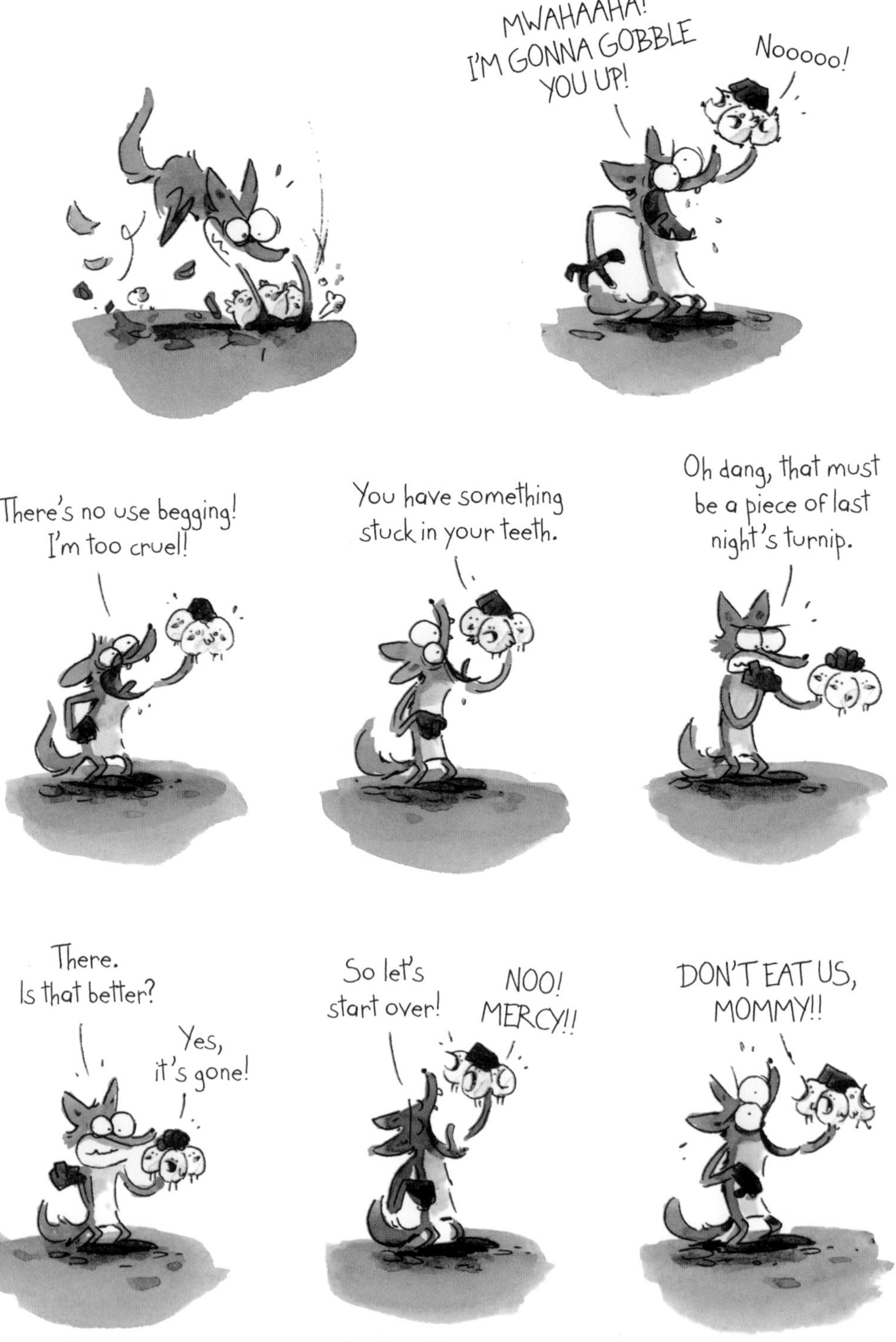
MWAHAAHA!
I'M GONNA GOBBLE
YOU UP!
Nooooo!
There's no use begging!
I'm too cruel!
You have something
stuck in your teeth.
Oh dang, that must
be a piece of last
night's turnip.
There.
Is that better?
Yes,
it's gone!
So let's
start over!
NOO!
MERCY!!
DON'T EAT US,
MOMMY!!

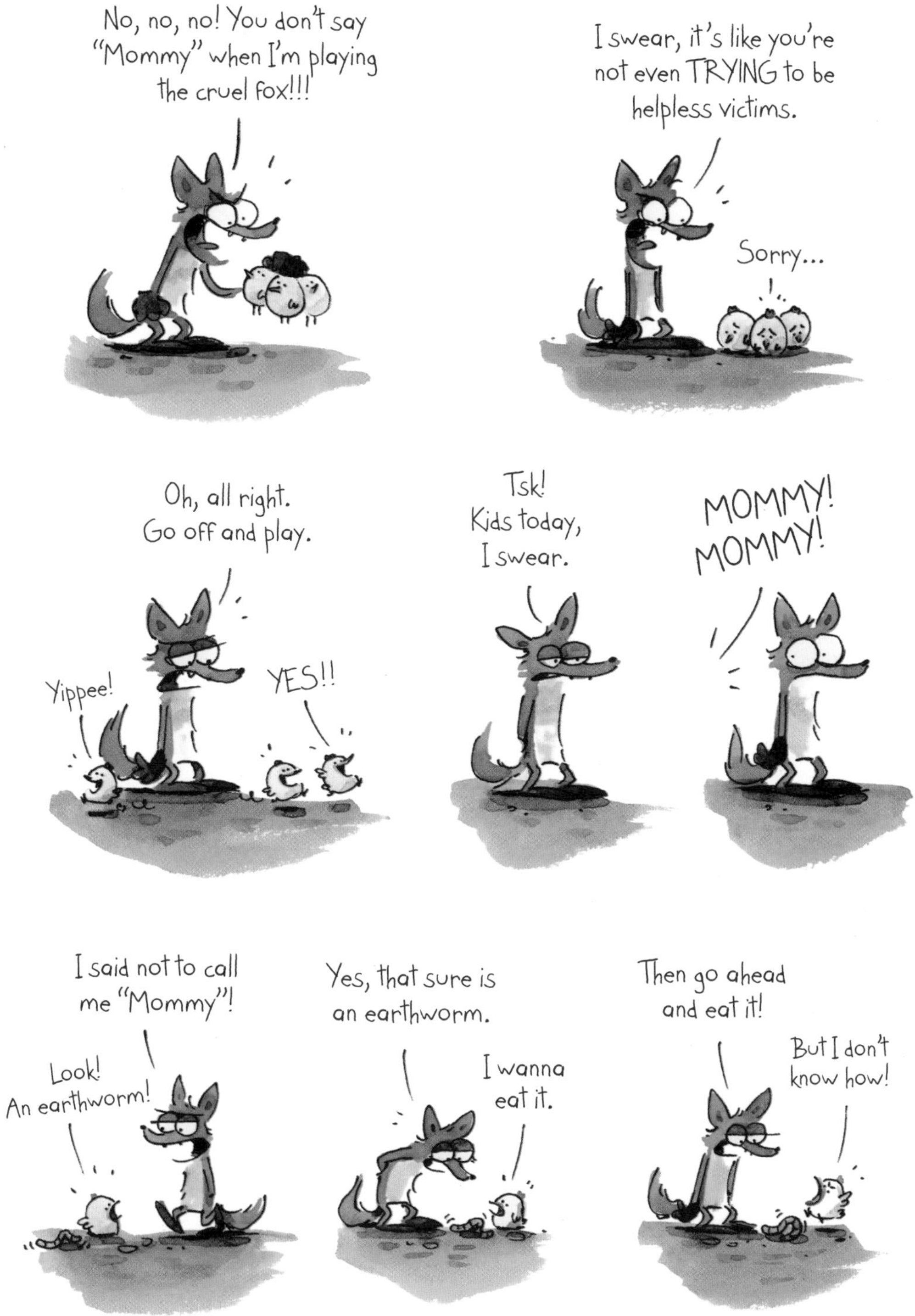

No, no, no! You don't say "Mommy" when I'm playing the cruel fox!!!
I swear, it's like you're not even TRYING to be helpless victims.
Sorry...
Oh, all right. Go off and play.
Yippee!
YES!!
Tsk! Kids today, I swear.
MOMMY! MOMMY!
I said not to call me "Mommy"!
Look! An earthworm!
Yes, that sure is an earthworm.
I wanna eat it.
Then go ahead and eat it!
But I don't know how!

Just do your thing.

NO, IT'S TOO HARD!

You gotta try before you can say it's too hard!

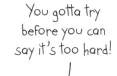

BUT I CAN'T!

JUST TRY!

BUT IT'S TOO HARD!

MOMMY!!

MOMMY, QUICK!!

What? What?

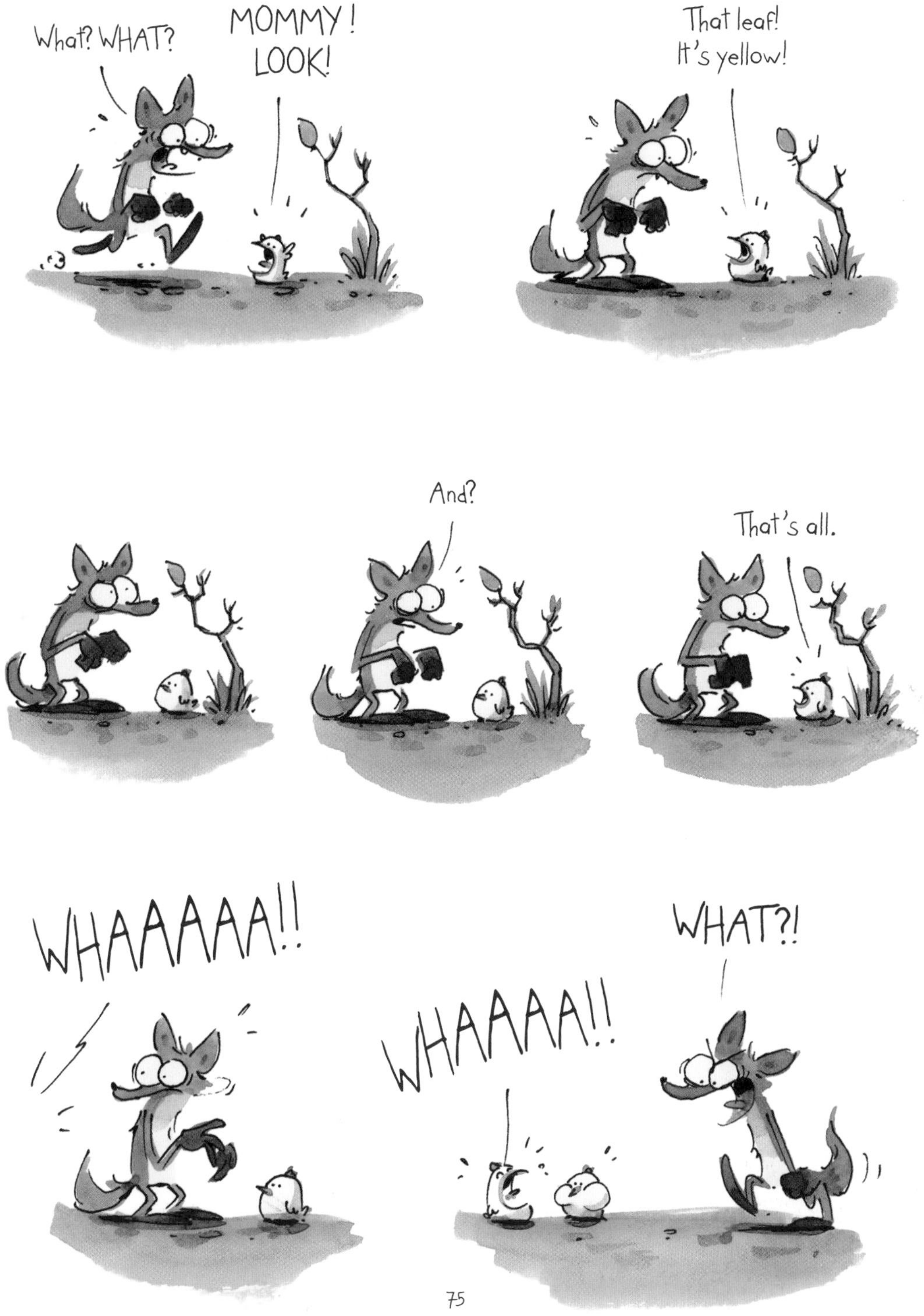
What? WHAT?
MOMMY! LOOK!
That leaf! It's yellow!
And?
That's all.
WHAAAAA!!
WHAAAAA!!
WHAT?!

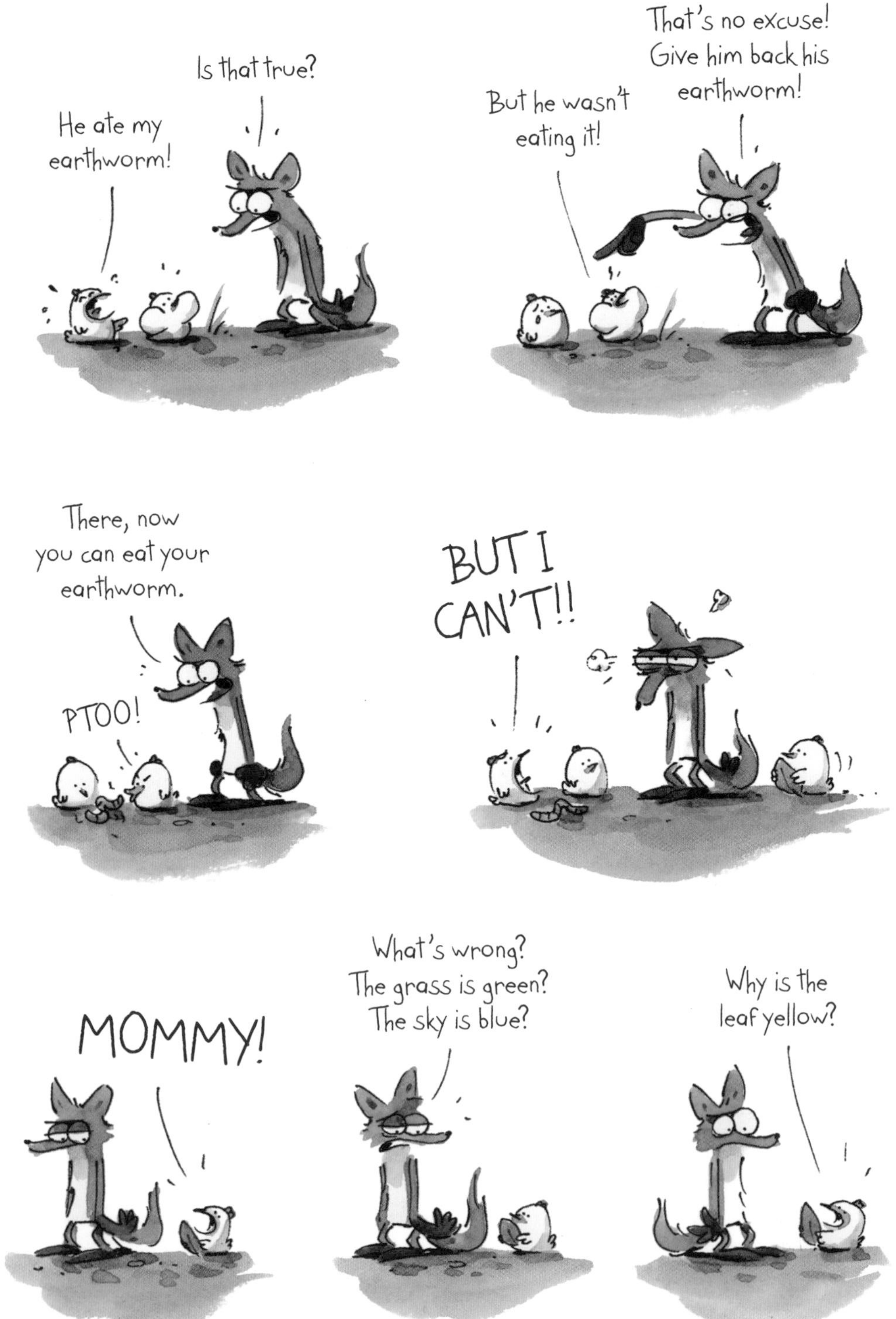
Is that true?
He ate my earthworm!
That's no excuse! Give him back his earthworm!
But he wasn't eating it!
There, now you can eat your earthworm.
PTOO!
BUT I CAN'T!!
MOMMY!
What's wrong? The grass is green? The sky is blue?
Why is the leaf yellow?

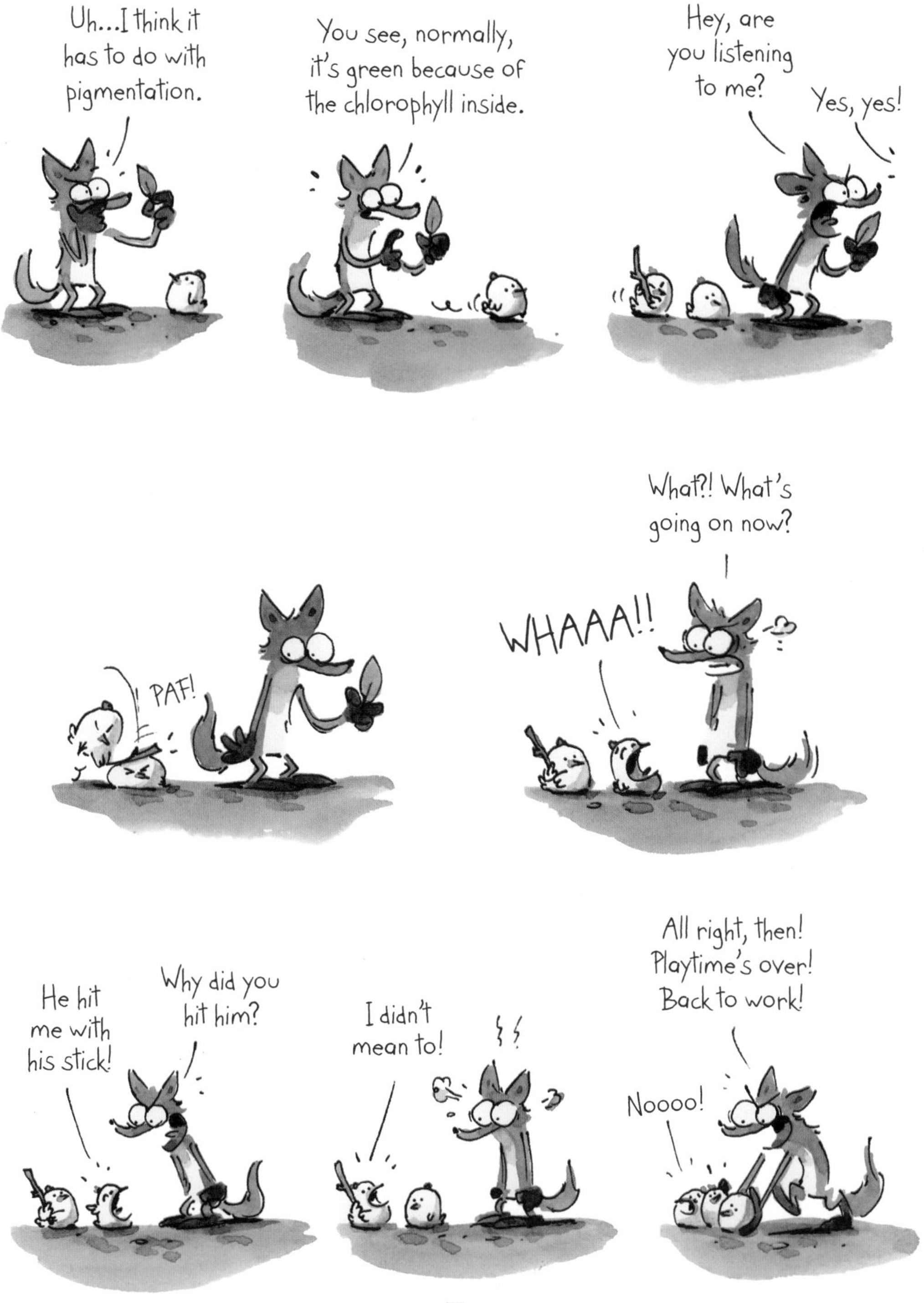
Uh...I think it has to do with pigmentation.
You see, normally, it's green because of the chlorophyll inside.
Hey, are you listening to me?
Yes, yes!
PAF!
What?! What's going on now?
WHAAA!!
He hit me with his stick!
Why did you hit him?
I didn't mean to!
All right, then! Playtime's over! Back to work!
Noooo!

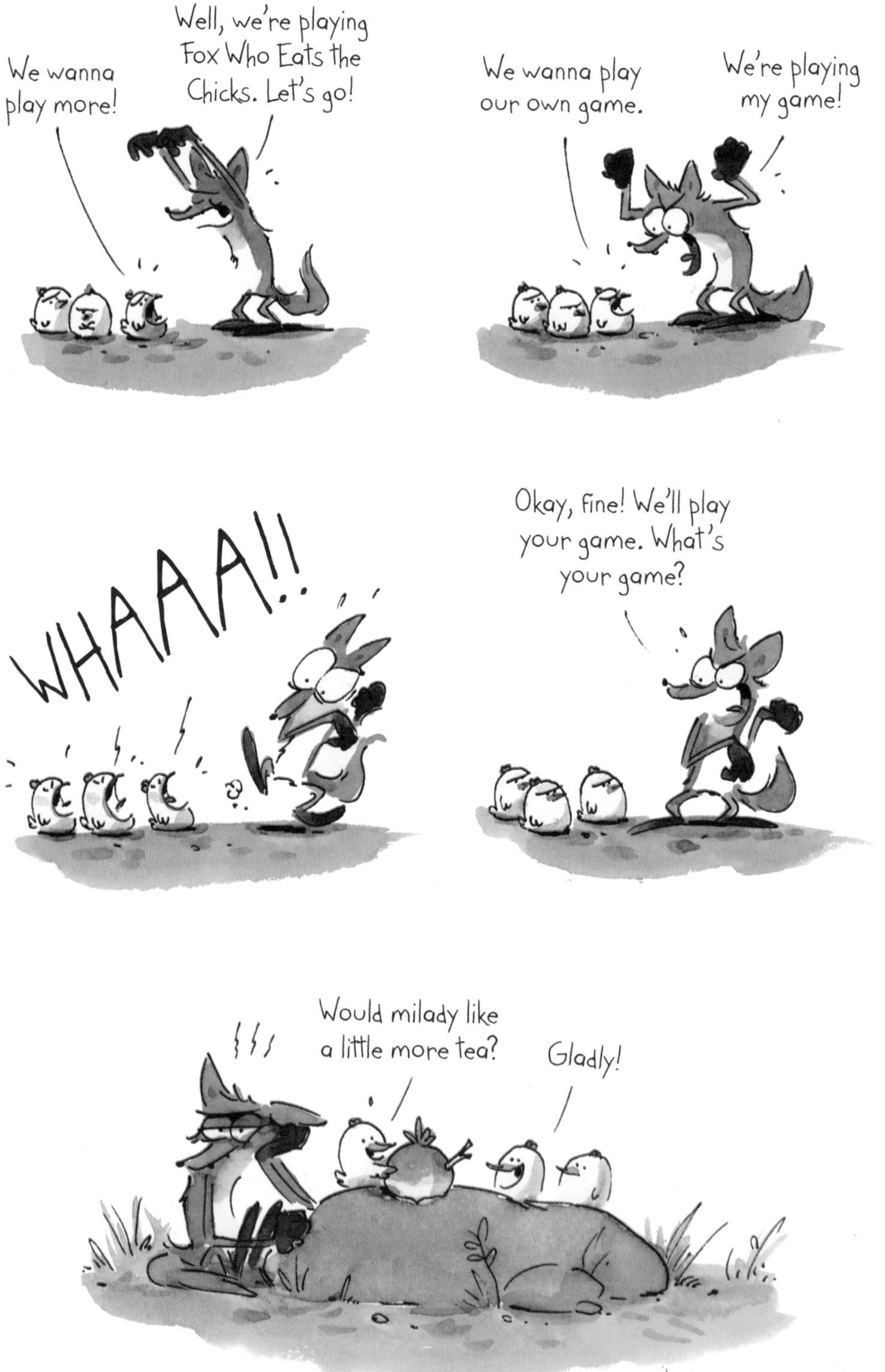
We wanna play more!
Well, we're playing Fox Who Eats the Chicks. Let's go!
We wanna play our own game.
We're playing my game!
WHAAAA!!
Okay, fine! We'll play your game. What's your game?
Would milady like a little more tea?
Gladly!

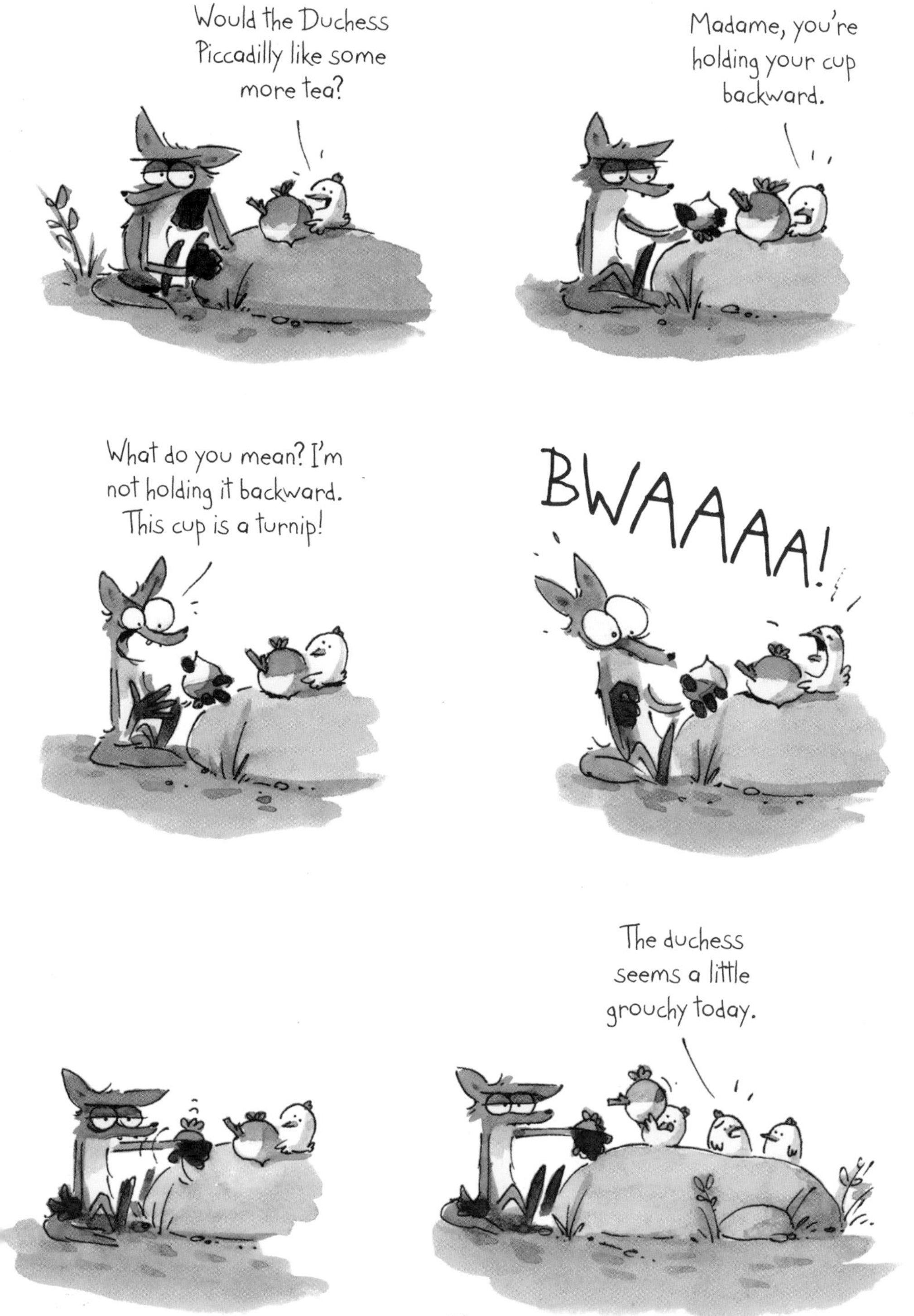
Would the Duchess Piccadilly like some more tea?
Madame, you're holding your cup backward.
What do you mean? I'm not holding it backward. This cup is a turnip!
BWAAAAA!
The duchess seems a little grouchy today.

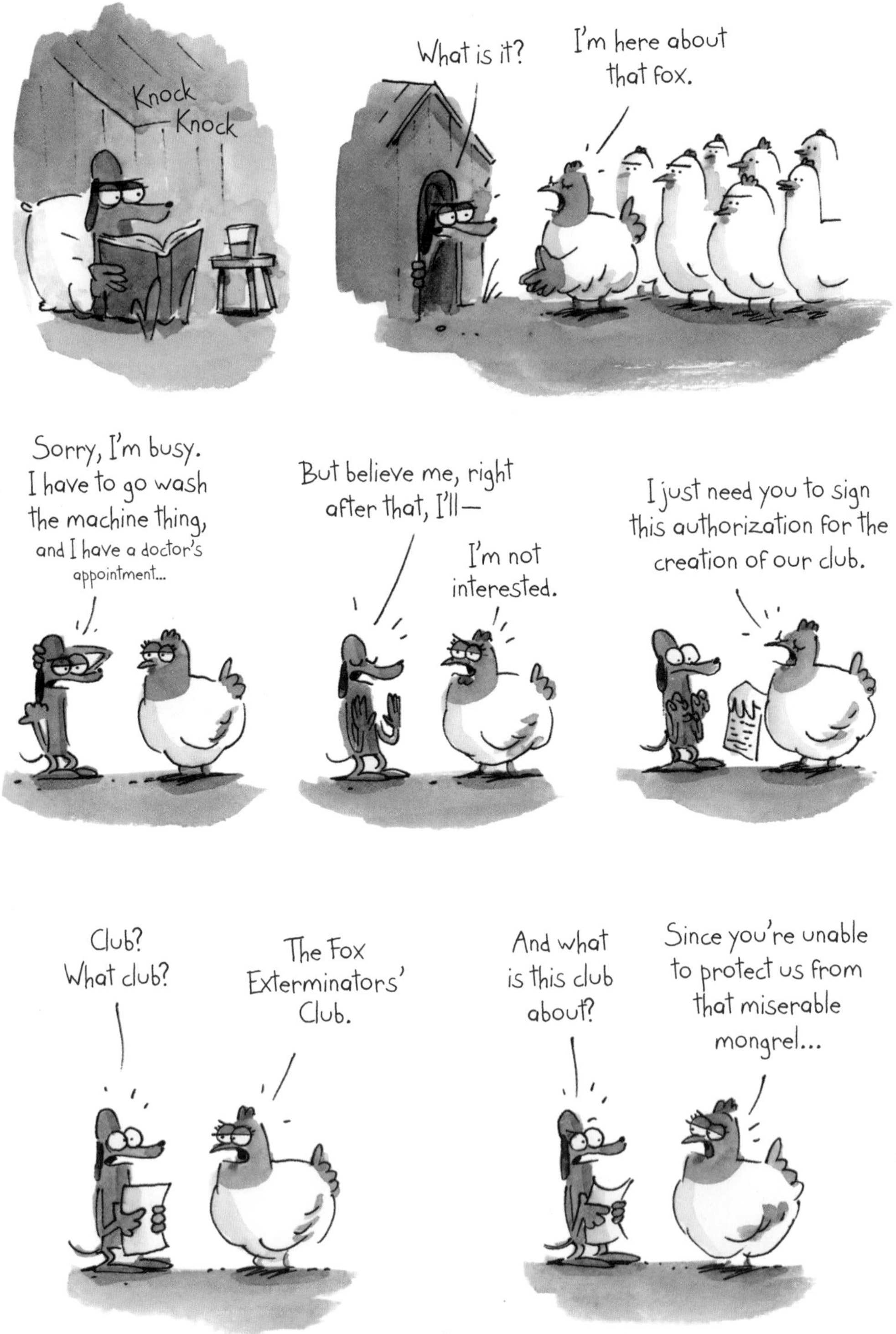
Knock
Knock
What is it?
I'm here about that fox.
Sorry, I'm busy. I have to go wash the machine thing, and I have a doctor's appointment...
But believe me, right after that, I'll—
I'm not interested.
I just need you to sign this authorization for the creation of our club.
Club? What club?
The Fox Exterminators' Club.
And what is this club about?
Since you're unable to protect us from that miserable mongrel...

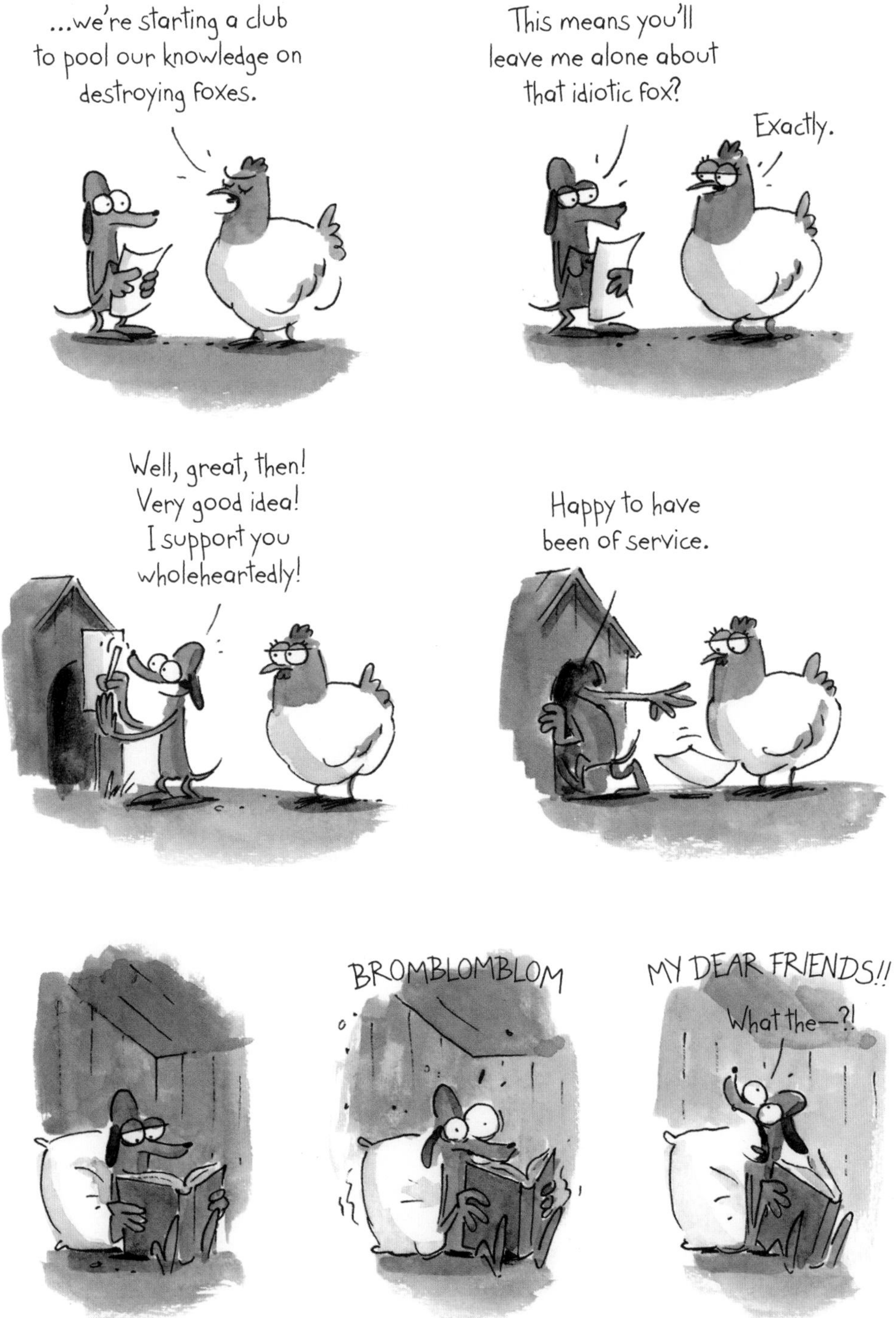
...we're starting a club to pool our knowledge on destroying foxes.
This means you'll leave me alone about that idiotic fox?
Exactly.
Well, great, then! Very good idea! I support you wholeheartedly!
Happy to have been of service.
BROMBLOMBLOM
MY DEAR FRIENDS!!
What the—?!

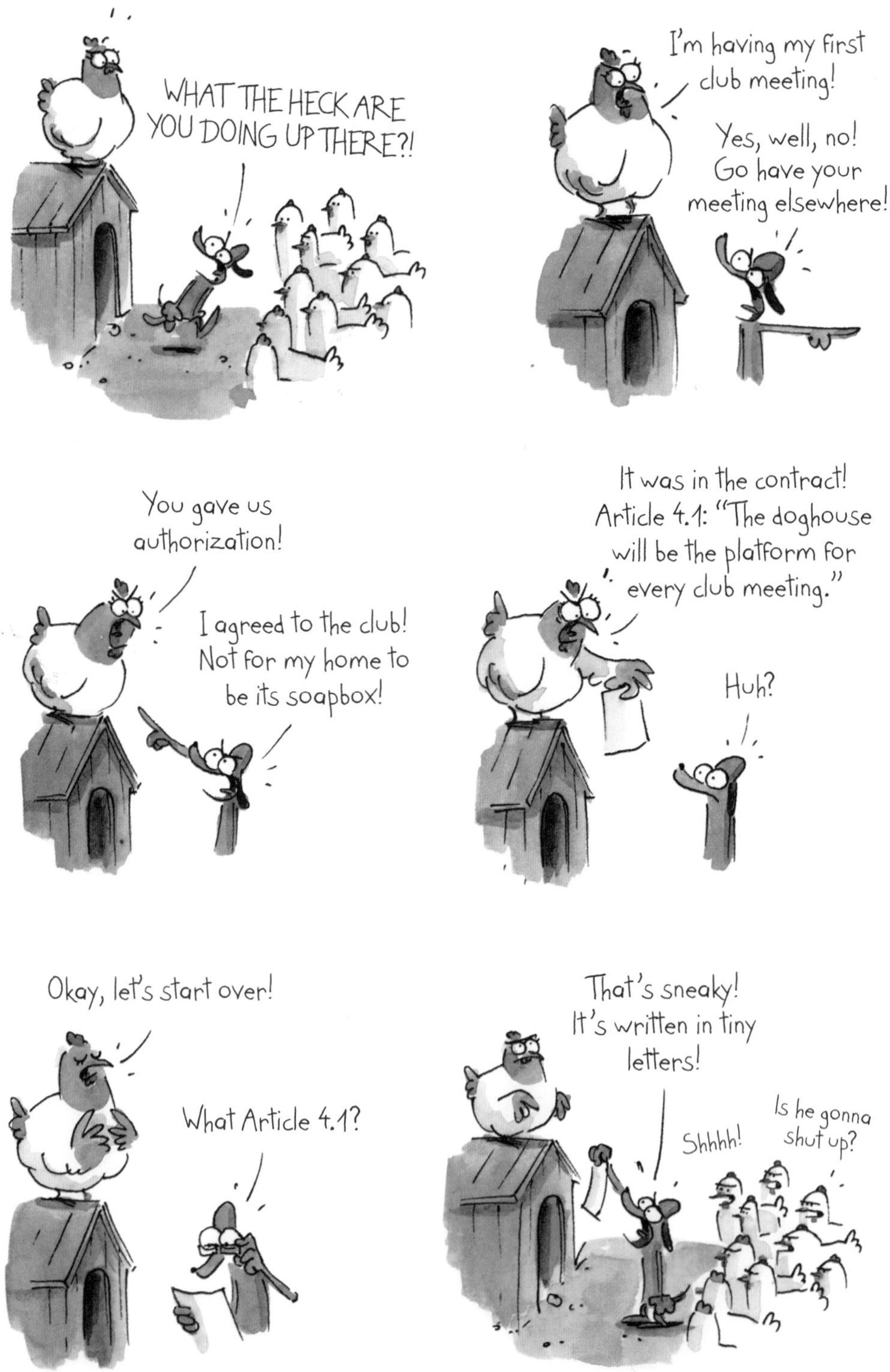
WHAT THE HECK ARE YOU DOING UP THERE?!
I'm having my first club meeting!
Yes, well, no! Go have your meeting elsewhere!
You gave us authorization!
I agreed to the club! Not for my home to be its soapbox!
It was in the contract! Article 4.1: "The doghouse will be the platform for every club meeting."
Huh?
Okay, let's start over!
What Article 4.1?
That's sneaky! It's written in tiny letters!
Shhhh!
Is he gonna shut up?

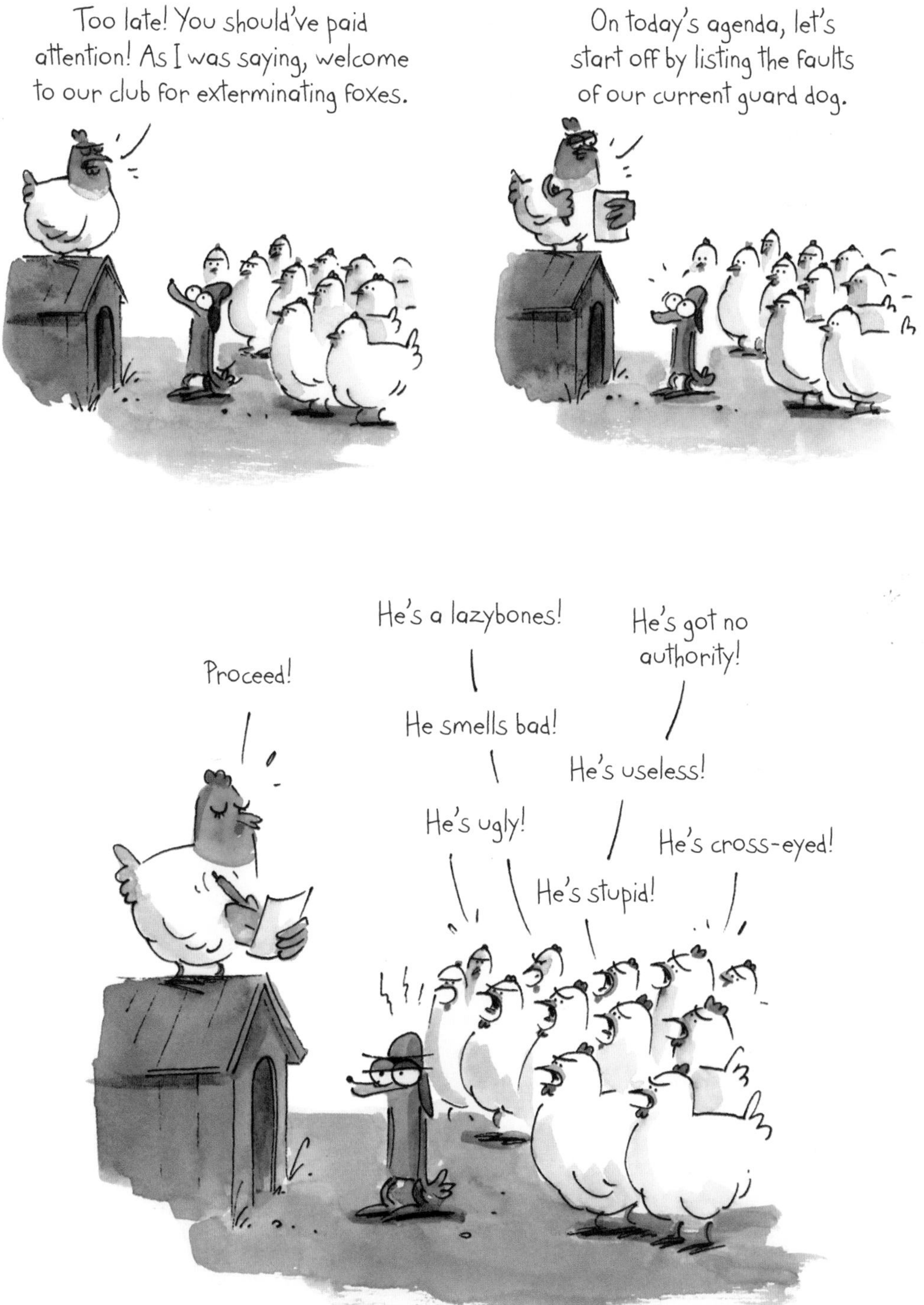
Too late! You should've paid attention! As I was saying, welcome to our club for exterminating foxes.
On today's agenda, let's start off by listing the faults of our current guard dog.
Proceed!
He's a lazybones!
He's got no authority!
He smells bad!
He's useless!
He's ugly!
He's cross-eyed!
He's stupid!

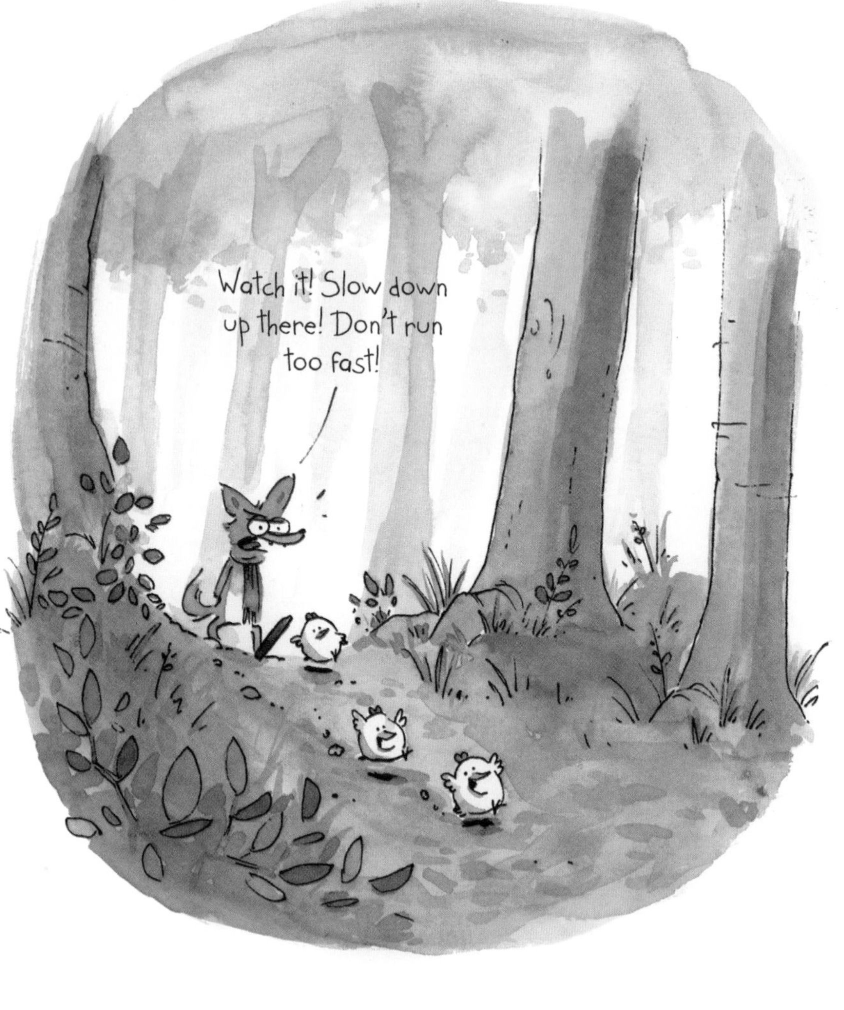
Watch it! Slow down up there! Don't run too fast!

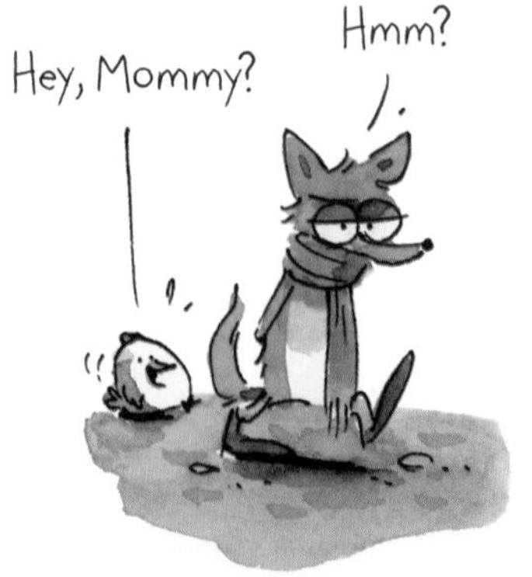
Hey, Mommy?
Hmm?

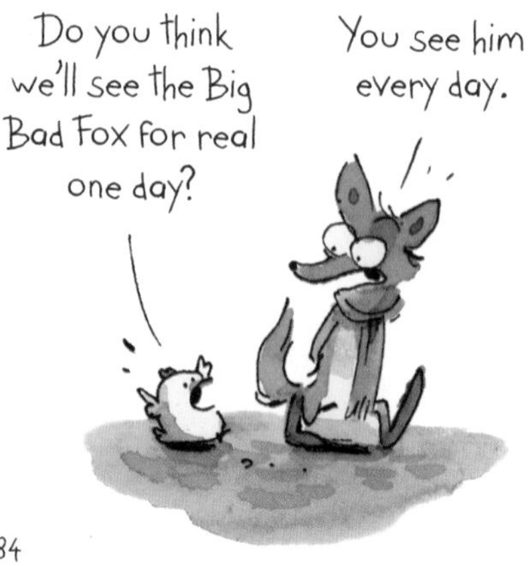
Do you think we'll see the Big Bad Fox for real one day?
You see him every day.

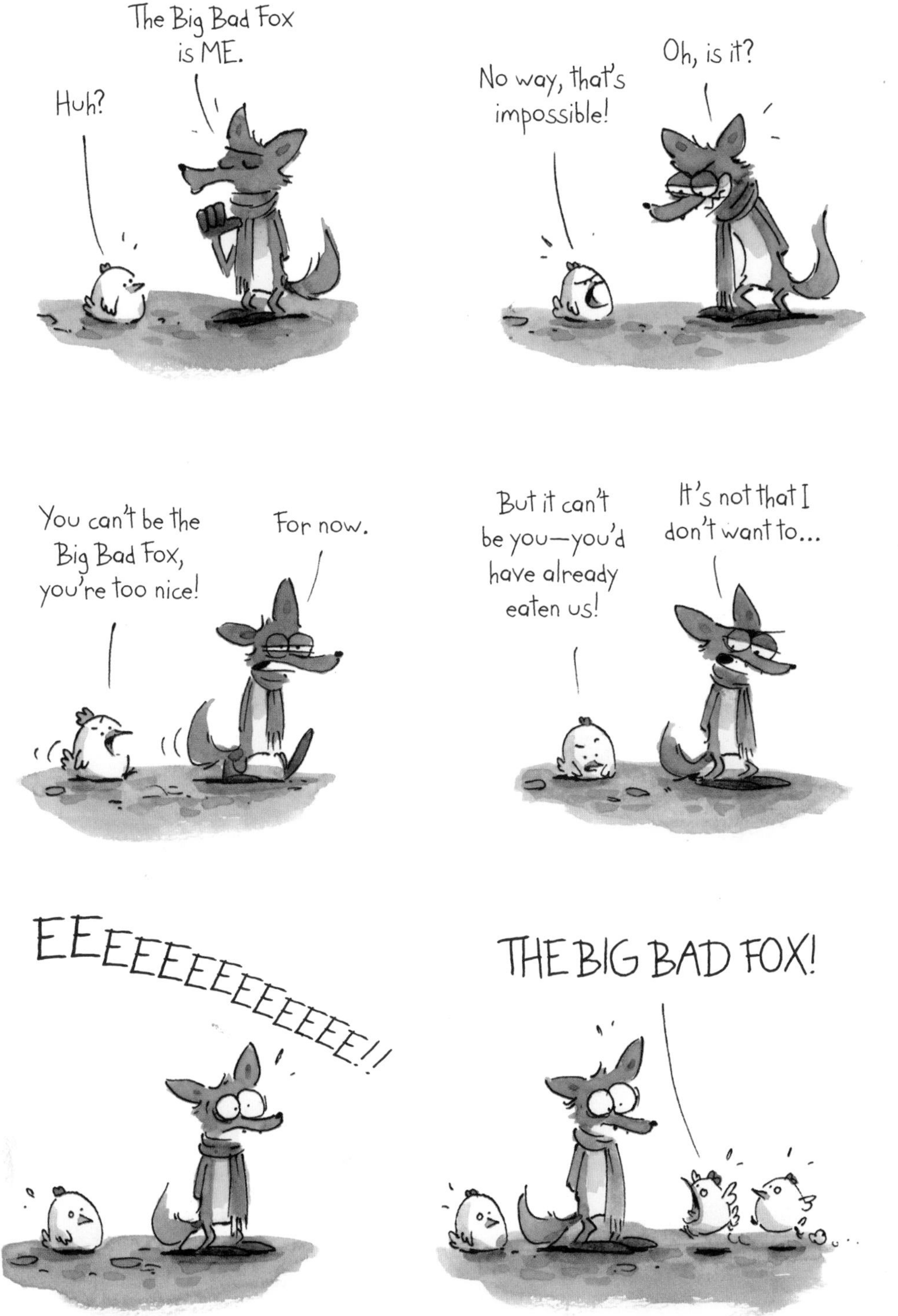
Huh?
The Big Bad Fox is ME.
No way, that's impossible!
Oh, is it?
You can't be the Big Bad Fox, you're too nice!
For now.
But it can't be you—you'd have already eaten us!
It's not that I don't want to...
EEEEEEEEEEEEEEEE!!
THE BIG BAD FOX!

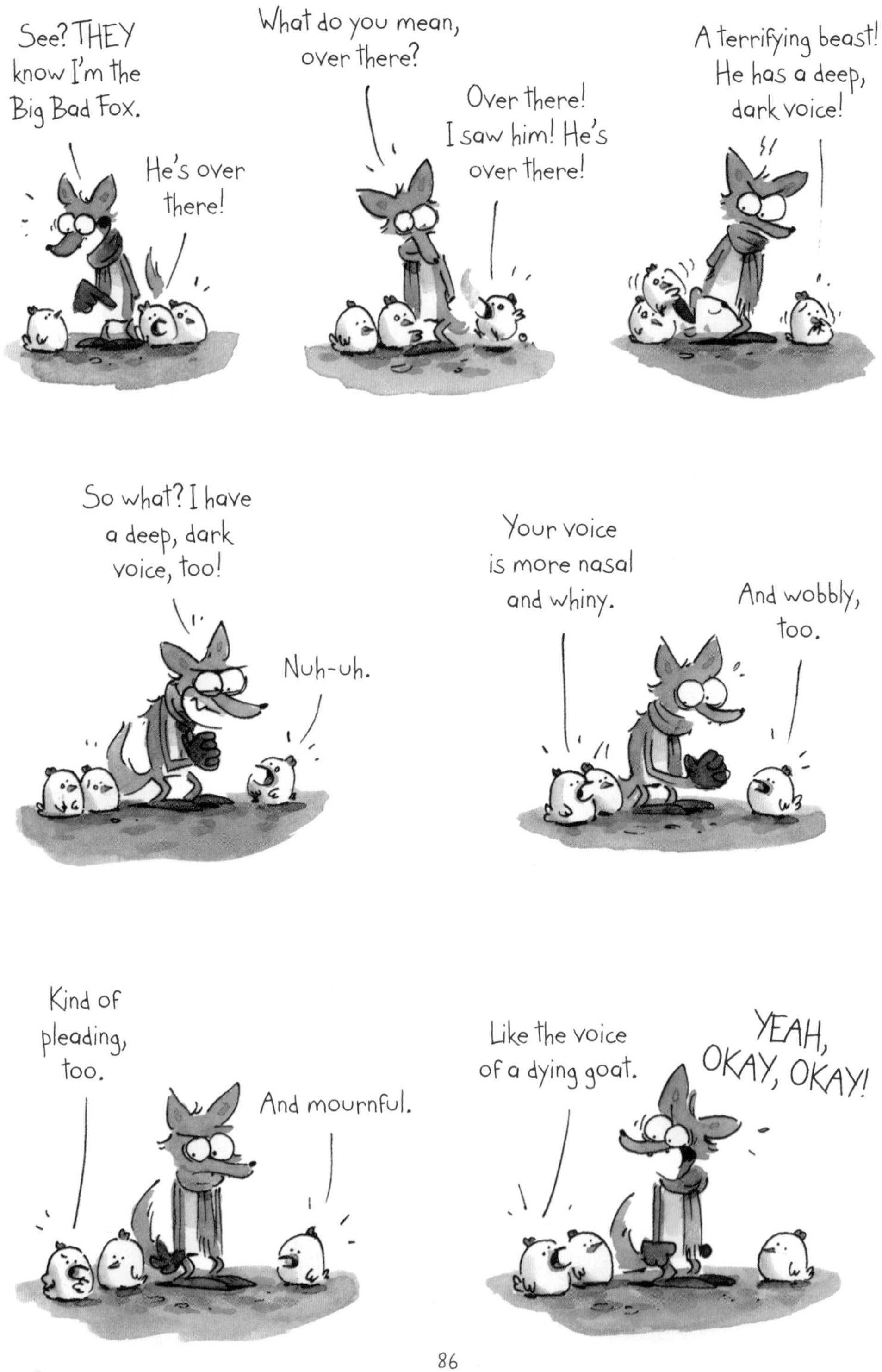
See? THEY know I'm the Big Bad Fox.
He's over there!
What do you mean, over there?
Over there! I saw him! He's over there!
A terrifying beast! He has a deep, dark voice!
So what? I have a deep, dark voice, too!
Nuh-uh.
Your voice is more nasal and whiny.
And wobbly, too.
Kind of pleading, too.
And mournful.
Like the voice of a dying goat.
YEAH, OKAY, OKAY!

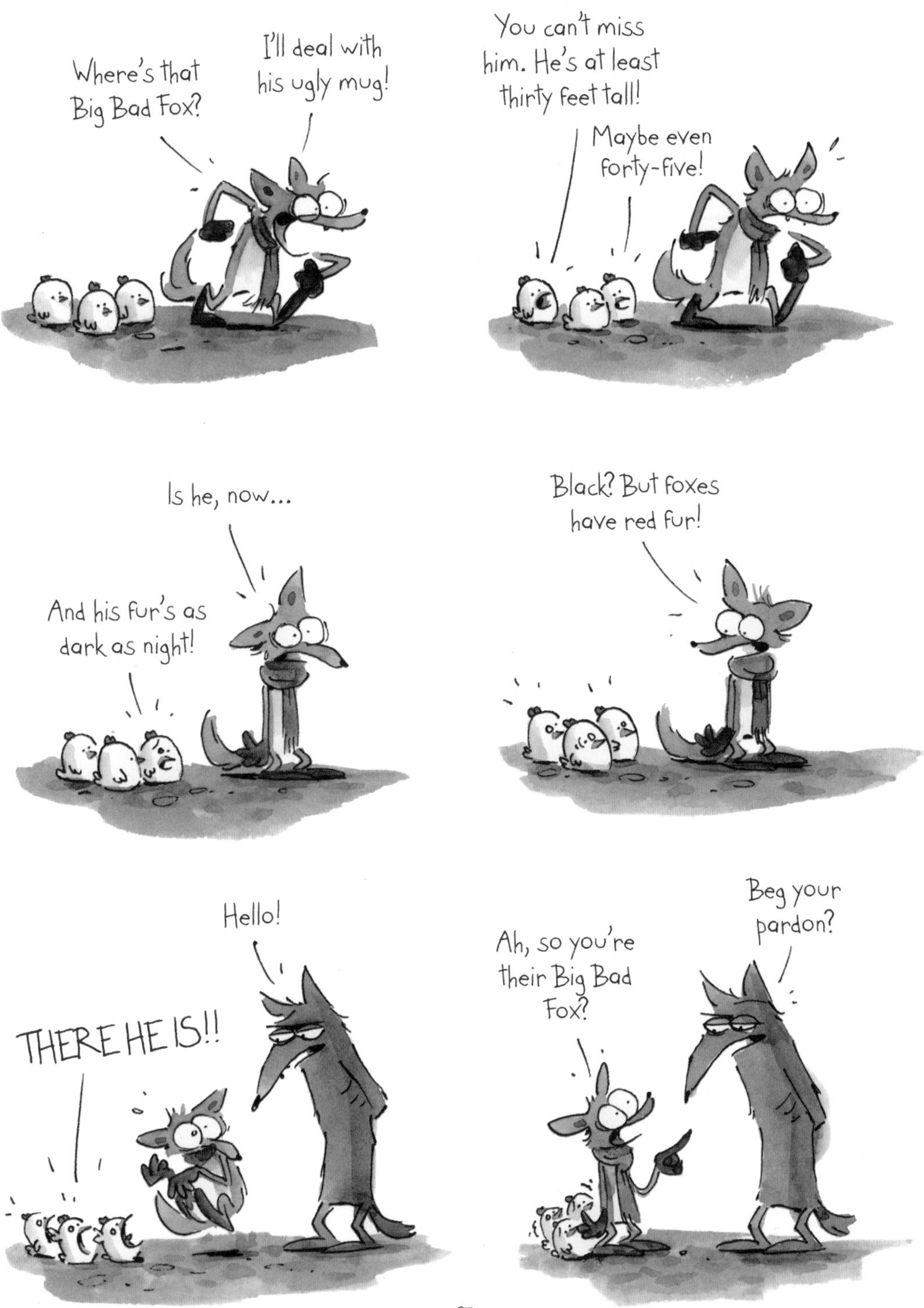
Where's that Big Bad Fox?
I'll deal with his ugly mug!
You can't miss him. He's at least thirty feet tall!
Maybe even forty-five!
And his fur's as dark as night!
Is he, now...
Black? But foxes have red fur!
Hello!
THERE HE IS!!
Ah, so you're their Big Bad Fox?
Beg your pardon?

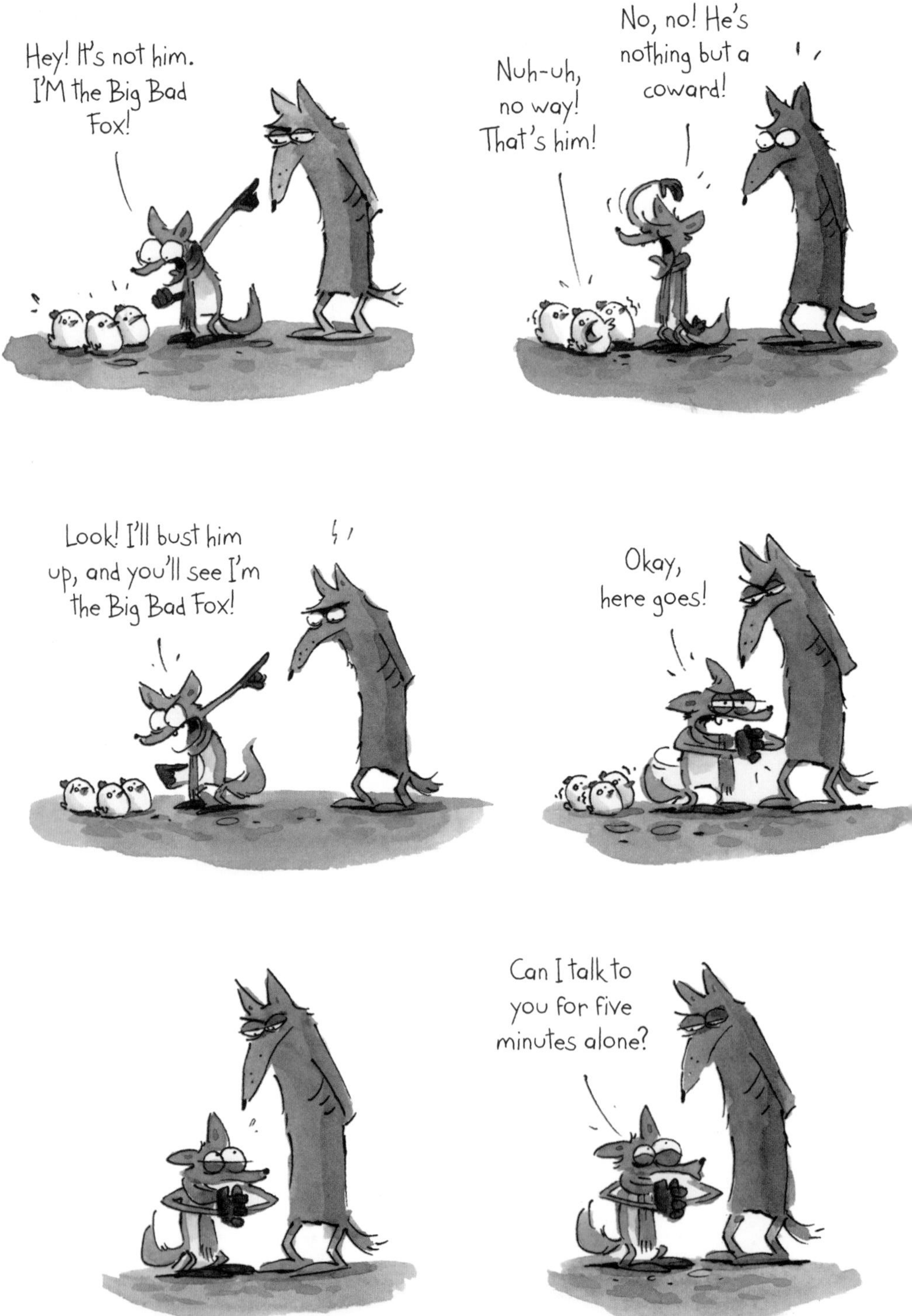
Hey! It's not him. I'M the Big Bad Fox!
Nuh-uh, no way! That's him!
No, no! He's nothing but a coward!
Look! I'll bust him up, and you'll see I'm the Big Bad Fox!
Okay, here goes!
Can I talk to you for five minutes alone?

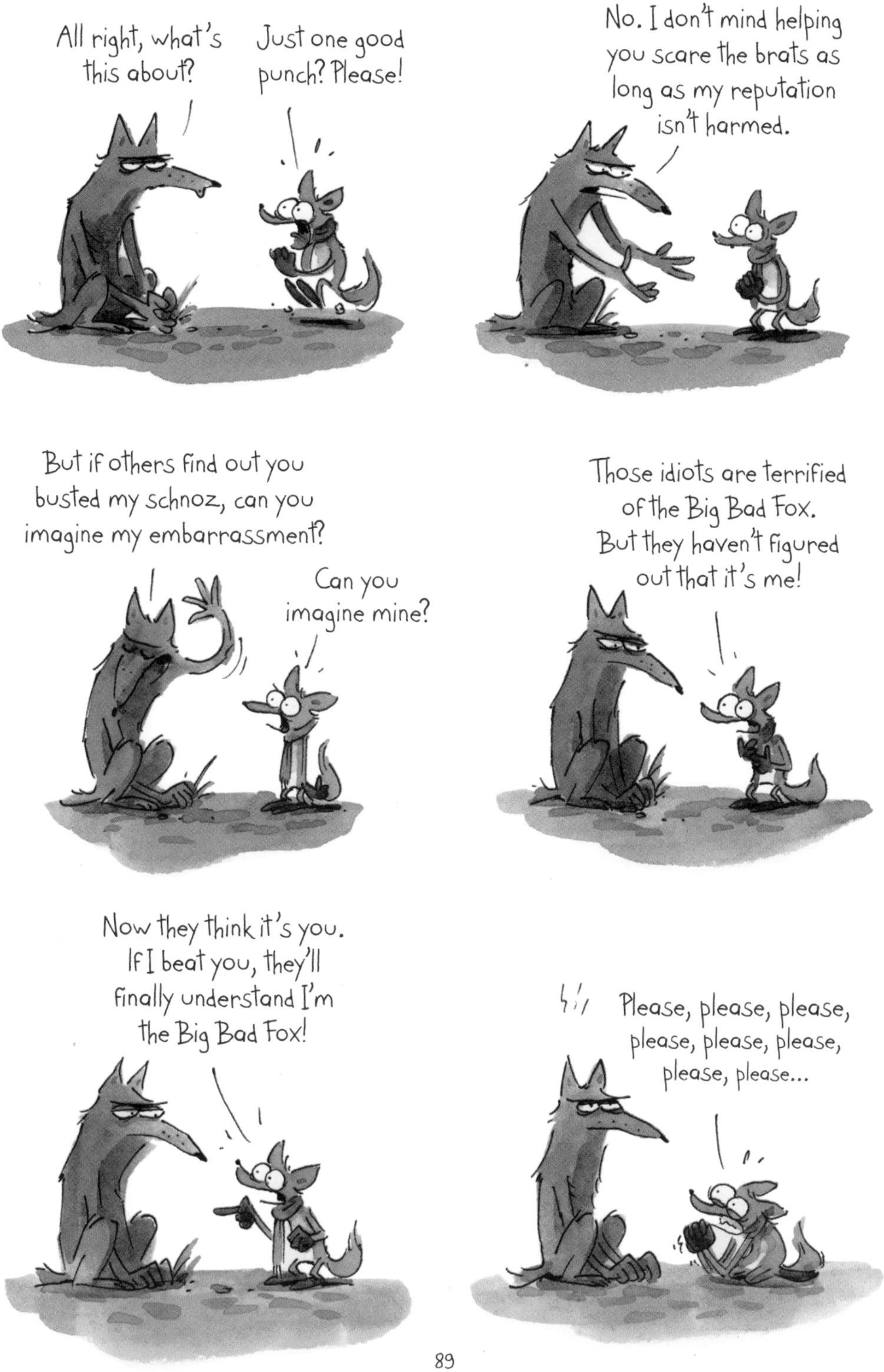
All right, what's this about?
Just one good punch? Please!
No. I don't mind helping you scare the brats as long as my reputation isn't harmed.
But if others find out you busted my schnoz, can you imagine my embarrassment?
Can you imagine mine?
Those idiots are terrified of the Big Bad Fox. But they haven't figured out that it's me!
Now they think it's you. If I beat you, they'll finally understand I'm the Big Bad Fox!
Please, please, please, please, please, please, please, please...

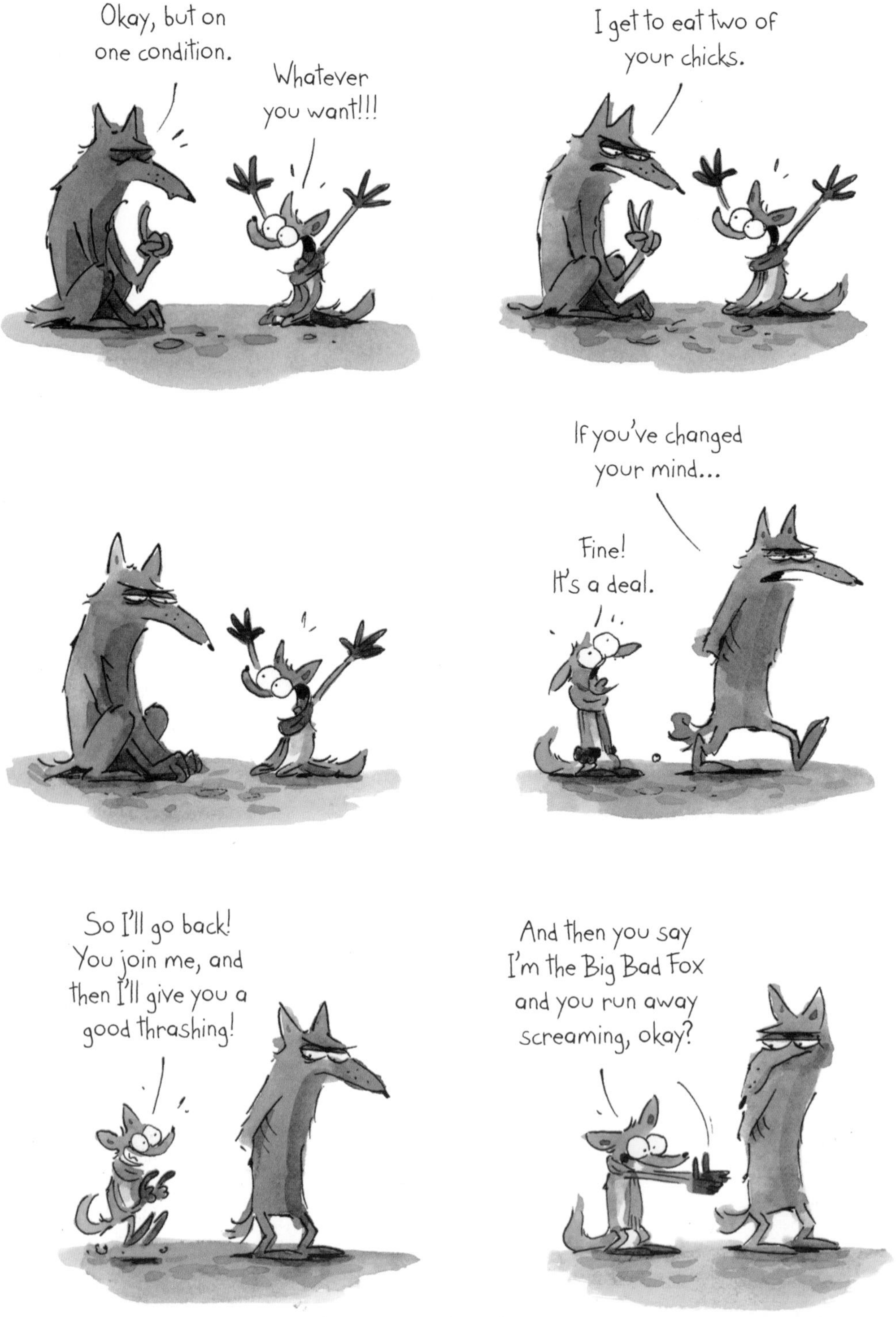
Okay, but on one condition.
Whatever you want!!!
I get to eat two of your chicks.
If you've changed your mind...
Fine! It's a deal.
So I'll go back! You join me, and then I'll give you a good thrashing!
And then you say I'm the Big Bad Fox and you run away screaming, okay?

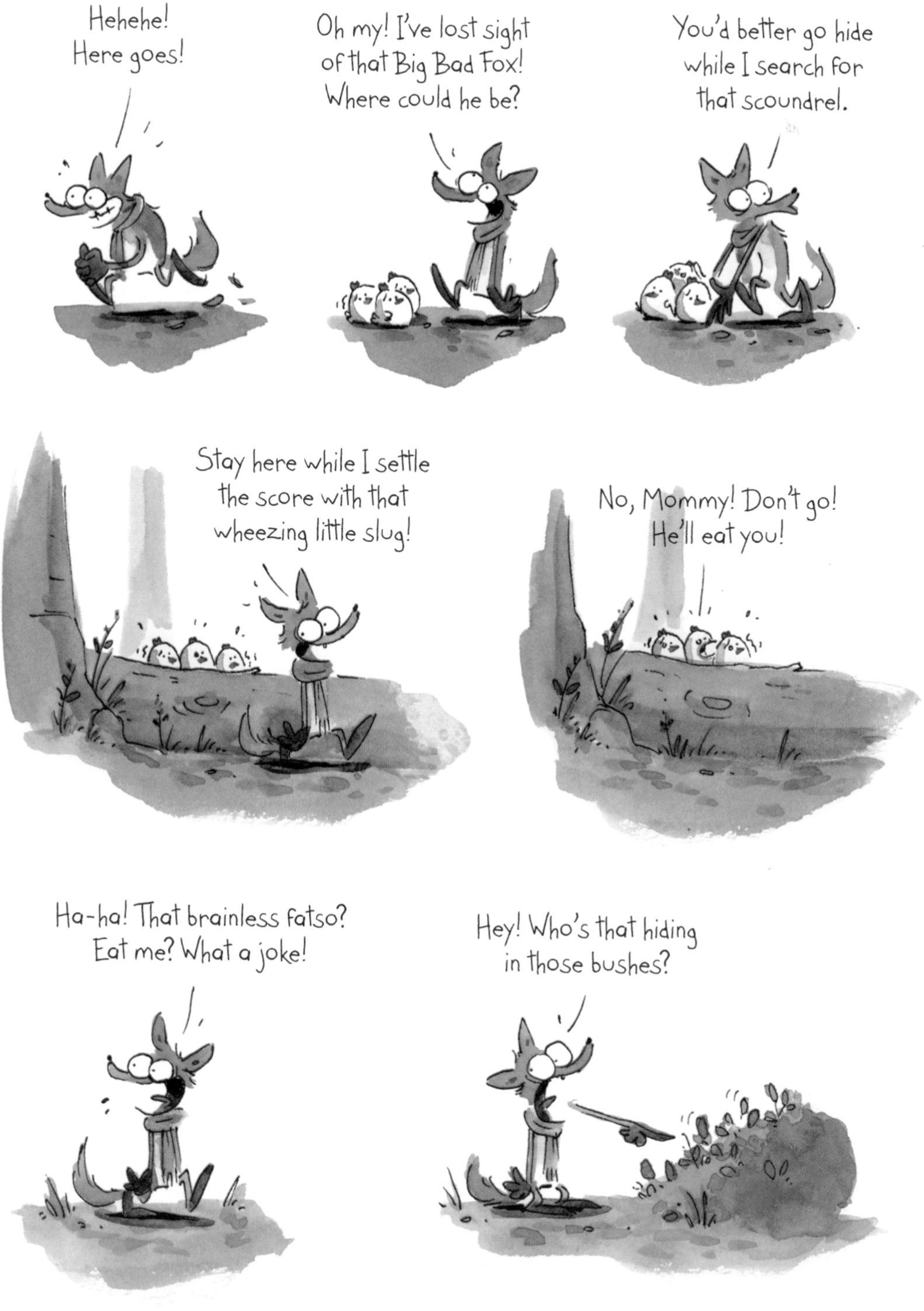
Hehehe! Here goes!
Oh my! I've lost sight of that Big Bad Fox! Where could he be?
You'd better go hide while I search for that scoundrel.
Stay here while I settle the score with that wheezing little slug!
No, Mommy! Don't go! He'll eat you!
Ha-ha! That brainless fatso? Eat me? What a joke!
Hey! Who's that hiding in those bushes?

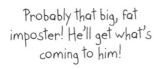

Probably that big, fat imposter! He'll get what's coming to him!

WHACK!

HEY, WHAT'S WRONG WITH YOU?!

WHEN DID YOU START HITTING FOLKS LIKE THAT?

It was a mistake!

THAT'S NO EXCUSE!!

BOMF

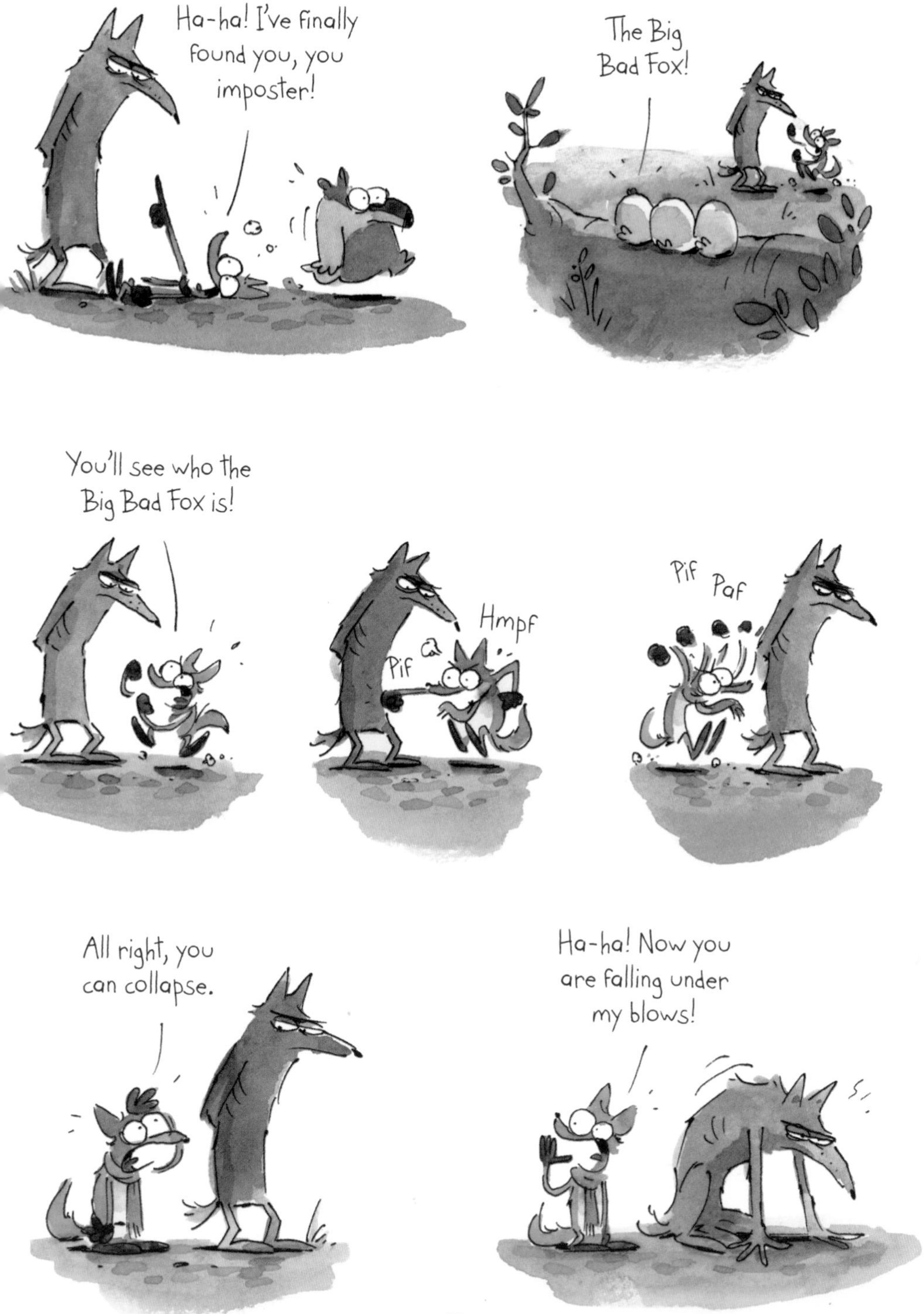

Ha-ha! I've finally found you, you imposter!
The Big Bad Fox!
You'll see who the Big Bad Fox is!
Hmpf
Pif
Pif
Paf
All right, you can collapse.
Ha-ha! Now you are falling under my blows!

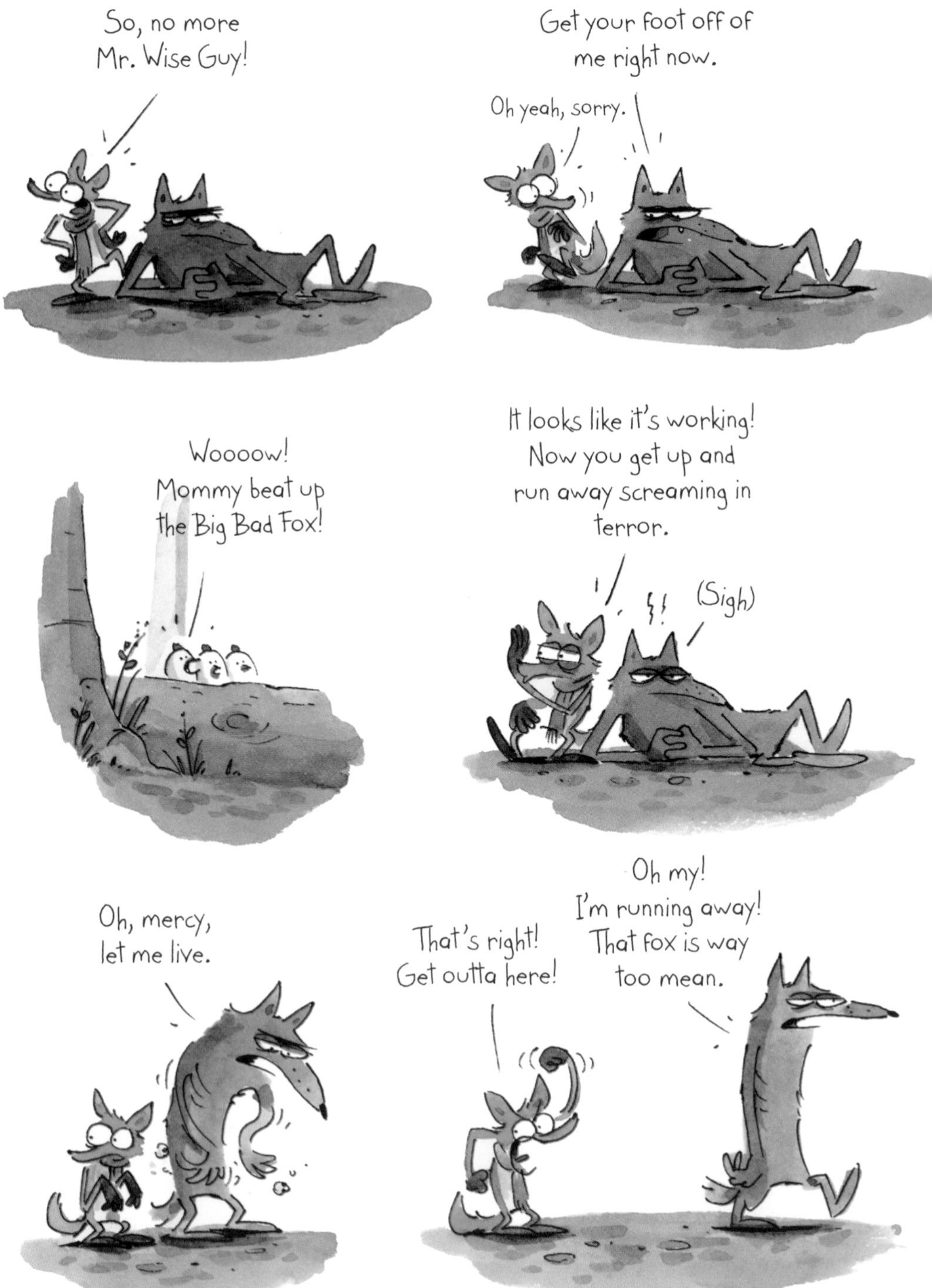

So, no more Mr. Wise Guy!
Get your foot off of me right now.
Oh yeah, sorry.
Wooooow! Mommy beat up the Big Bad Fox!
It looks like it's working! Now you get up and run away screaming in terror.
(Sigh)
Oh, mercy, let me live.
That's right! Get outta here!
Oh my! I'm running away! That fox is way too mean.

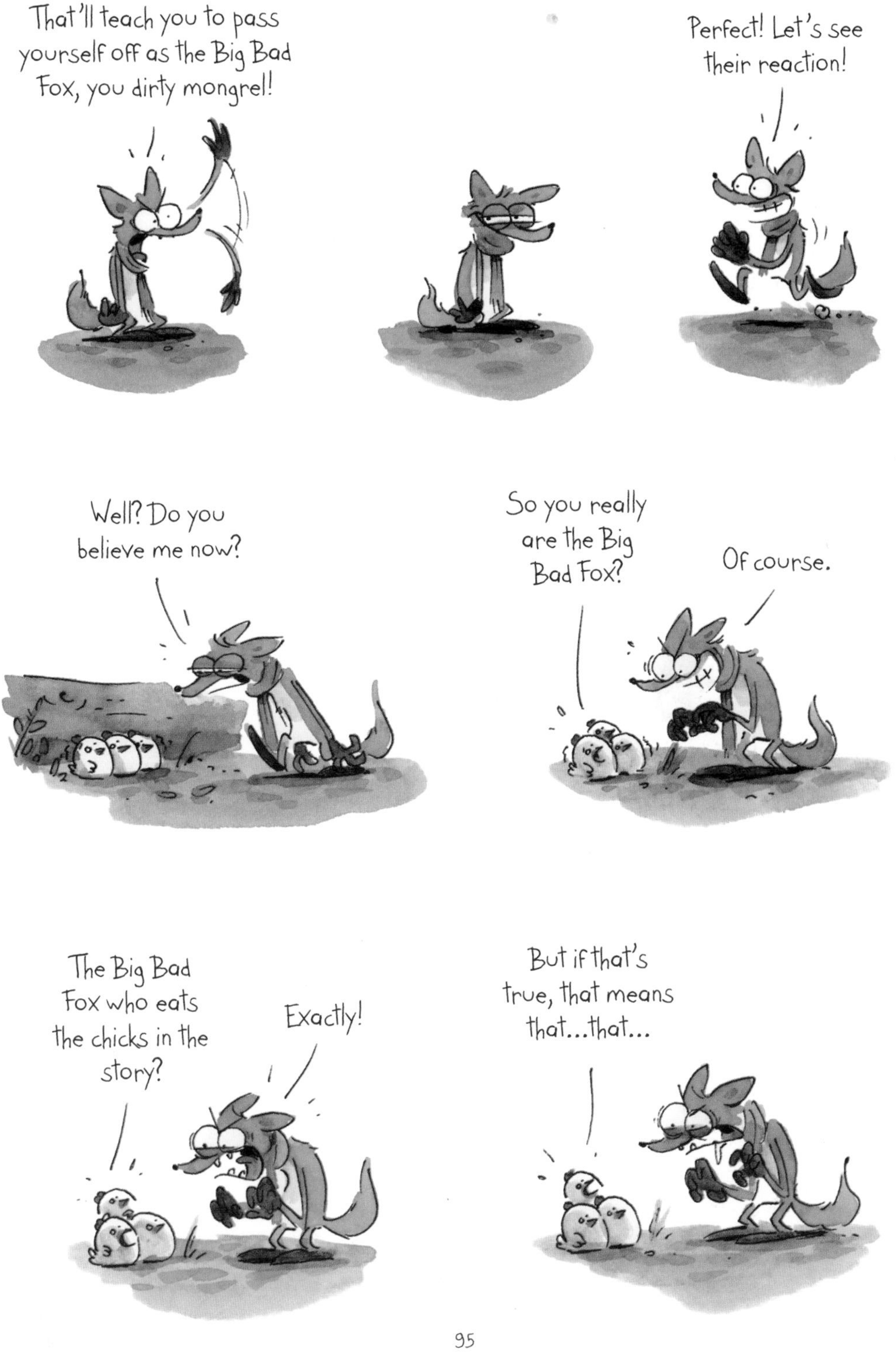
That'll teach you to pass yourself off as the Big Bad Fox, you dirty mongrel!
Perfect! Let's see their reaction!
Well? Do you believe me now?
So you really are the Big Bad Fox?
Of course.
The Big Bad Fox who eats the chicks in the story?
Exactly!
But if that's true, that means that...that...

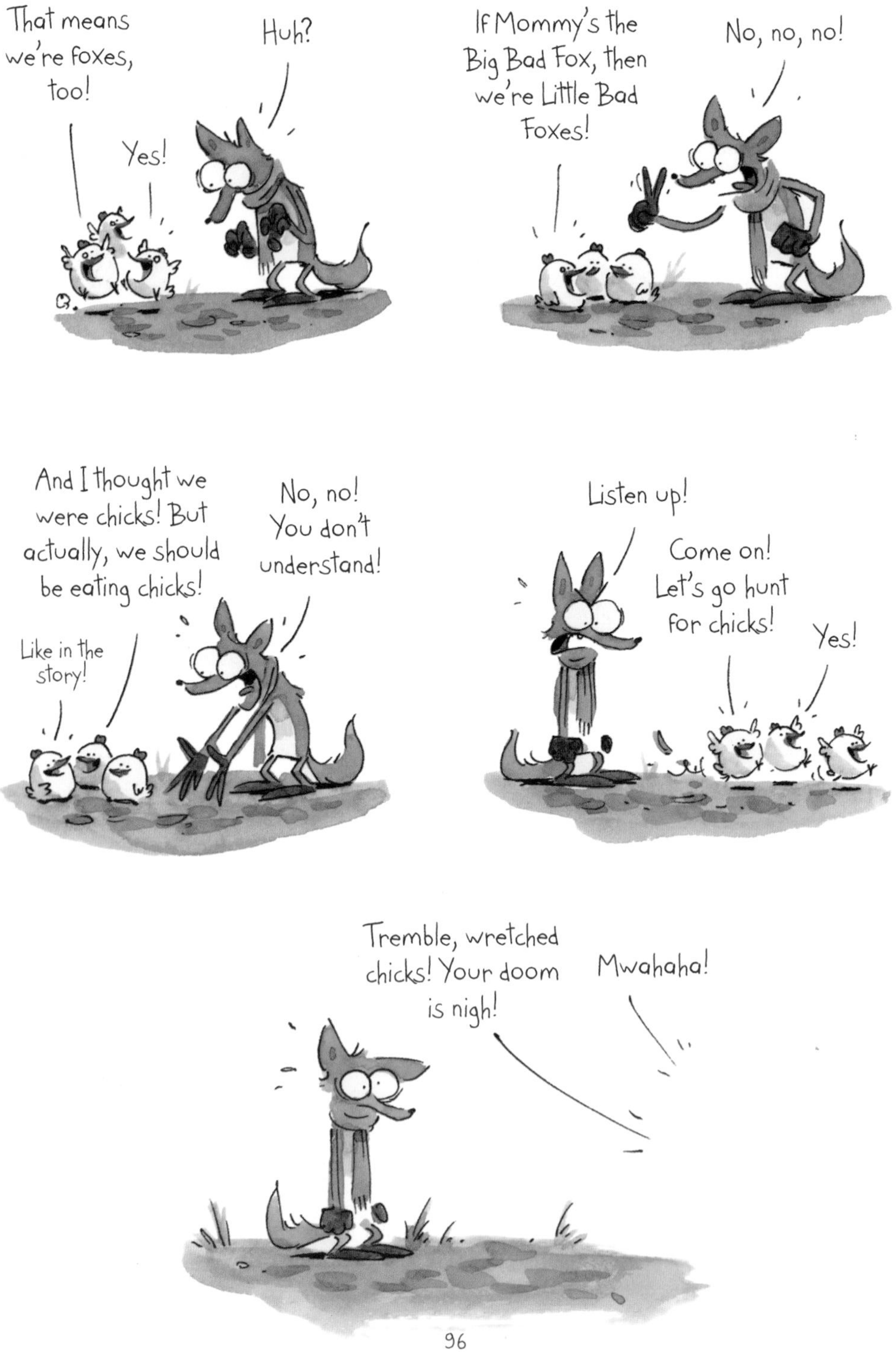

That means we're foxes, too!
Huh?
Yes!
If Mommy's the Big Bad Fox, then we're Little Bad Foxes!
No, no, no!
And I thought we were chicks! But actually, we should be eating chicks!
Like in the story!
No, no! You don't understand!
Listen up!
Come on! Let's go hunt for chicks!
Yes!
Tremble, wretched chicks! Your doom is nigh!
Mwahaha!

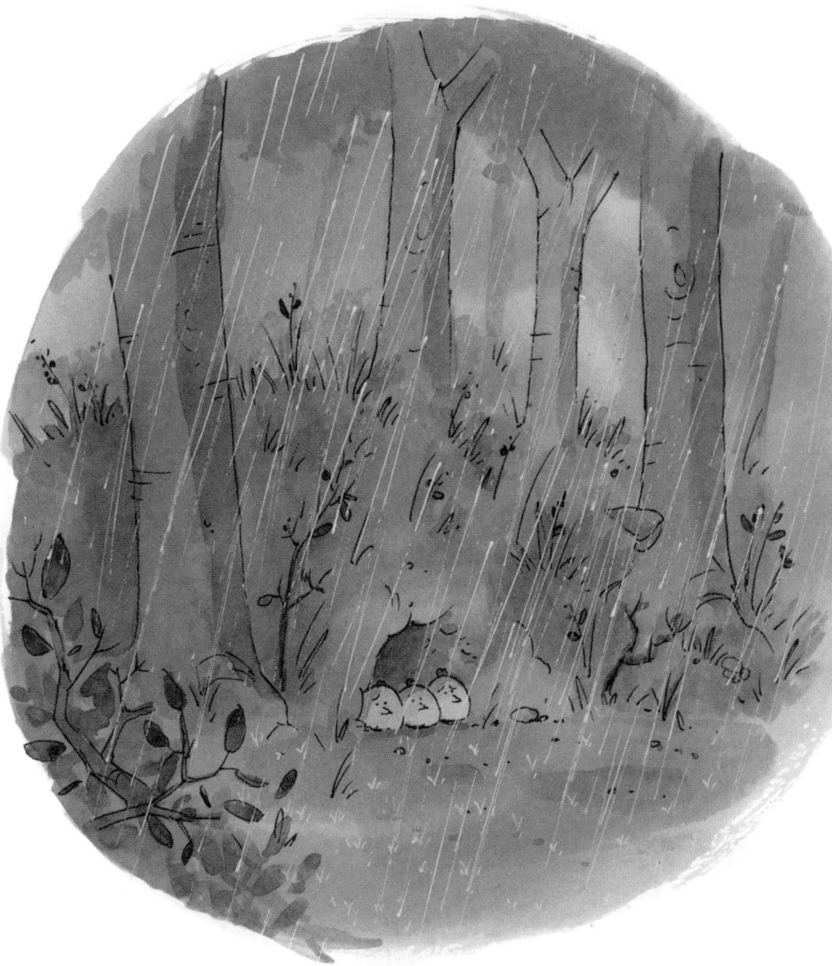

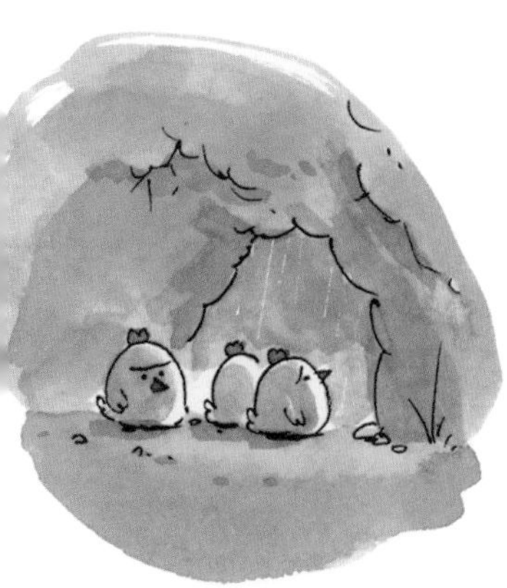

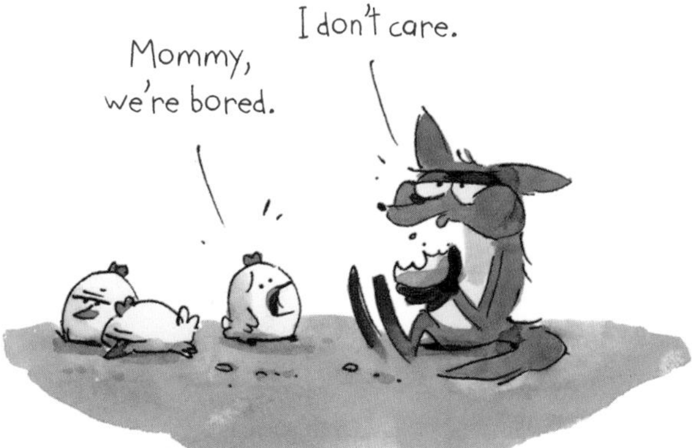
Mommy, we're bored.
I don't care.

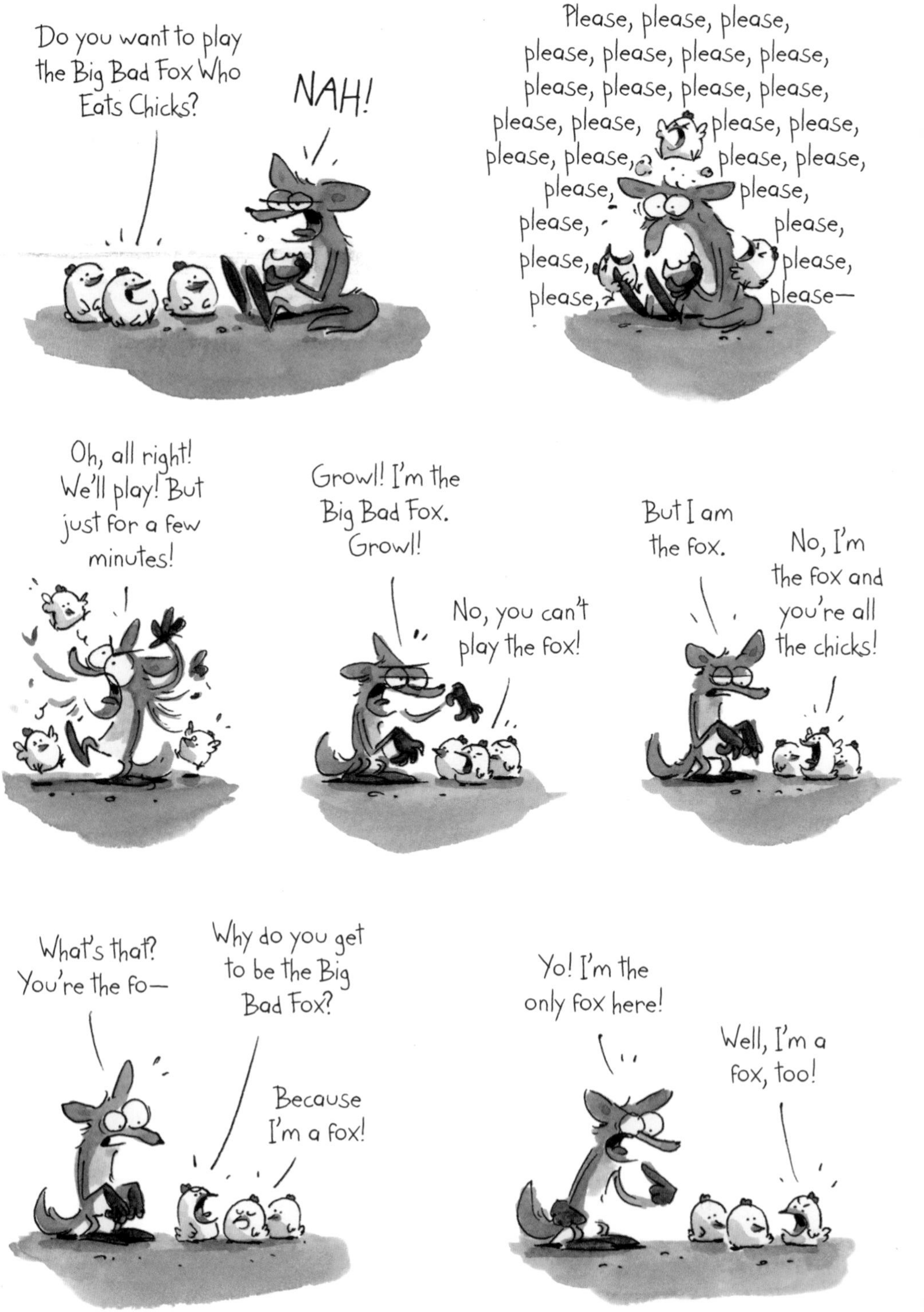
Do you want to play the Big Bad Fox Who Eats Chicks?
NAH!
Please, please—
Oh, all right! We'll play! But just for a few minutes!
Growl! I'm the Big Bad Fox. Growl!
No, you can't play the fox!
But I am the fox.
No, I'm the fox and you're all the chicks!
What's that? You're the fo—
Why do you get to be the Big Bad Fox?
Because I'm a fox!
Yo! I'm the only fox here!
Well, I'm a fox, too!

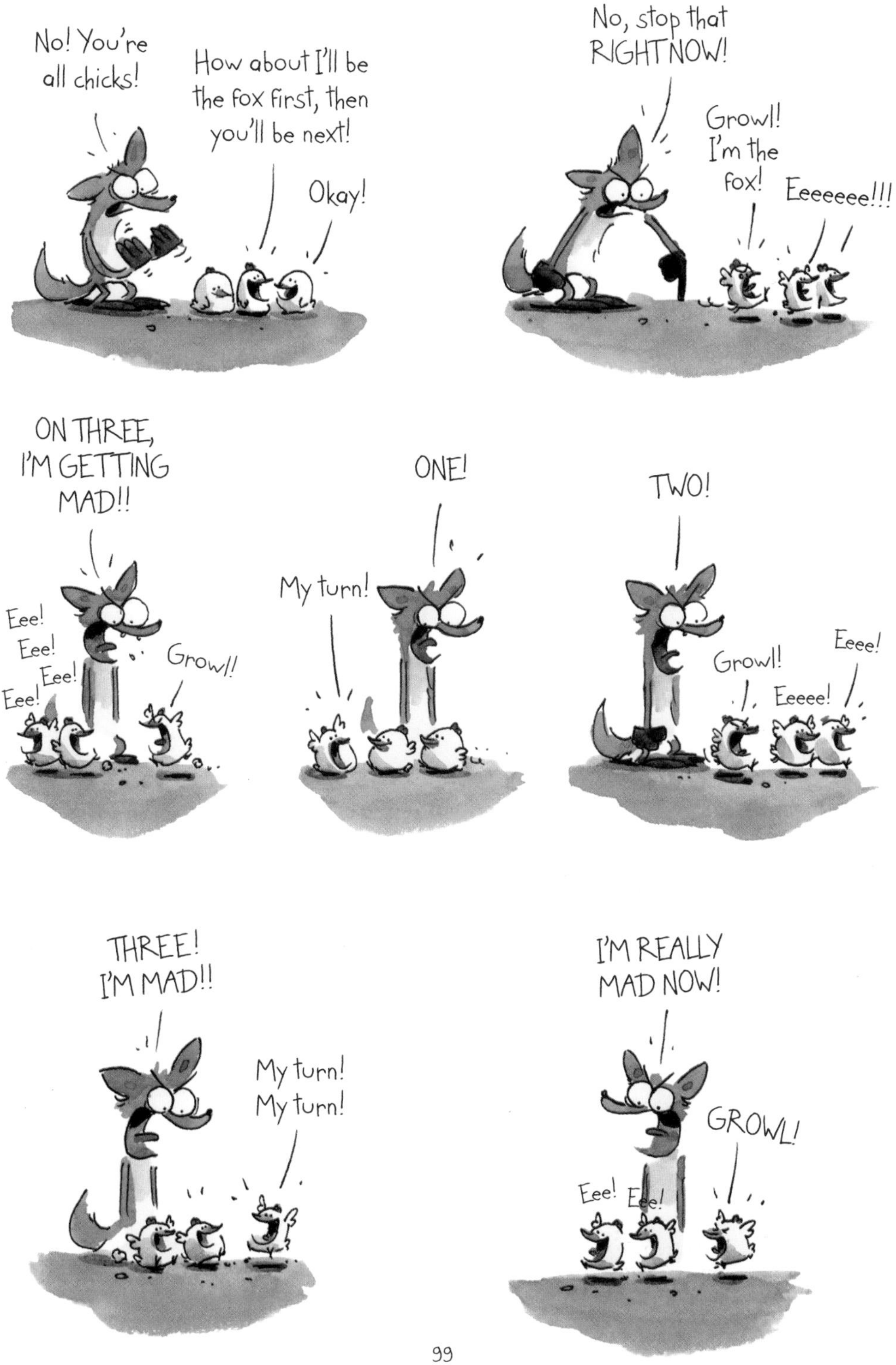
No! You're all chicks!
How about I'll be the fox first, then you'll be next!
Okay!
No, stop that RIGHT NOW!
Growl! I'm the fox!
Eeeeeee!!!
ON THREE, I'M GETTING MAD!!
Eee!
Eee!
Eee!
Eee!
Growl!
ONE!
My turn!
TWO!
Growl!
Eeeee!
Eeee!
THREE! I'M MAD!!
My turn! My turn!
I'M REALLY MAD NOW!
GROWL!
Eee!
Eee!

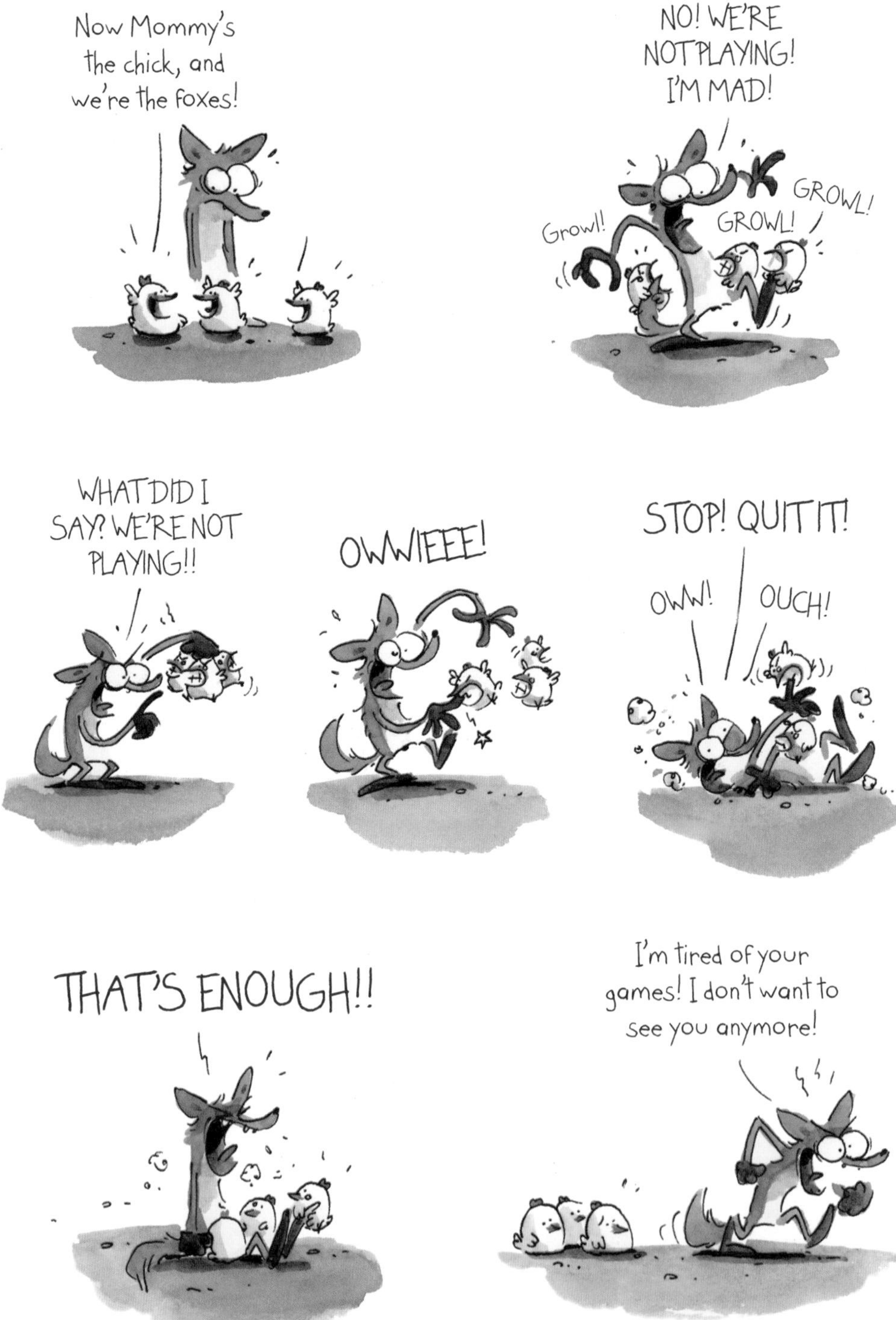
Now Mommy's the chick, and we're the foxes!
NO! WE'RE NOT PLAYING! I'M MAD!
Growl!
GROWL!
GROWL!
WHAT DID I SAY? WE'RE NOT PLAYING!!
OWWIEEE!
STOP! QUIT IT!
OWW!
OUCH!
THAT'S ENOUGH!!
I'm tired of your games! I don't want to see you anymore!

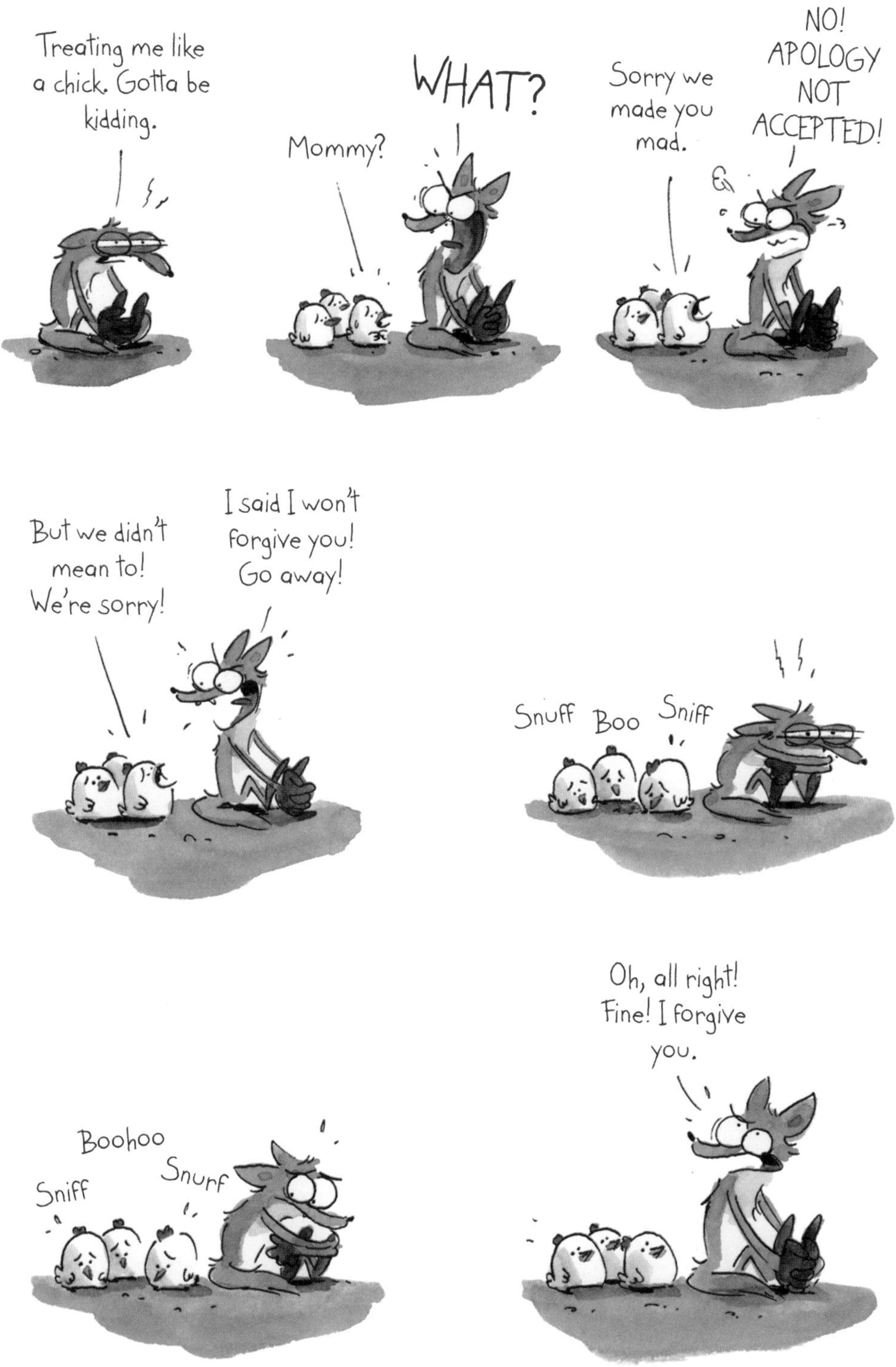
Treating me like a chick. Gotta be kidding.
Mommy?
WHAT?
Sorry we made you mad.
NO! APOLOGY NOT ACCEPTED!
But we didn't mean to! We're sorry!
I said I won't forgive you! Go away!
Snuff
Boo
Sniff
Boohoo
Sniff
Snurf
Oh, all right! Fine! I forgive you.

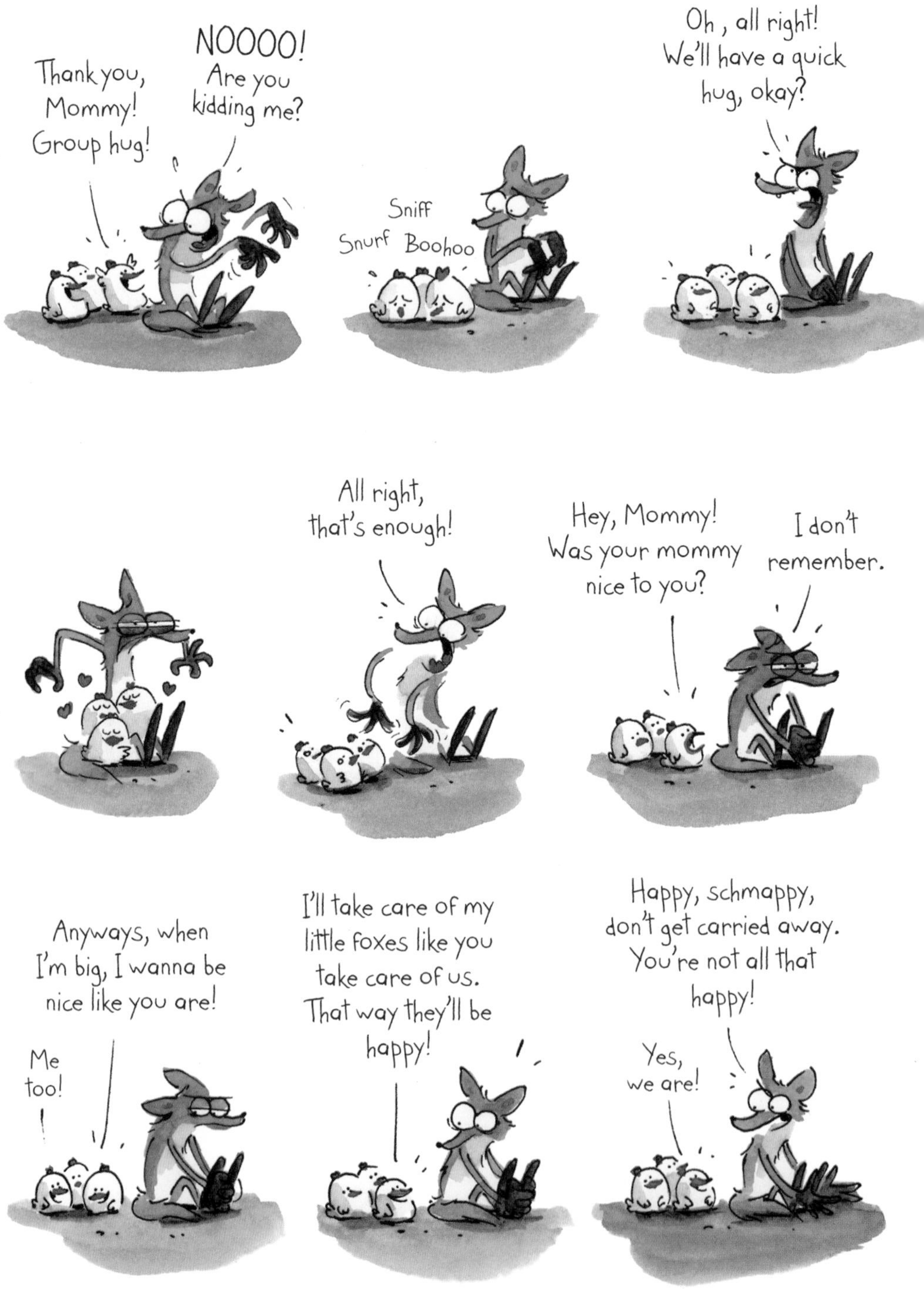
Thank you, Mommy! Group hug!
NOOOO! Are you kidding me?
Sniff
Snurf
Boohoo
Oh, all right! We'll have a quick hug, okay?
All right, that's enough!
Hey, Mommy! Was your mommy nice to you?
I don't remember.
Anyways, when I'm big, I wanna be nice like you are!
Me too!
I'll take care of my little foxes like you take care of us. That way they'll be happy!
Happy, schmappy, don't get carried away. You're not all that happy!
Yes, we are!

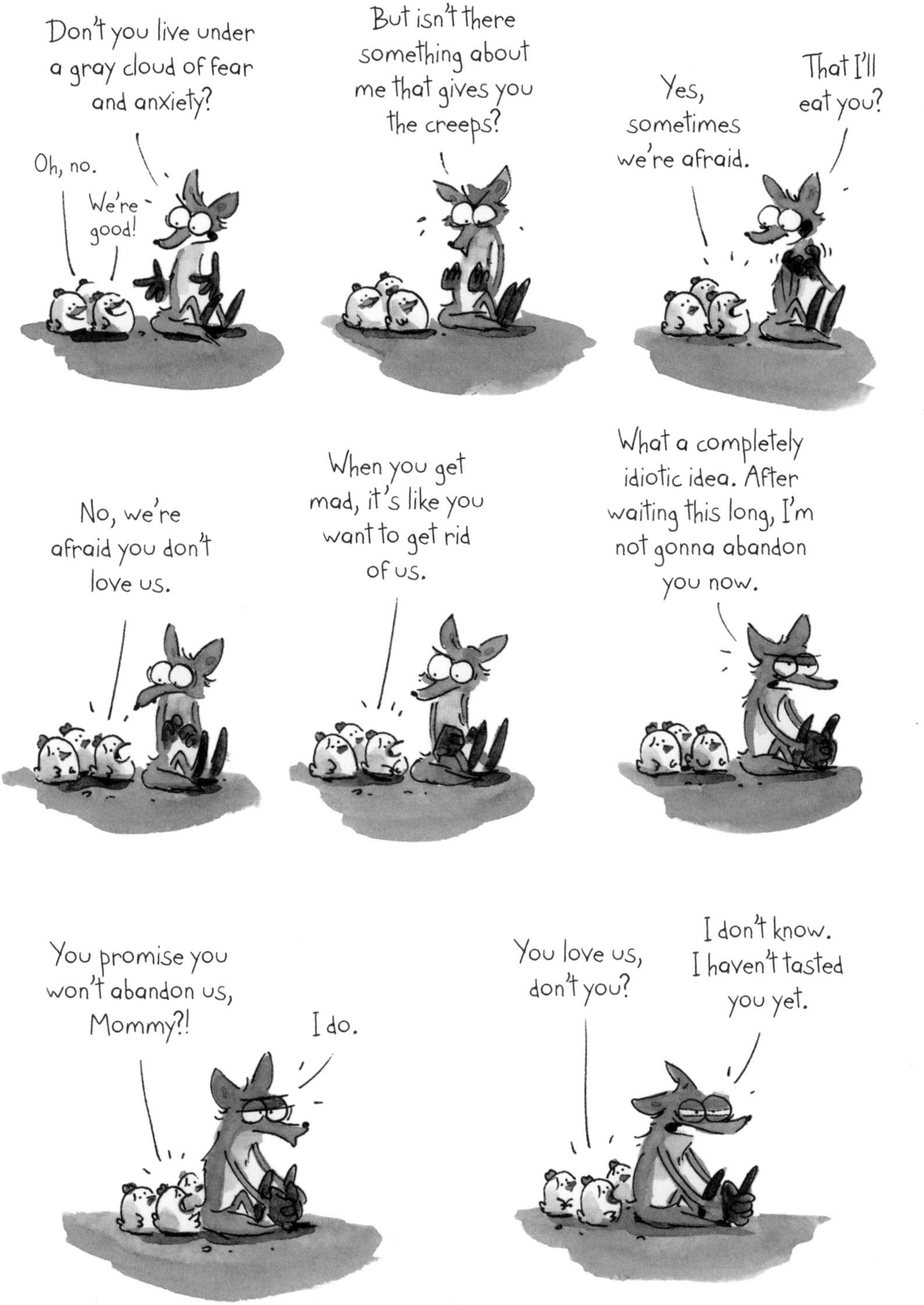
Don't you live under a gray cloud of fear and anxiety?
Oh, no.
We're good!
But isn't there something about me that gives you the creeps?
Yes, sometimes we're afraid.
That I'll eat you?
No, we're afraid you don't love us.
When you get mad, it's like you want to get rid of us.
What a completely idiotic idea. After waiting this long, I'm not gonna abandon you now.
You promise you won't abandon us, Mommy?!
I do.
You love us, don't you?
I don't know. I haven't tasted you yet.

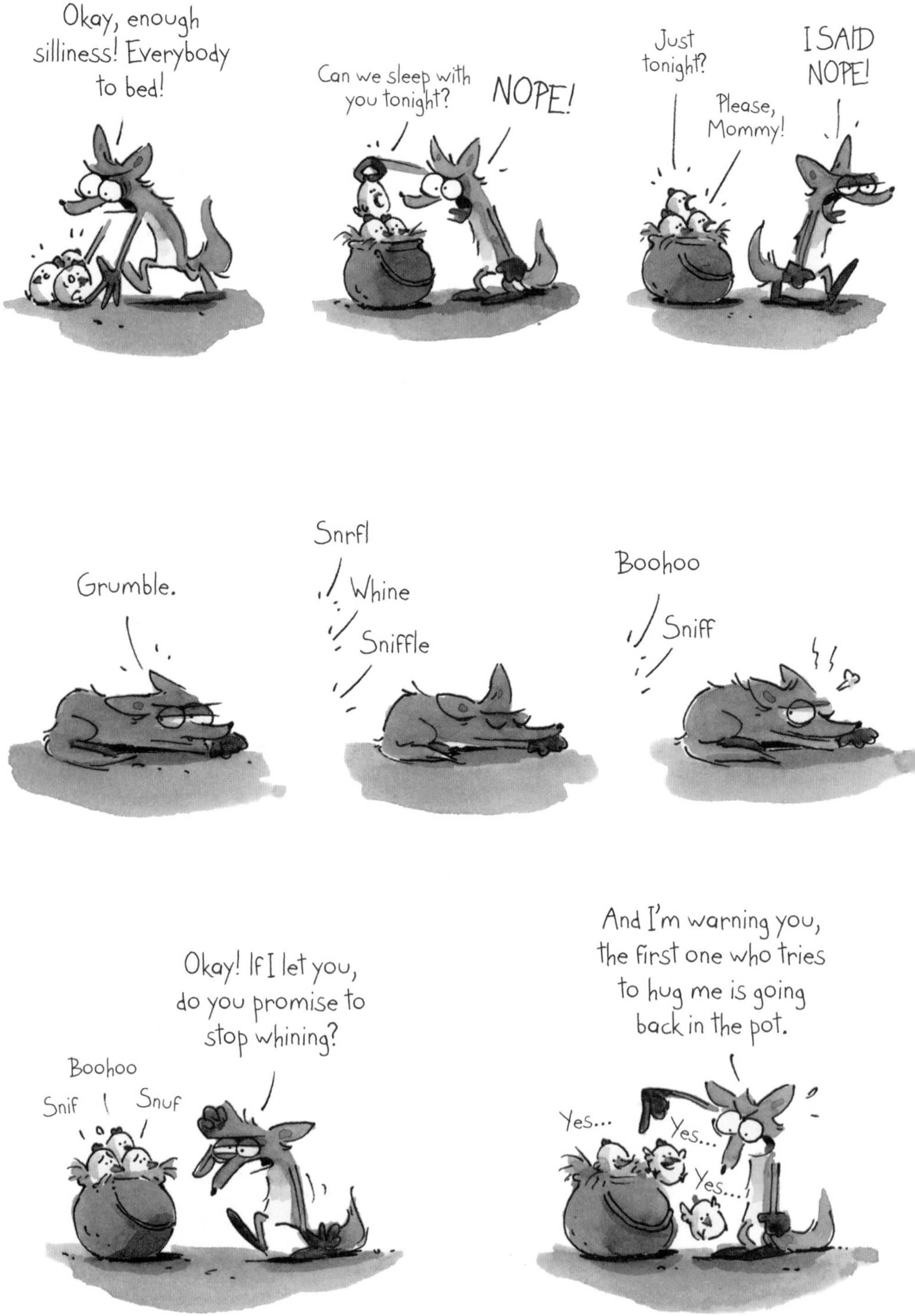

Okay, enough silliness! Everybody to bed!
Can we sleep with you tonight?
NOPE!
Just tonight?
Please, Mommy!
I SAID NOPE!
Grumble.
Snrfl
Whine
Sniffle
Boohoo
Sniff
Okay! If I let you, do you promise to stop whining?
Boohoo
Snif
Snuf
And I'm warning you, the first one who tries to hug me is going back in the pot.
Yes...
Yes...
Yes...

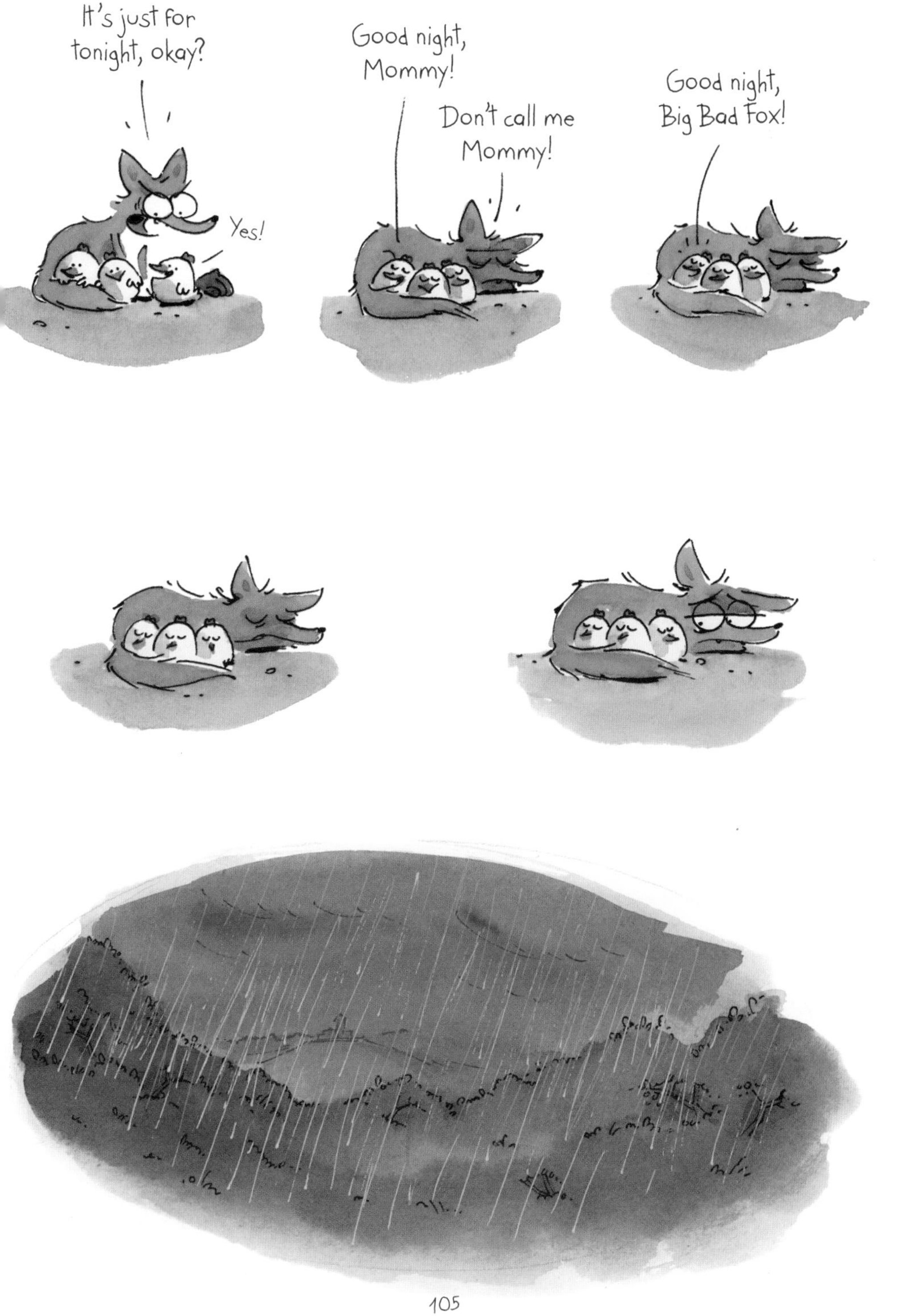
It's just for tonight, okay?
Yes!
Good night, Mommy!
Don't call me Mommy!
Good night, Big Bad Fox!

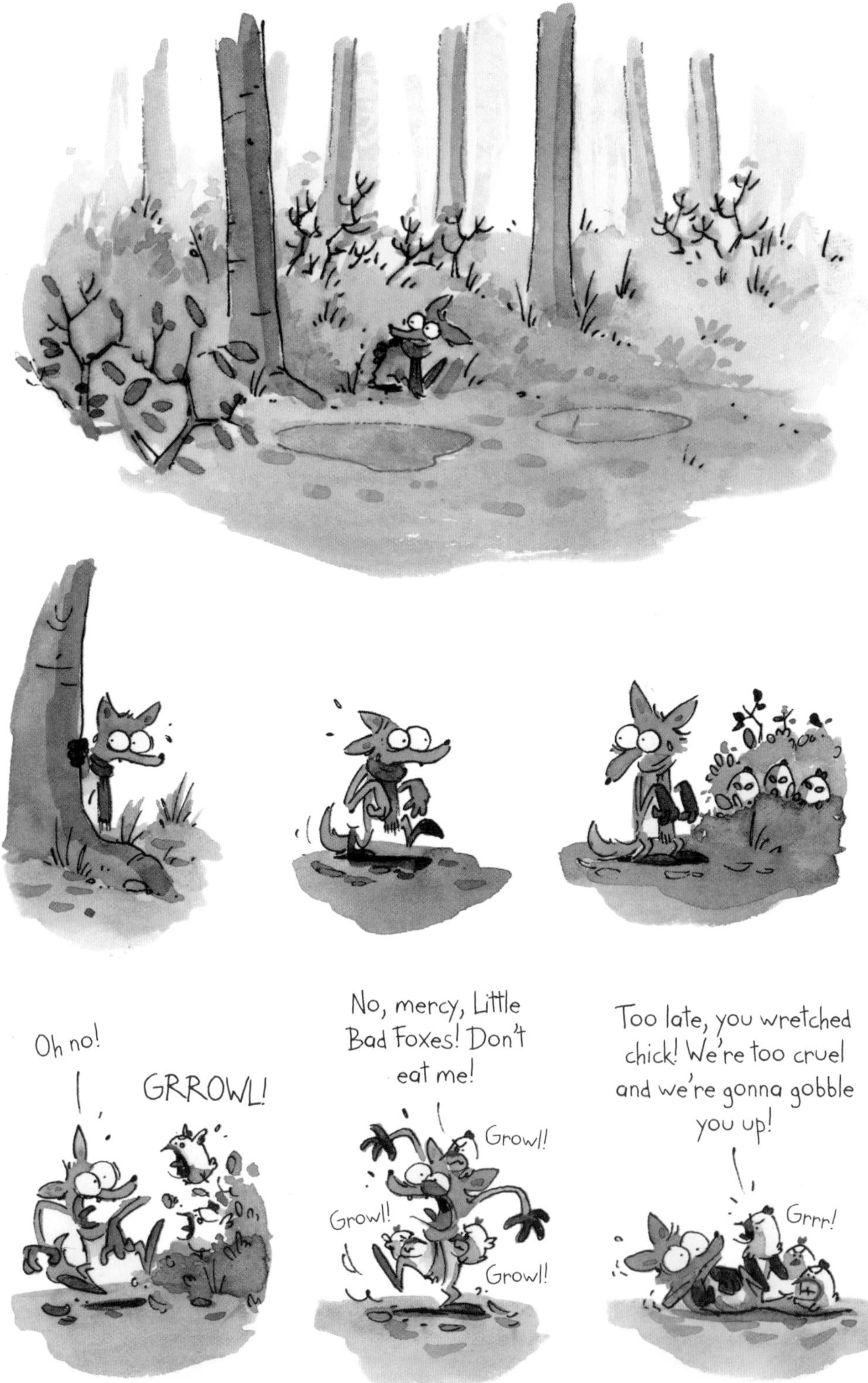
Oh no!
GRROWL!
No, mercy, Little Bad Foxes! Don't eat me!
Growl!
Growl!
Growl!
Too late, you wretched chick! We're too cruel and we're gonna gobble you up!
Grrr!

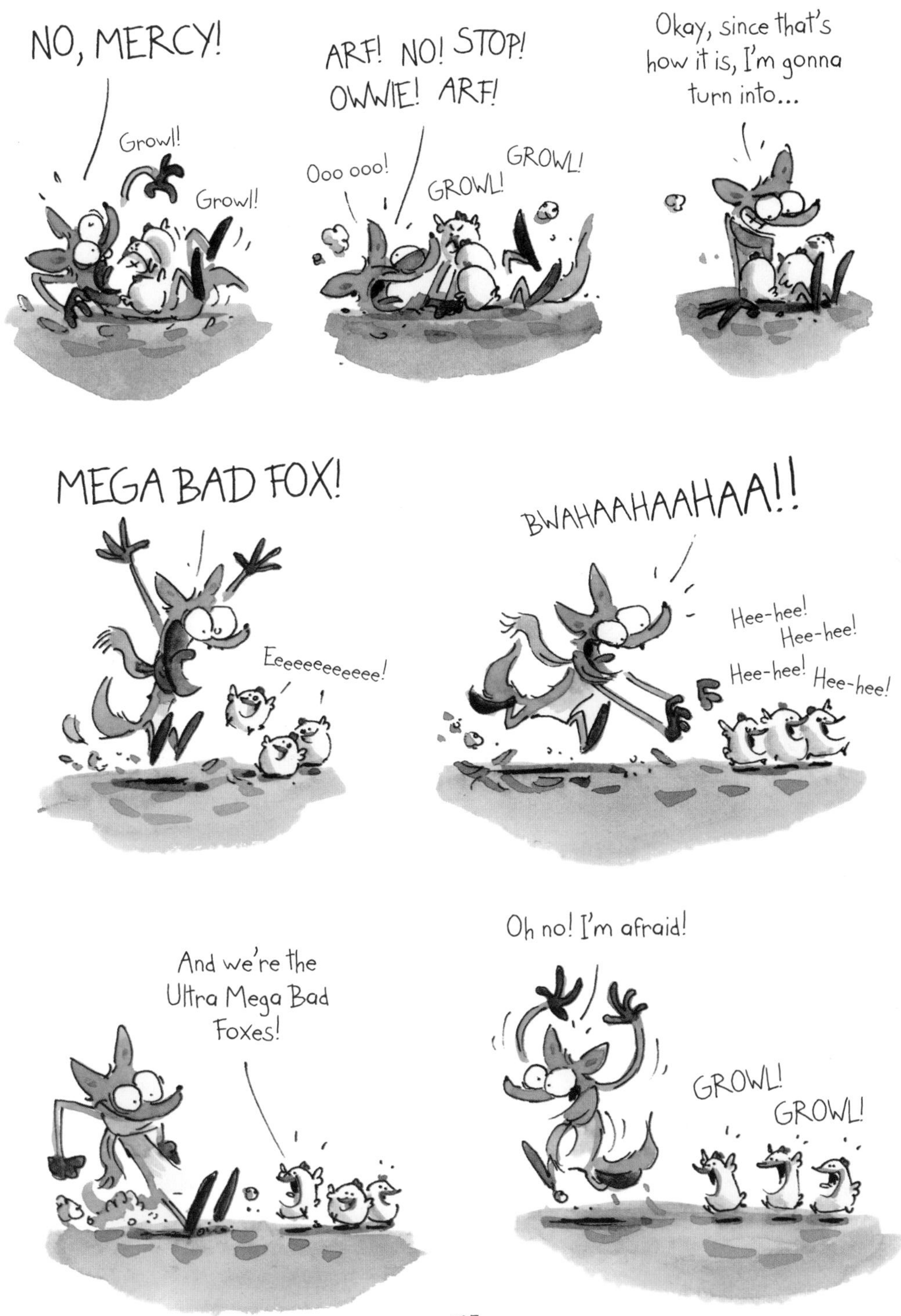
NO, MERCY!
Growl!
Growl!
ARF! NO! STOP! OWWIE! ARF!
Ooo ooo!
GROWL!
GROWL!
Okay, since that's how it is, I'm gonna turn into...
MEGA BAD FOX!
Eeeeeeeeeeee!
BWAHAAHAAHAA!!
Hee-hee!
Hee-hee!
Hee-hee!
Hee-hee!
And we're the Ultra Mega Bad Foxes!
Oh no! I'm afraid!
GROWL!
GROWL!

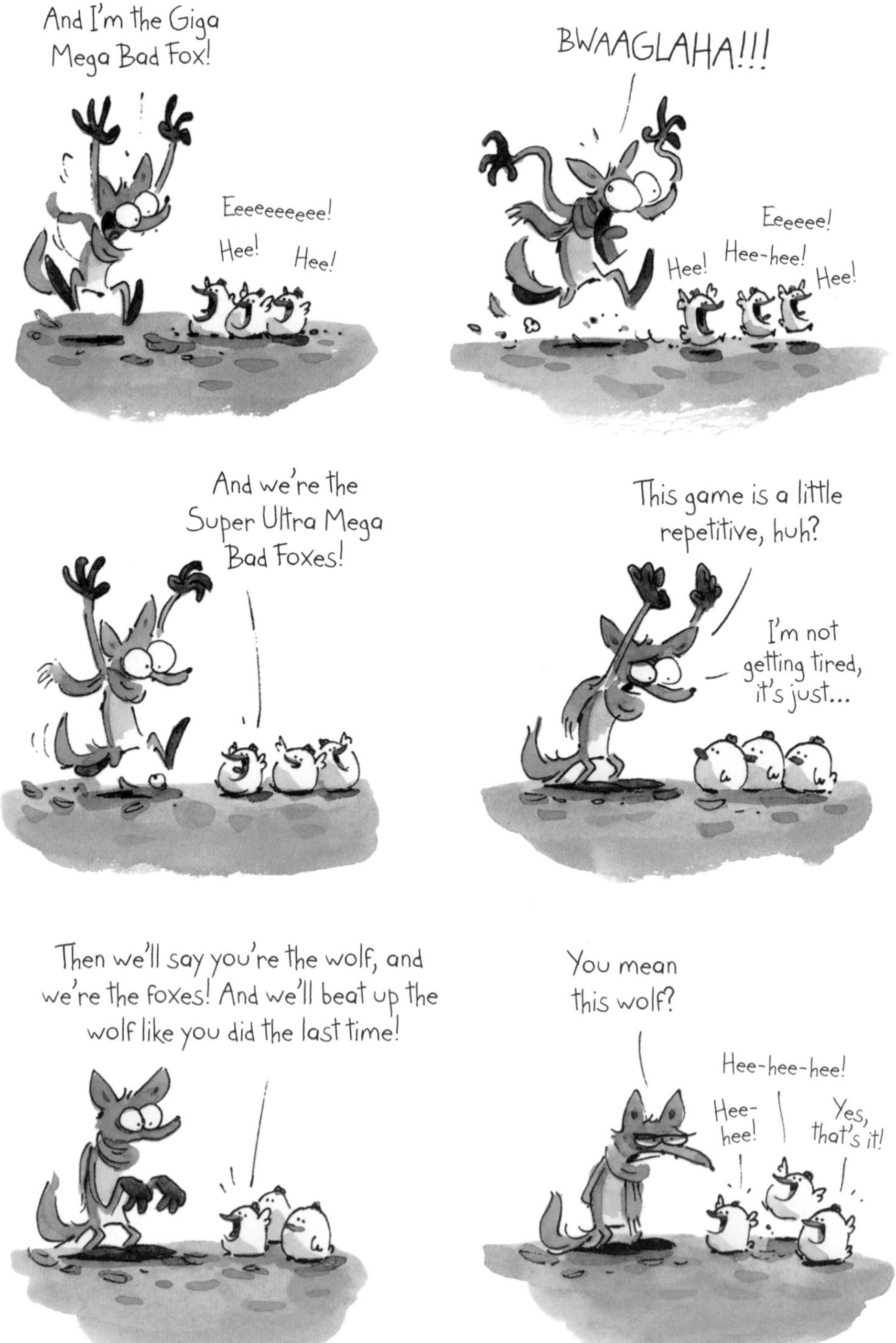

And I'm the Giga Mega Bad Fox!
Eeeeeeeeee!
Hee!
Hee!
BWAAGLAHA!!!
Eeeeee!
Hee!
Hee-hee!
Hee!
And we're the Super Ultra Mega Bad Foxes!
This game is a little repetitive, huh?
I'm not getting tired, it's just...
Then we'll say you're the wolf, and we're the foxes! And we'll beat up the wolf like you did the last time!
You mean this wolf?
Hee-hee-hee!
Hee-hee!
Yes, that's it!

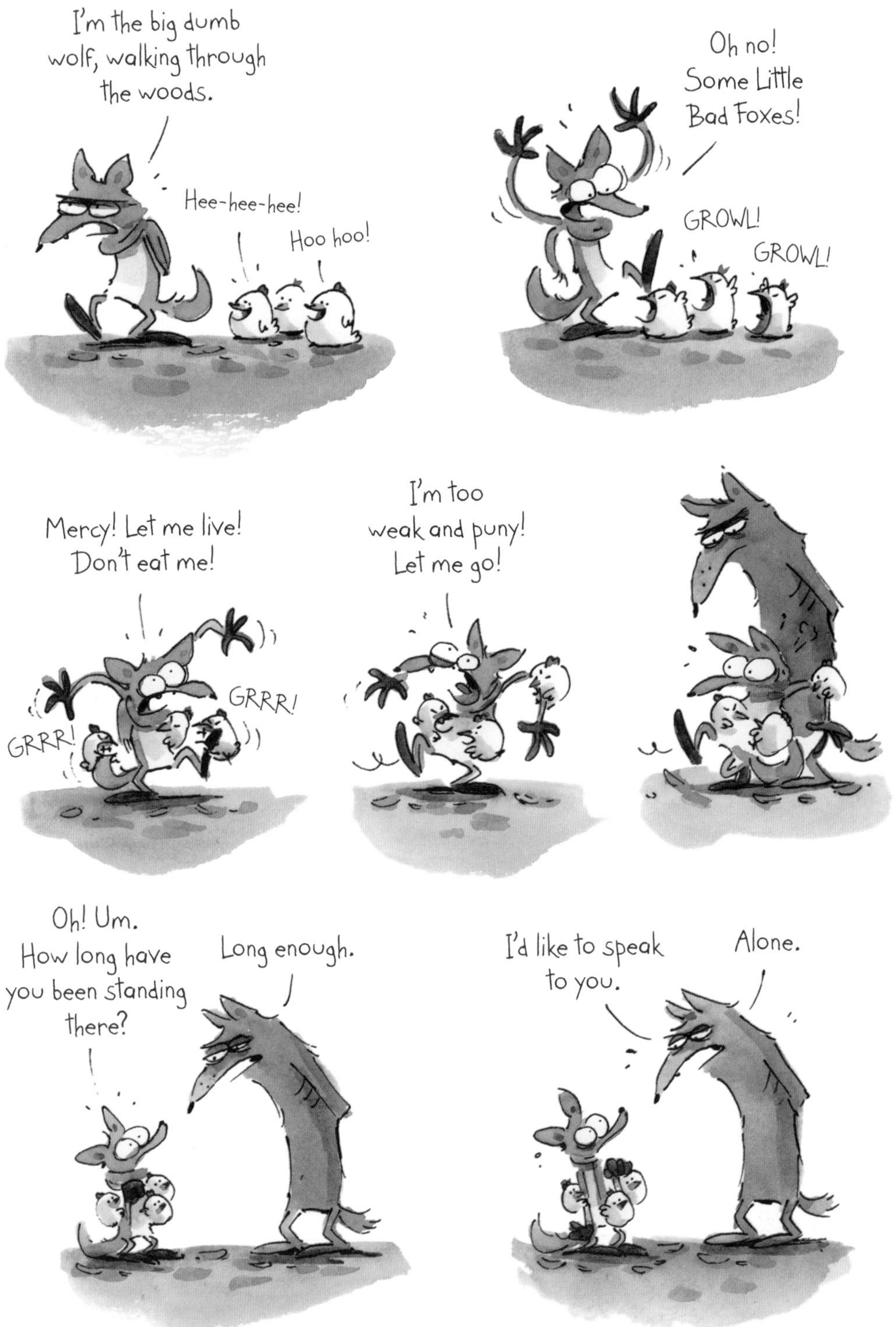

I'm the big dumb wolf, walking through the woods.
Hee-hee-hee!
Hoo hoo!
Oh no! Some Little Bad Foxes!
GROWL!
GROWL!
Mercy! Let me live! Don't eat me!
GRRR!
GRRR!
I'm too weak and puny! Let me go!
Oh! Um. How long have you been standing there?
Long enough.
I'd like to speak to you.
Alone.

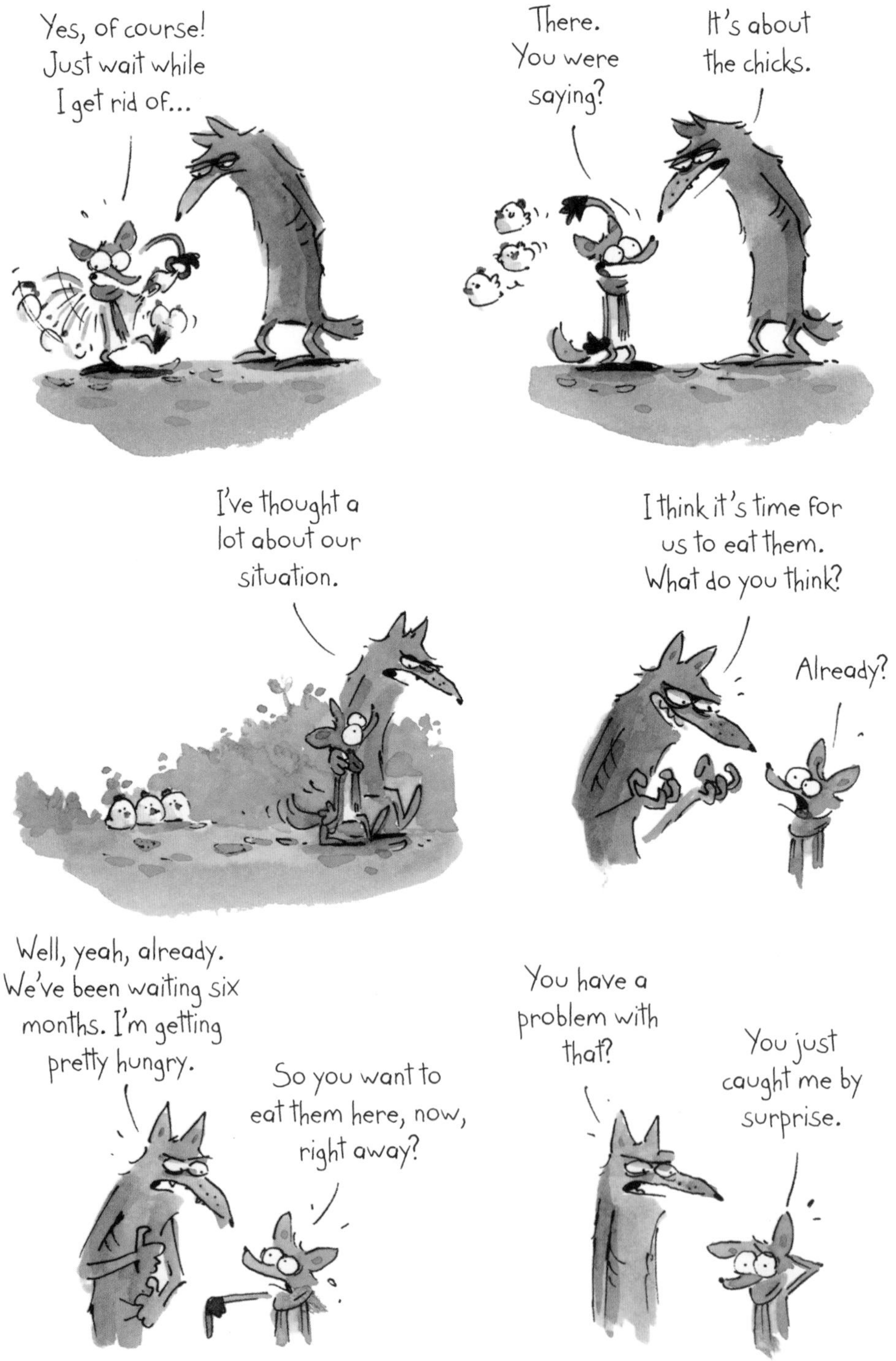
Yes, of course! Just wait while I get rid of...
There. You were saying?
It's about the chicks.
I've thought a lot about our situation.
I think it's time for us to eat them. What do you think?
Already?
Well, yeah, already. We've been waiting six months. I'm getting pretty hungry.
So you want to eat them here, now, right away?
You have a problem with that?
You just caught me by surprise.

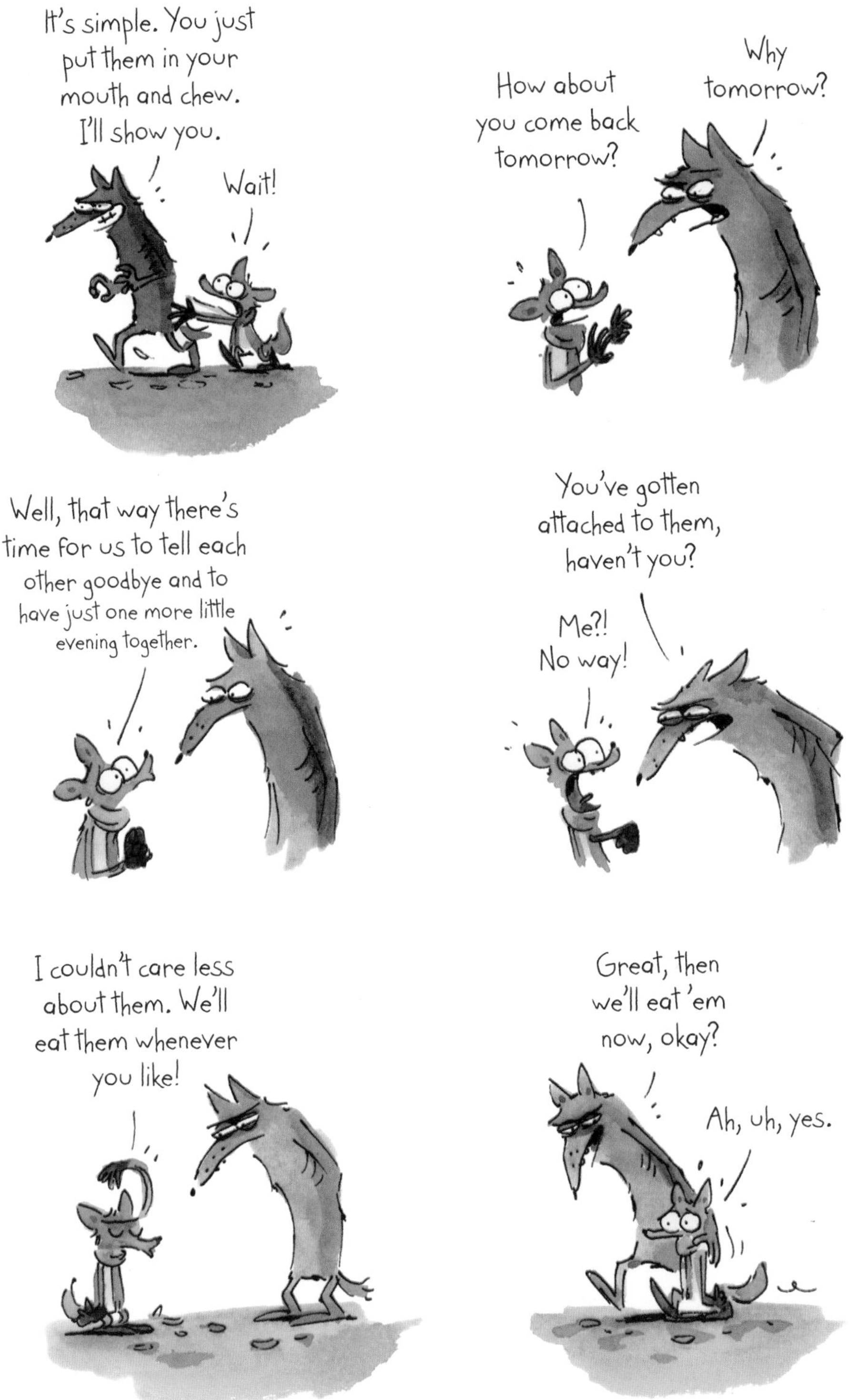
It's simple. You just put them in your mouth and chew. I'll show you.
Wait!
How about you come back tomorrow?
Why tomorrow?
Well, that way there's time for us to tell each other goodbye and to have just one more little evening together.
You've gotten attached to them, haven't you?
Me?! No way!
I couldn't care less about them. We'll eat them whenever you like!
Great, then we'll eat 'em now, okay?
Ah, uh, yes.

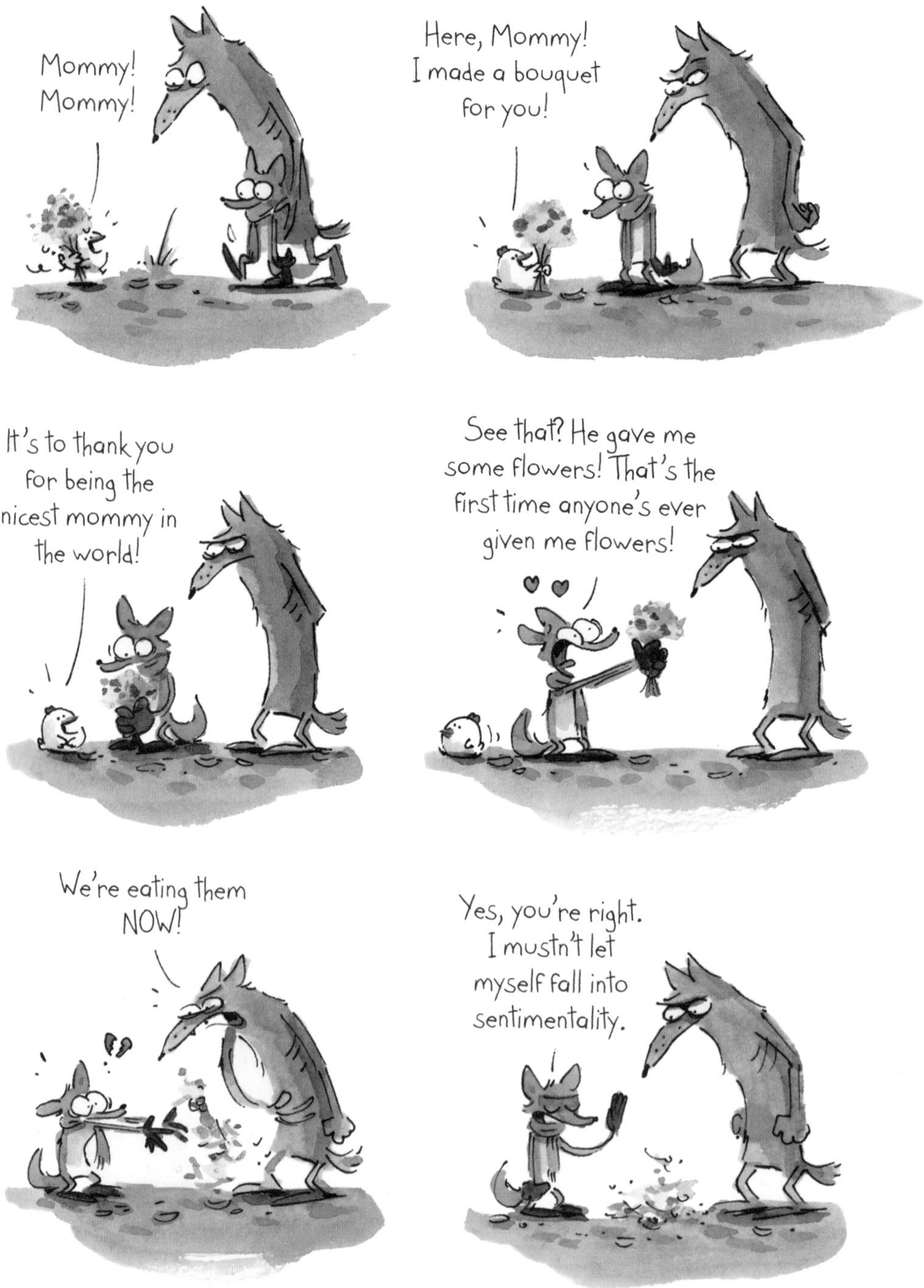
Mommy!
Mommy!
Here, Mommy!
I made a bouquet
for you!
It's to thank you
for being the
nicest mommy in
the world!
See that? He gave me
some flowers! That's the
first time anyone's ever
given me flowers!
We're eating them
NOW!
Yes, you're right.
I mustn't let
myself fall into
sentimentality.

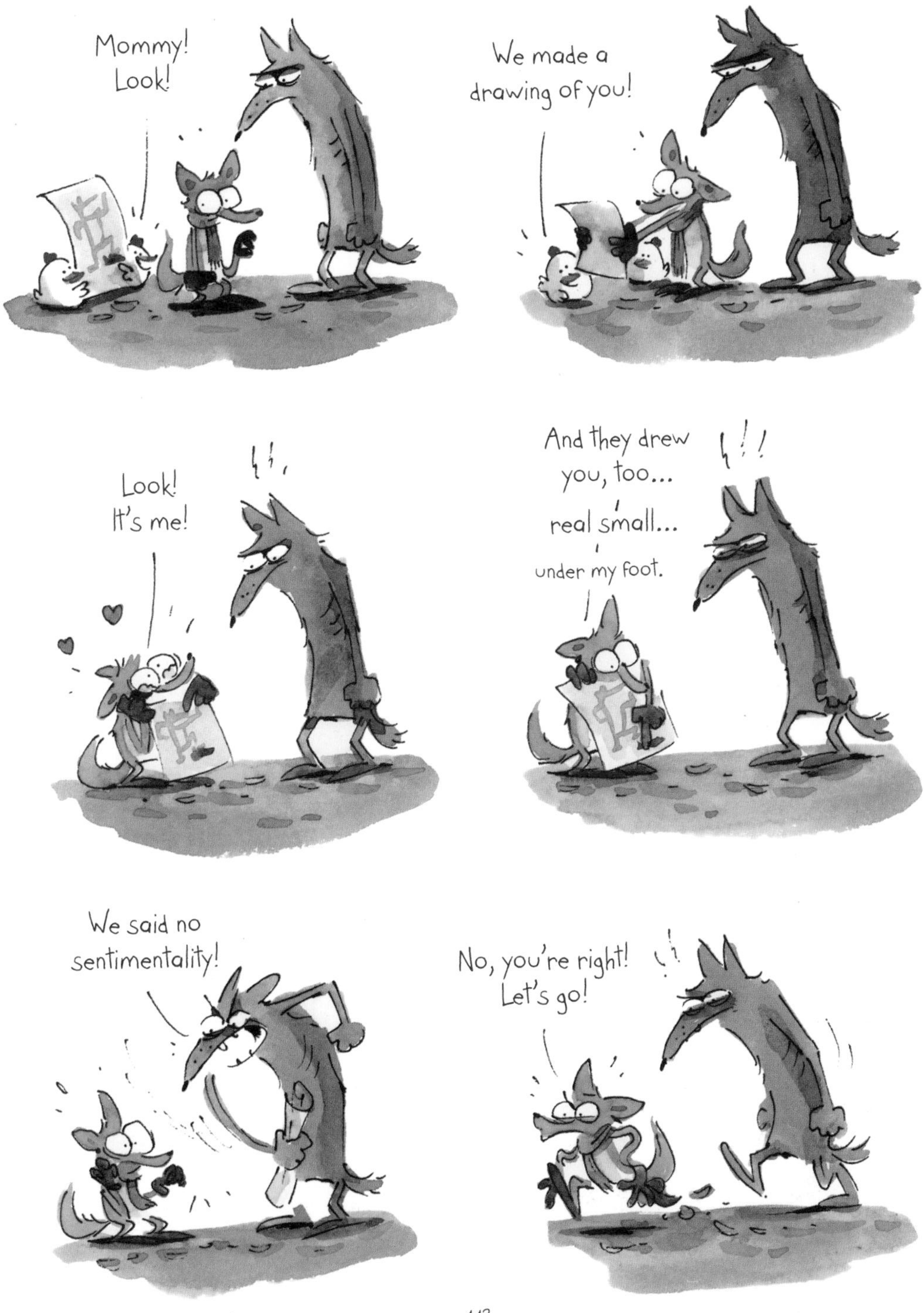
Mommy!
Look!
We made a drawing of you!
Look!
It's me!
And they drew you, too...
real small...
under my foot.
We said no sentimentality!
No, you're right!
Let's go!

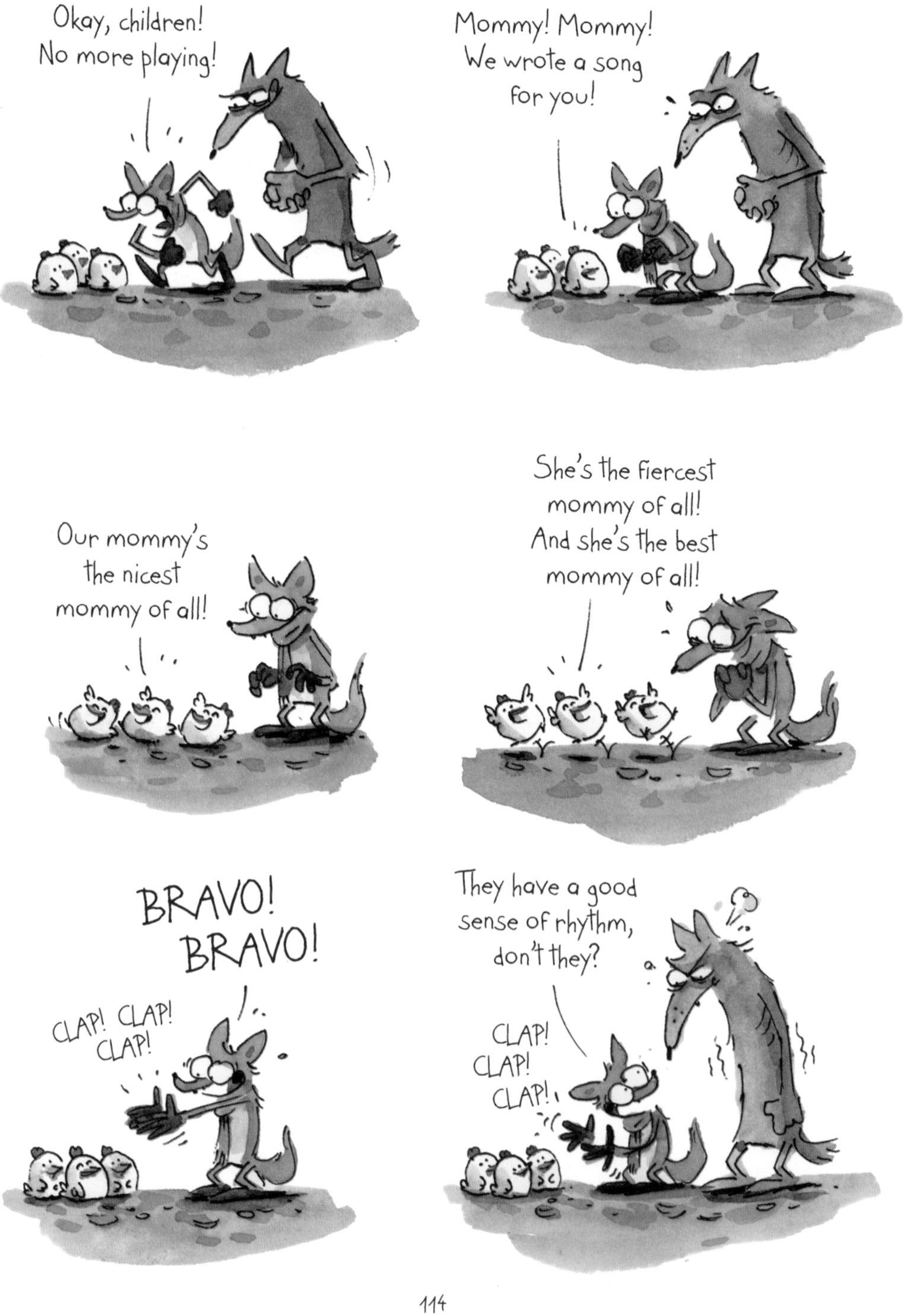
Okay, children!
No more playing!
Mommy! Mommy!
We wrote a song
for you!
Our mommy's
the nicest
mommy of all!
She's the fiercest
mommy of all!
And she's the best
mommy of all!
BRAVO!
BRAVO!
CLAP! CLAP!
CLAP!
They have a good
sense of rhythm,
don't they?
CLAP!
CLAP!
CLAP!

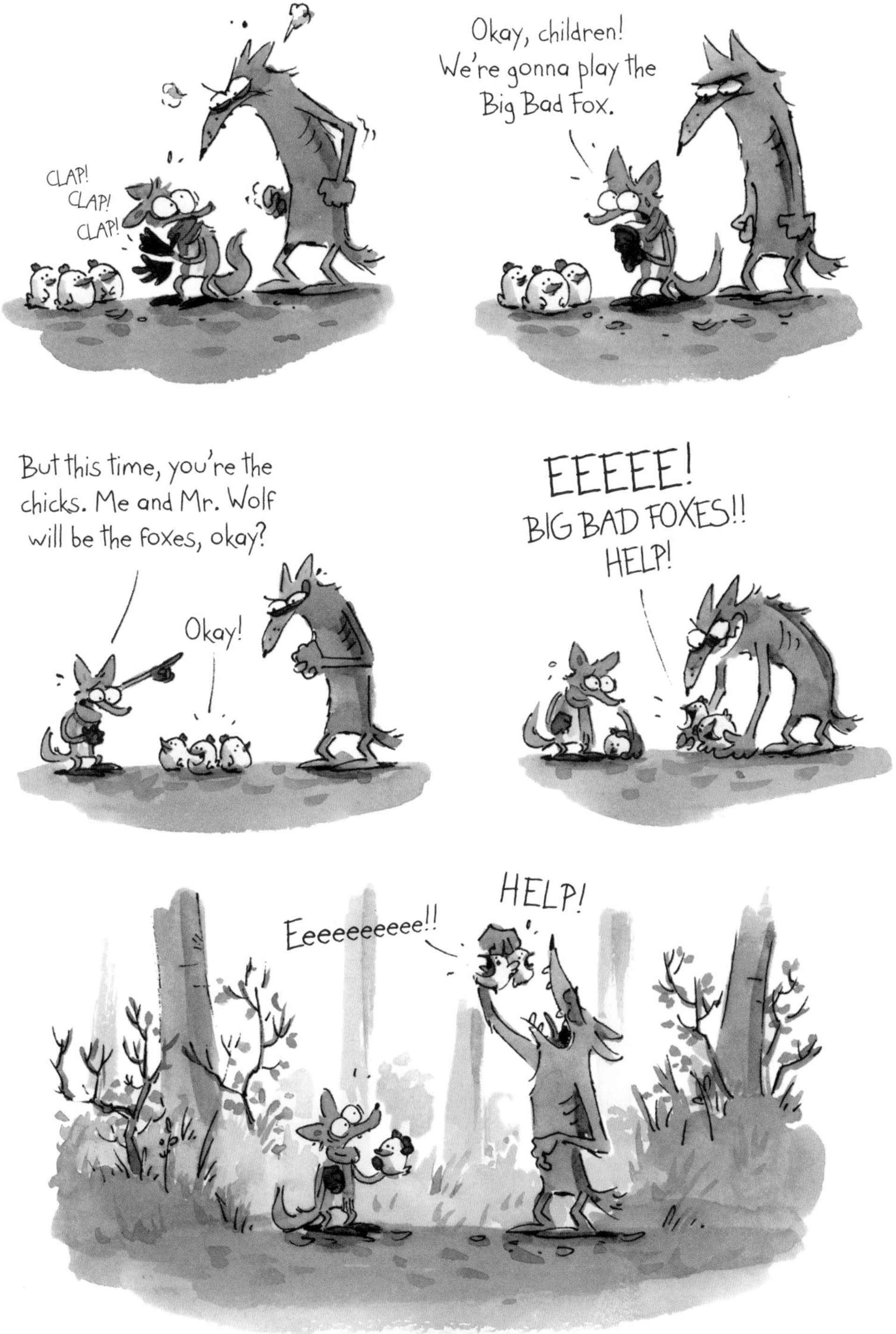
CLAP!
CLAP!
CLAP!
Okay, children! We're gonna play the Big Bad Fox.
But this time, you're the chicks. Me and Mr. Wolf will be the foxes, okay?
Okay!
EEEEE!
BIG BAD FOXES!! HELP!
HELP!
Eeeeeeeee!!

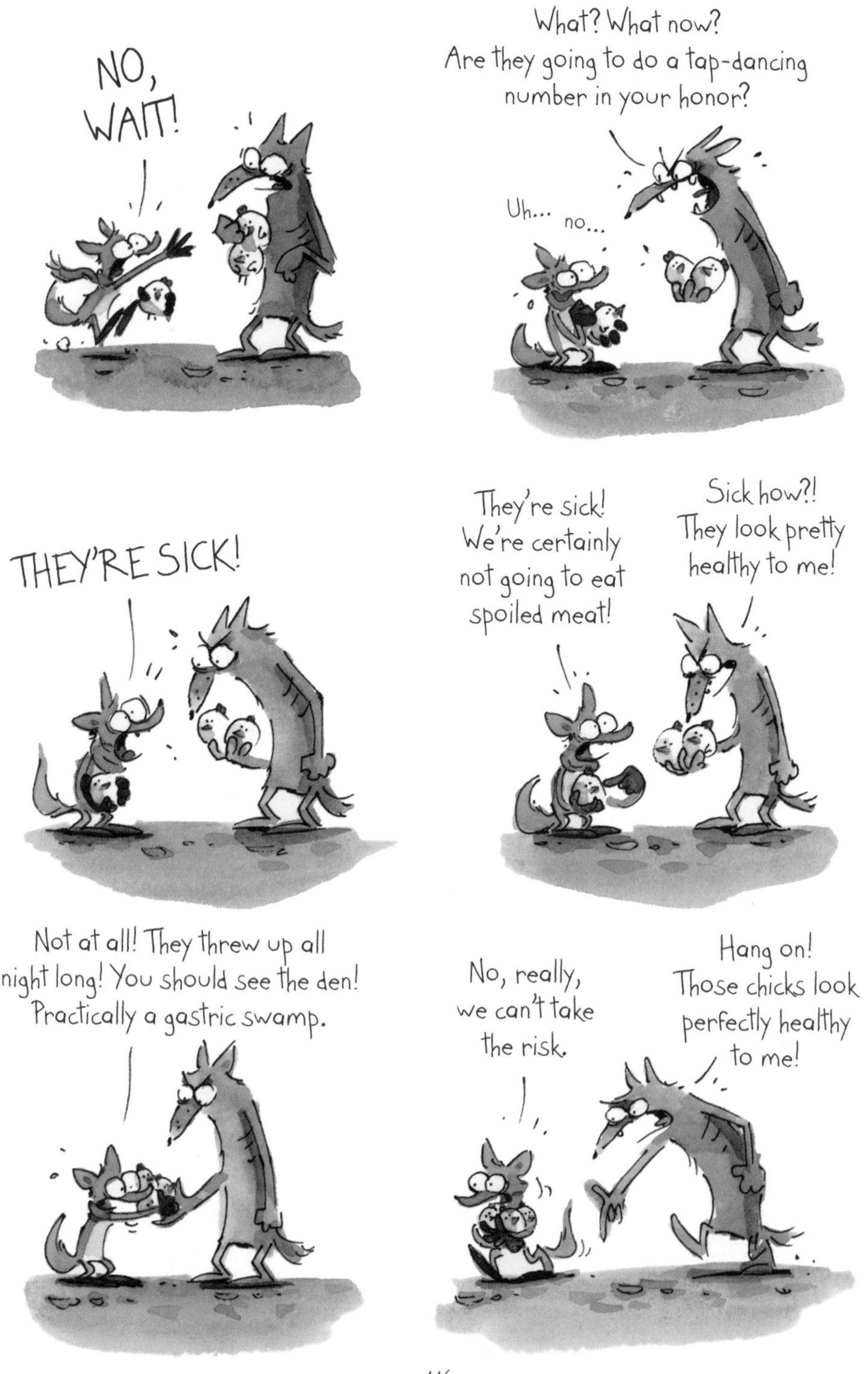
NO, WAIT!
What? What now? Are they going to do a tap-dancing number in your honor?
Uh... no...
THEY'RE SICK!
They're sick! We're certainly not going to eat spoiled meat!
Sick how?! They look pretty healthy to me!
Not at all! They threw up all night long! You should see the den! Practically a gastric swamp.
No, really, we can't take the risk.
Hang on! Those chicks look perfectly healthy to me!

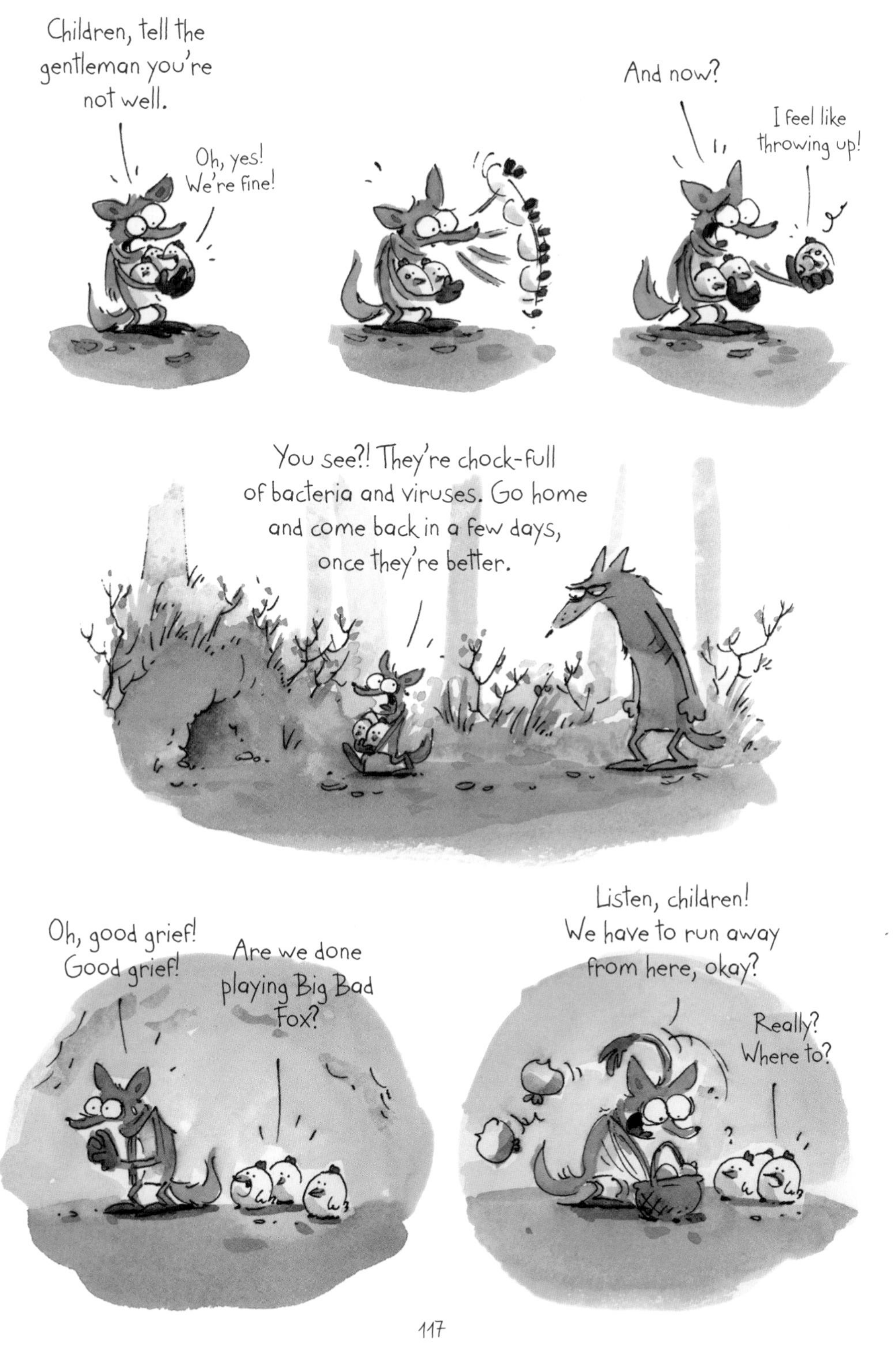

Children, tell the gentleman you're not well.
Oh, yes! We're fine!
And now?
I feel like throwing up!
You see?! They're chock-full of bacteria and viruses. Go home and come back in a few days, once they're better.
Oh, good grief! Good grief!
Are we done playing Big Bad Fox?
Listen, children! We have to run away from here, okay?
Really? Where to?

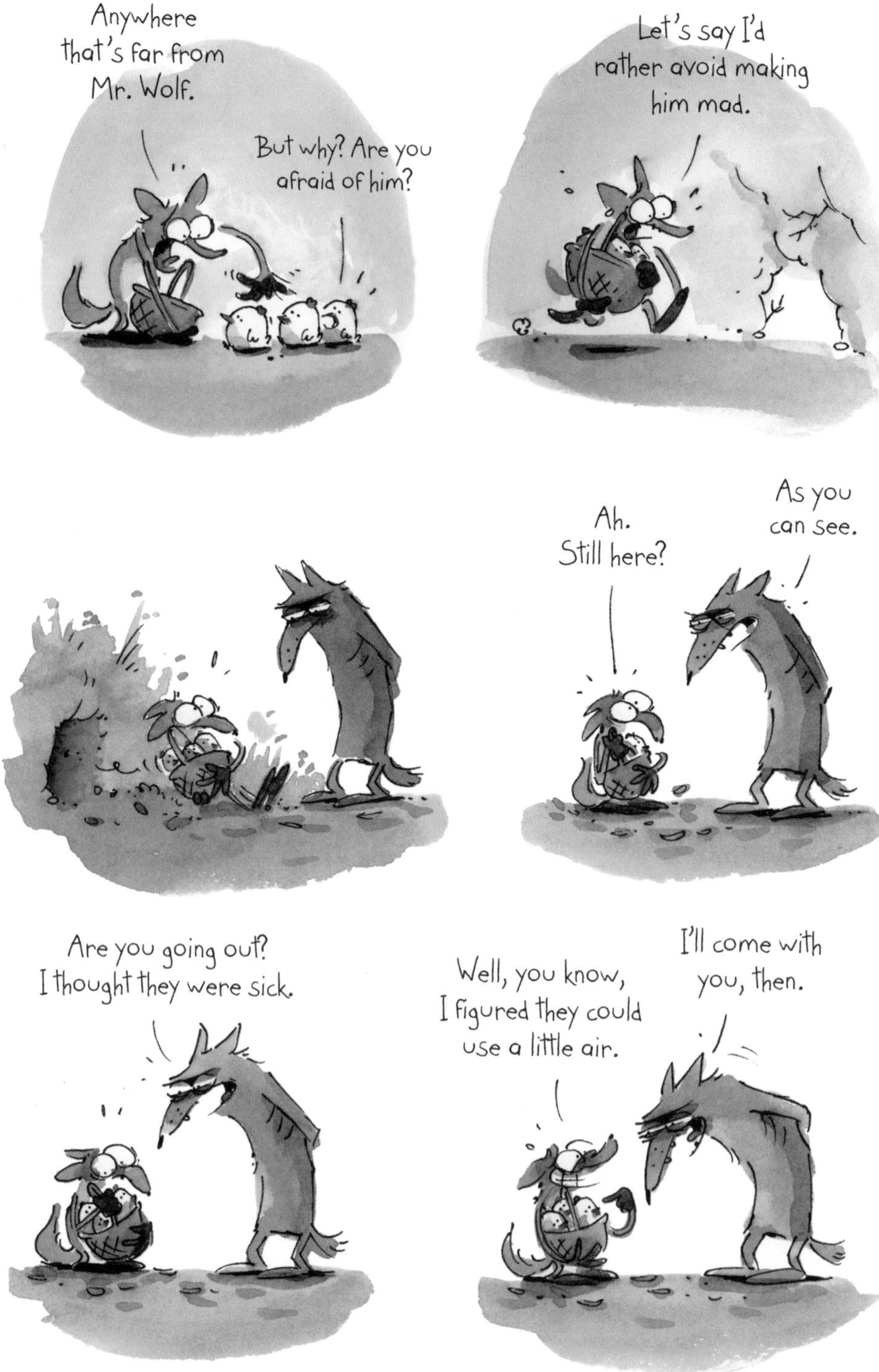
Anywhere that's far from Mr. Wolf.
But why? Are you afraid of him?
Let's say I'd rather avoid making him mad.
Ah. Still here?
As you can see.
Are you going out? I thought they were sick.
Well, you know, I figured they could use a little air.
I'll come with you, then.

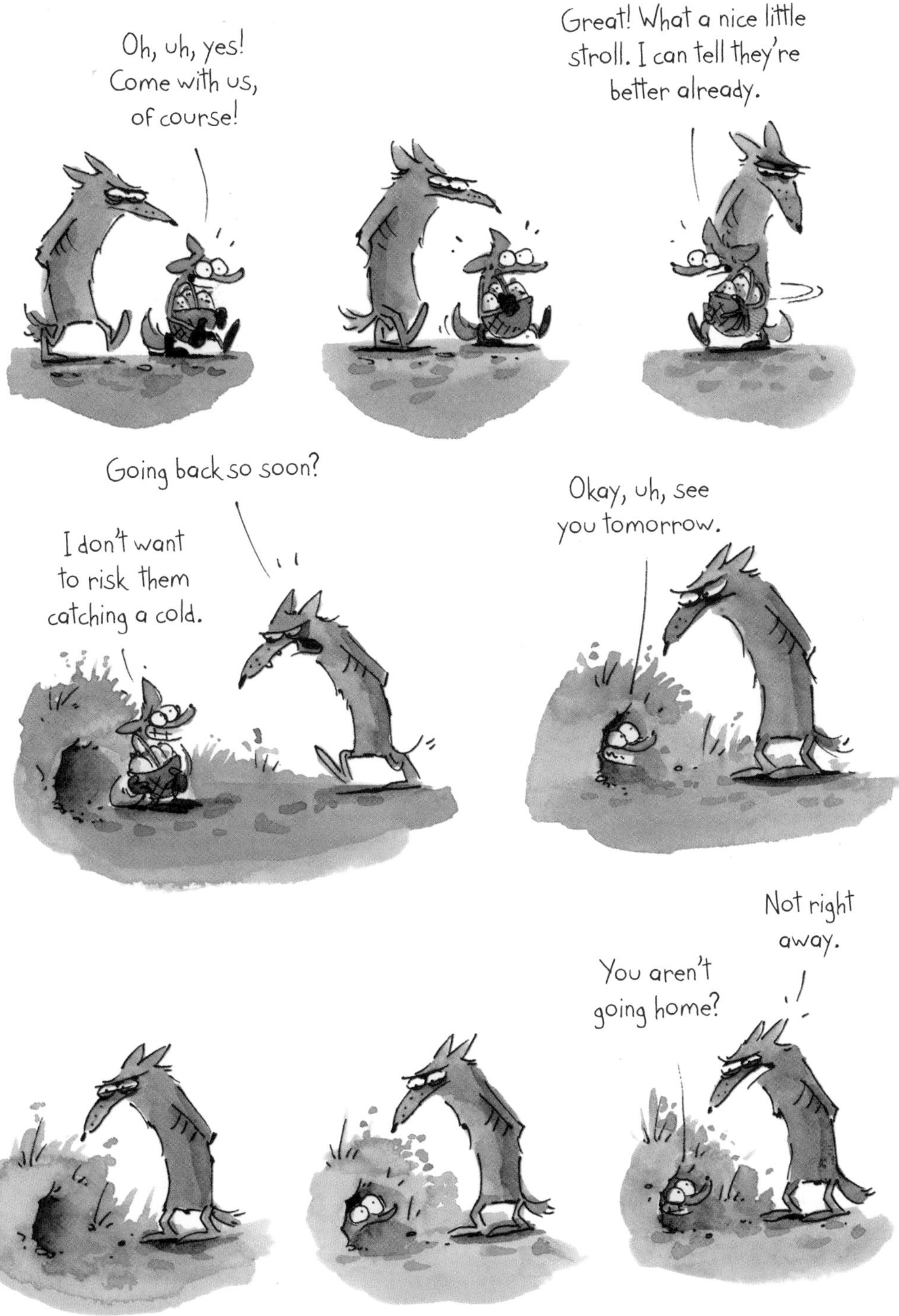
Oh, uh, yes! Come with us, of course!
Great! What a nice little stroll. I can tell they're better already.
Going back so soon?
I don't want to risk them catching a cold.
Okay, uh, see you tomorrow.
You aren't going home?
Not right away.

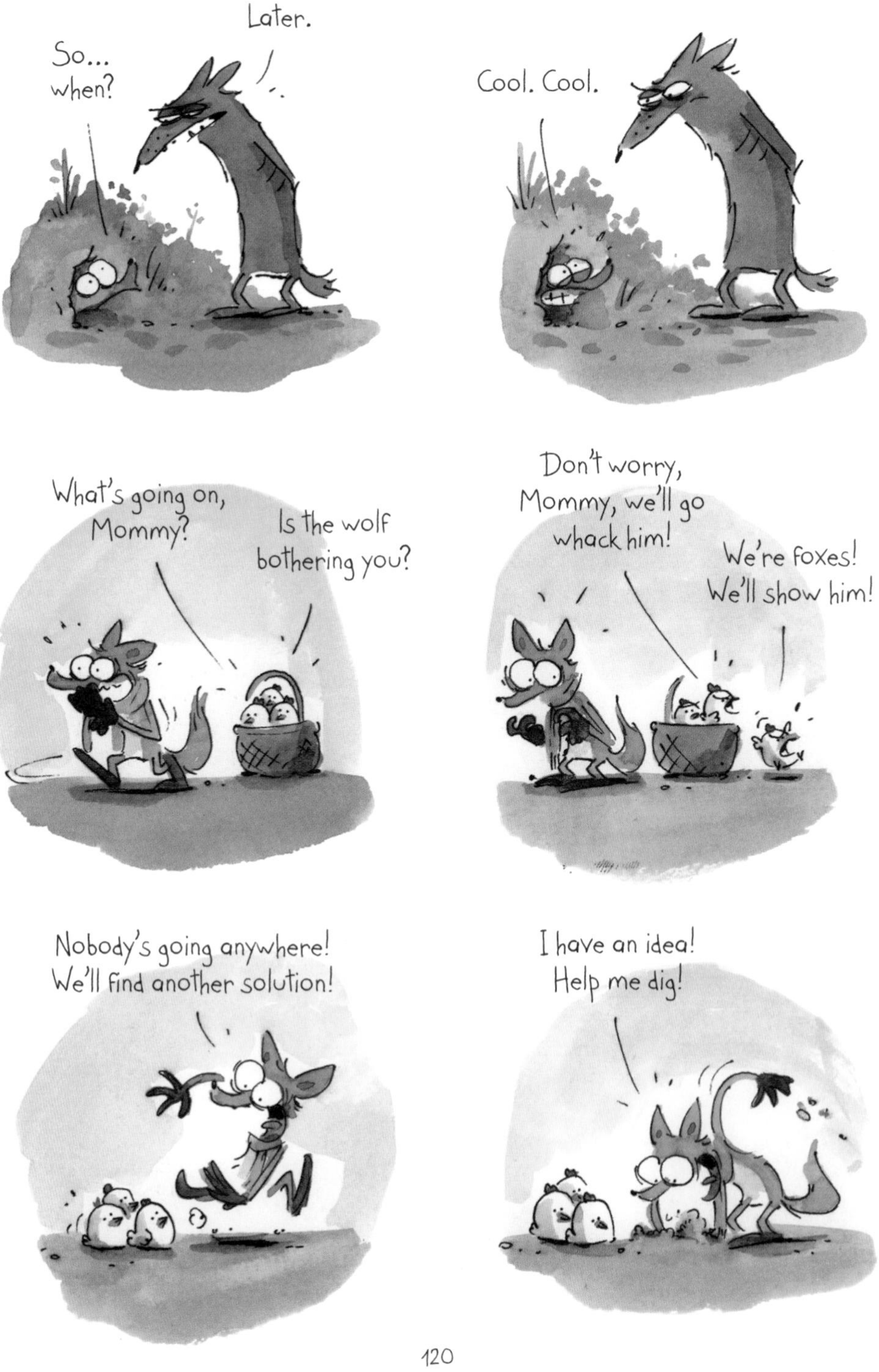

So... when?
Later.
Cool. Cool.
What's going on, Mommy?
Is the wolf bothering you?
Don't worry, Mommy, we'll go whack him!
We're foxes! We'll show him!
Nobody's going anywhere! We'll find another solution!
I have an idea! Help me dig!

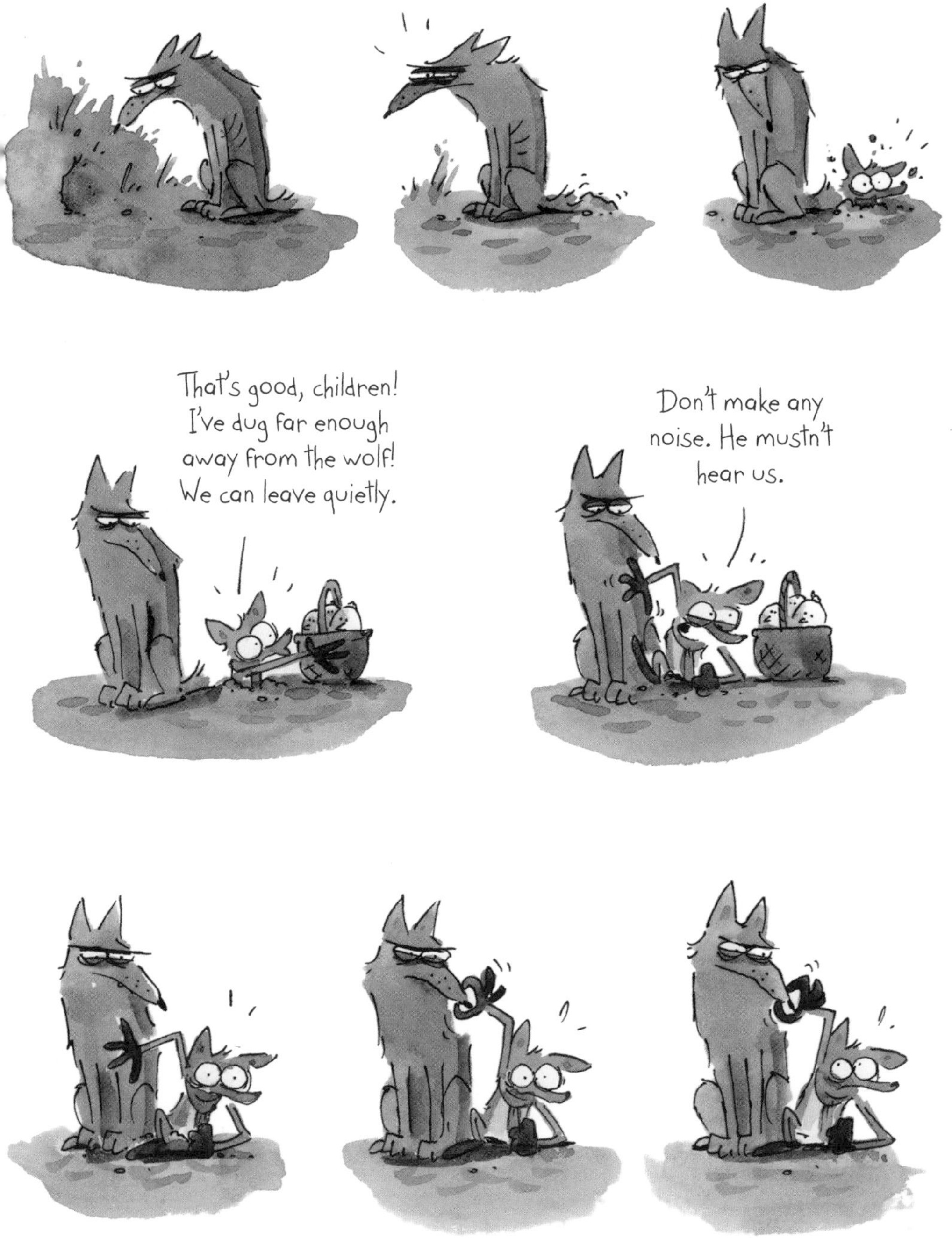
That's good, children! I've dug far enough away from the wolf! We can leave quietly.
Don't make any noise. He mustn't hear us.

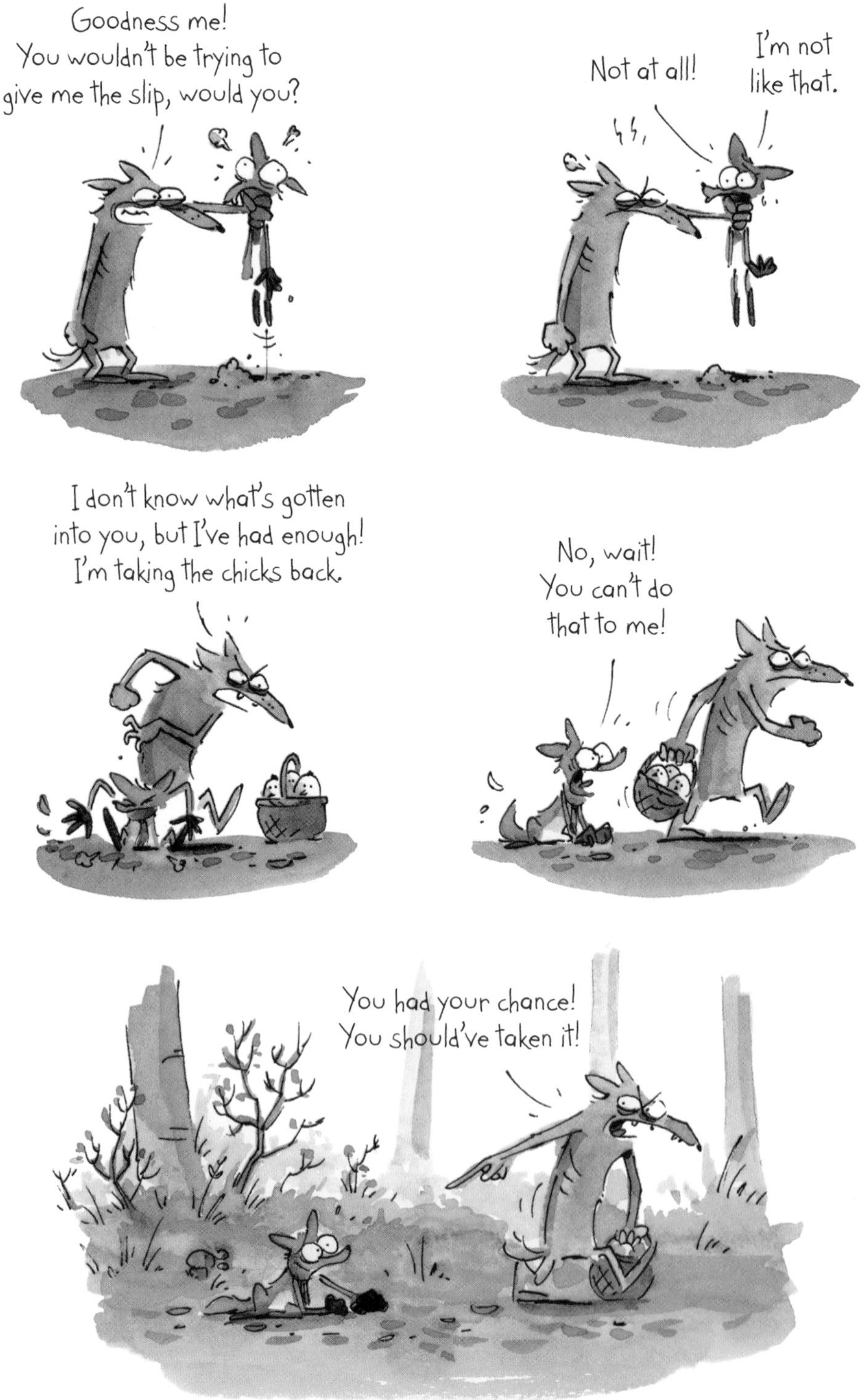
Goodness me!
You wouldn't be trying to give me the slip, would you?
Not at all!
I'm not like that.
I don't know what's gotten into you, but I've had enough!
I'm taking the chicks back.
No, wait!
You can't do that to me!
You had your chance!
You should've taken it!

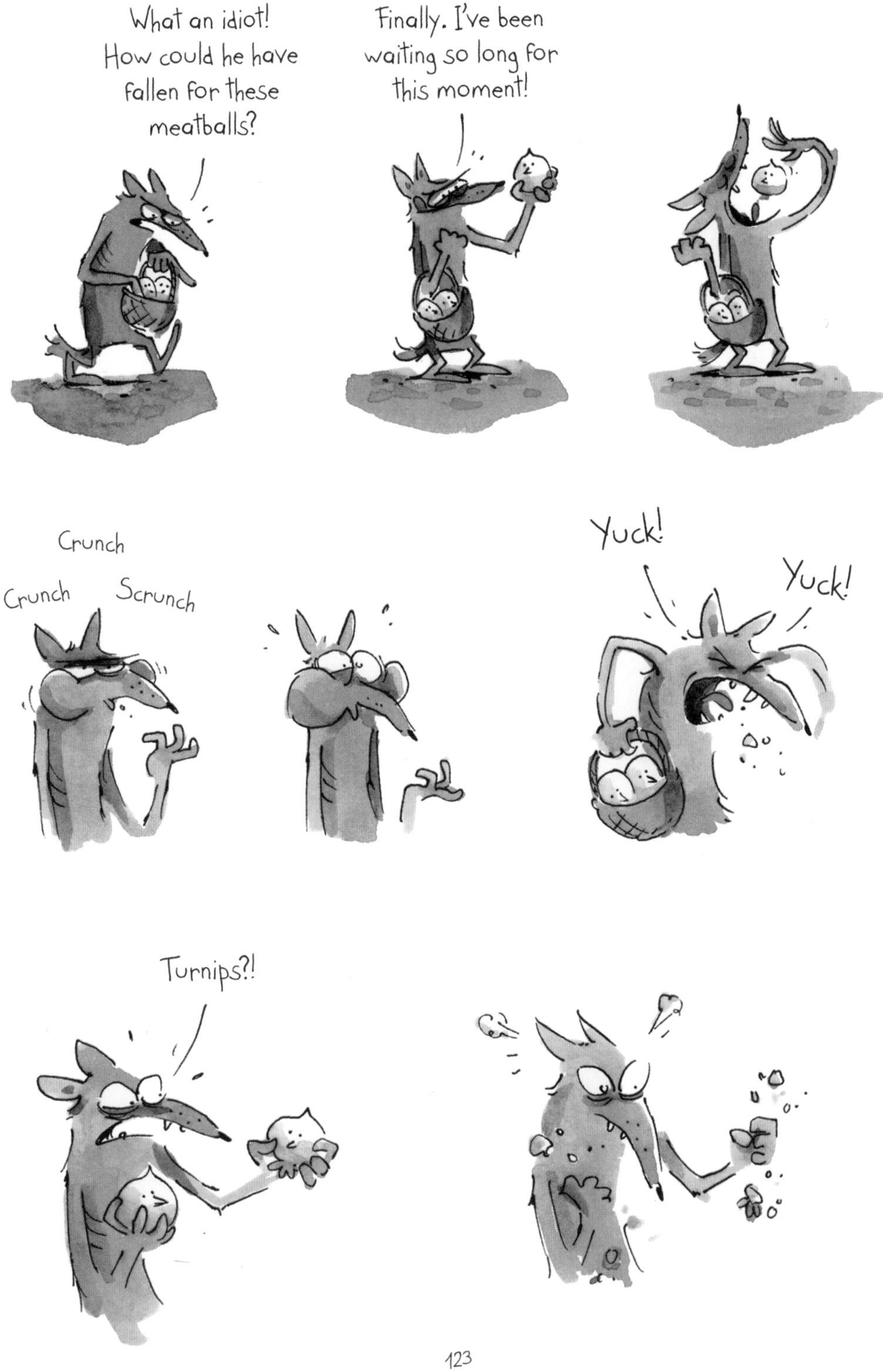
What an idiot! How could he have fallen for these meatballs?
Finally. I've been waiting so long for this moment!
Crunch
Crunch
Scrunch
Yuck!
Yuck!
Turnips?!

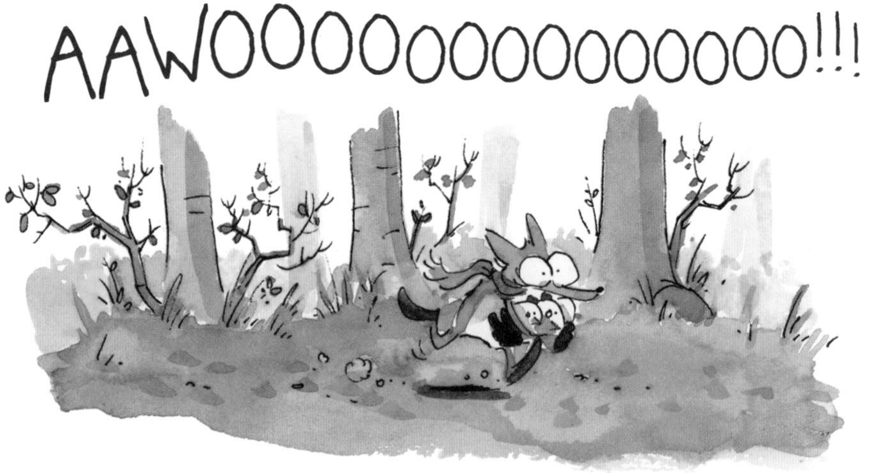
AAWOOOOOOOOOOOOOOO!!!

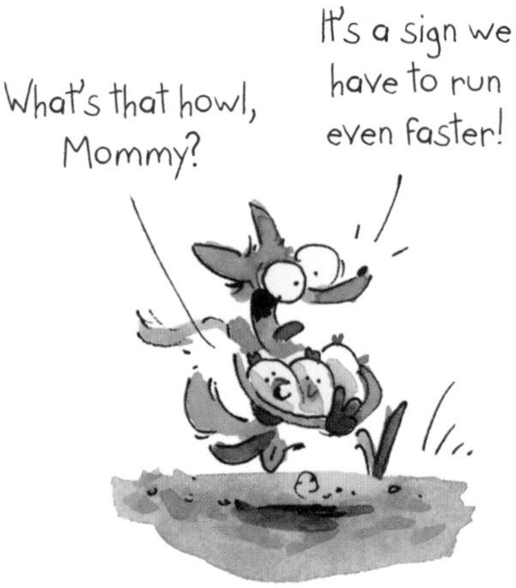
What's that howl, Mommy?
It's a sign we have to run even faster!

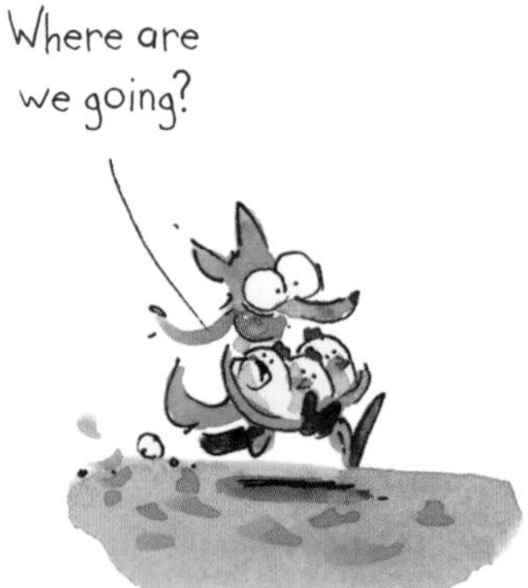
Where are we going?

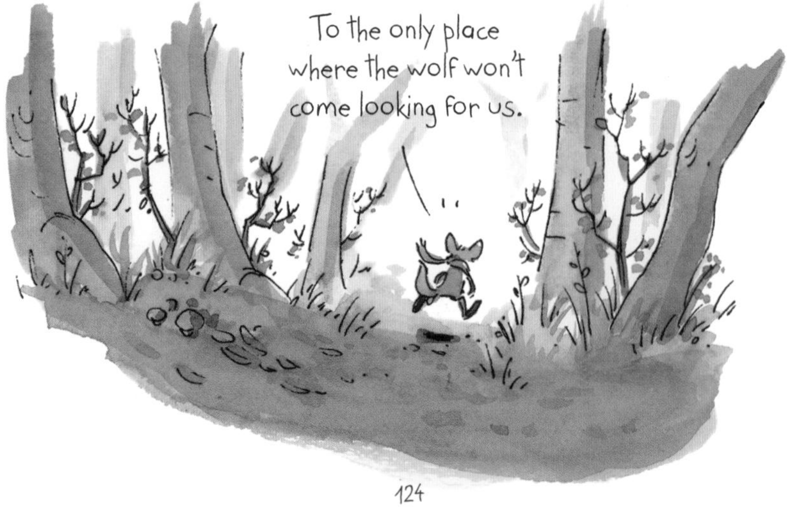
To the only place where the wolf won't come looking for us.

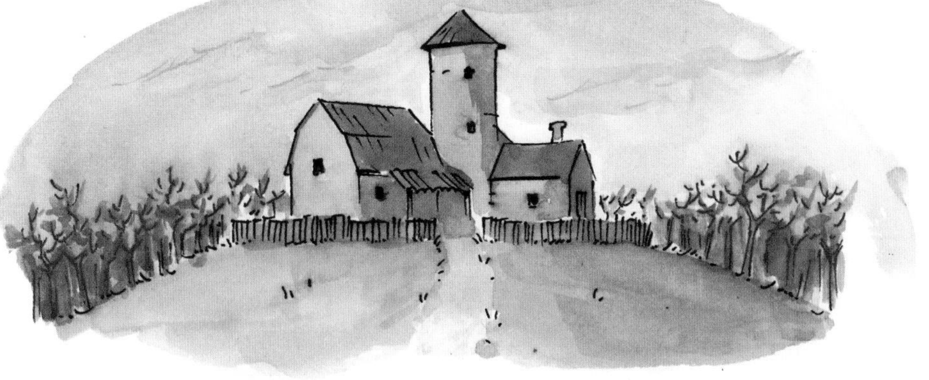

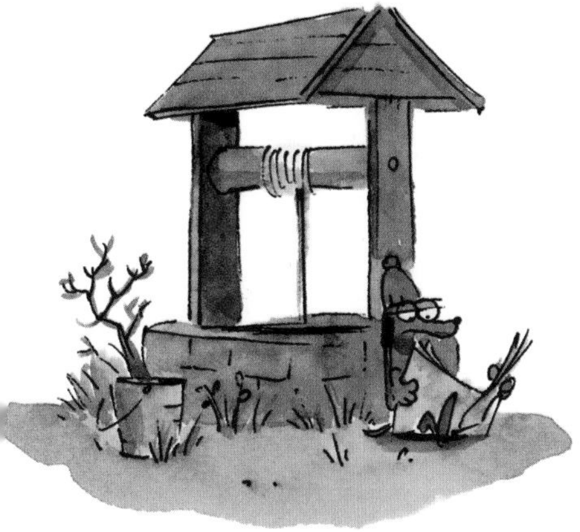

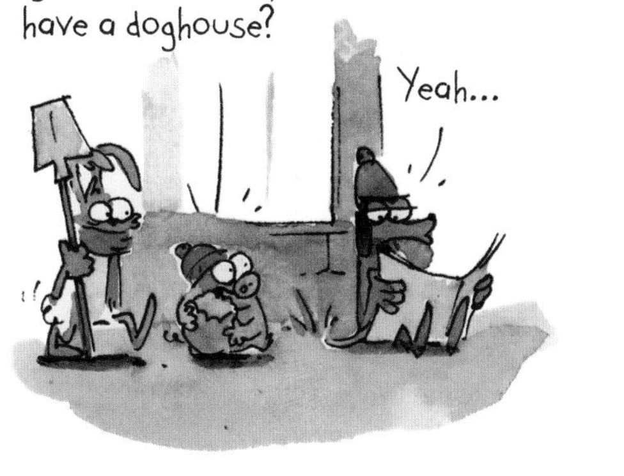
Oh my! What are you doing outside? Don't you have a doghouse?
Yeah...

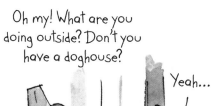

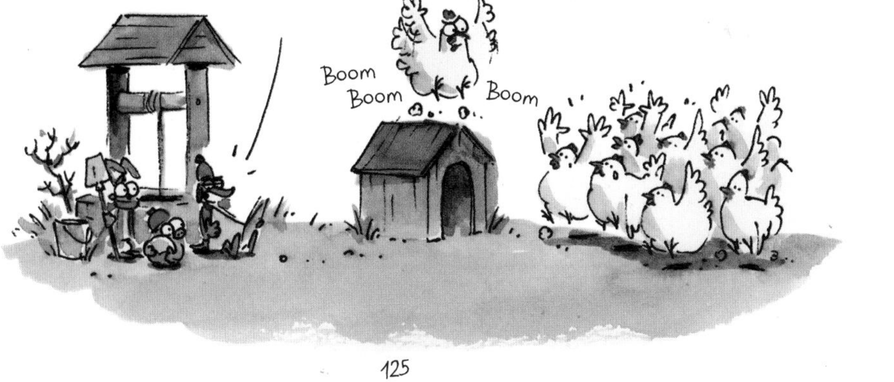
But it's time for the aerobics class at the Fox Exterminators' Club.
And one, and two!
And one, and two!
Boom
Boom
Boom

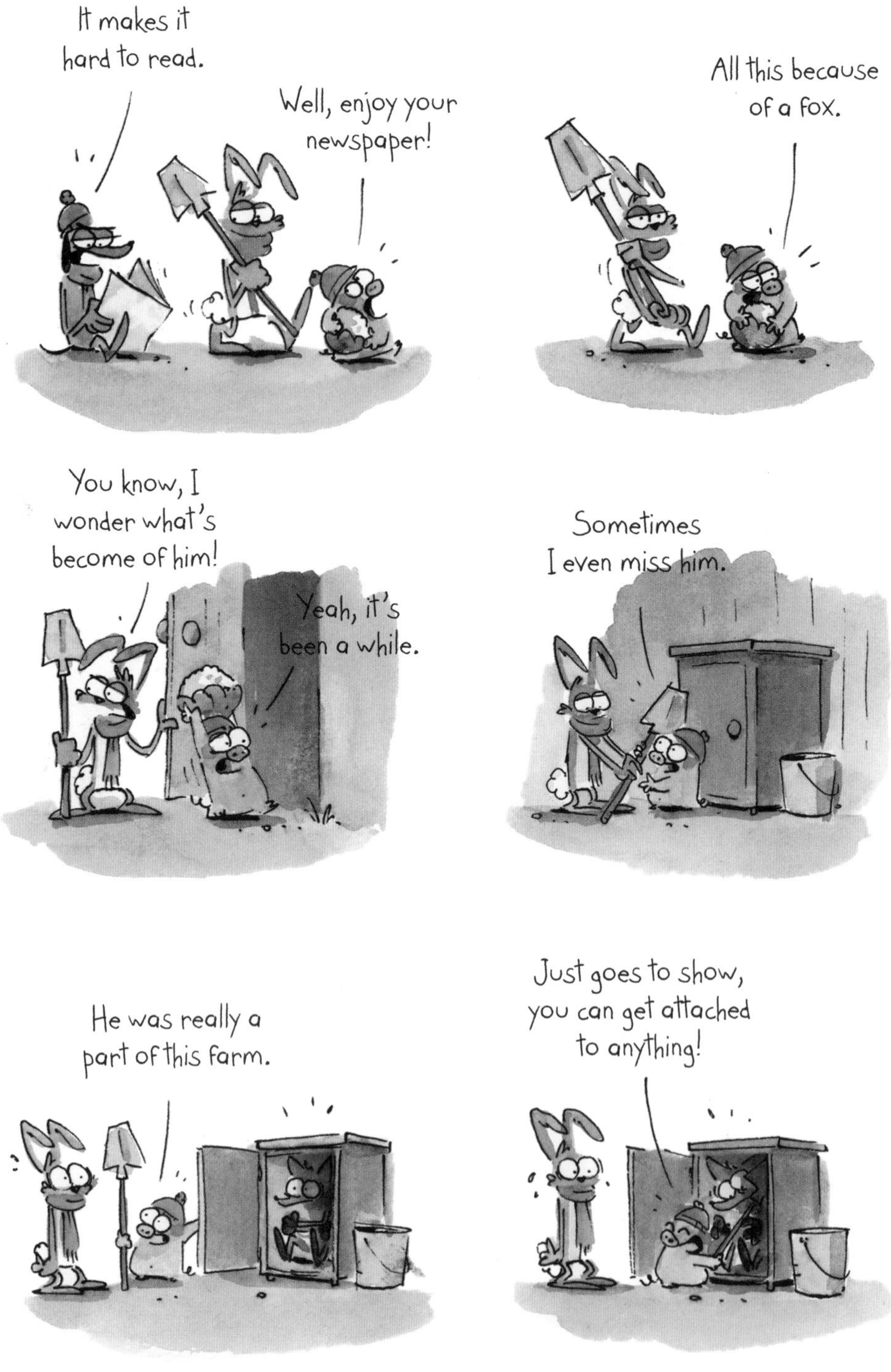
It makes it hard to read.
Well, enjoy your newspaper!
All this because of a fox.
You know, I wonder what's become of him!
Yeah, it's been a while.
Sometimes I even miss him.
He was really a part of this farm.
Just goes to show, you can get attached to anything!

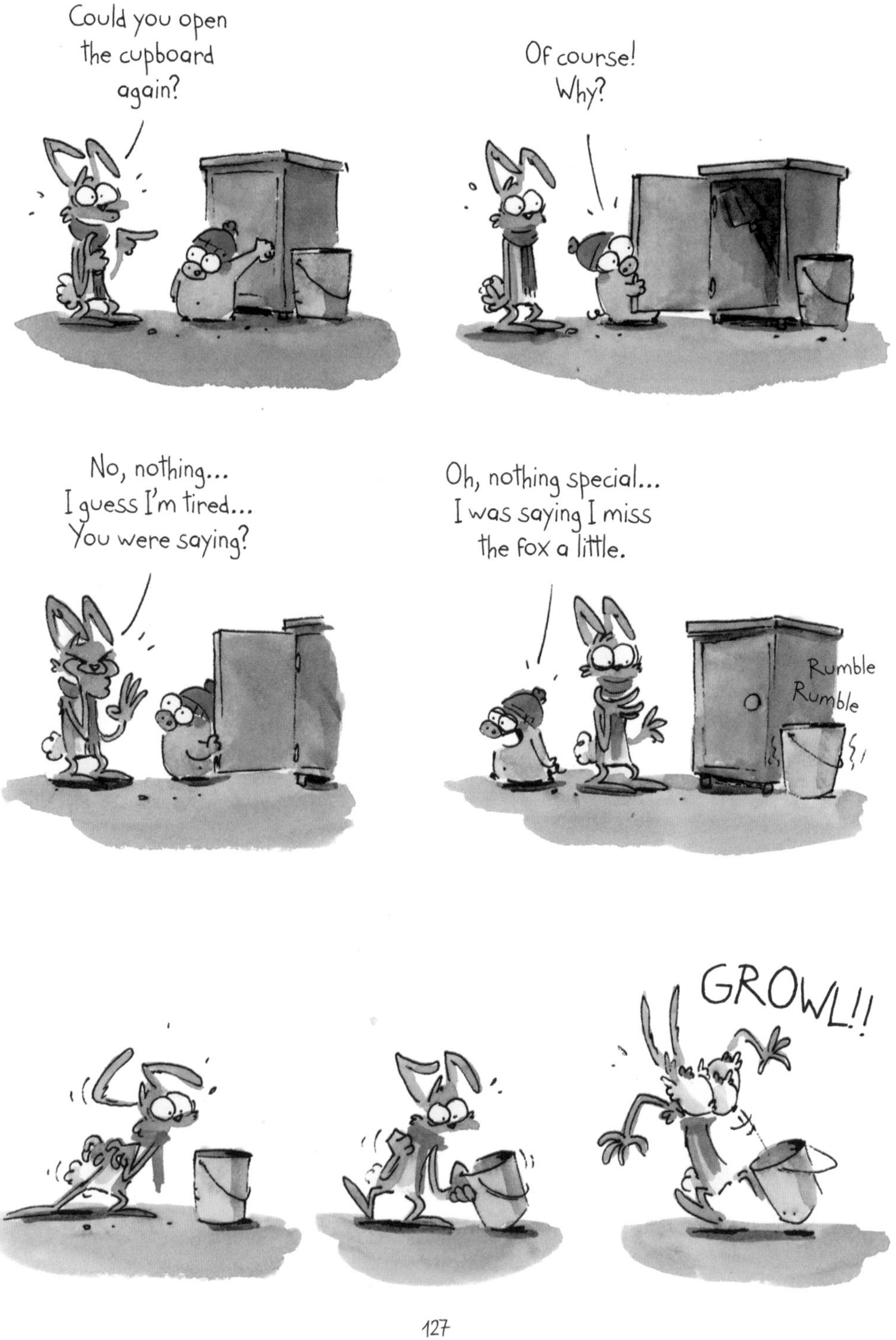
Could you open the cupboard again?
Of course! Why?
No, nothing... I guess I'm tired... You were saying?
Oh, nothing special... I was saying I miss the fox a little.
Rumble Rumble
GROWL!!

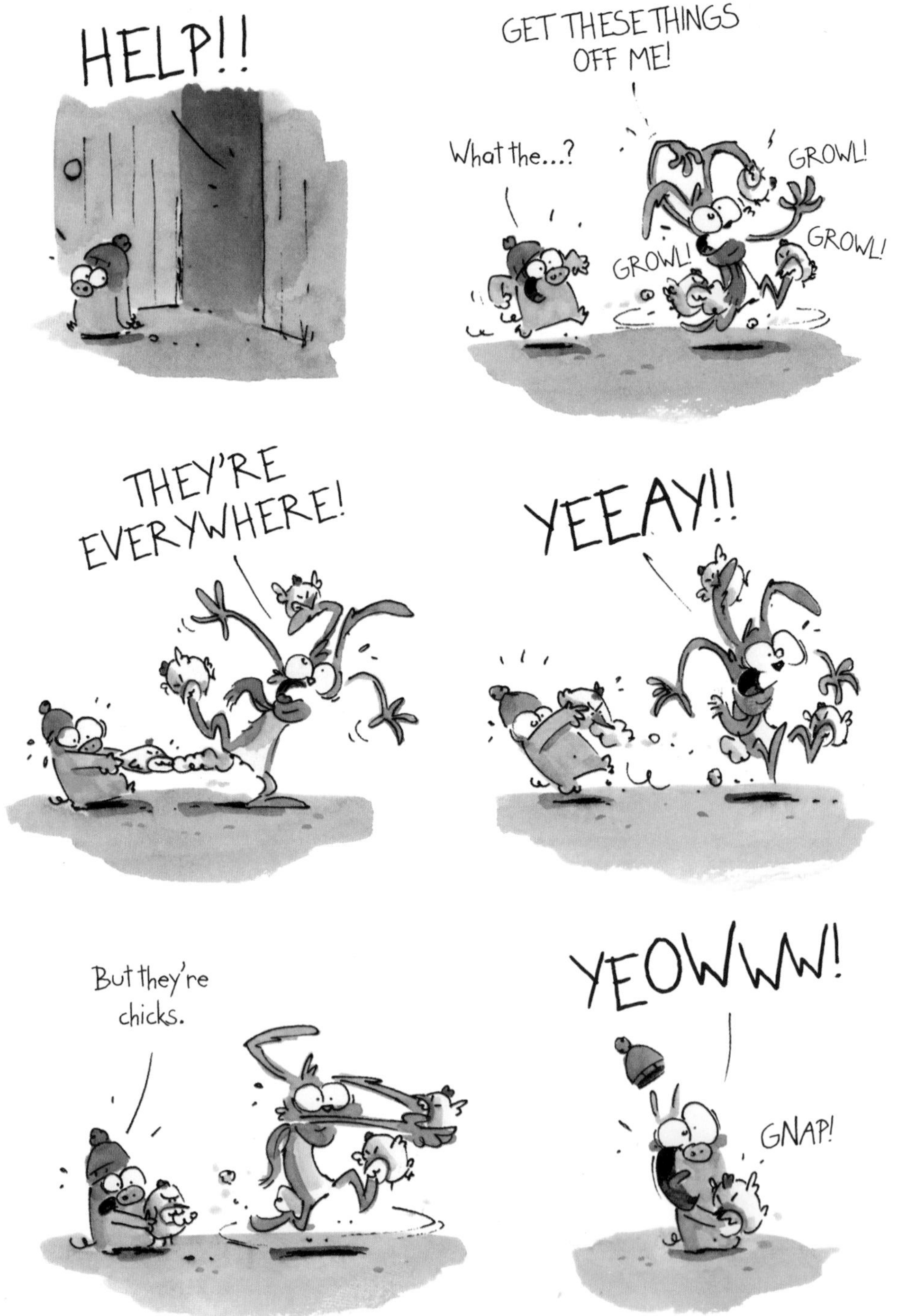
HELP!!
GET THESE THINGS OFF ME!
What the...?
GROWL!
GROWL!
GROWL!
THEY'RE EVERYWHERE!
YEEAY!!
But they're chicks.
YEOWW!
GNAP!

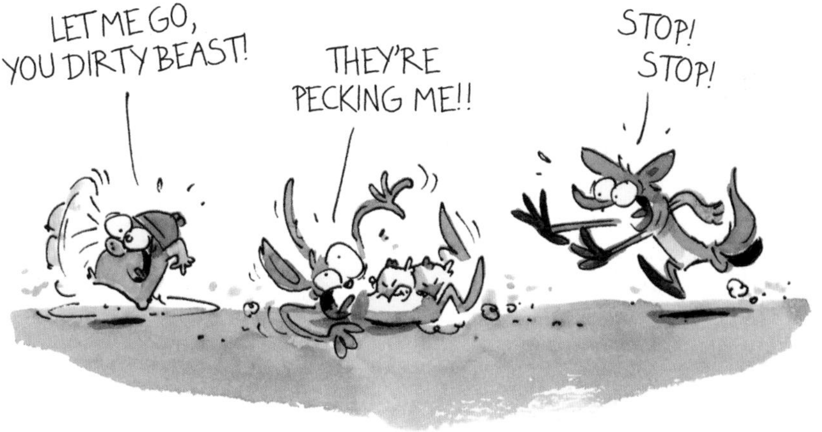
LET ME GO, YOU DIRTY BEAST!
THEY'RE PECKING ME!!
STOP! STOP!

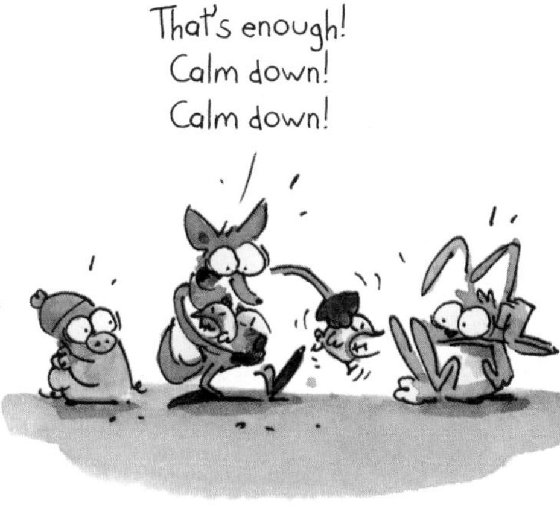
That's enough! Calm down! Calm down!

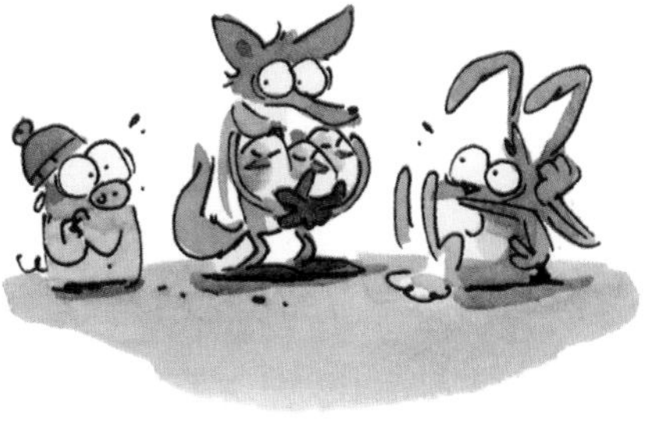

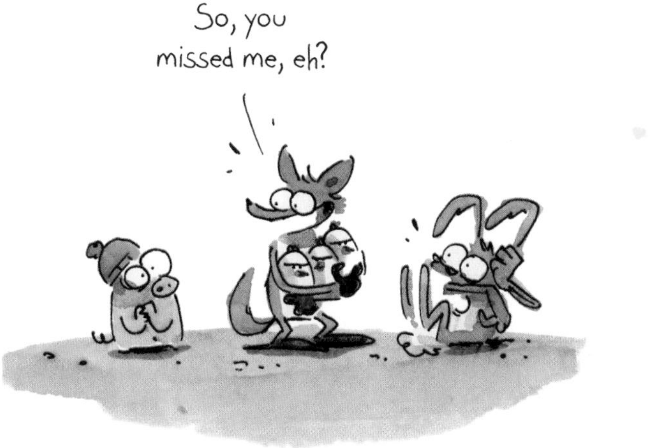
So, you missed me, eh?

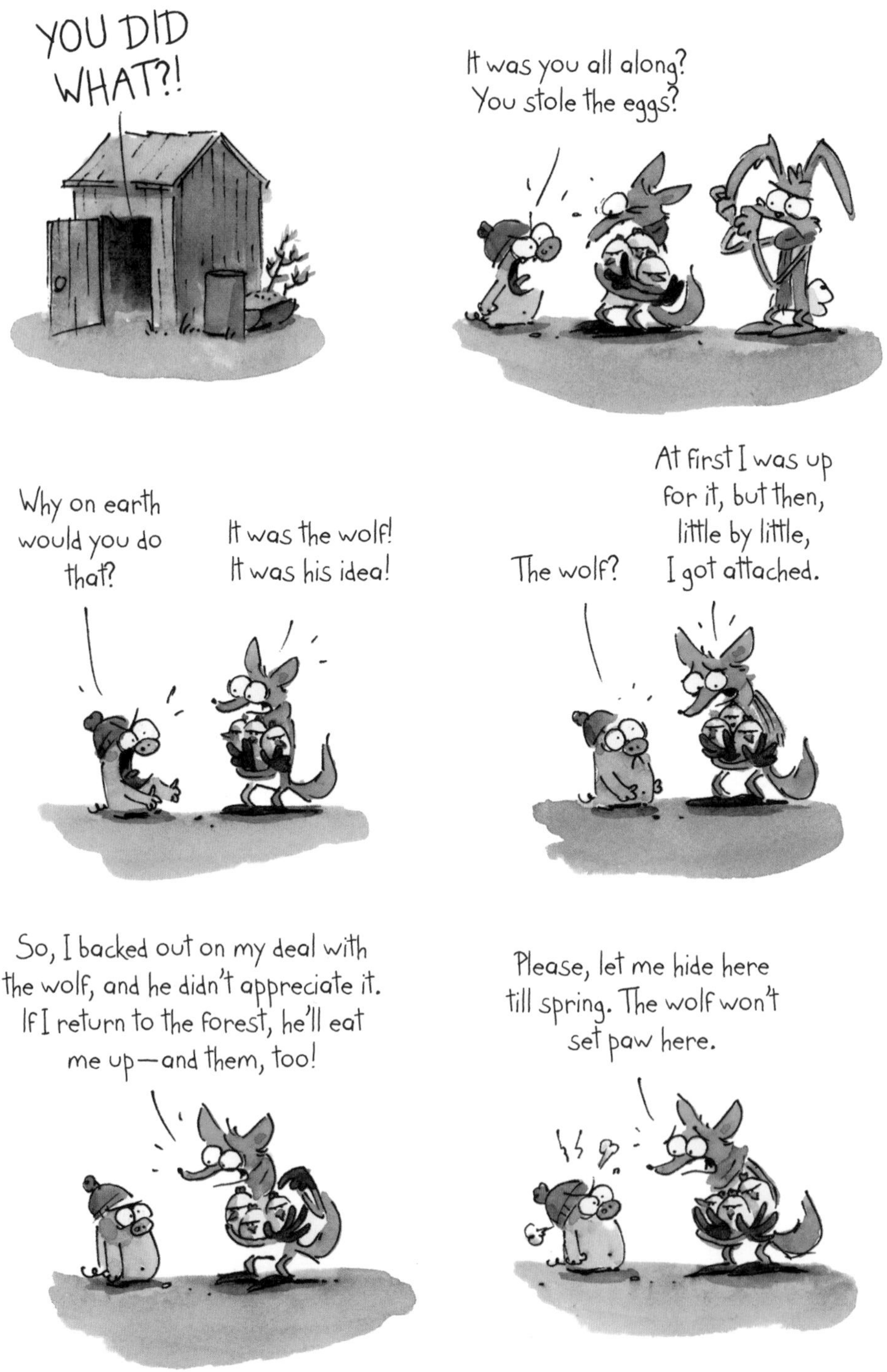
YOU DID WHAT?!
It was you all along? You stole the eggs?
Why on earth would you do that?
It was the wolf! It was his idea!
The wolf?
At first I was up for it, but then, little by little, I got attached.
So, I backed out on my deal with the wolf, and he didn't appreciate it. If I return to the forest, he'll eat me up—and them, too!
Please, let me hide here till spring. The wolf won't set paw here.

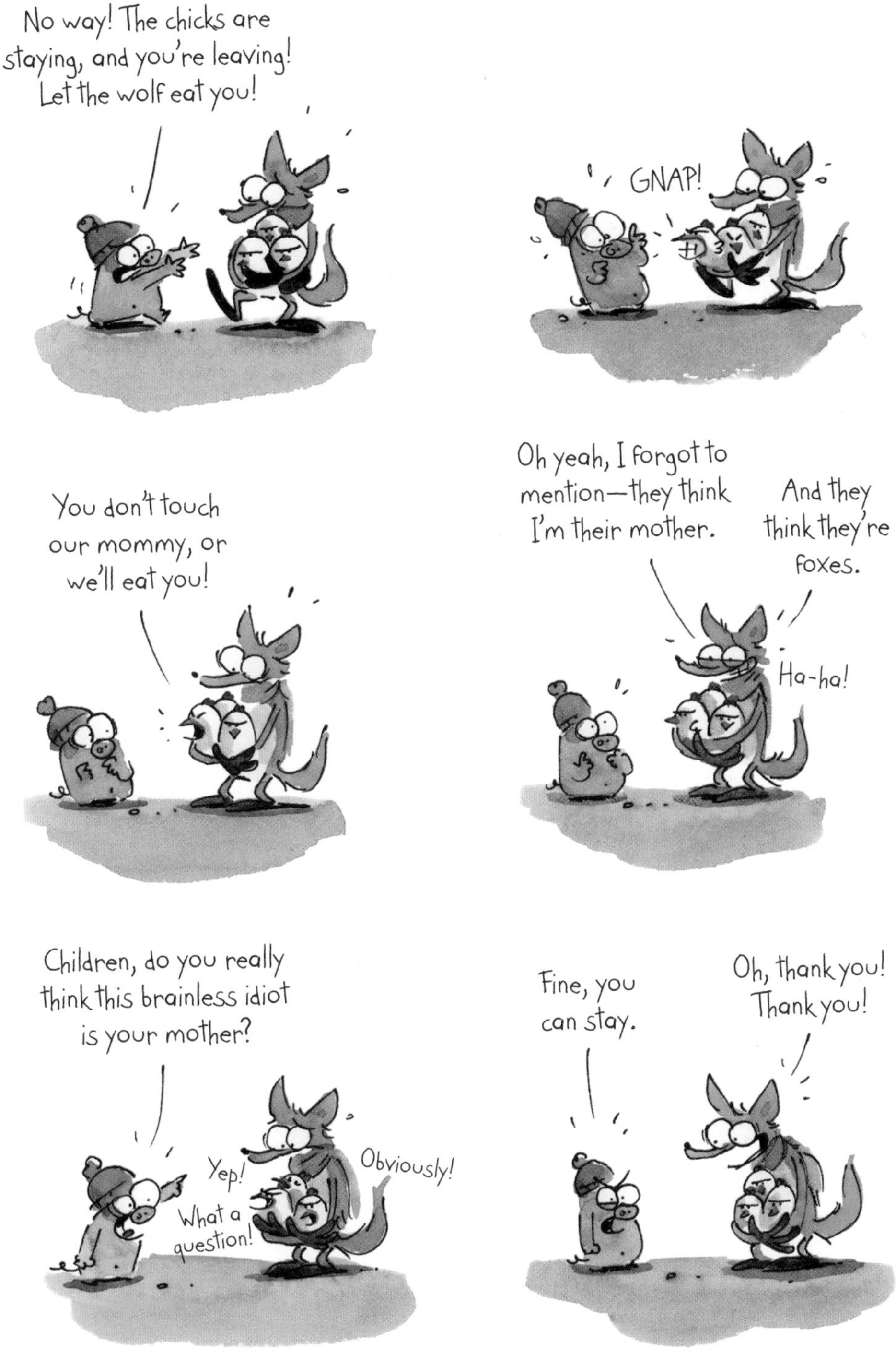
No way! The chicks are staying, and you're leaving! Let the wolf eat you!
GNAP!
You don't touch our mommy, or we'll eat you!
Oh yeah, I forgot to mention—they think I'm their mother.
And they think they're foxes.
Ha-ha!
Children, do you really think this brainless idiot is your mother?
Yep!
What a question!
Obviously!
Fine, you can stay.
Oh, thank you! Thank you!

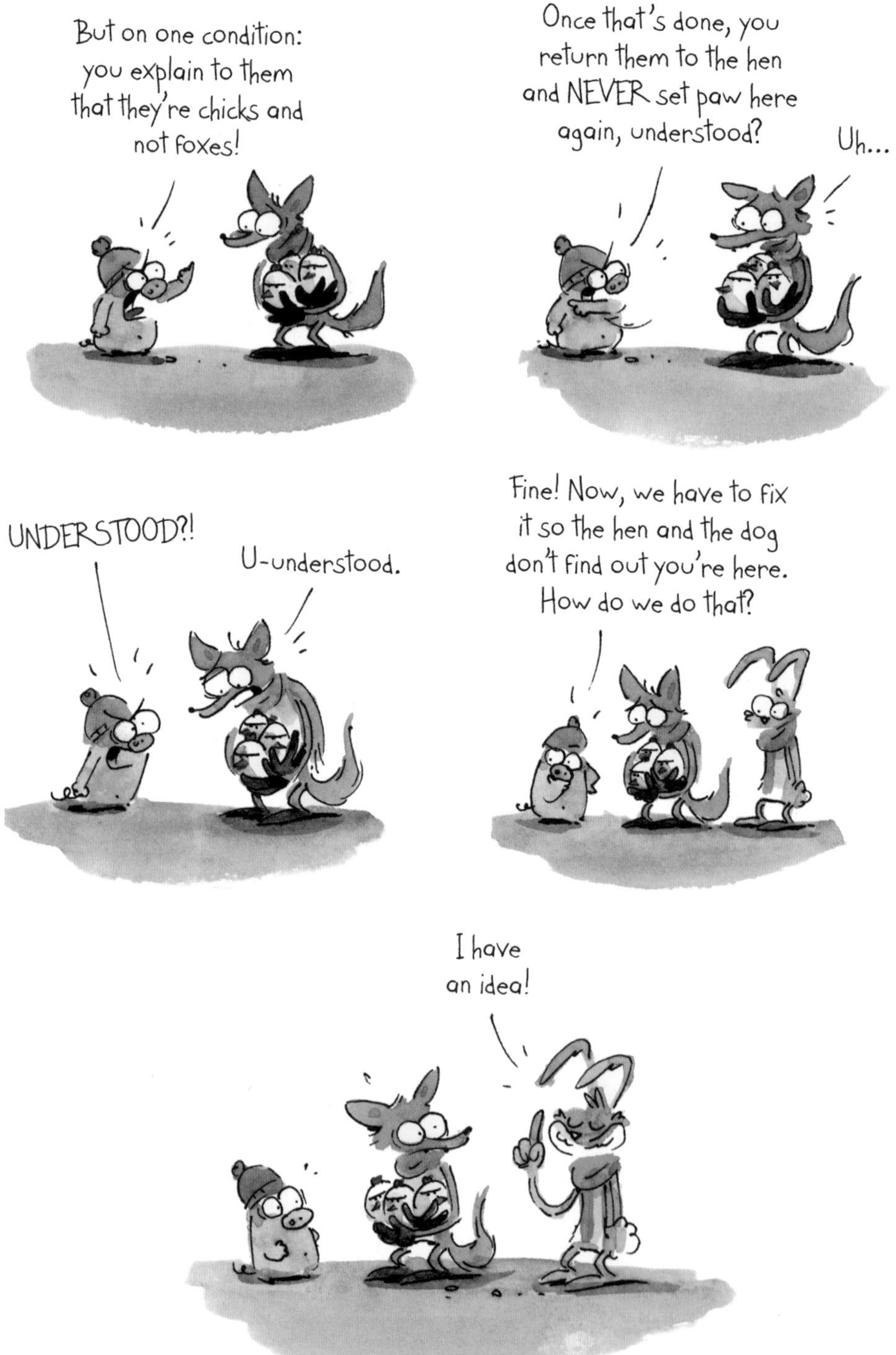
But on one condition: you explain to them that they're chicks and not foxes!
Once that's done, you return them to the hen and NEVER set paw here again, understood?
Uh...
UNDERSTOOD?!
U-understood.
Fine! Now, we have to fix it so the hen and the dog don't find out you're here. How do we do that?
I have an idea!

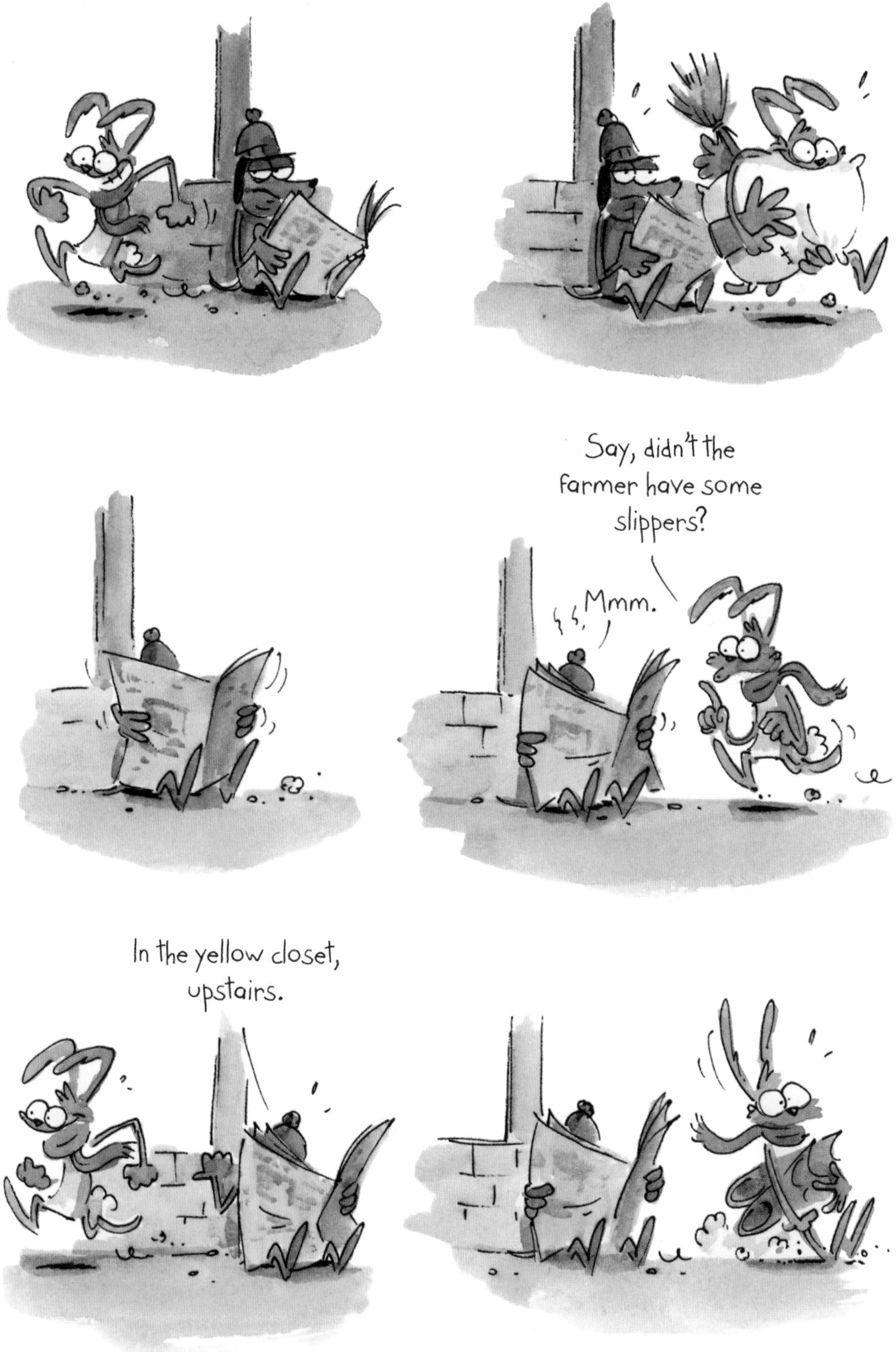
Say, didn't the farmer have some slippers?
Mmm.
In the yellow closet, upstairs.

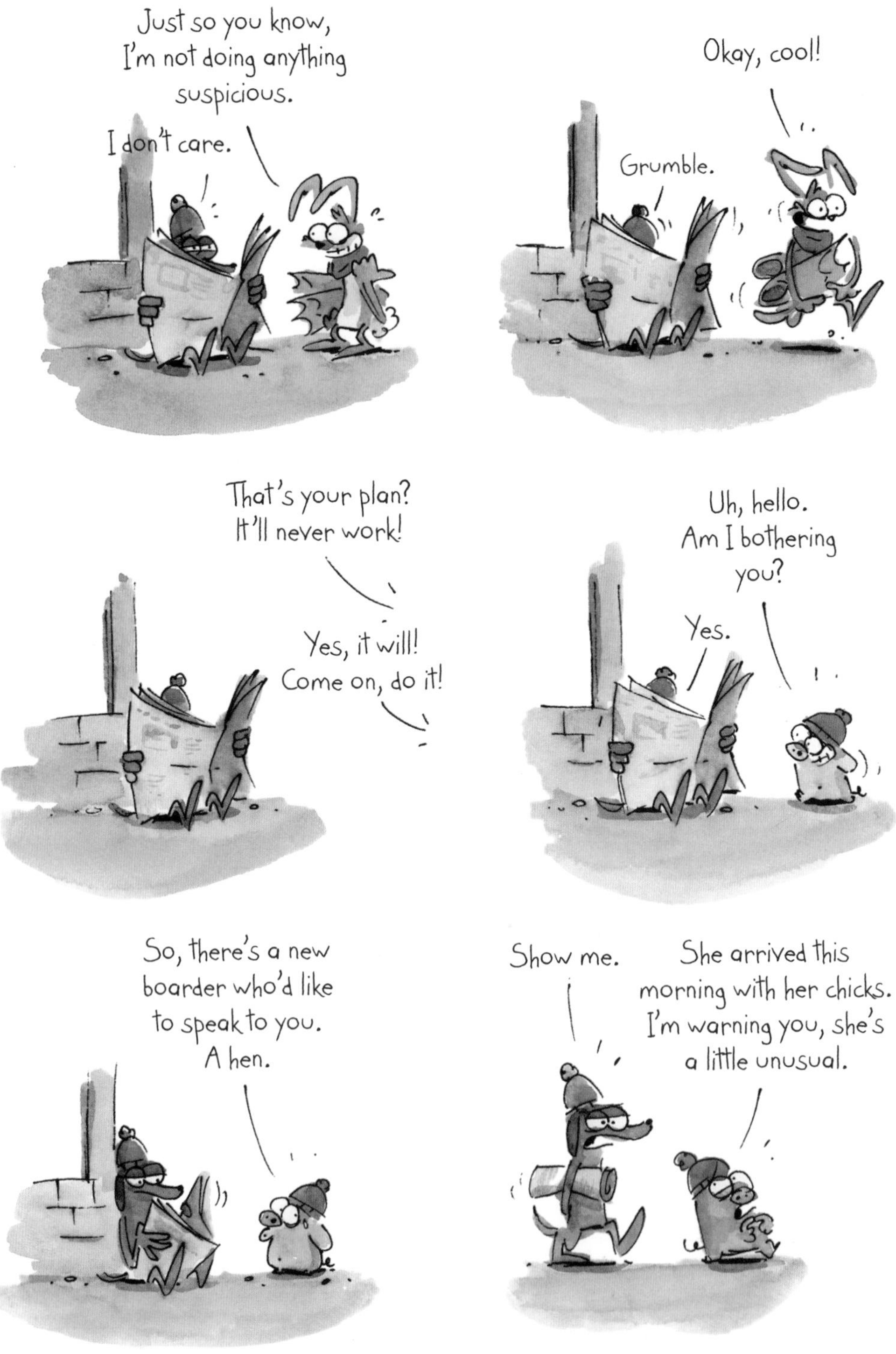
Just so you know, I'm not doing anything suspicious.
I don't care.
Okay, cool!
Grumble.
That's your plan? It'll never work!
Yes, it will! Come on, do it!
Uh, hello. Am I bothering you?
Yes.
So, there's a new boarder who'd like to speak to you. A hen.
Show me.
She arrived this morning with her chicks. I'm warning you, she's a little unusual.

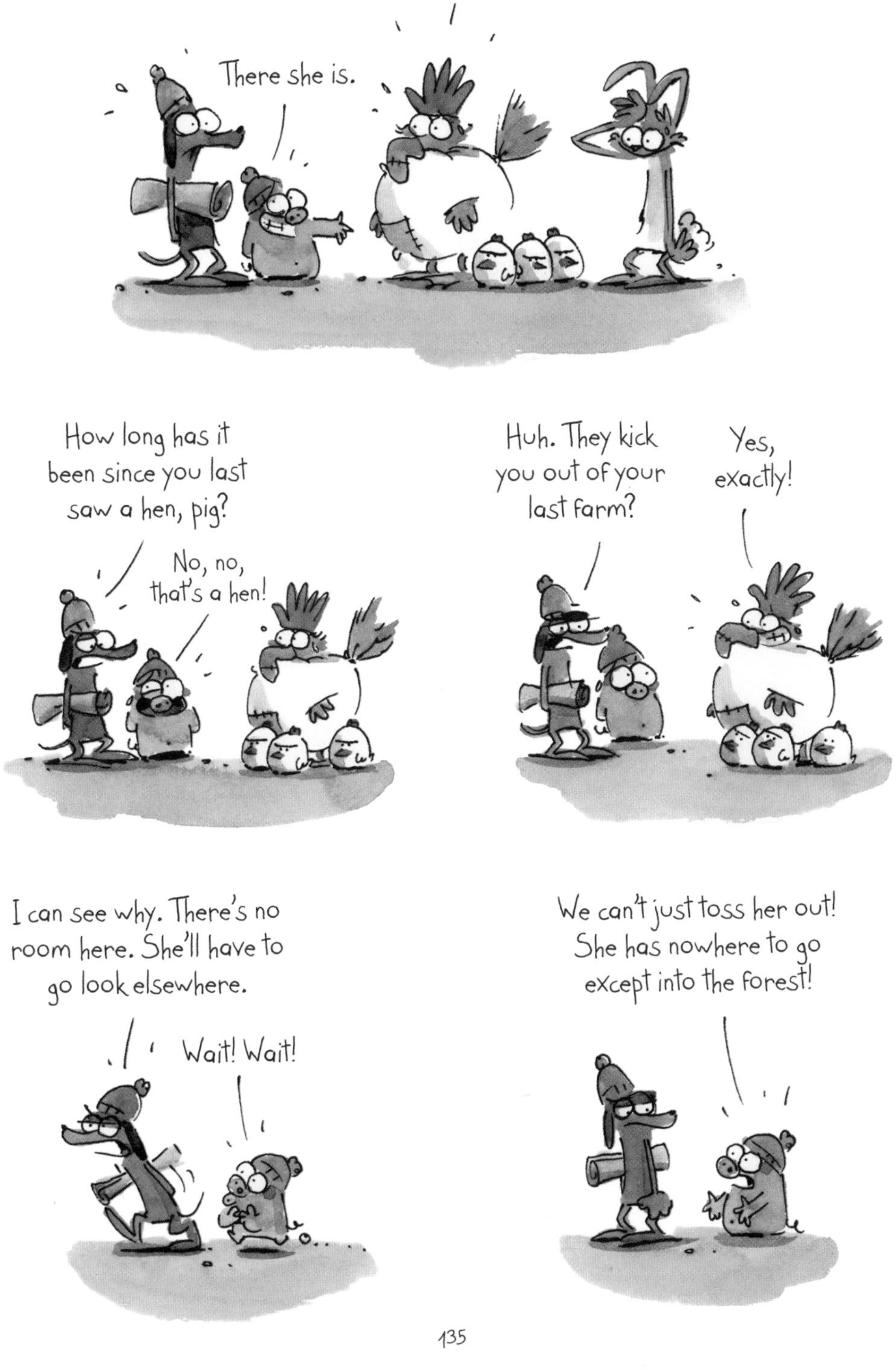
There she is.
How long has it been since you last saw a hen, pig?
No, no, that's a hen!
Huh. They kick you out of your last farm?
Yes, exactly!
I can see why. There's no room here. She'll have to go look elsewhere.
Wait! Wait!
We can't just toss her out! She has nowhere to go except into the forest!

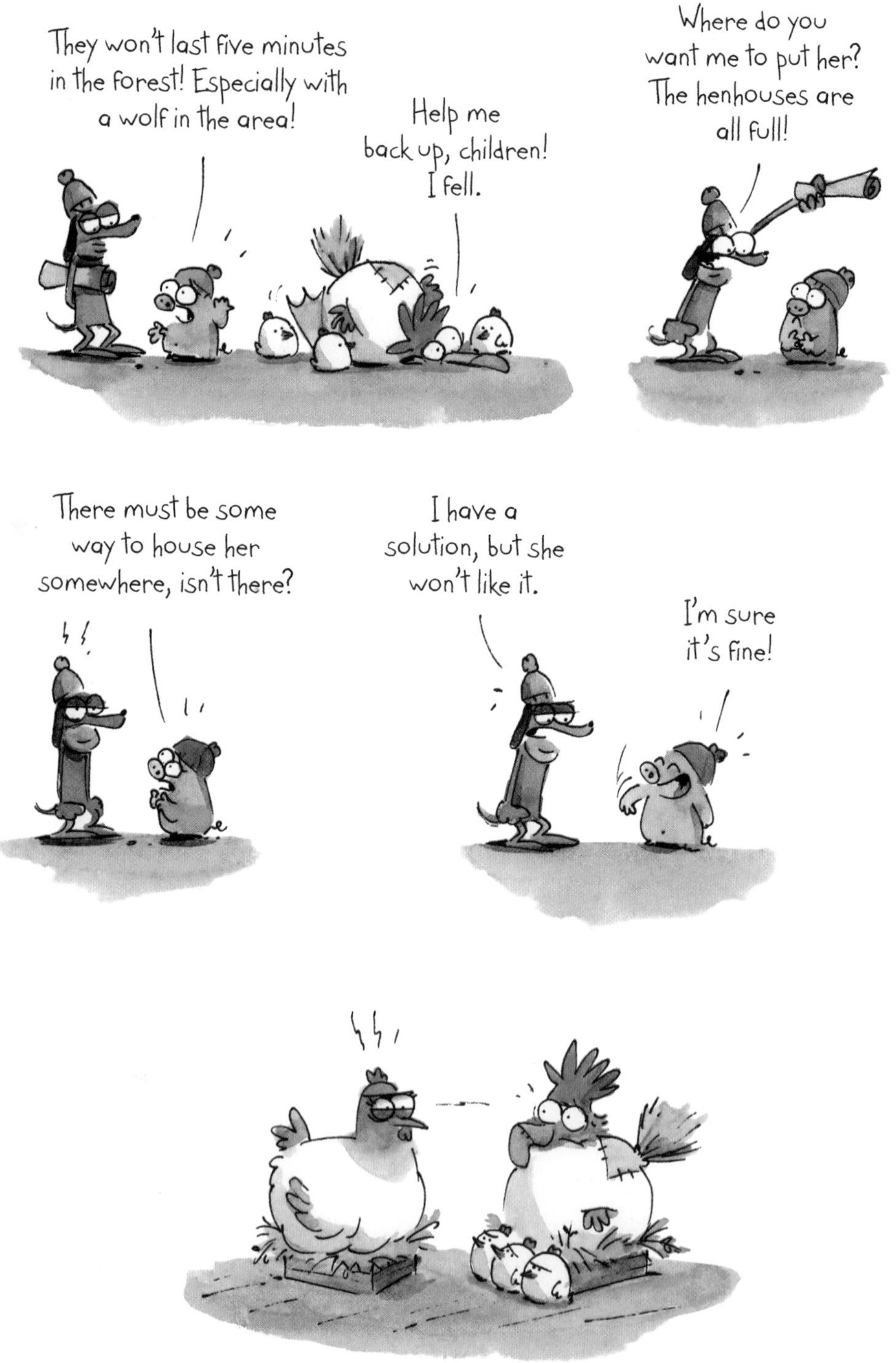
They won't last five minutes in the forest! Especially with a wolf in the area!
Help me back up, children! I fell.
Where do you want me to put her? The henhouses are all full!
There must be some way to house her somewhere, isn't there?
I have a solution, but she won't like it.
I'm sure it's fine!

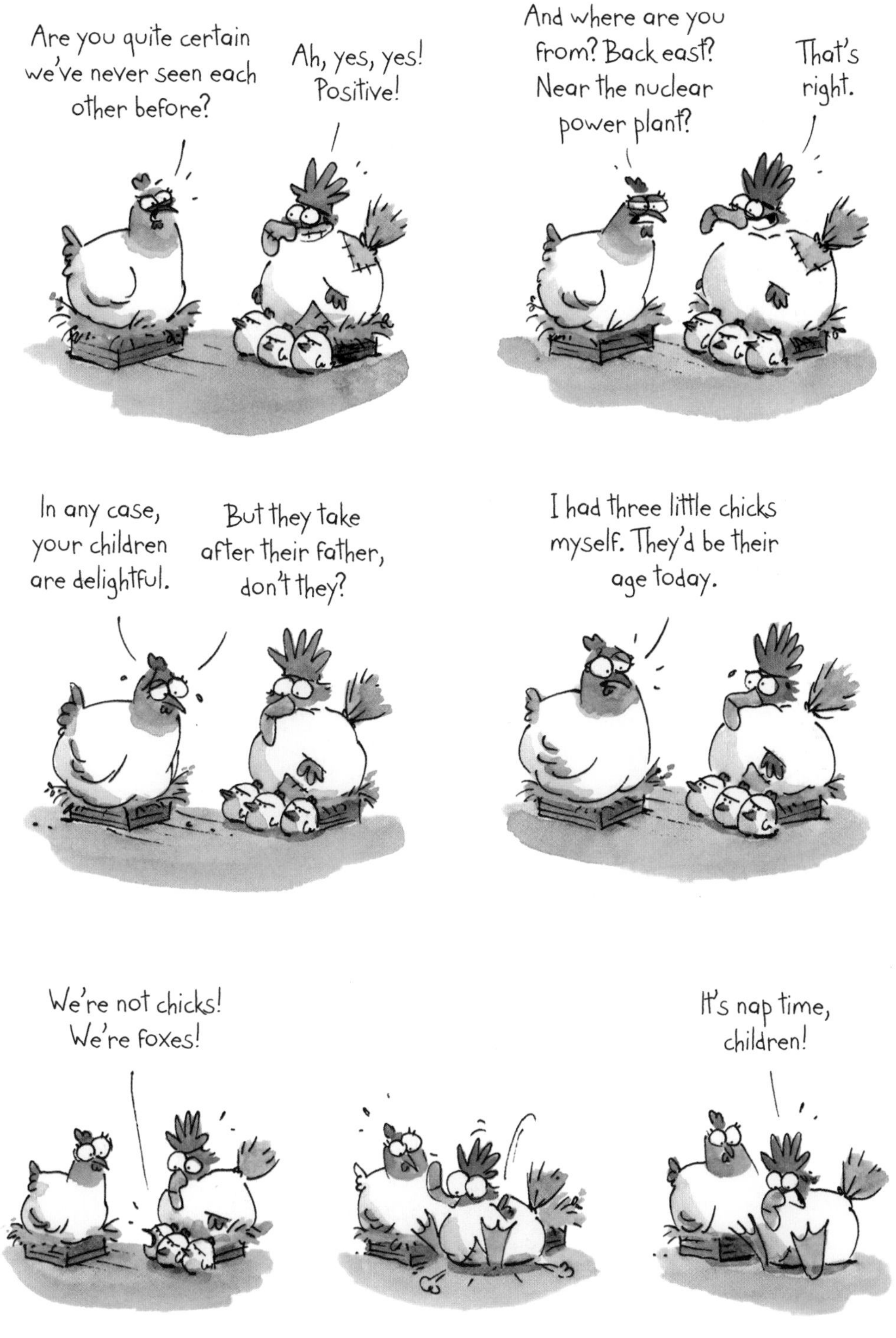
Are you quite certain we've never seen each other before?
Ah, yes, yes! Positive!
And where are you from? Back east? Near the nuclear power plant?
That's right.
In any case, your children are delightful.
But they take after their father, don't they?
I had three little chicks myself. They'd be their age today.
We're not chicks! We're foxes!
It's nap time, children!

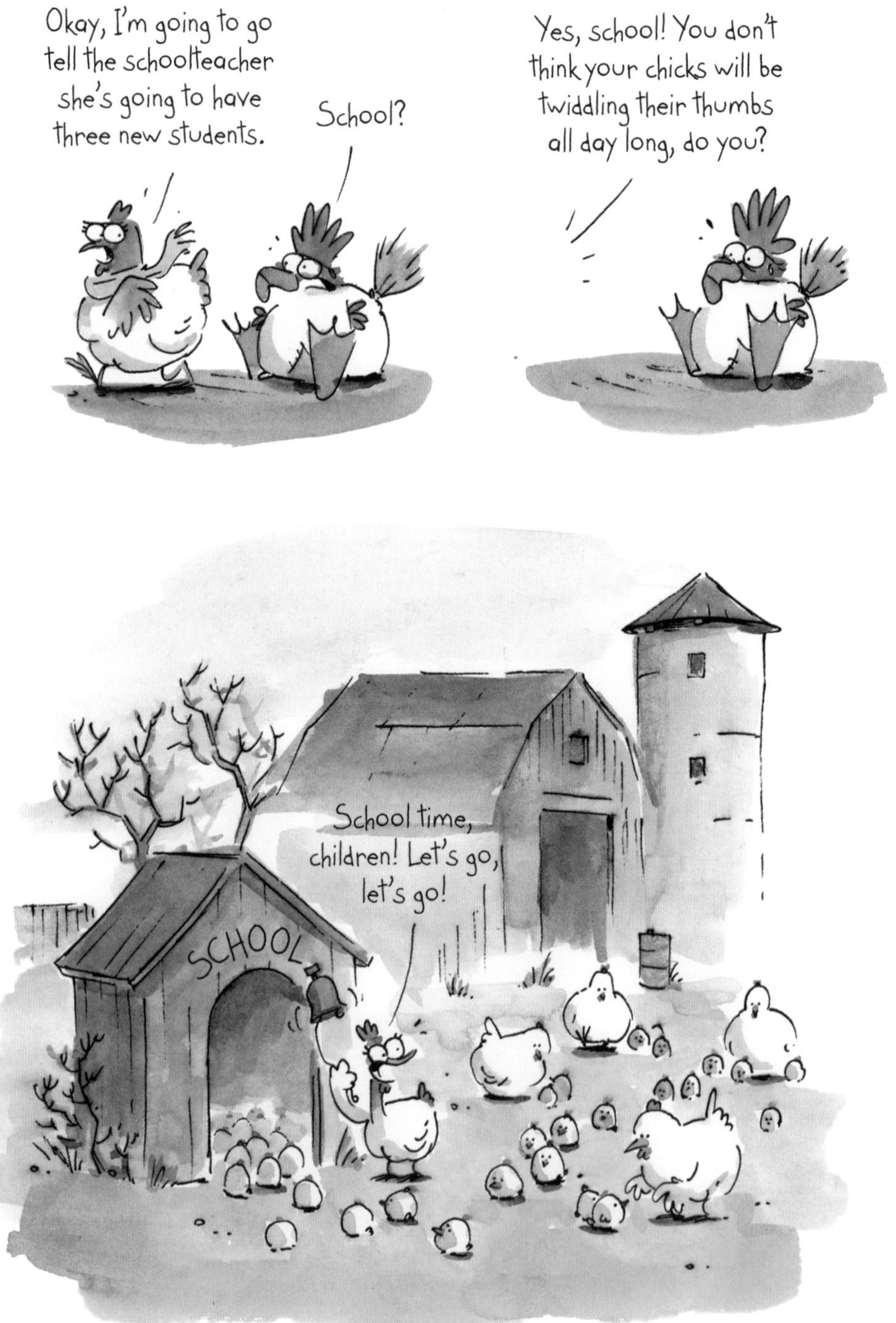
Okay, I'm going to go tell the schoolteacher she's going to have three new students.
School?
Yes, school! You don't think your chicks will be twiddling their thumbs all day long, do you?
School time, children! Let's go, let's go!
SCHOOL

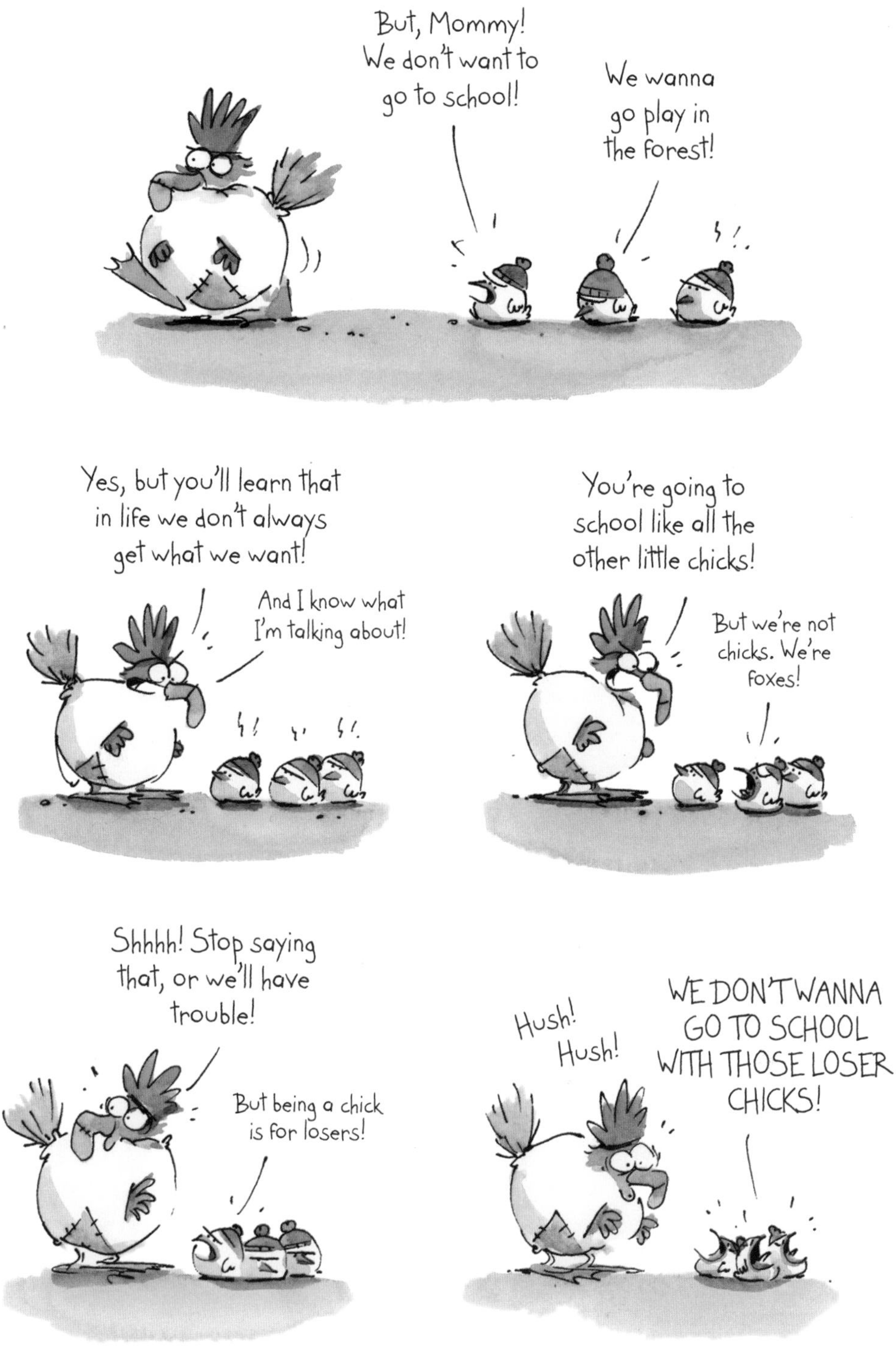

But, Mommy! We don't want to go to school!
We wanna go play in the forest!
Yes, but you'll learn that in life we don't always get what we want!
And I know what I'm talking about!
You're going to school like all the other little chicks!
But we're not chicks. We're foxes!
Shhhh! Stop saying that, or we'll have trouble!
But being a chick is for losers!
Hush! Hush!
WE DON'T WANNA GO TO SCHOOL WITH THOSE LOSER CHICKS!

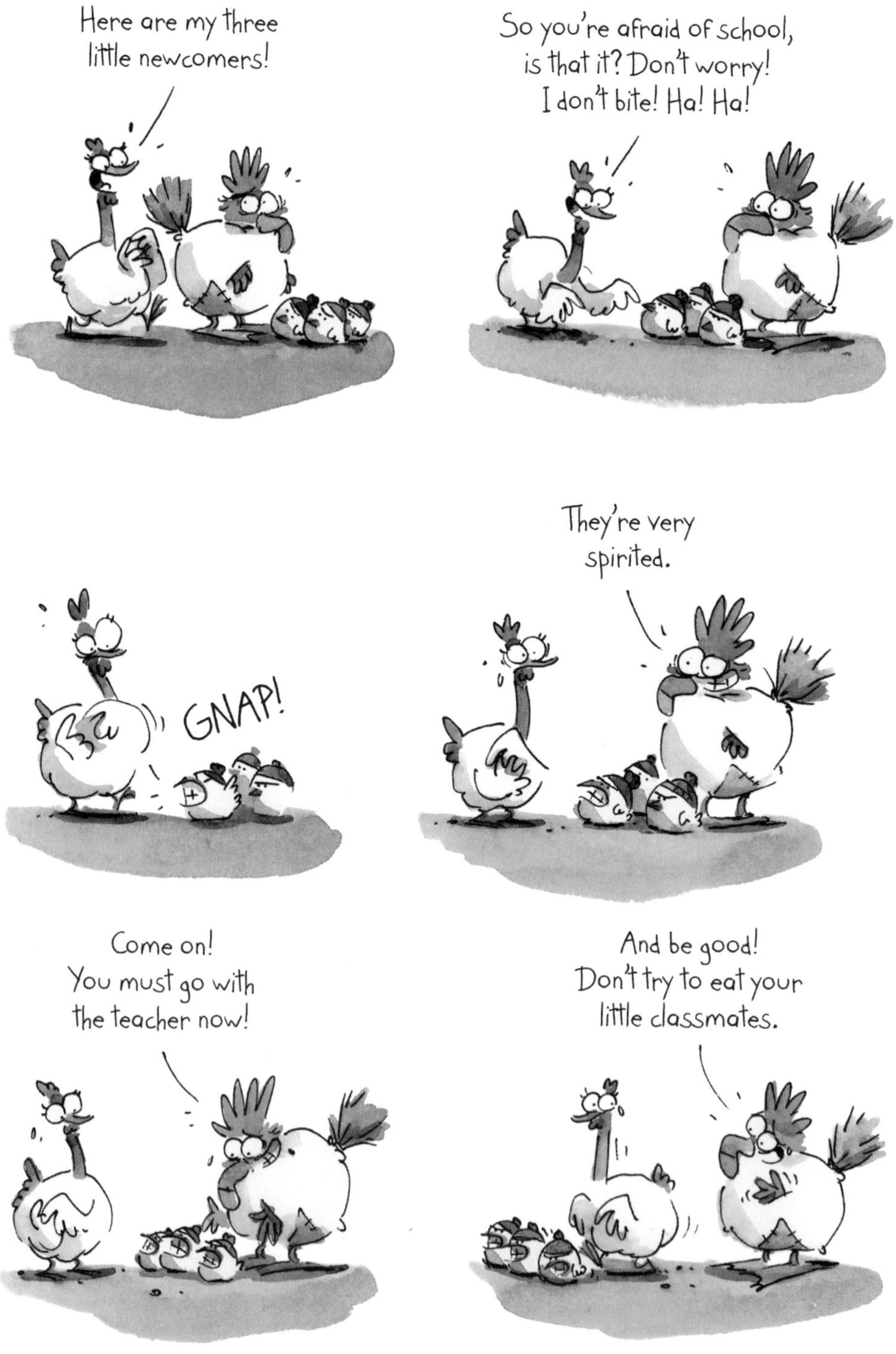
Here are my three little newcomers!
So you're afraid of school, is that it? Don't worry! I don't bite! Ha! Ha!
GNAP!
They're very spirited.
Come on! You must go with the teacher now!
And be good! Don't try to eat your little classmates.

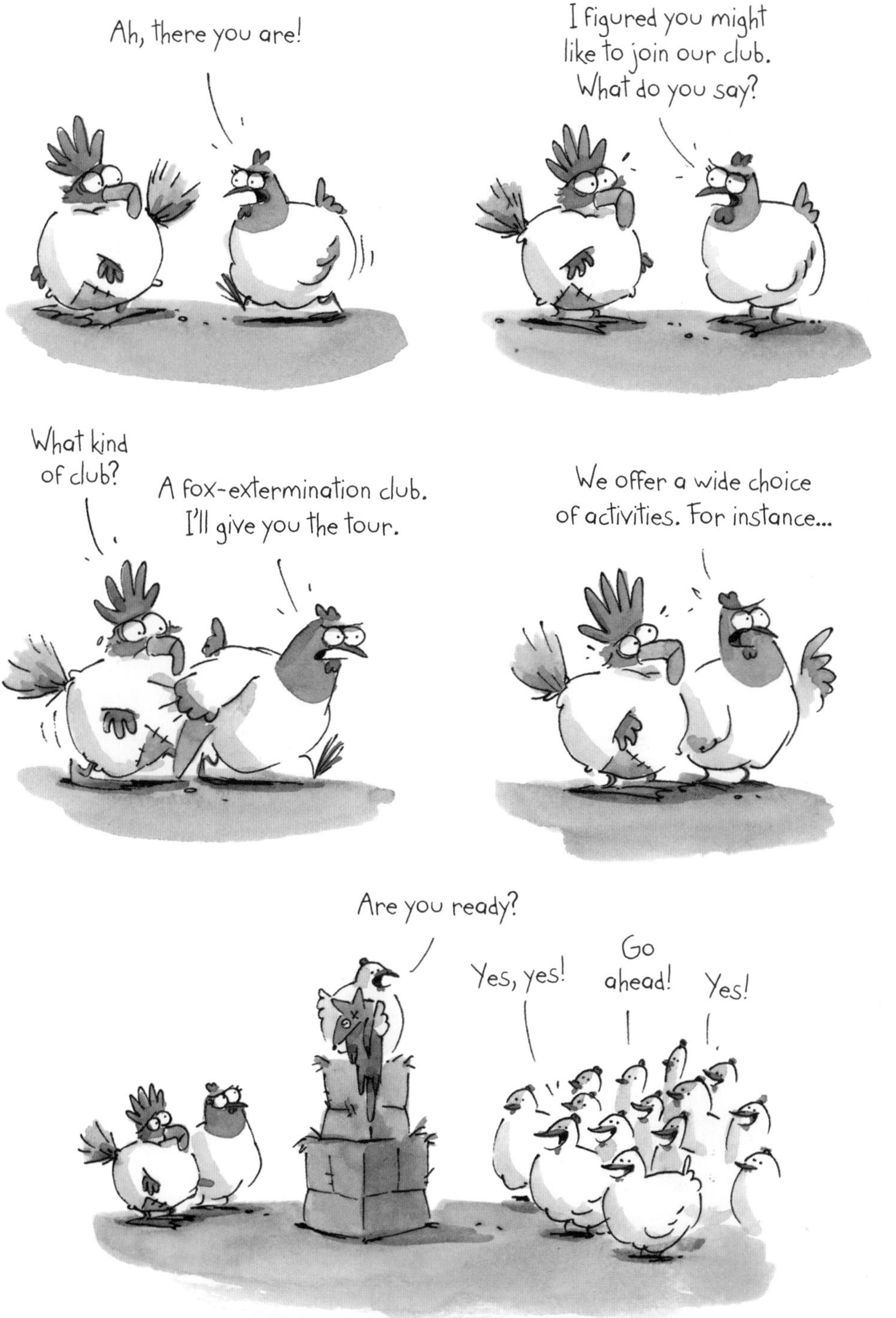
Ah, there you are!
I figured you might like to join our club. What do you say?
What kind of club?
A fox-extermination club. I'll give you the tour.
We offer a wide choice of activities. For instance...
Are you ready?
Yes, yes!
Go ahead!
Yes!

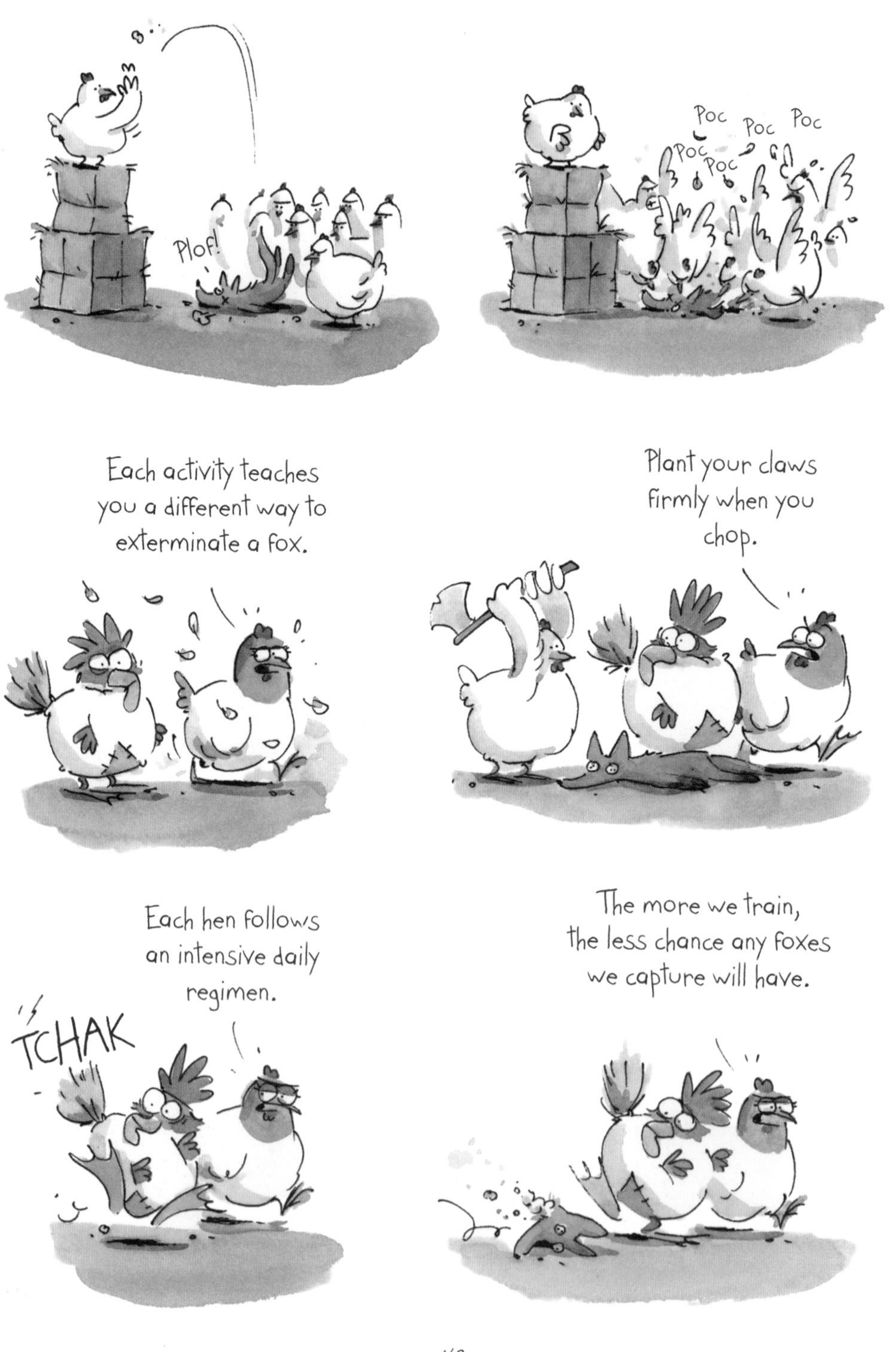
Plof!
Poc
Poc
Poc
Poc
Poc
Each activity teaches you a different way to exterminate a fox.
Plant your claws firmly when you chop.
Each hen follows an intensive daily regimen.
TCHAK
The more we train, the less chance any foxes we capture will have.

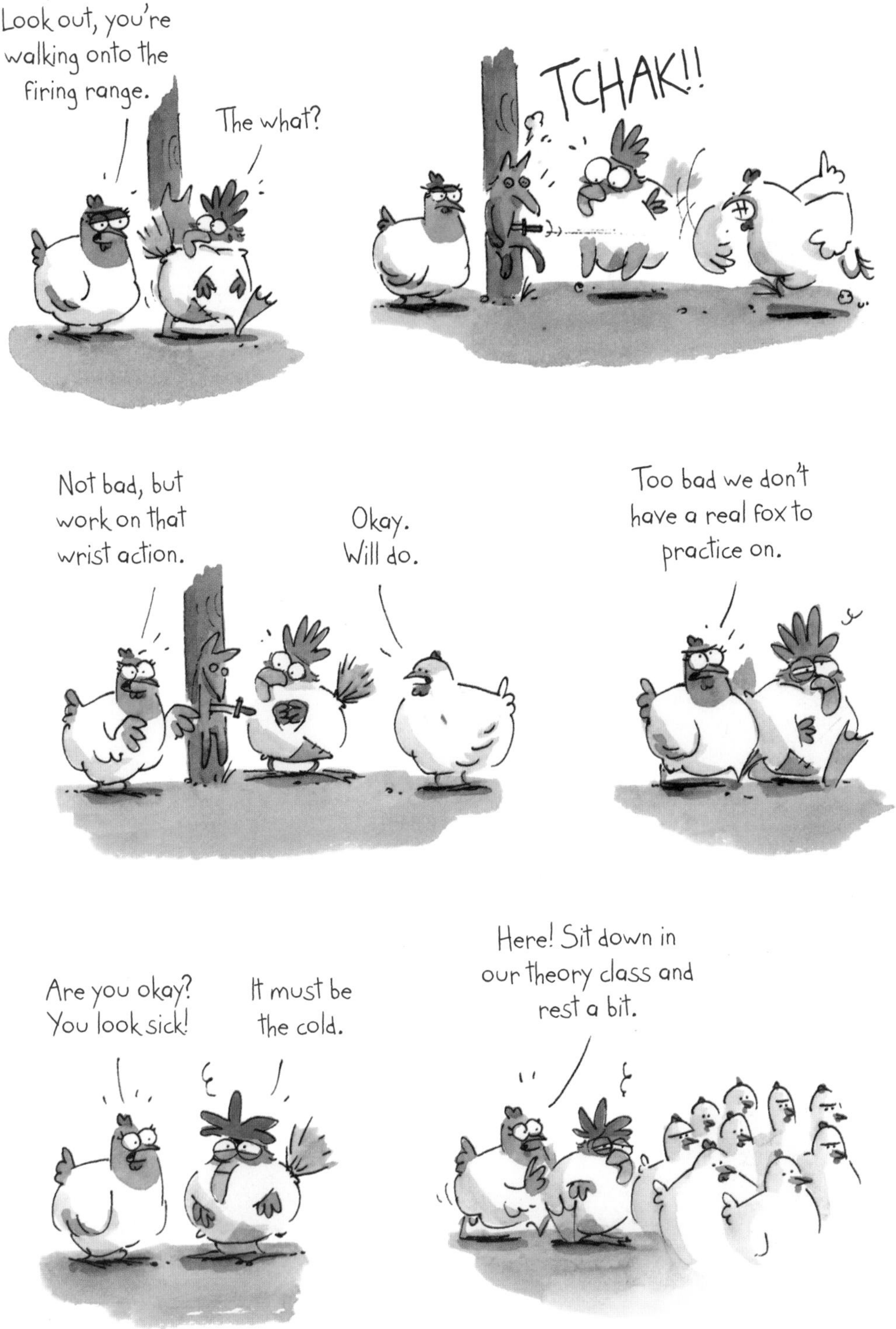

Look out, you're walking onto the firing range.
The what?
TCHAK!!
Not bad, but work on that wrist action.
Okay. Will do.
Too bad we don't have a real fox to practice on.
Are you okay? You look sick!
It must be the cold.
Here! Sit down in our theory class and rest a bit.

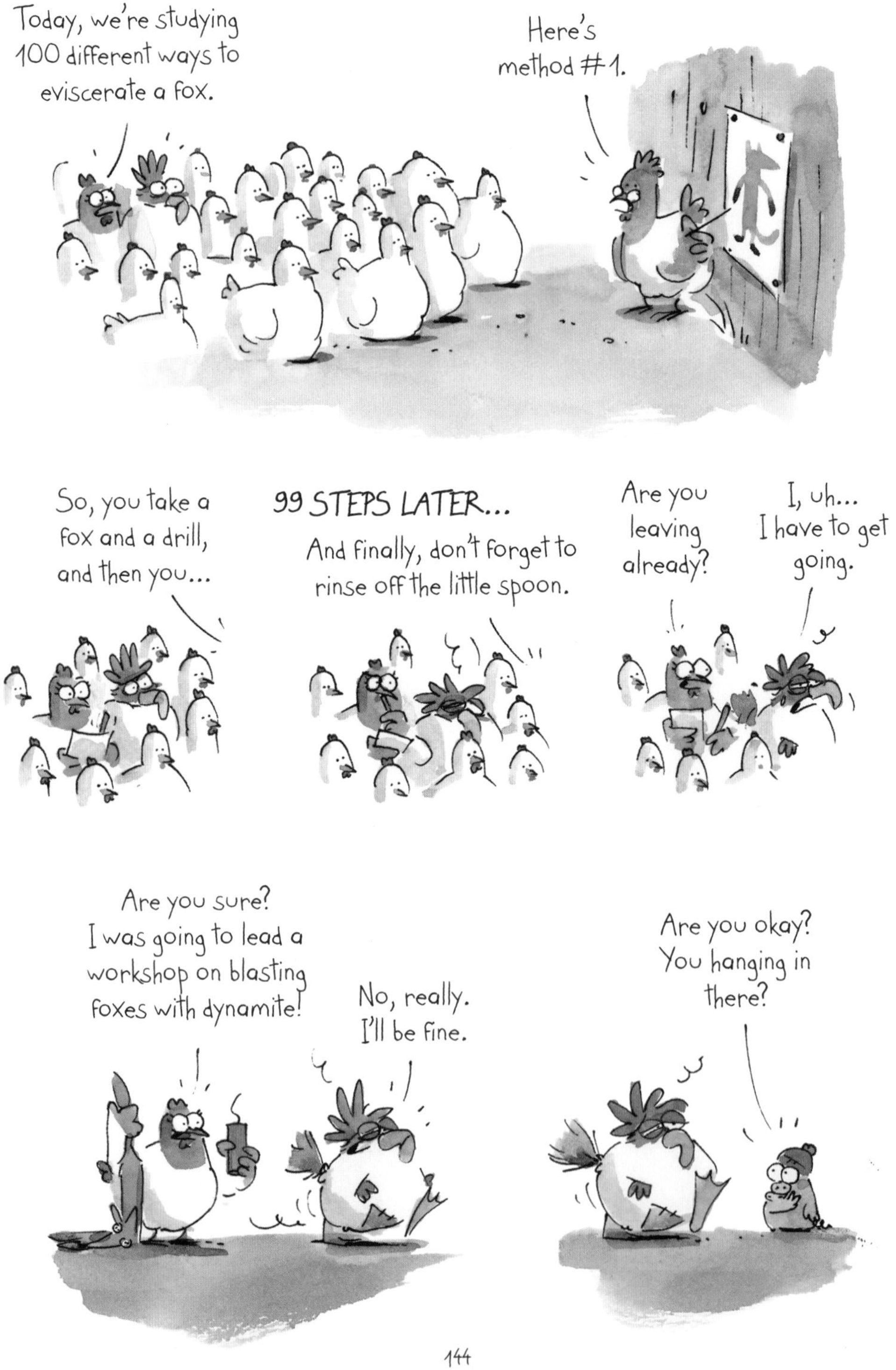
Today, we're studying 100 different ways to eviscerate a fox.
Here's method #1.
So, you take a fox and a drill, and then you...
99 STEPS LATER...
And finally, don't forget to rinse off the little spoon.
Are you leaving already?
I, uh... I have to get going.
Are you sure? I was going to lead a workshop on blasting foxes with dynamite!
No, really. I'll be fine.
Are you okay? You hanging in there?

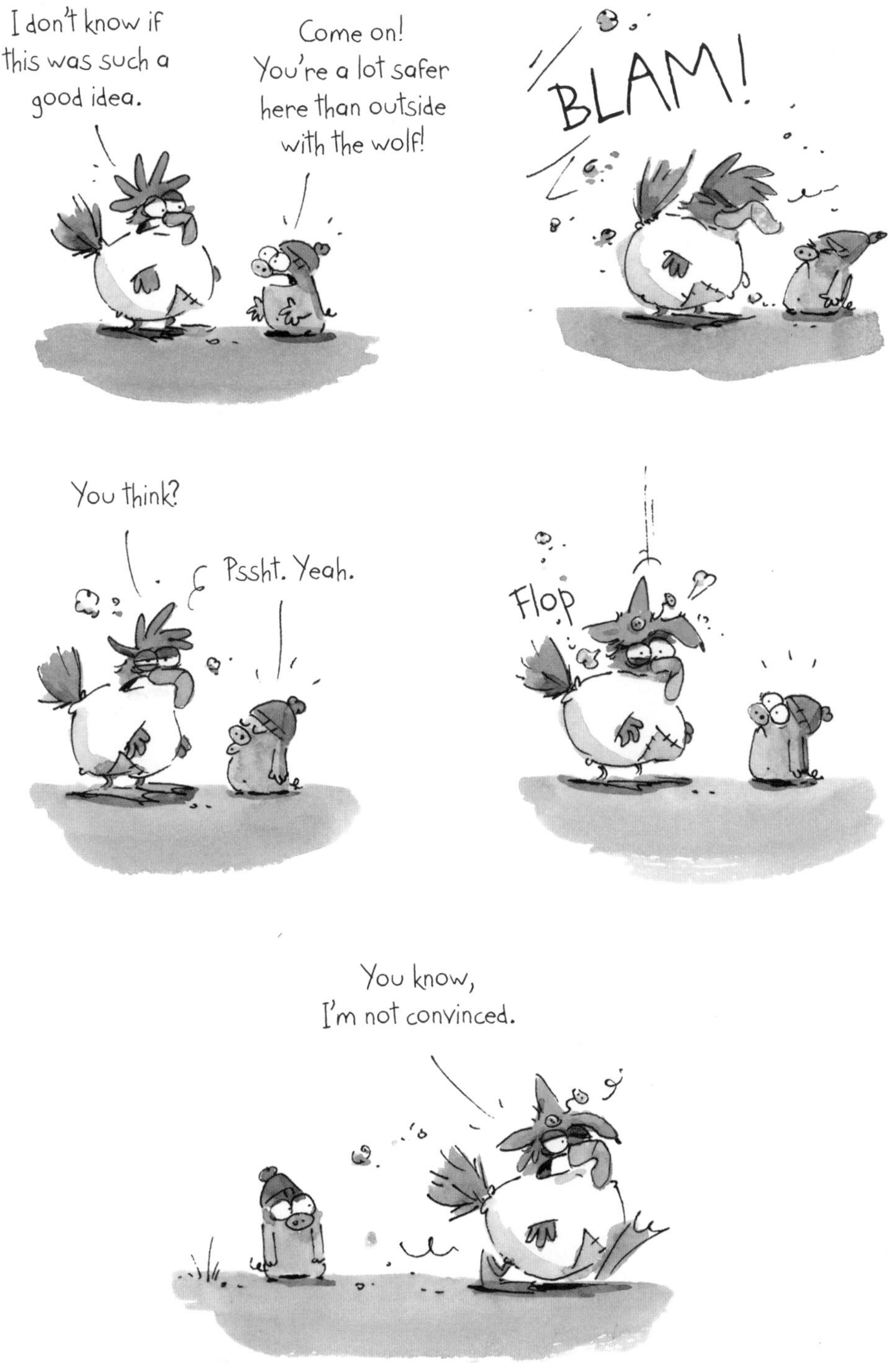
I don't know if this was such a good idea.
Come on! You're a lot safer here than outside with the wolf!
BLAM!
You think?
Pssht. Yeah.
Flop
You know, I'm not convinced.

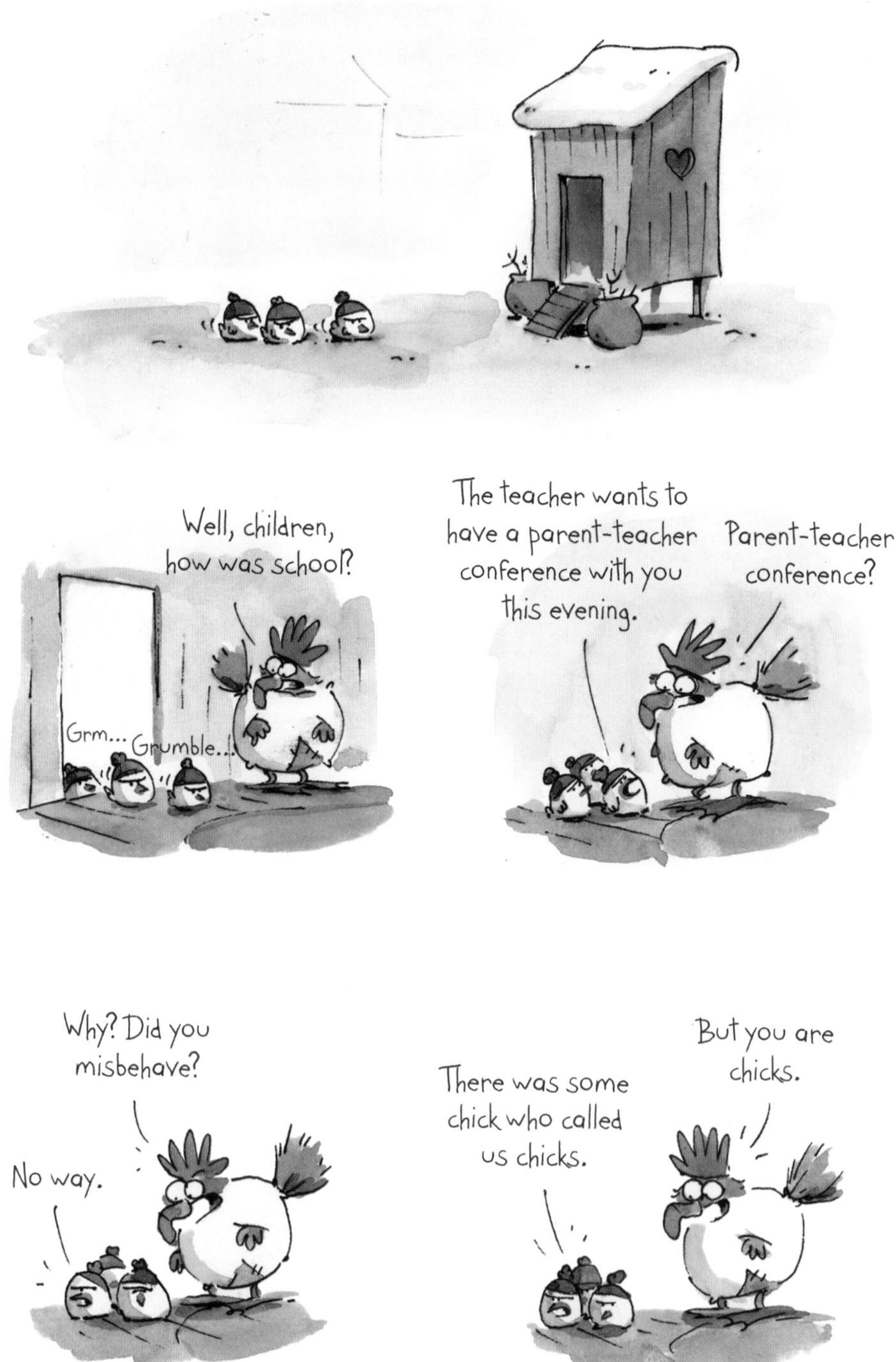
Well, children, how was school?
Grm...
Grumble...
The teacher wants to have a parent-teacher conference with you this evening.
Parent-teacher conference?
Why? Did you misbehave?
No way.
There was some chick who called us chicks.
But you are chicks.

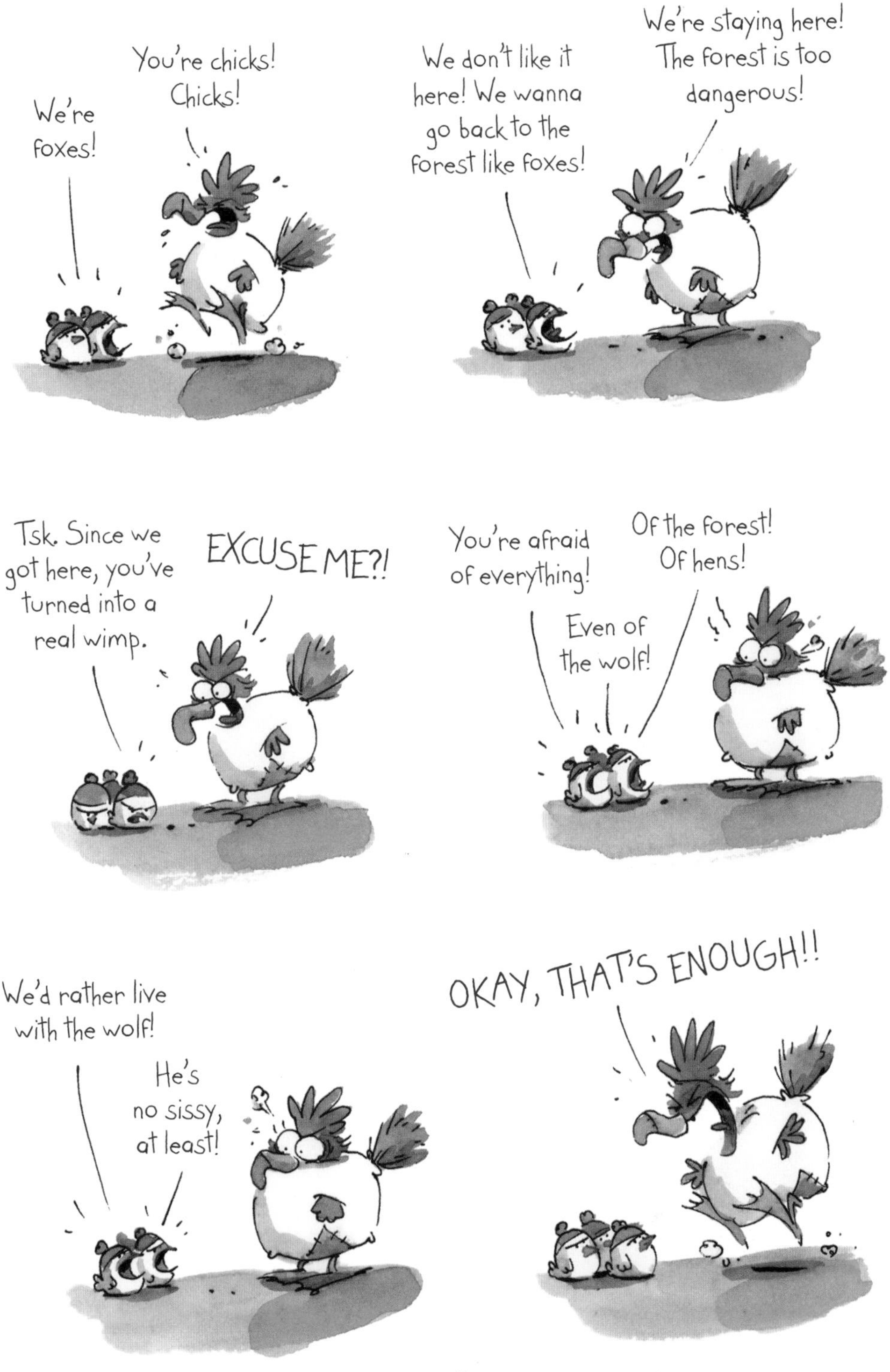
We're foxes!
You're chicks! Chicks!
We don't like it here! We wanna go back to the forest like foxes!
We're staying here! The forest is too dangerous!
Tsk. Since we got here, you've turned into a real wimp.
EXCUSE ME?!
You're afraid of everything!
Of the forest! Of hens!
Even of the wolf!
We'd rather live with the wolf!
He's no sissy, at least!
OKAY, THAT'S ENOUGH!!

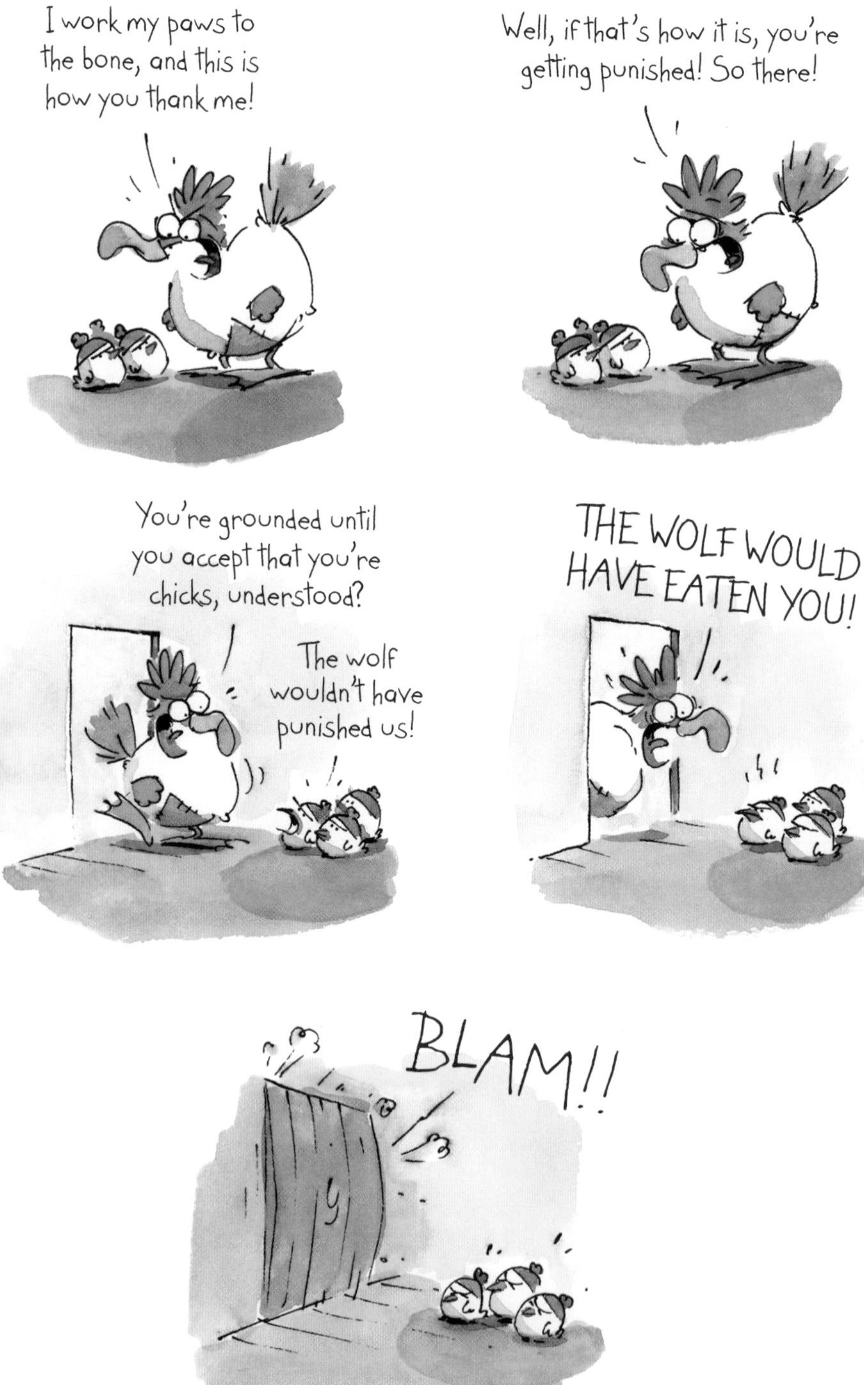
I work my paws to the bone, and this is how you thank me!
Well, if that's how it is, you're getting punished! So there!
You're grounded until you accept that you're chicks, understood?
The wolf wouldn't have punished us!
THE WOLF WOULD HAVE EATEN YOU!
BLAM!!

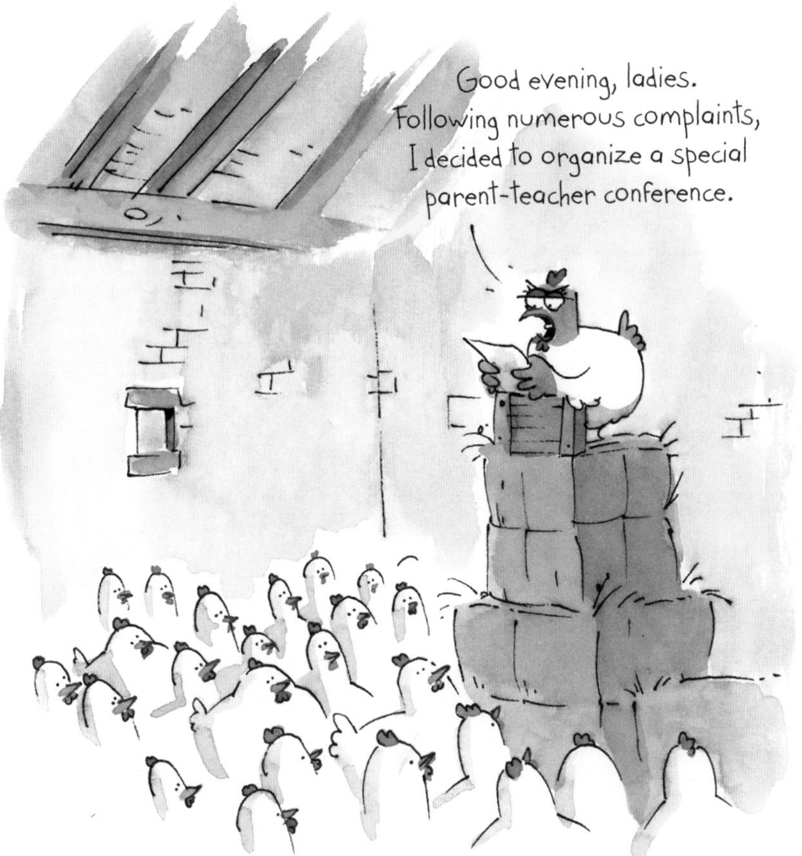
Good evening, ladies. Following numerous complaints, I decided to organize a special parent-teacher conference.

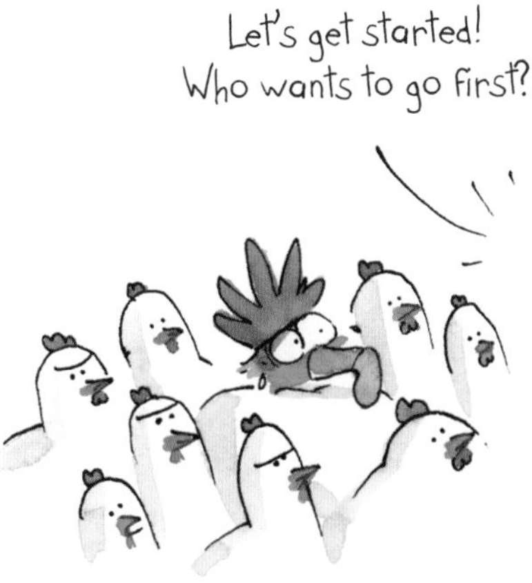
Let's get started! Who wants to go first?

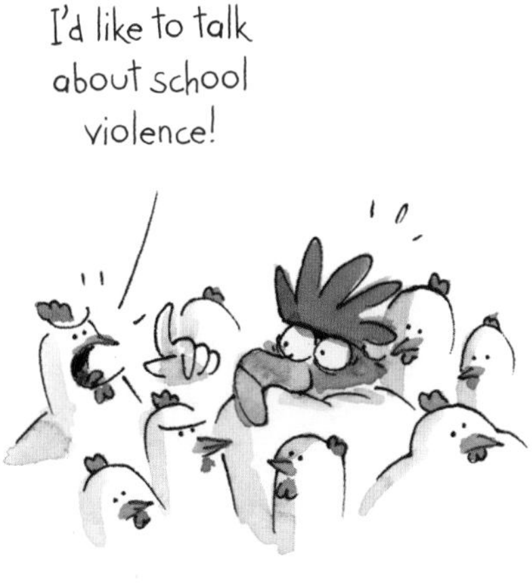
I'd like to talk about school violence!

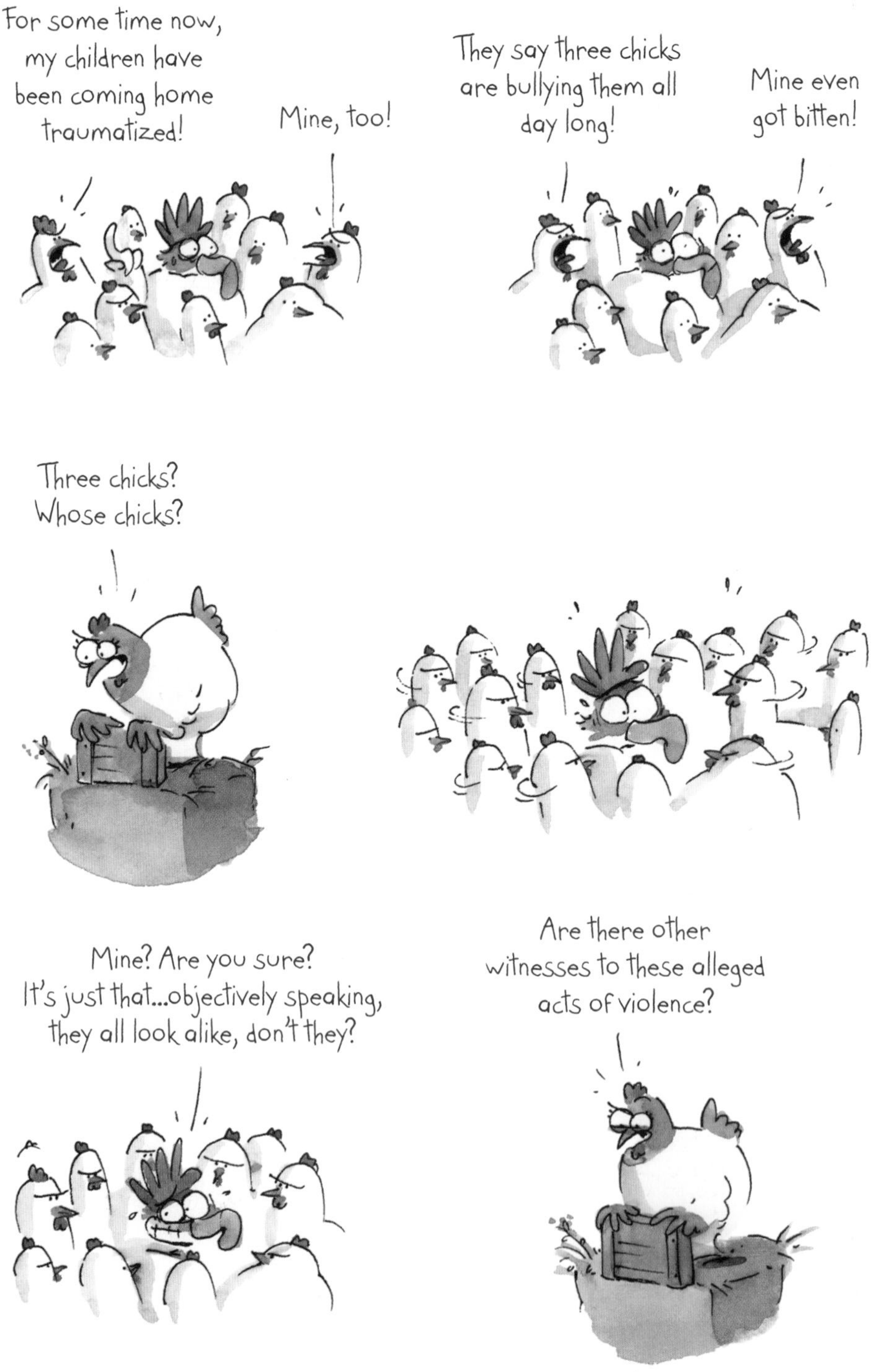
For some time now, my children have been coming home traumatized!
Mine, too!
They say three chicks are bullying them all day long!
Mine even got bitten!
Three chicks? Whose chicks?
Mine? Are you sure? It's just that...objectively speaking, they all look alike, don't they?
Are there other witnesses to these alleged acts of violence?

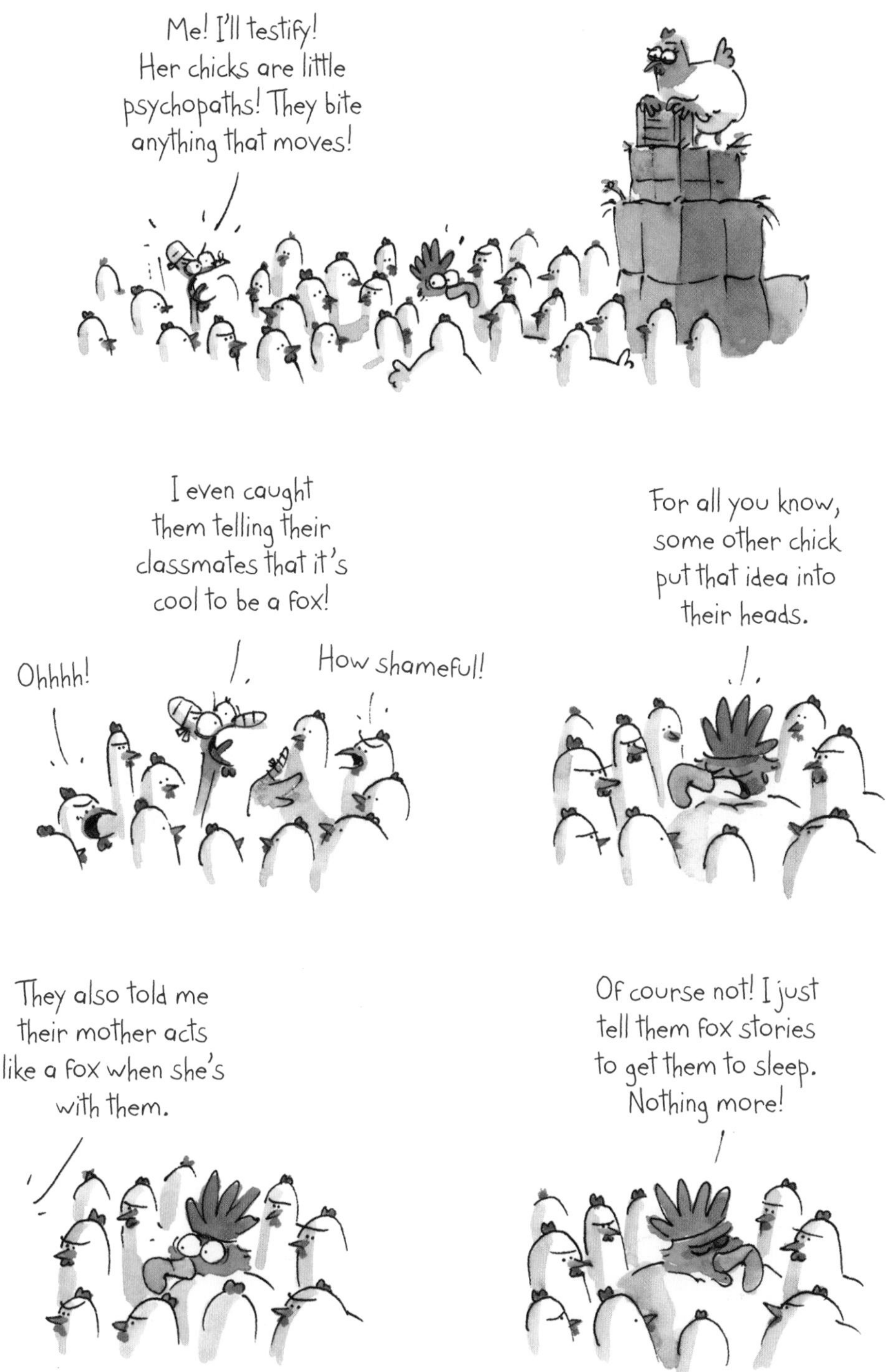
Me! I'll testify! Her chicks are little psychopaths! They bite anything that moves!
I even caught them telling their classmates that it's cool to be a fox!
Ohhhh!
How shameful!
For all you know, some other chick put that idea into their heads.
They also told me their mother acts like a fox when she's with them.
Of course not! I just tell them fox stories to get them to sleep. Nothing more!

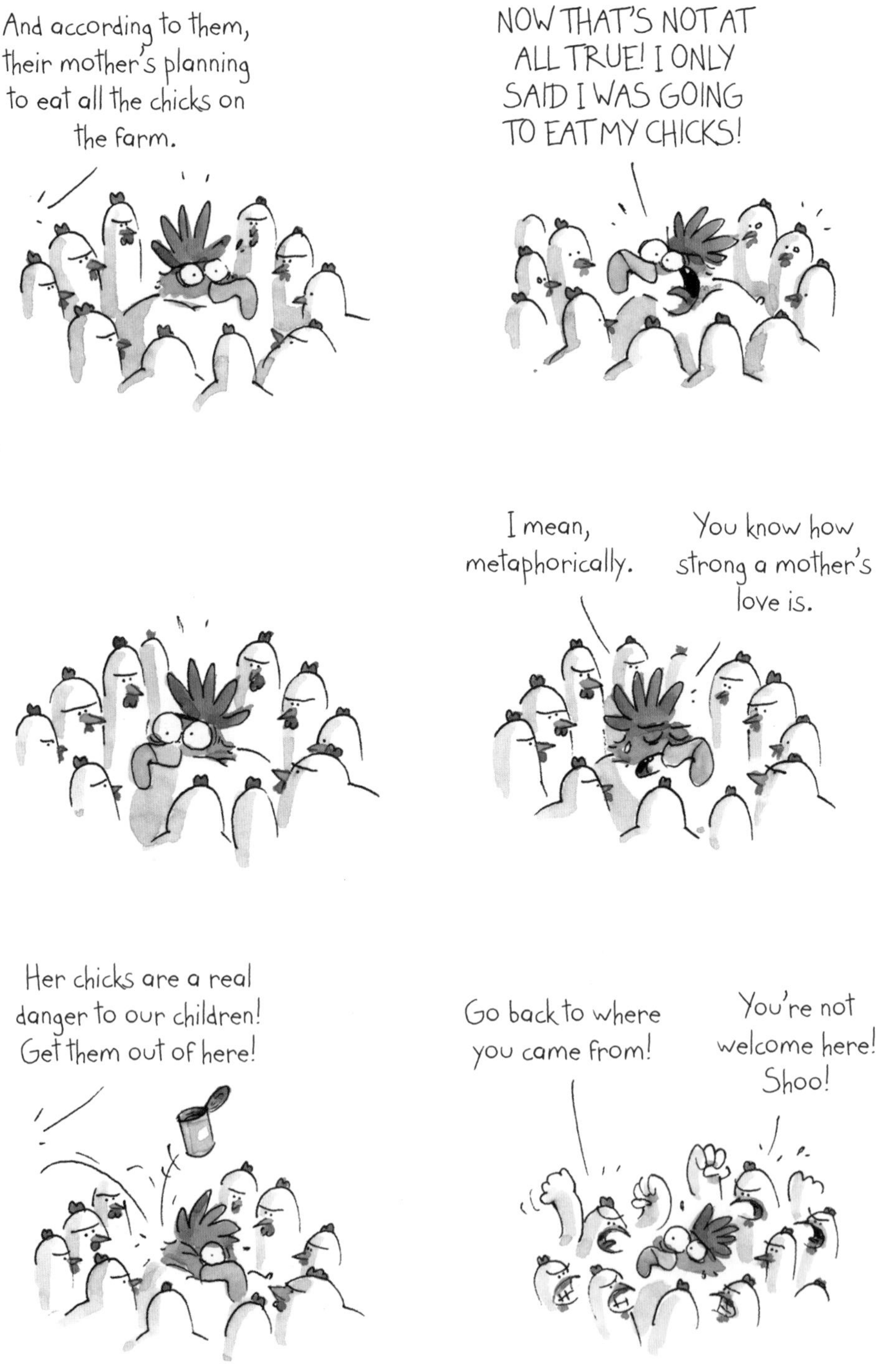
And according to them, their mother's planning to eat all the chicks on the farm.
NOW THAT'S NOT AT ALL TRUE! I ONLY SAID I WAS GOING TO EAT MY CHICKS!
I mean, metaphorically.
You know how strong a mother's love is.
Her chicks are a real danger to our children! Get them out of here!
Go back to where you came from!
You're not welcome here! Shoo!

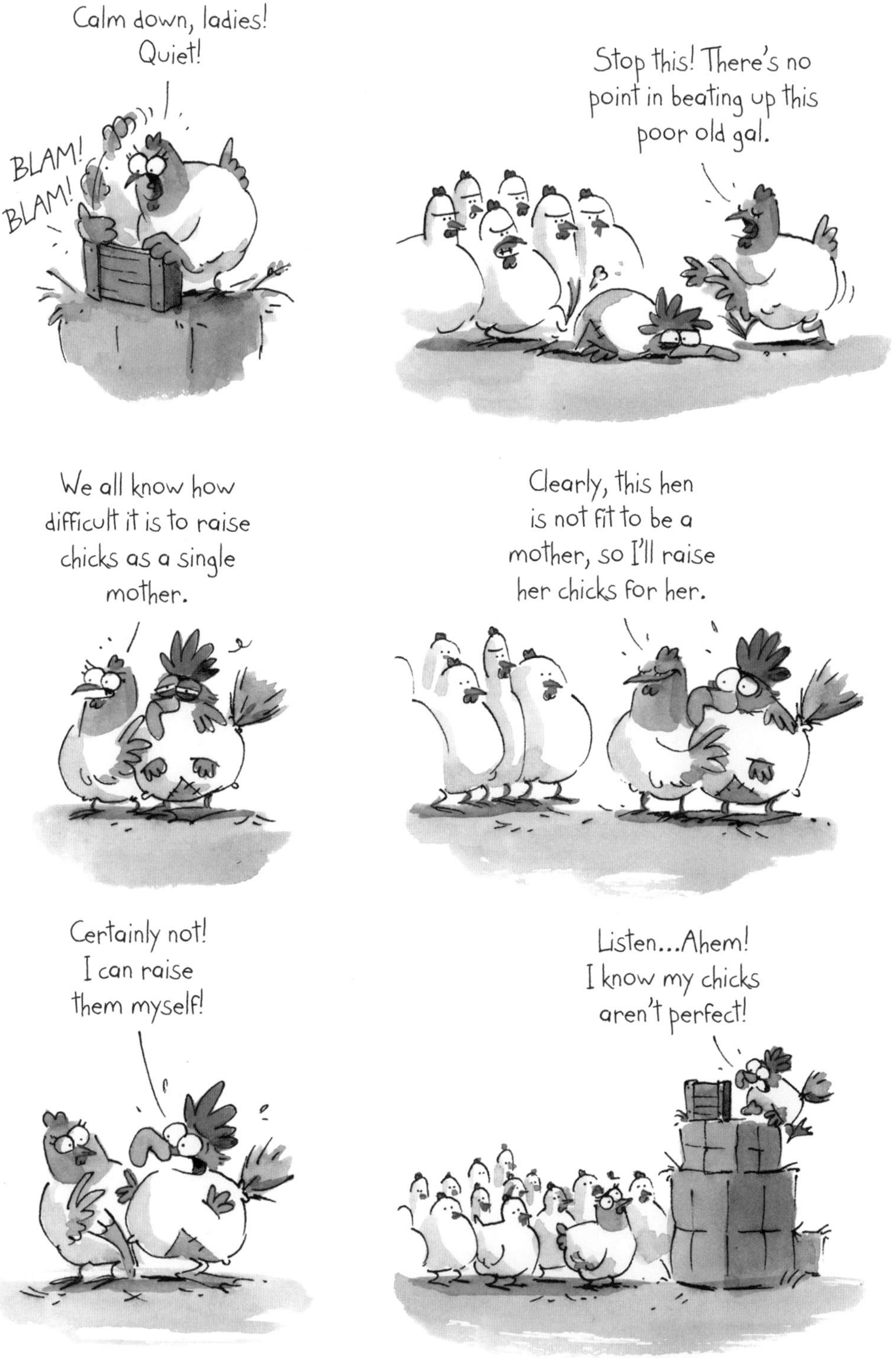
Calm down, ladies! Quiet!
BLAM! BLAM!
Stop this! There's no point in beating up this poor old gal.
We all know how difficult it is to raise chicks as a single mother.
Clearly, this hen is not fit to be a mother, so I'll raise her chicks for her.
Certainly not! I can raise them myself!
Listen...Ahem! I know my chicks aren't perfect!

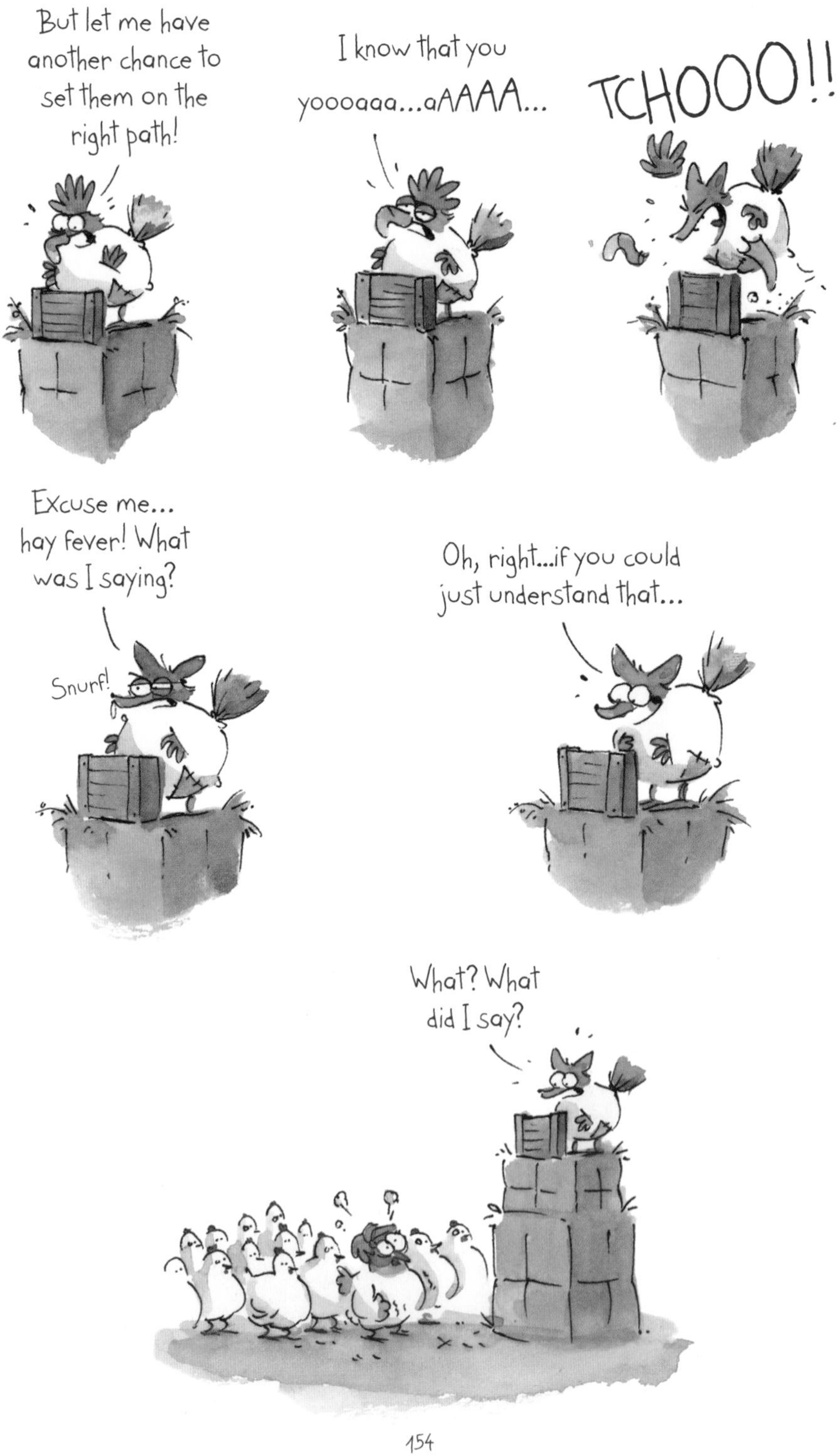
But let me have another chance to set them on the right path!
I know that you yoooaaa...aAAAA...
TCHOOO!!
Excuse me... hay fever! What was I saying?
Snurf!
Oh, right...if you could just understand that...
What? What did I say?

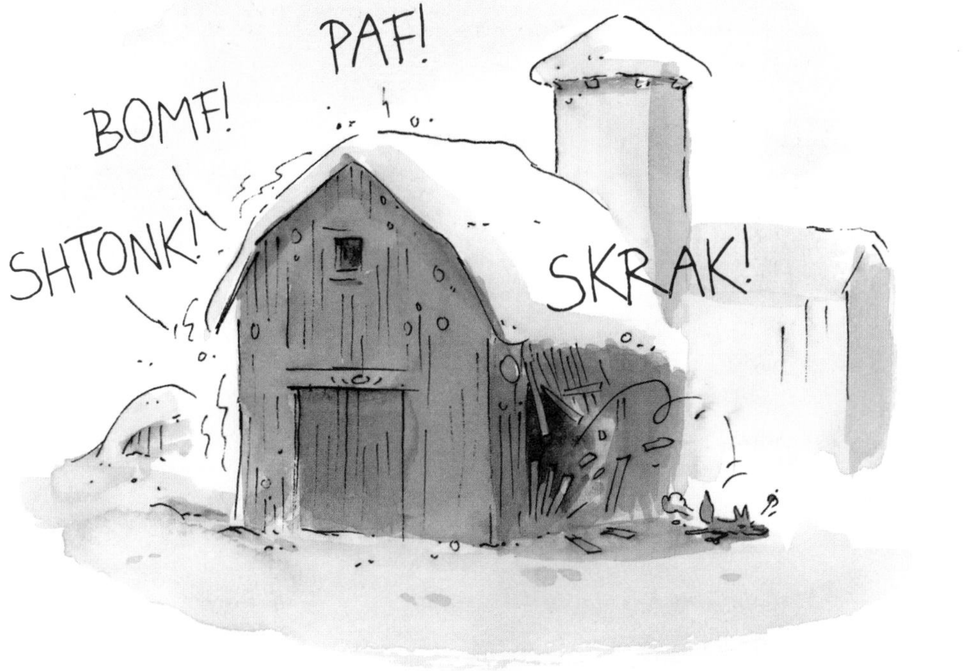
PAF!
BOMF!
SHTONK!
SKRAK!

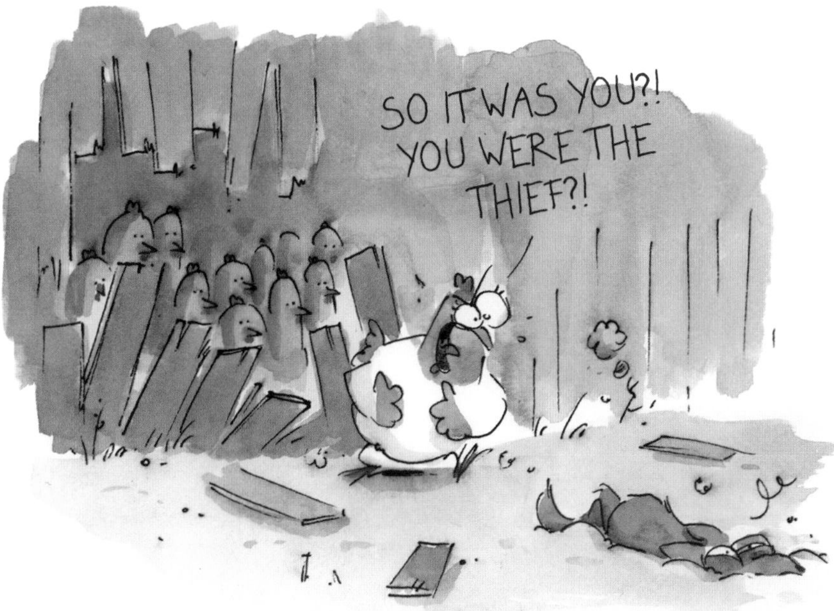
SO IT WAS YOU?! YOU WERE THE THIEF?!

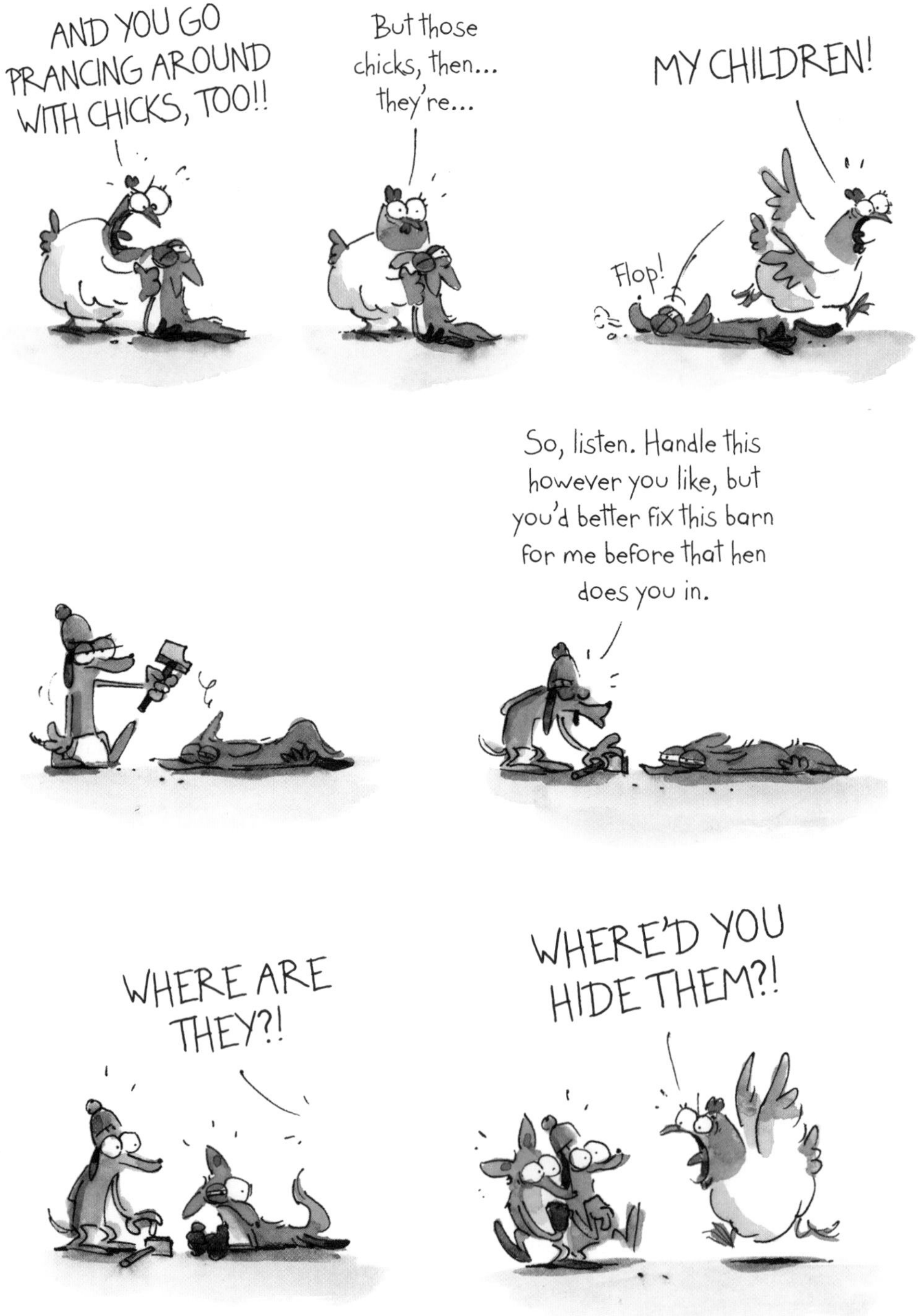
AND YOU GO PRANCING AROUND WITH CHICKS, TOO!!
But those chicks, then... they're...
MY CHILDREN!
Flop!
So, listen. Handle this however you like, but you'd better fix this barn for me before that hen does you in.
WHERE ARE THEY?!
WHERE'D YOU HIDE THEM?!

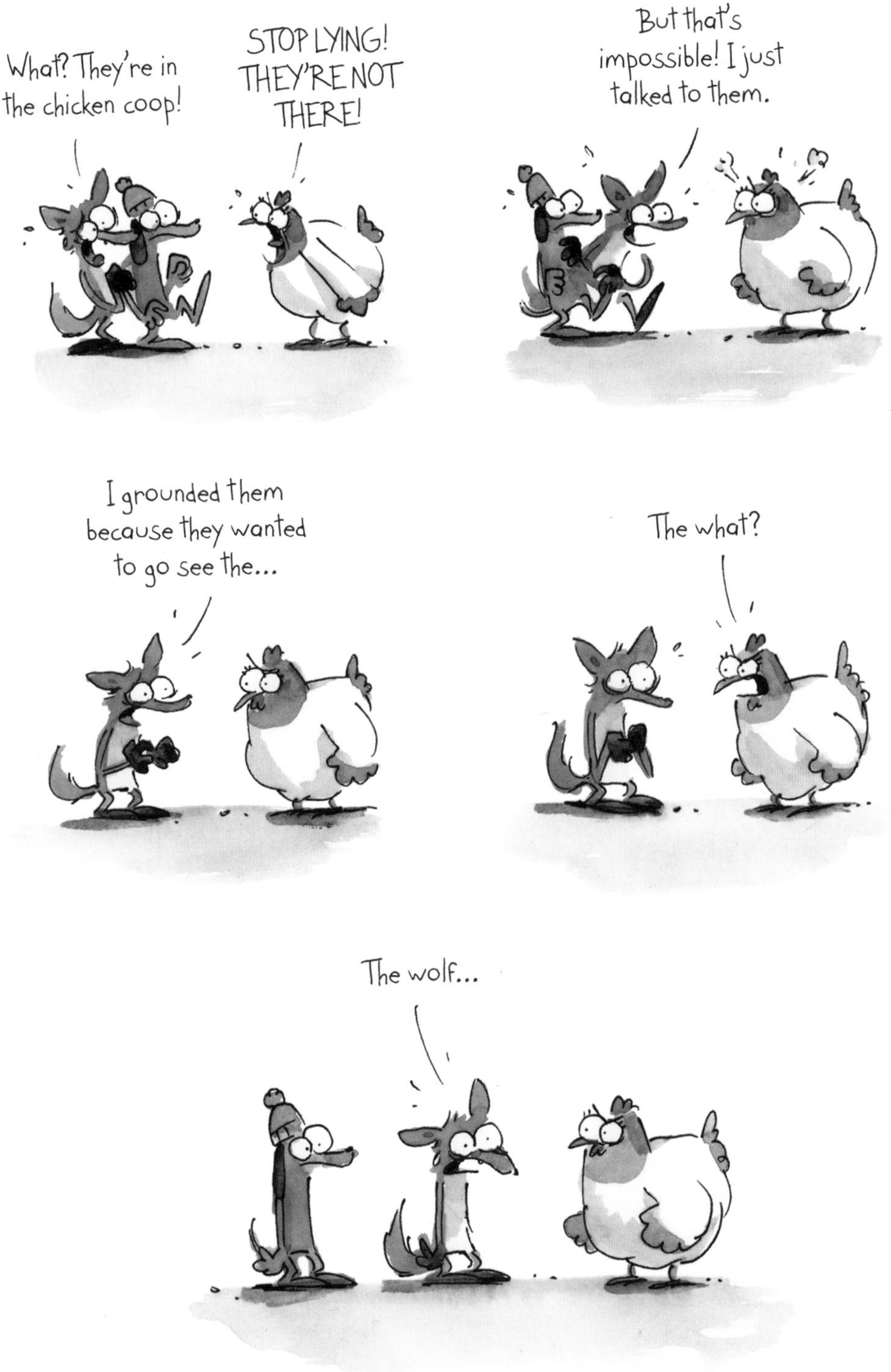
What? They're in the chicken coop!
STOP LYING! THEY'RE NOT THERE!
But that's impossible! I just talked to them.
I grounded them because they wanted to go see the...
The what?
The wolf...

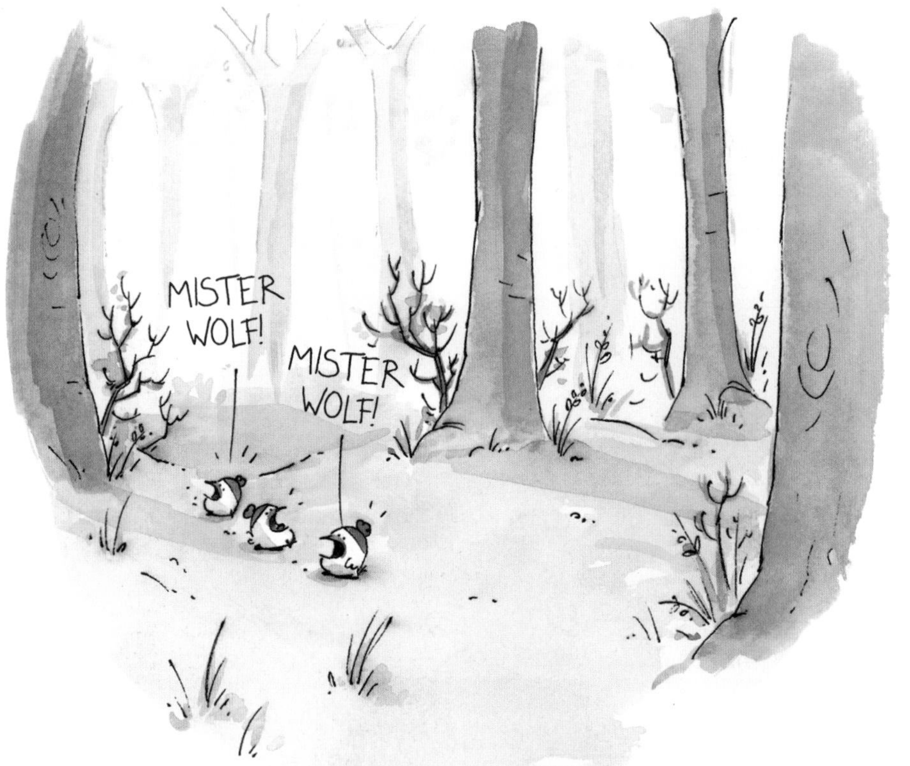
MISTER WOLF!
MISTER WOLF!

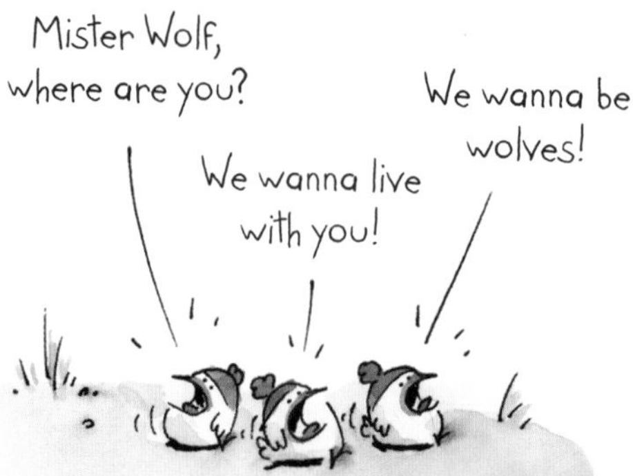
Mister Wolf, where are you?
We wanna live with you!
We wanna be wolves!

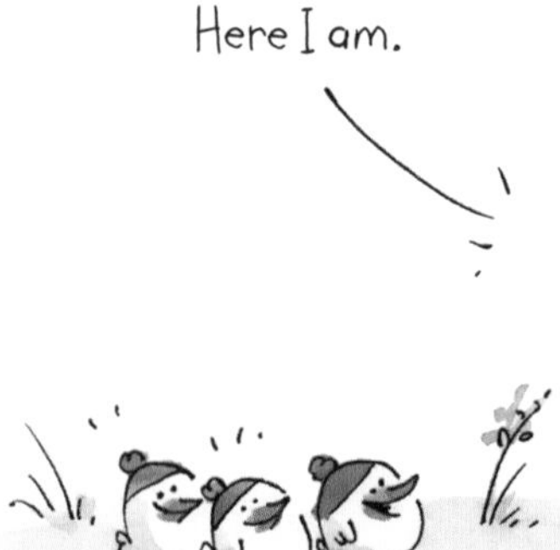
Here I am.

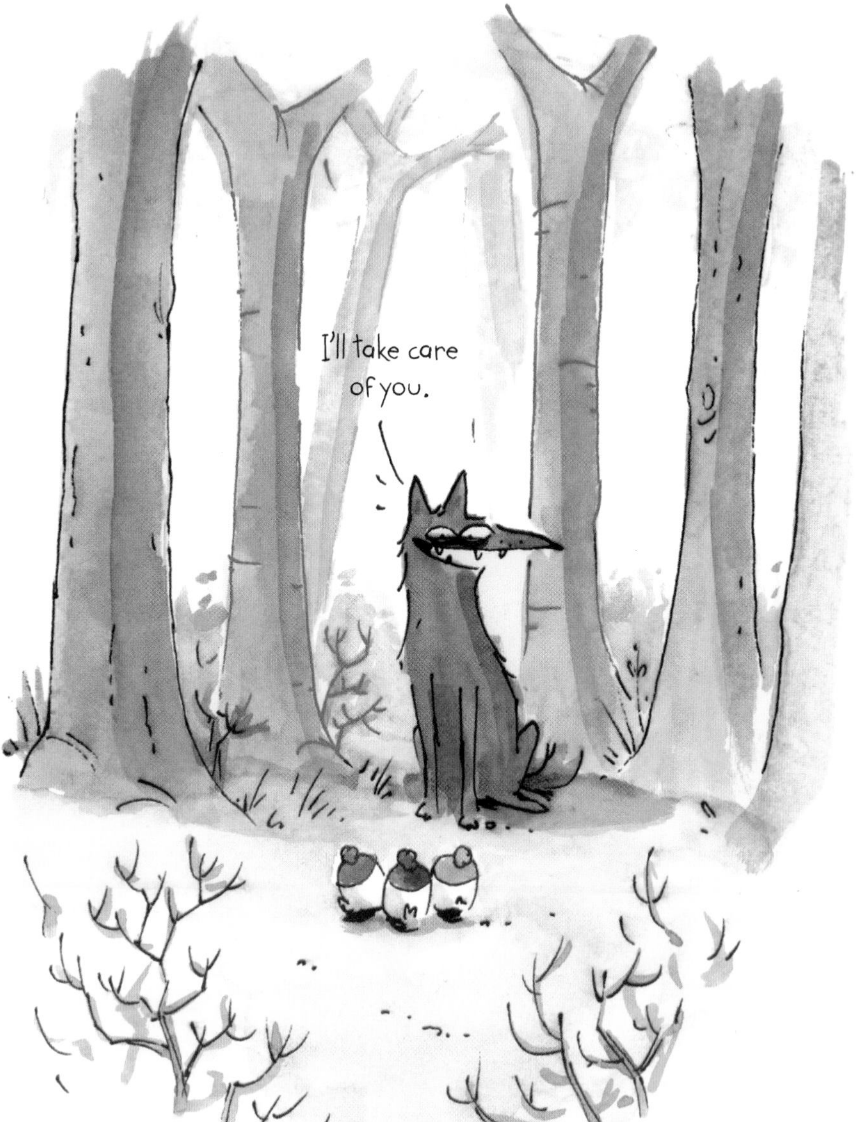
I'll take care of you.

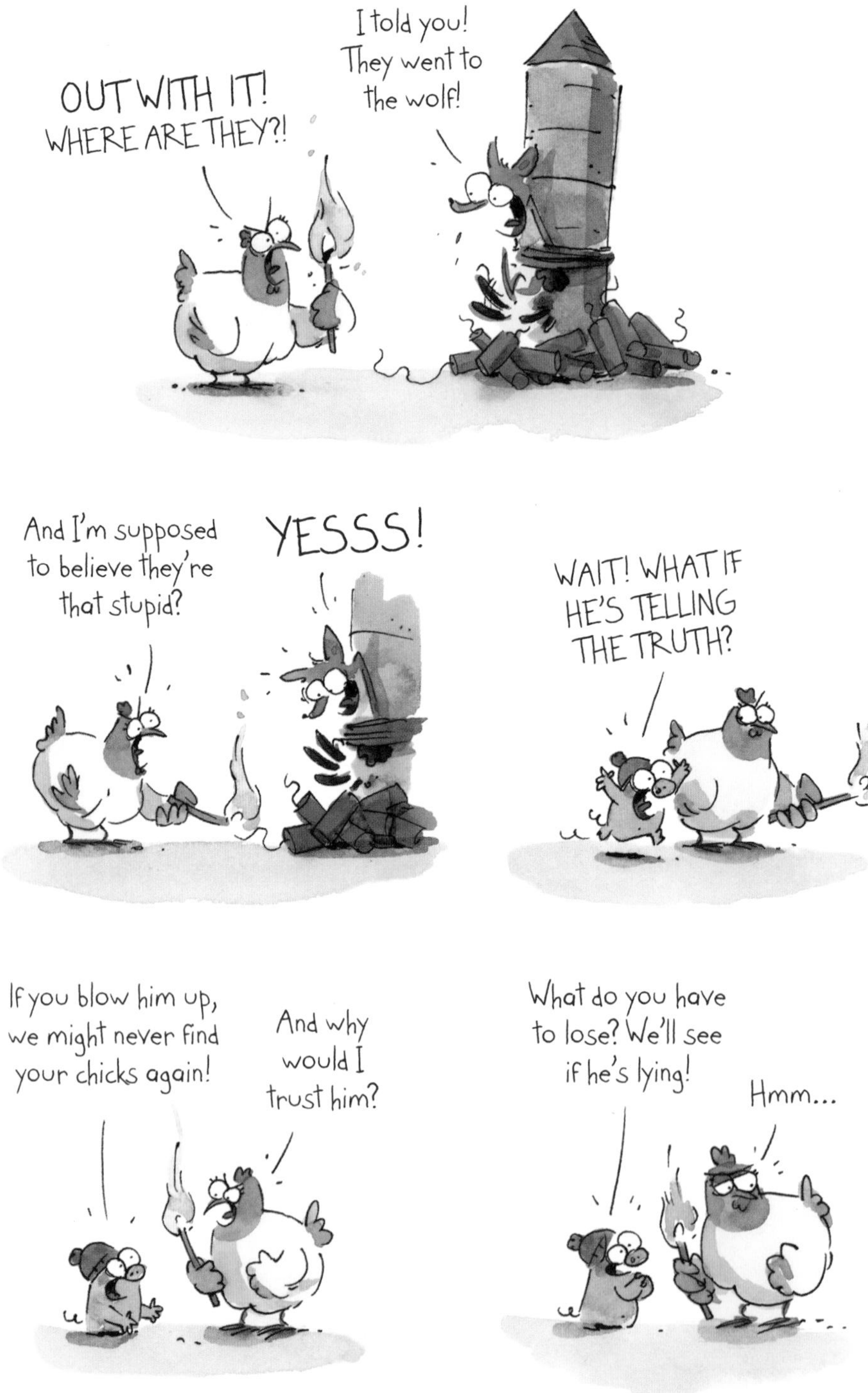
OUT WITH IT! WHERE ARE THEY?!
I told you! They went to the wolf!
And I'm supposed to believe they're that stupid?
YESSS!
WAIT! WHAT IF HE'S TELLING THE TRUTH?
If you blow him up, we might never find your chicks again!
And why would I trust him?
What do you have to lose? We'll see if he's lying!
Hmm...

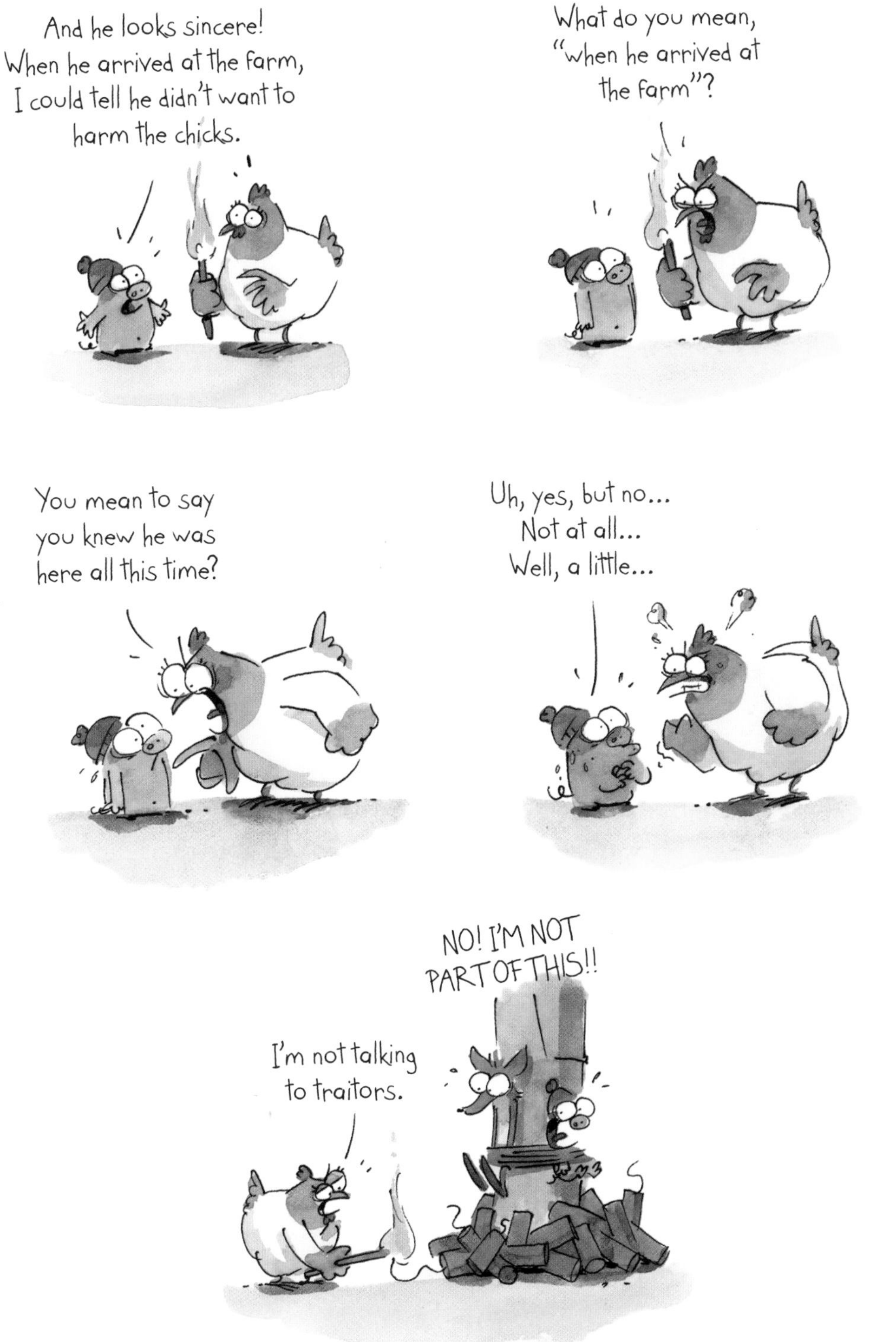
And he looks sincere! When he arrived at the farm, I could tell he didn't want to harm the chicks.
What do you mean, "when he arrived at the farm"?
You mean to say you knew he was here all this time?
Uh, yes, but no... Not at all... Well, a little...
NO! I'M NOT PART OF THIS!!
I'm not talking to traitors.

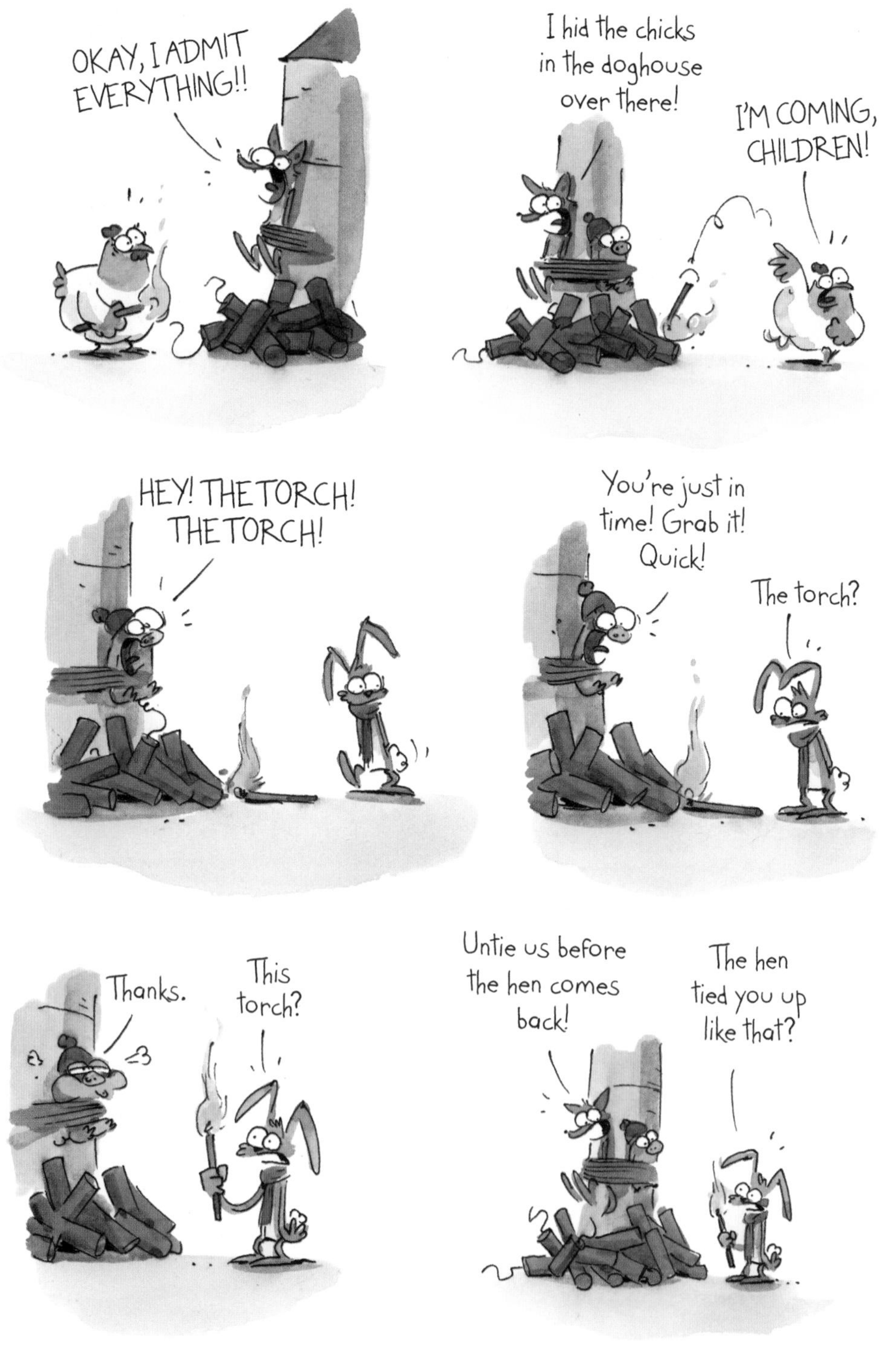
OKAY, I ADMIT EVERYTHING!!
I hid the chicks in the doghouse over there!
I'M COMING, CHILDREN!
HEY! THE TORCH! THE TORCH!
You're just in time! Grab it! Quick!
The torch?
Thanks.
This torch?
Untie us before the hen comes back!
The hen tied you up like that?

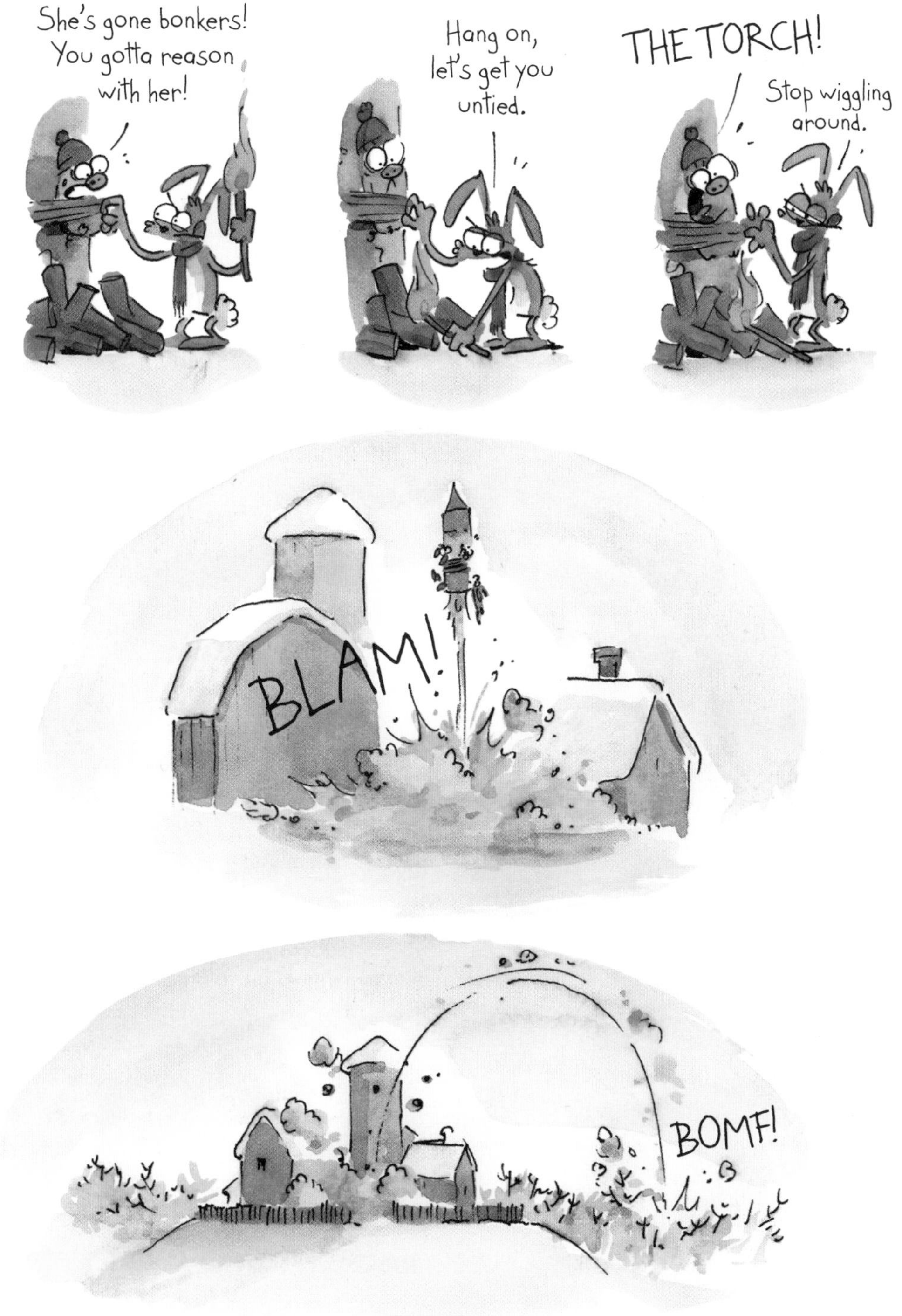
She's gone bonkers! You gotta reason with her!
Hang on, let's get you untied.
THE TORCH!
Stop wiggling around.
BLAM!
BOMF!

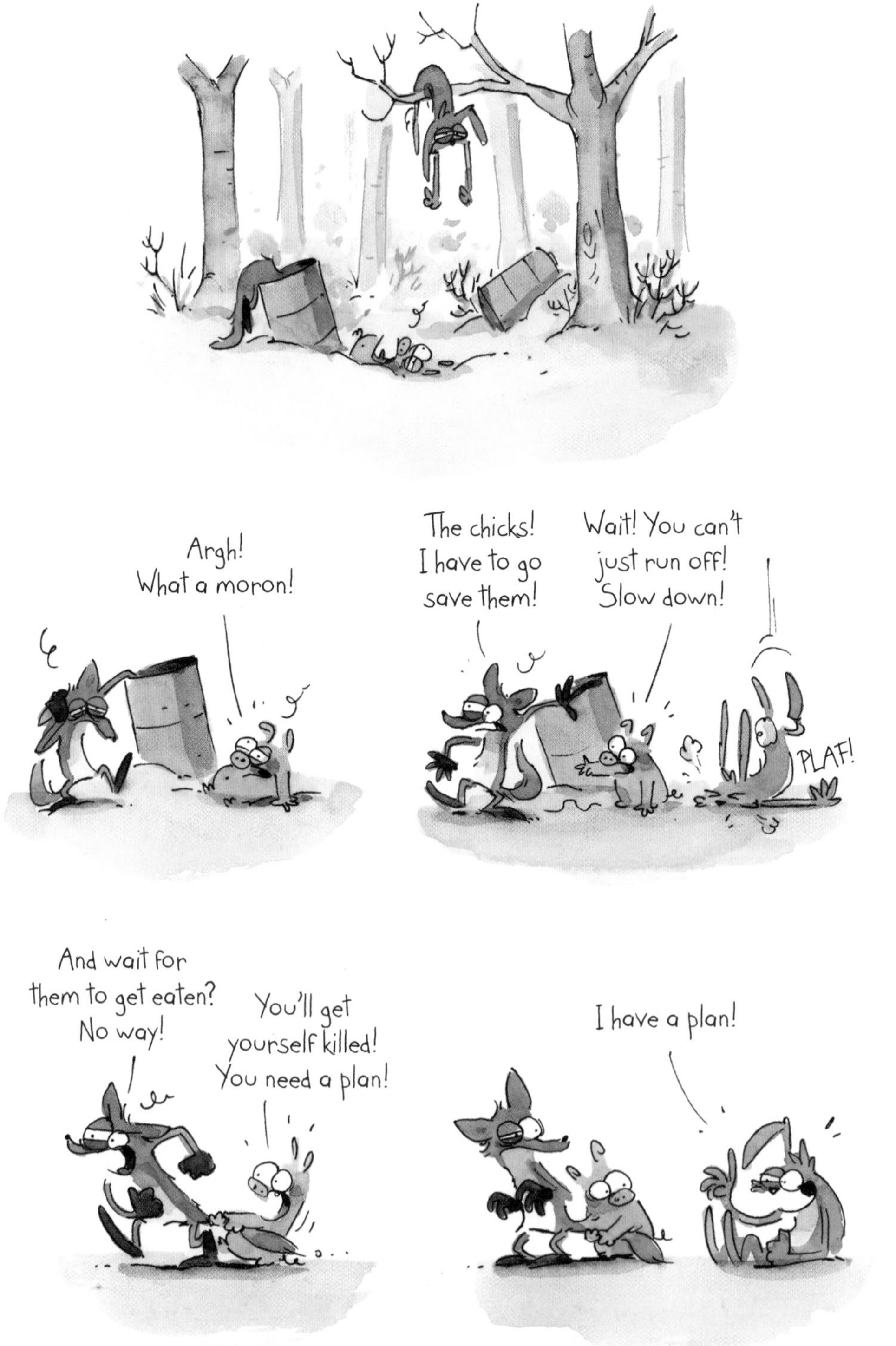
Argh!
What a moron!
The chicks!
I have to go
save them!
Wait! You can't
just run off!
Slow down!
PLAF!
And wait for
them to get eaten?
No way!
You'll get
yourself killed!
You need a plan!
I have a plan!

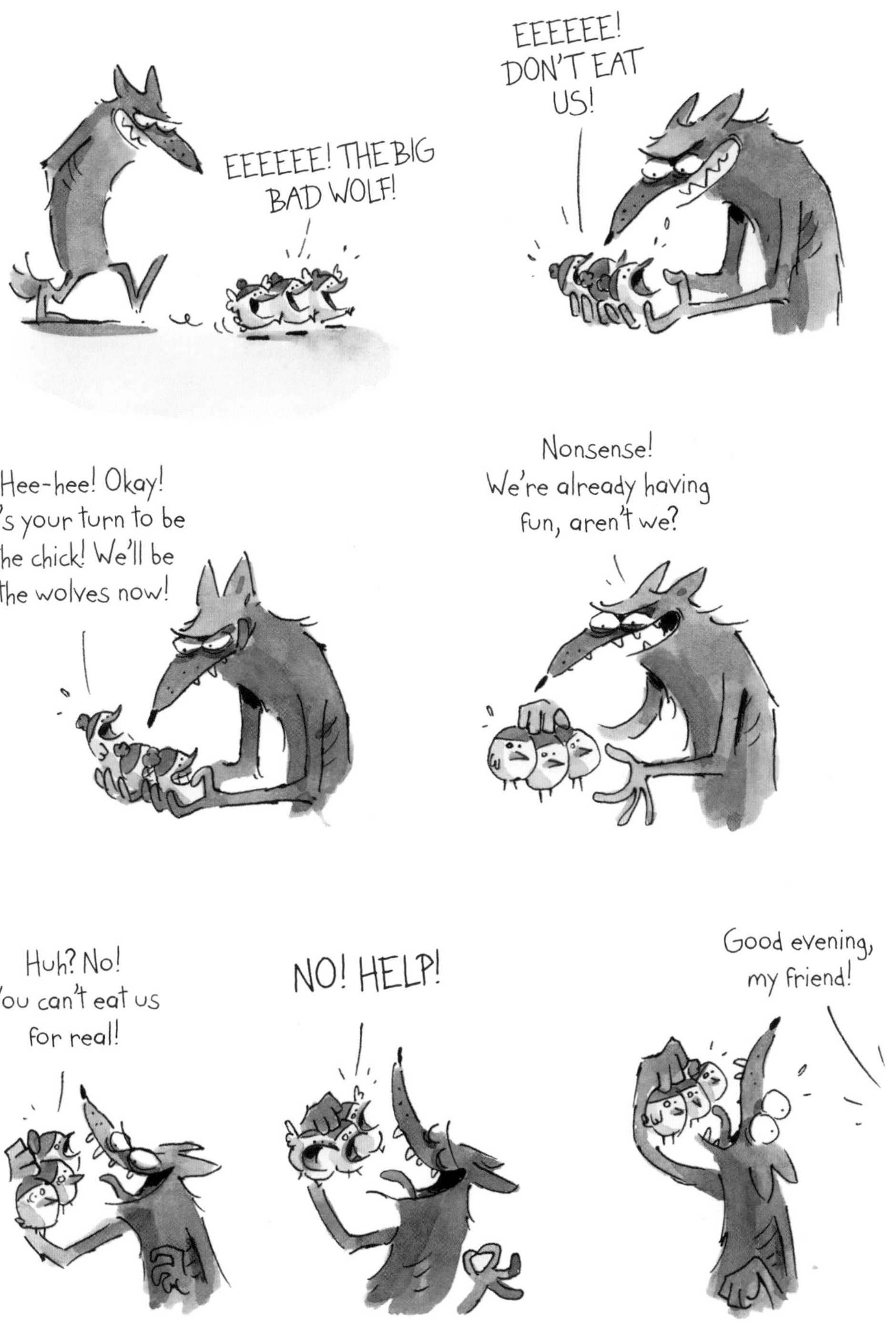
EEEEEE! THE BIG BAD WOLF!
EEEEEE! DON'T EAT US!
Hee-hee! Okay! It's your turn to be the chick! We'll be the wolves now!
Nonsense! We're already having fun, aren't we?
Huh? No! You can't eat us for real!
NO! HELP!
Good evening, my friend!

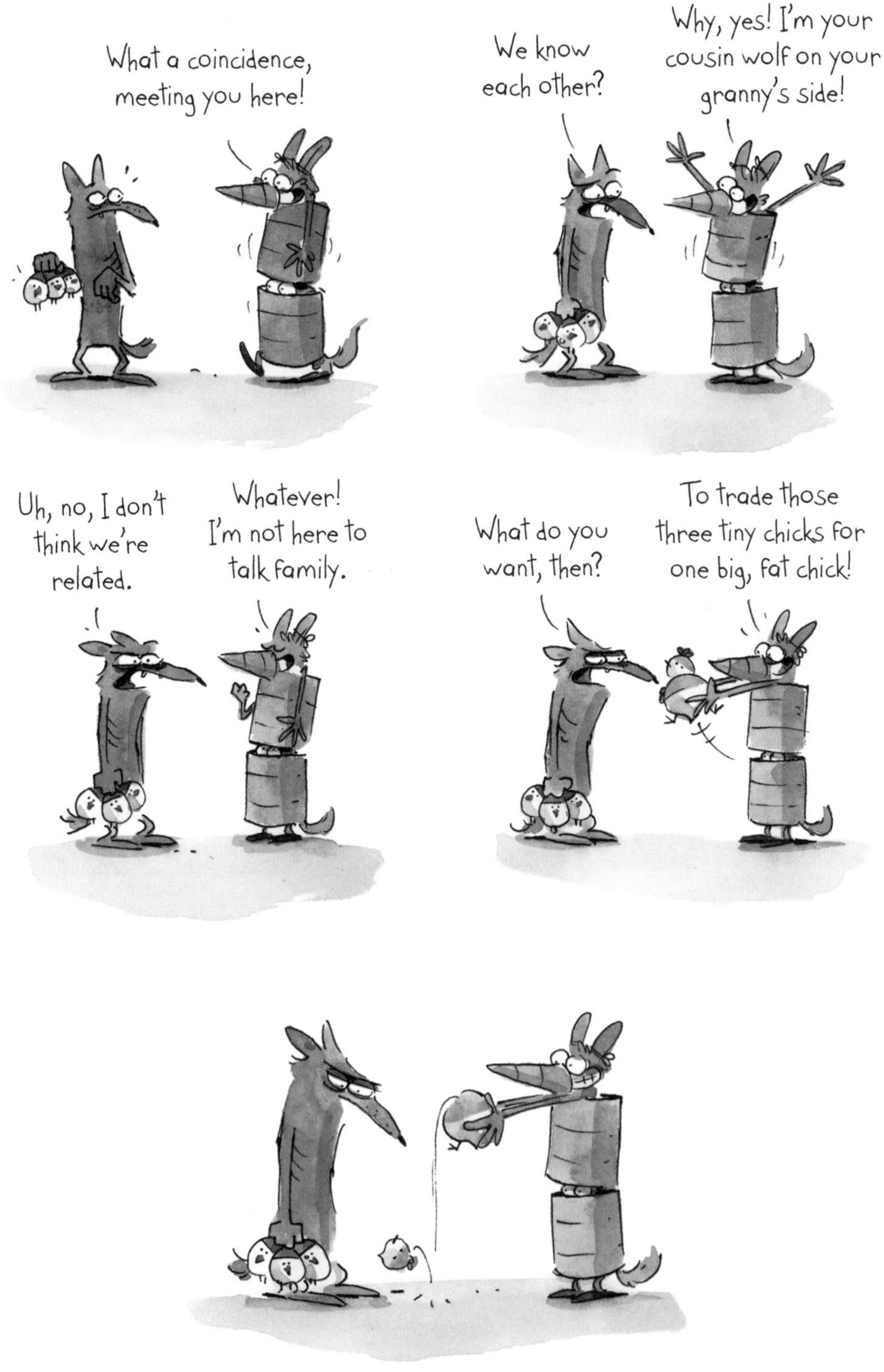
What a coincidence, meeting you here!
We know each other?
Why, yes! I'm your cousin wolf on your granny's side!
Uh, no, I don't think we're related.
Whatever! I'm not here to talk family.
What do you want, then?
To trade those three tiny chicks for one big, fat chick!

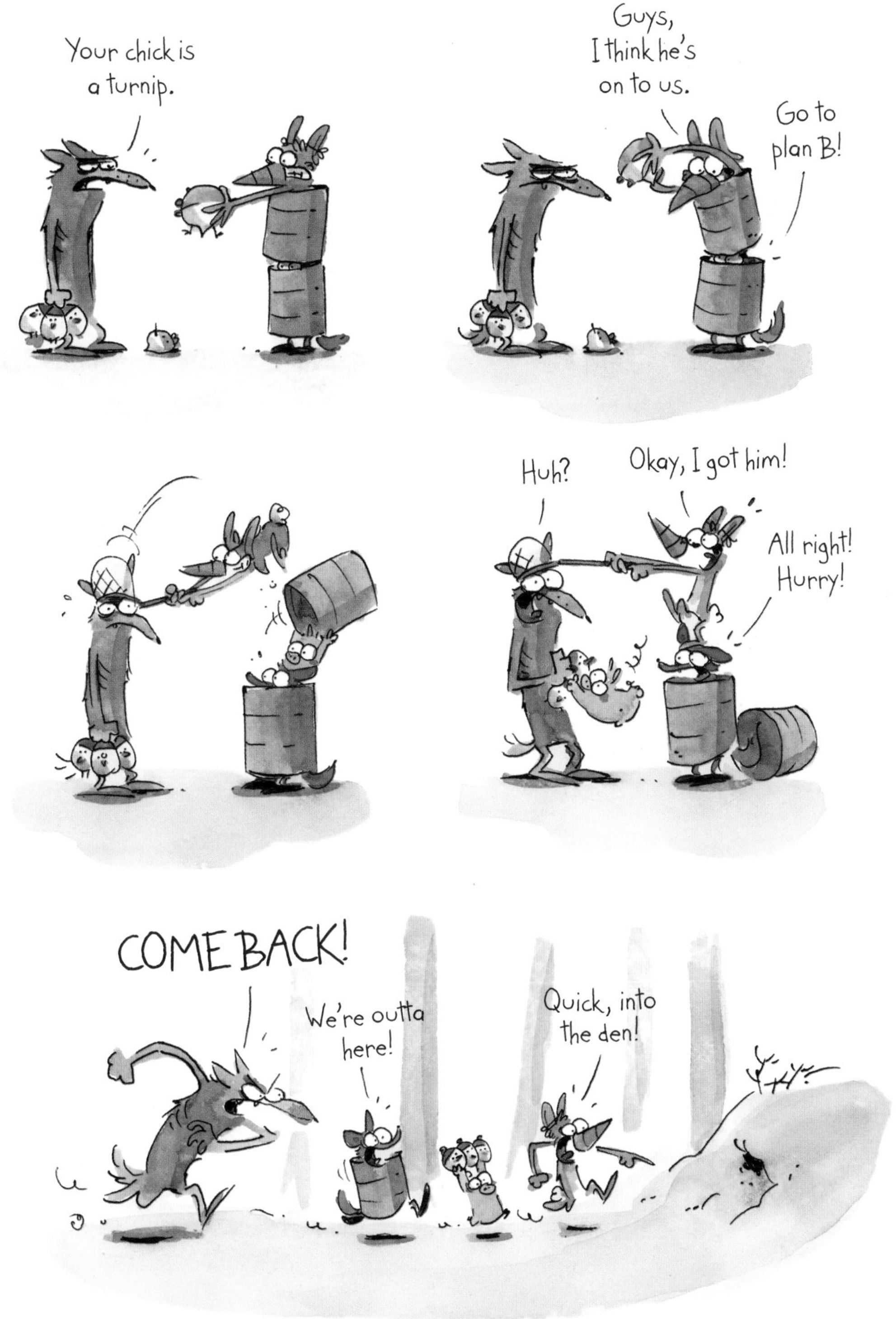
Your chick is a turnip.
Guys, I think he's on to us.
Go to plan B!
Huh?
Okay, I got him!
All right! Hurry!
COME BACK!
We're outta here!
Quick, into the den!

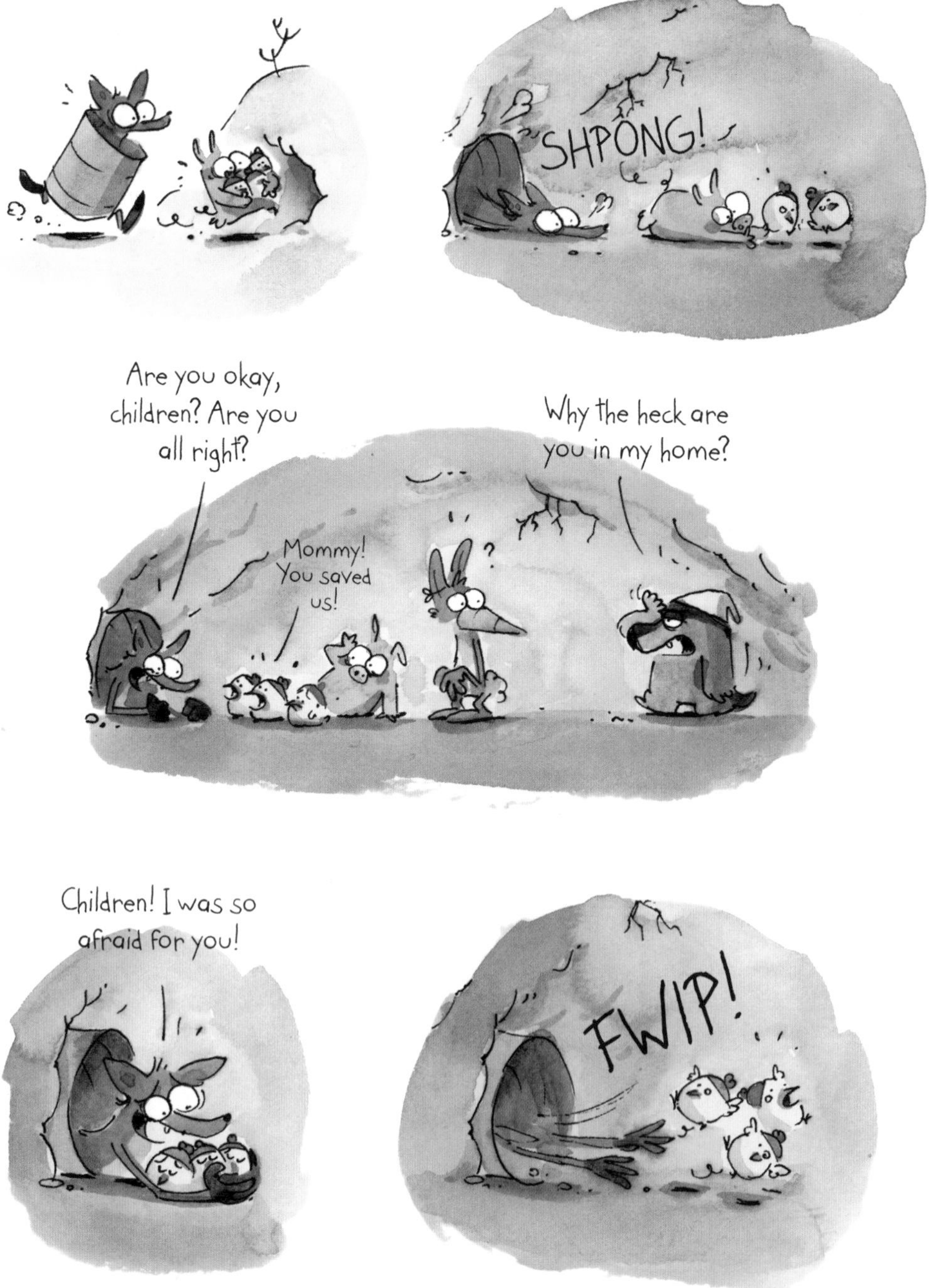

SHPONG!
Are you okay, children? Are you all right?
Mommy! You saved us!
Why the heck are you in my home?
Children! I was so afraid for you!
FWIP!

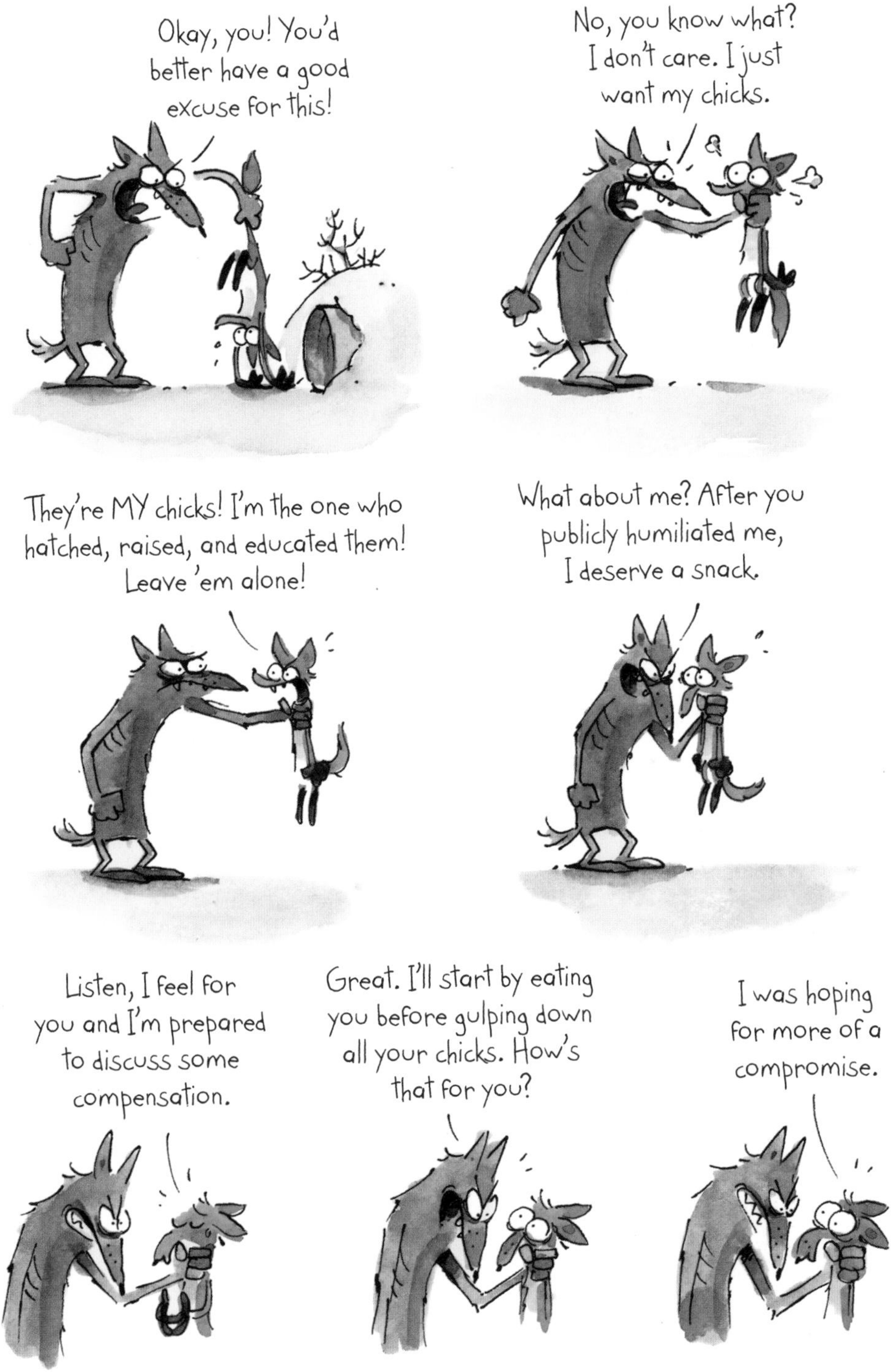
Okay, you! You'd better have a good excuse for this!
No, you know what? I don't care. I just want my chicks.
They're MY chicks! I'm the one who hatched, raised, and educated them! Leave 'em alone!
What about me? After you publicly humiliated me, I deserve a snack.
Listen, I feel for you and I'm prepared to discuss some compensation.
Great. I'll start by eating you before gulping down all your chicks. How's that for you?
I was hoping for more of a compromise.

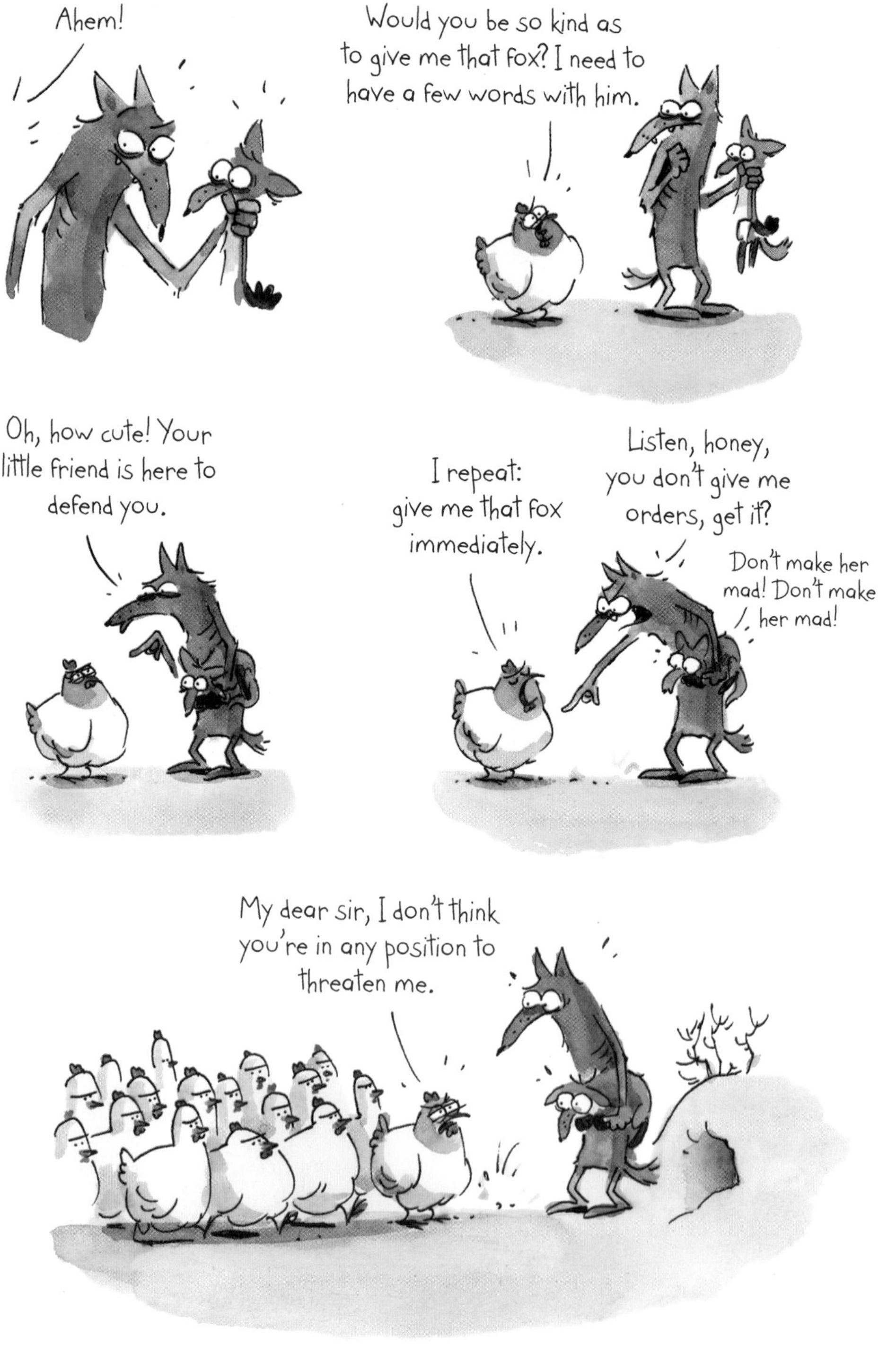
Ahem!
Would you be so kind as to give me that fox? I need to have a few words with him.
Oh, how cute! Your little friend is here to defend you.
I repeat: give me that fox immediately.
Listen, honey, you don't give me orders, get it?
Don't make her mad! Don't make her mad!
My dear sir, I don't think you're in any position to threaten me.

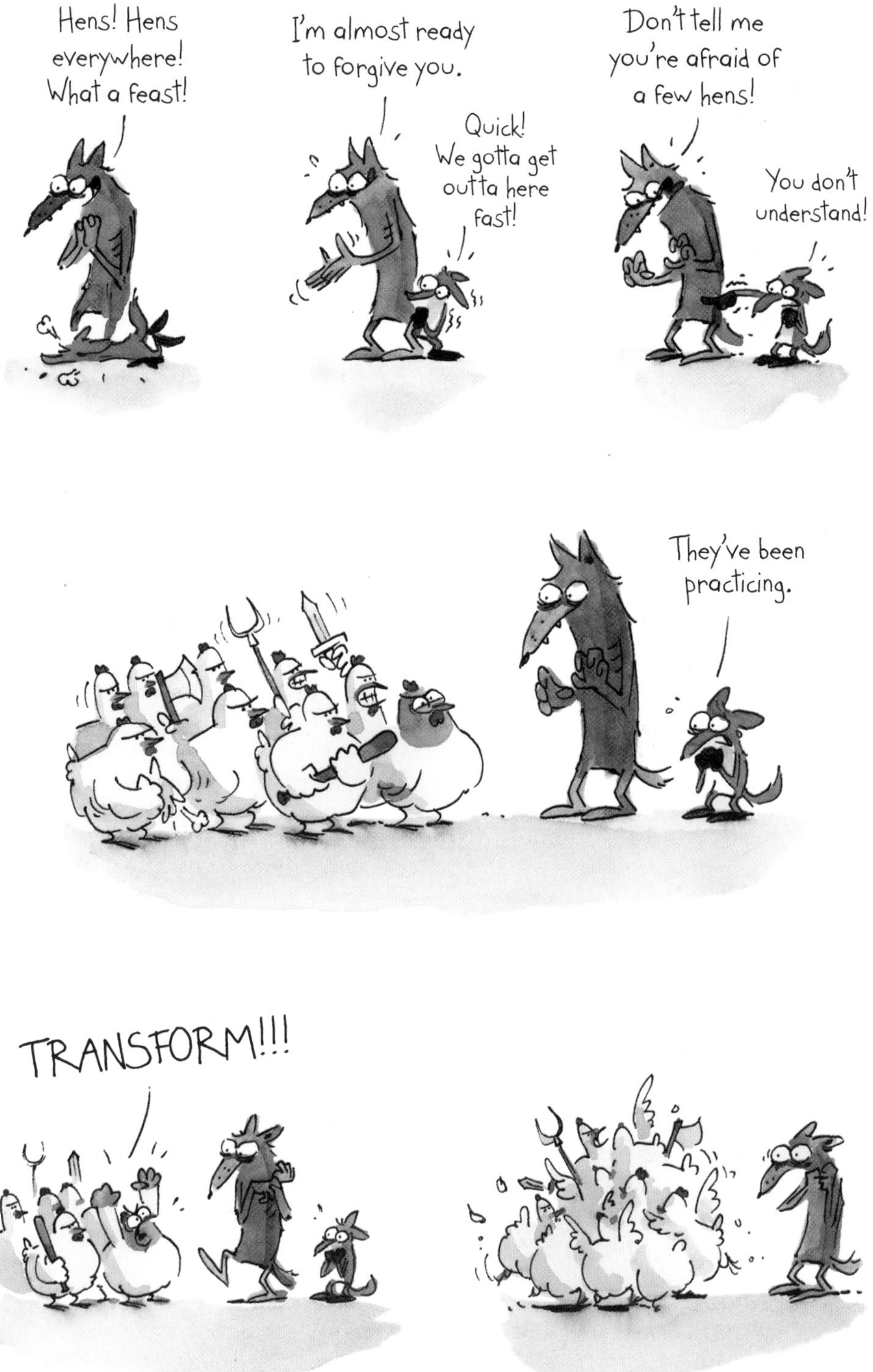
Hens! Hens everywhere! What a feast!
I'm almost ready to forgive you.
Quick! We gotta get outta here fast!
Don't tell me you're afraid of a few hens!
You don't understand!
They've been practicing.
TRANSFORM!!!

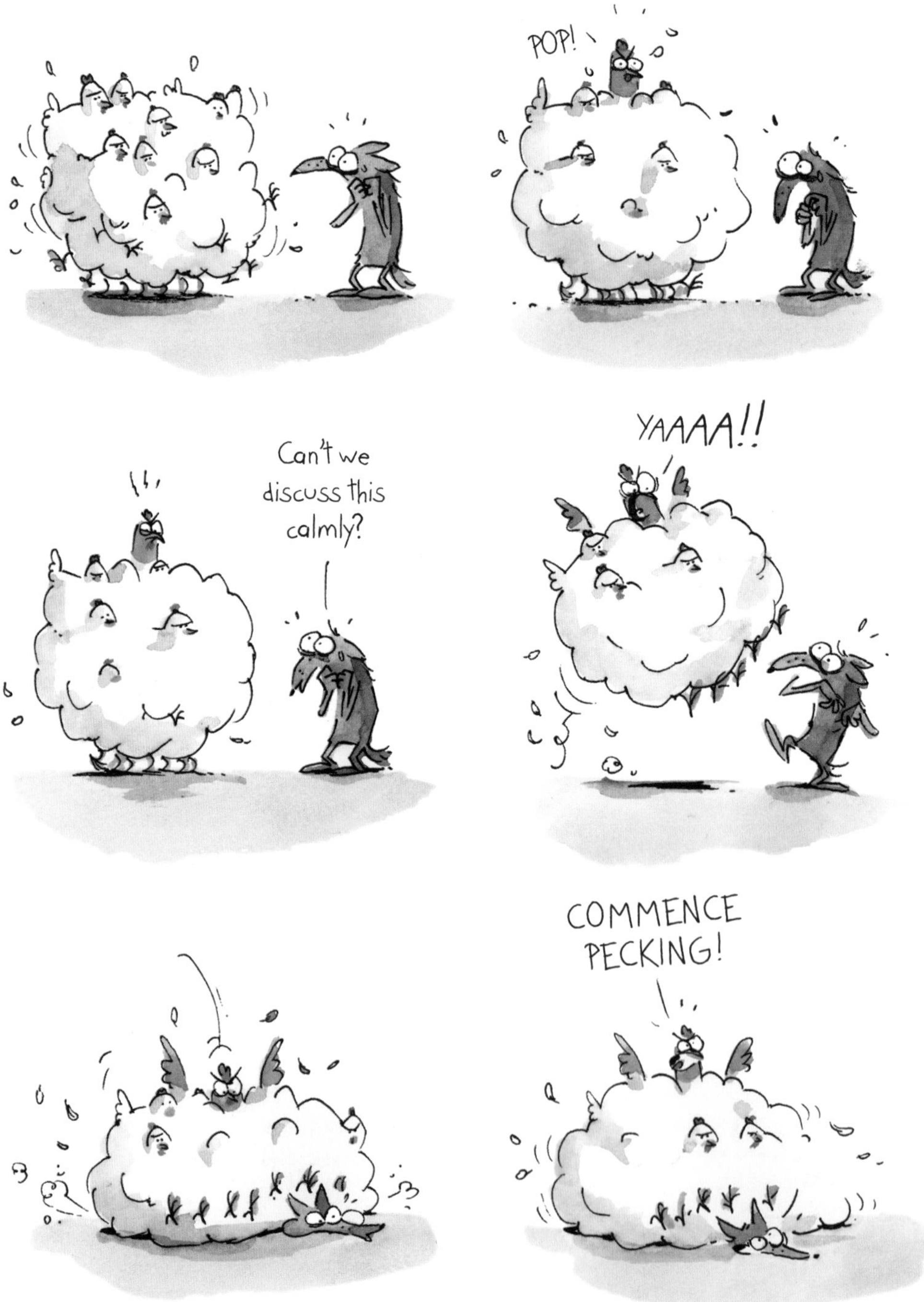
POP!
Can't we discuss this calmly?
YAAAA!!
COMMENCE PECKING!

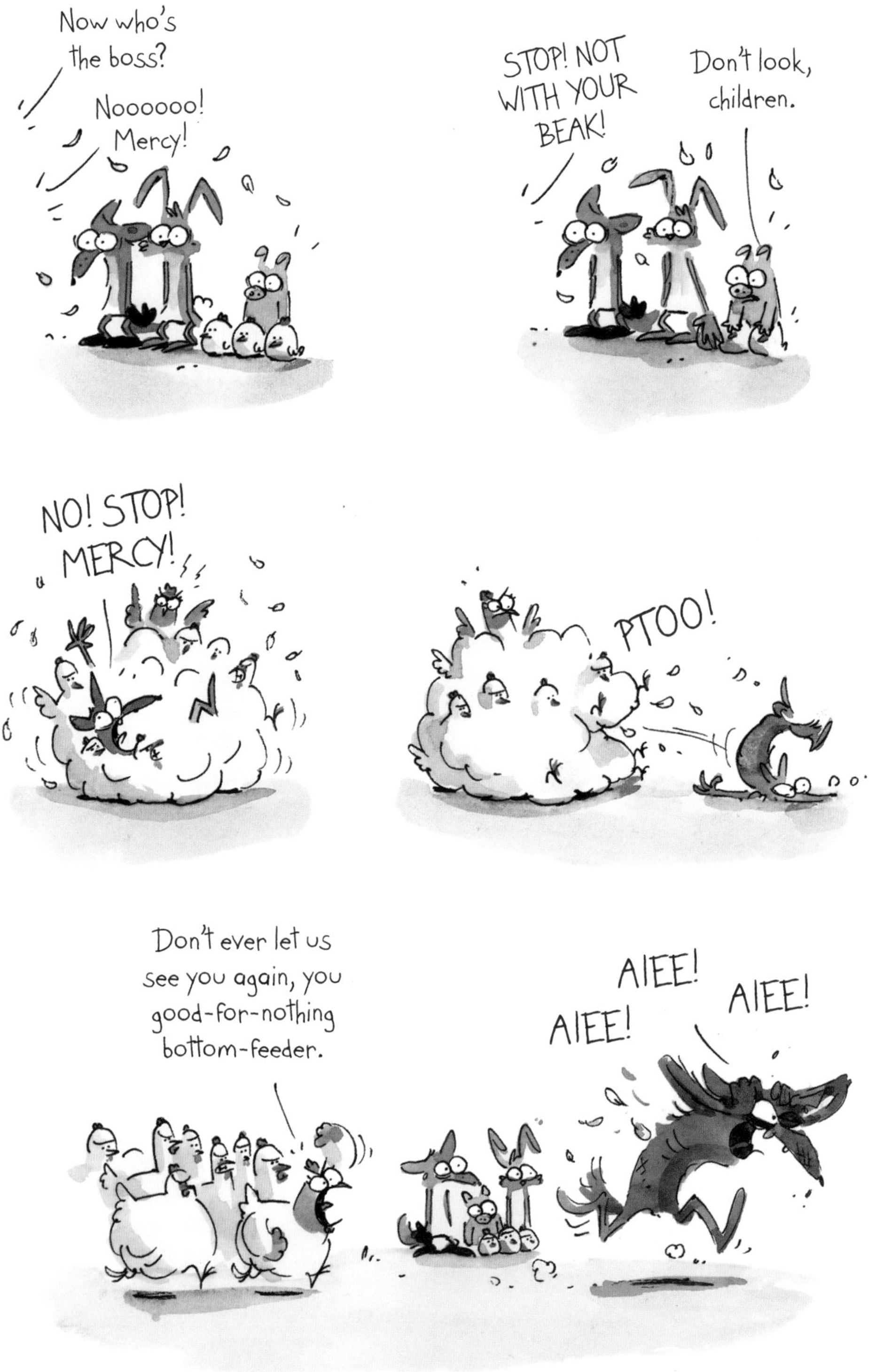
Now who's the boss?
Noooooo! Mercy!
STOP! NOT WITH YOUR BEAK!
Don't look, children.
NO! STOP! MERCY!
PTOO!
Don't ever let us see you again, you good-for-nothing bottom-feeder.
AIEE!
AIEE!
AIEE!

Your turn!
Are you ready?

WAIT!

Hmpf...

Before you do
me in, let me just
say goodbye.

Listen, children. I'm not
your mommy. The truth is
that I stole you from the hen
when you were just eggs.

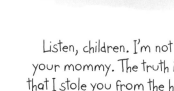

She's your
real mommy.

What?!

So when we grow
up, we'll be hens like
that lady? Not foxes?

That's right.

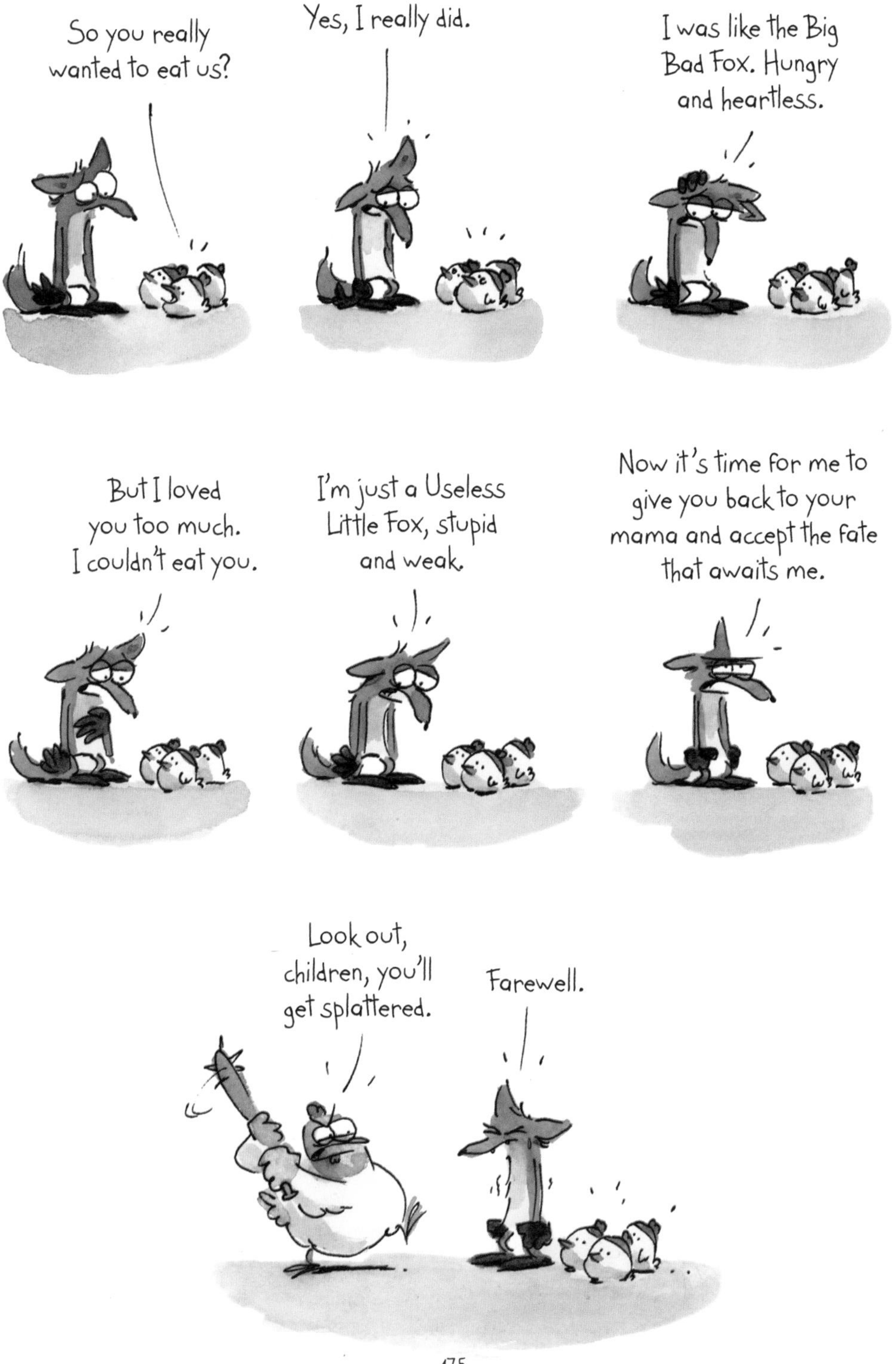
So you really wanted to eat us?
Yes, I really did.
I was like the Big Bad Fox. Hungry and heartless.
But I loved you too much. I couldn't eat you.
I'm just a Useless Little Fox, stupid and weak.
Now it's time for me to give you back to your mama and accept the fate that awaits me.
Look out, children, you'll get splattered.
Farewell.

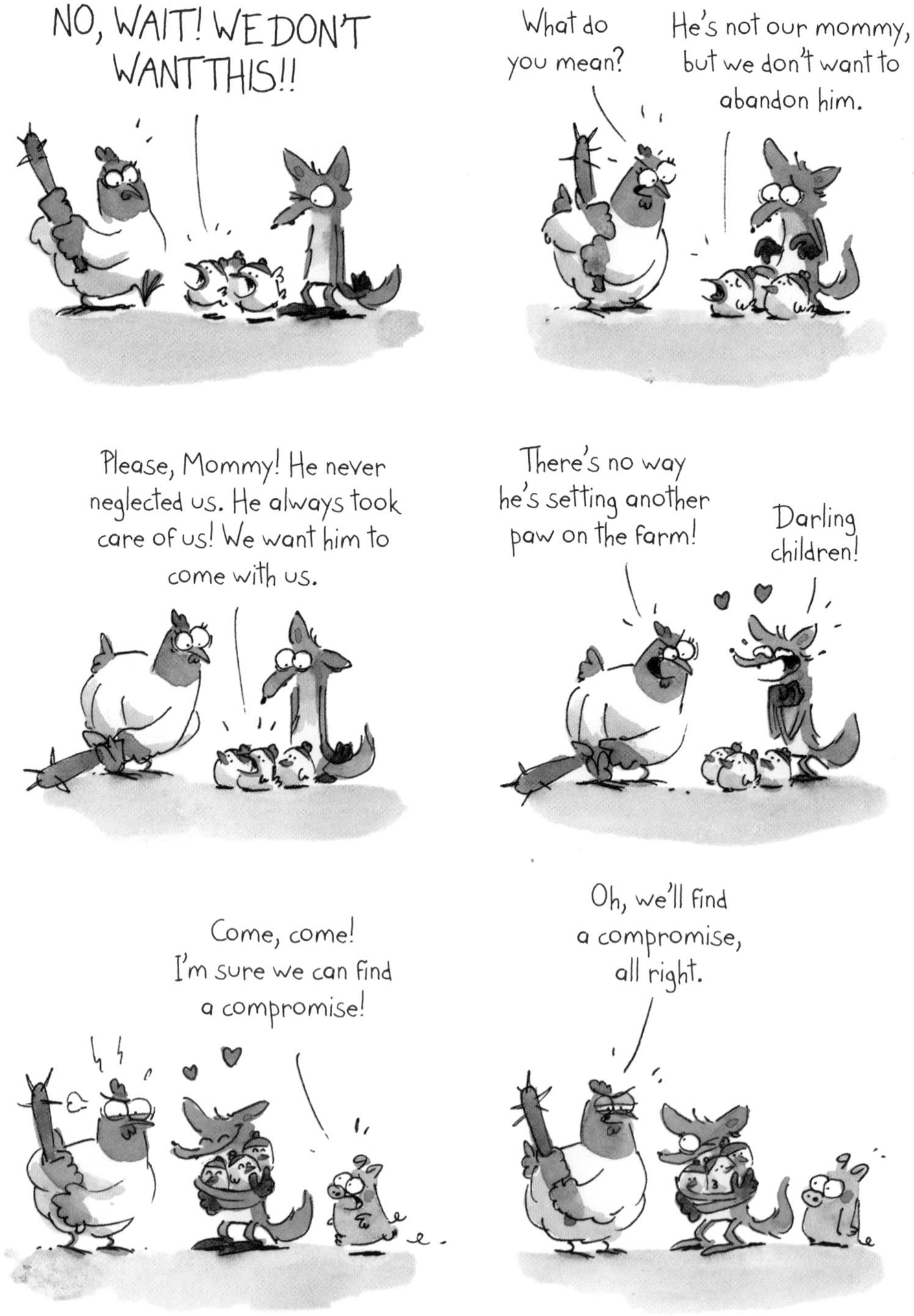
NO, WAIT! WE DON'T WANT THIS!!
What do you mean?
He's not our mommy, but we don't want to abandon him.
Please, Mommy! He never neglected us. He always took care of us! We want him to come with us.
There's no way he's setting another paw on the farm!
Darling children!
Come, come! I'm sure we can find a compromise!
Oh, we'll find a compromise, all right.

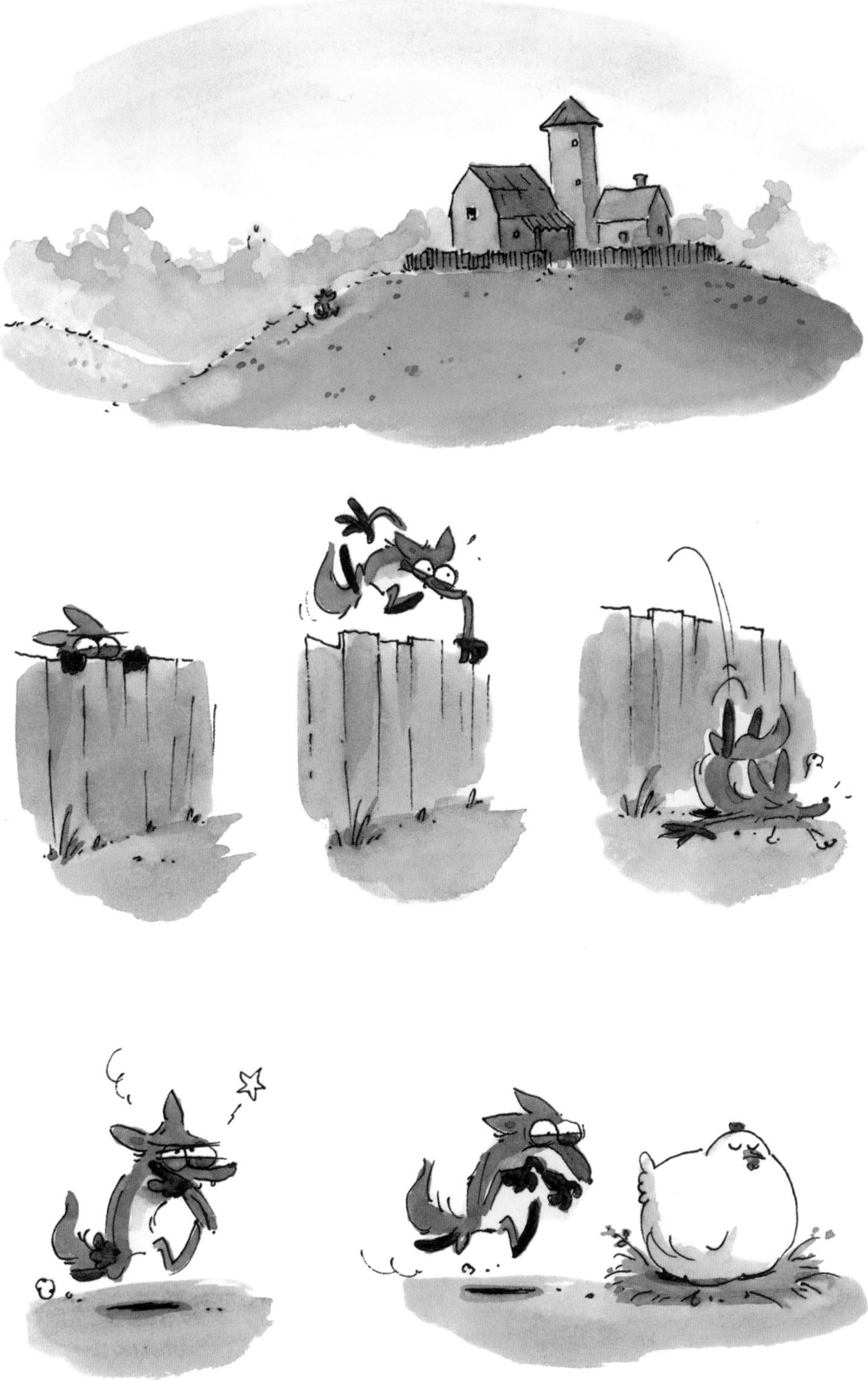

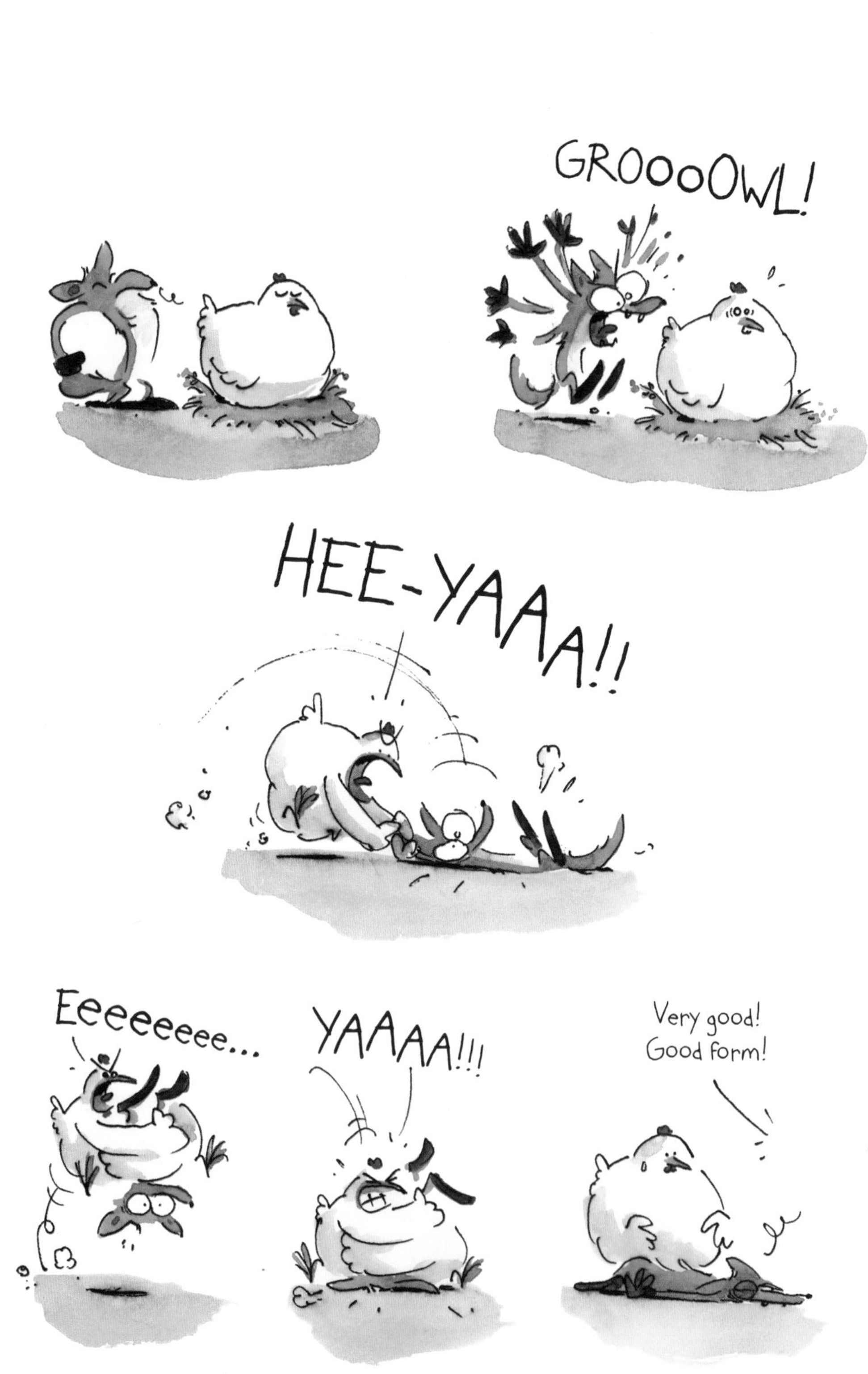
GROOOOWL!
HEE-YAAAA!!
Eeeeeeee...
YAAAA!!!
Very good! Good form!

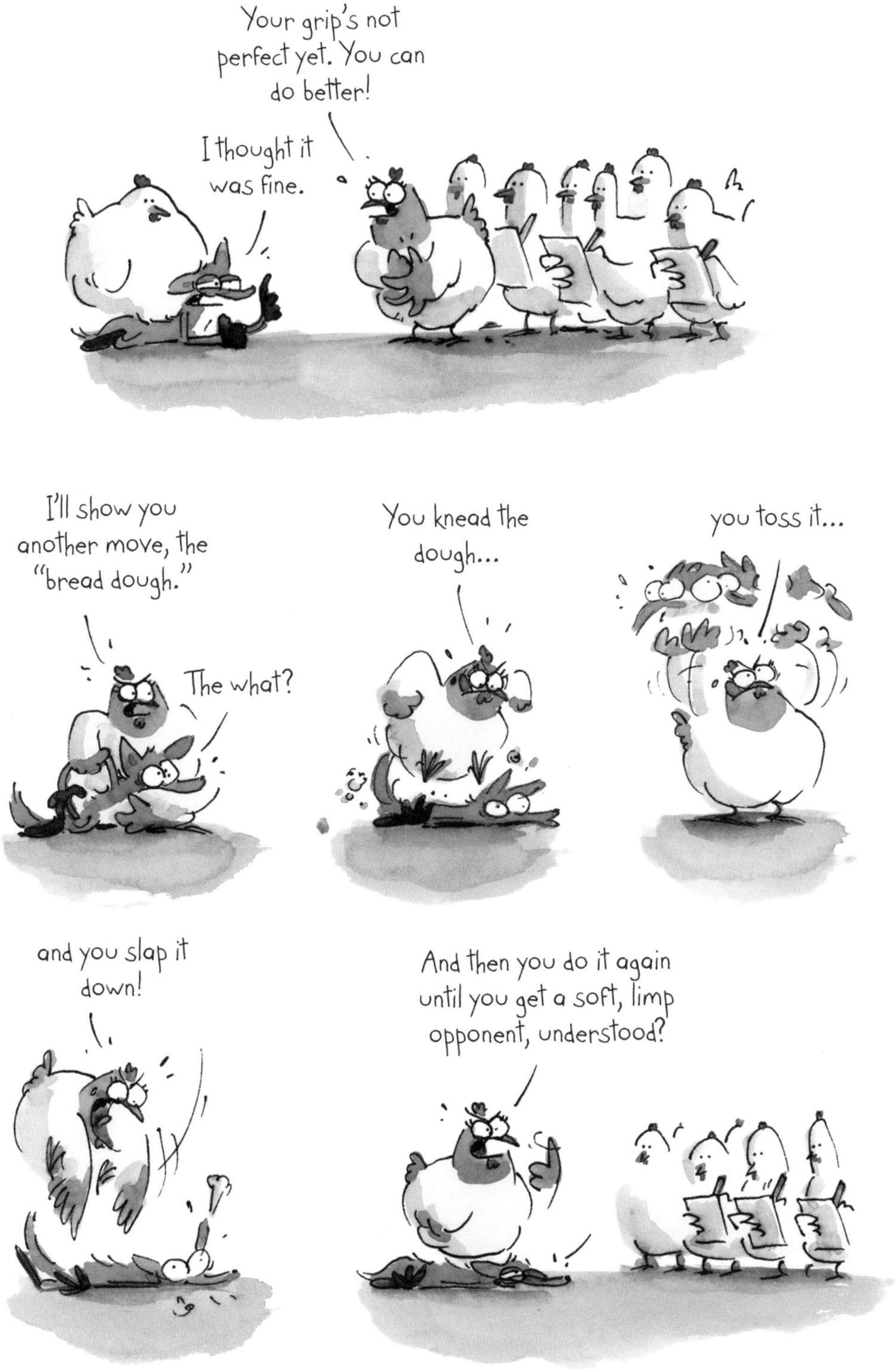

Your grip's not perfect yet. You can do better!
I thought it was fine.
I'll show you another move, the "bread dough."
The what?
You knead the dough...
you toss it...
and you slap it down!
And then you do it again until you get a soft, limp opponent, understood?

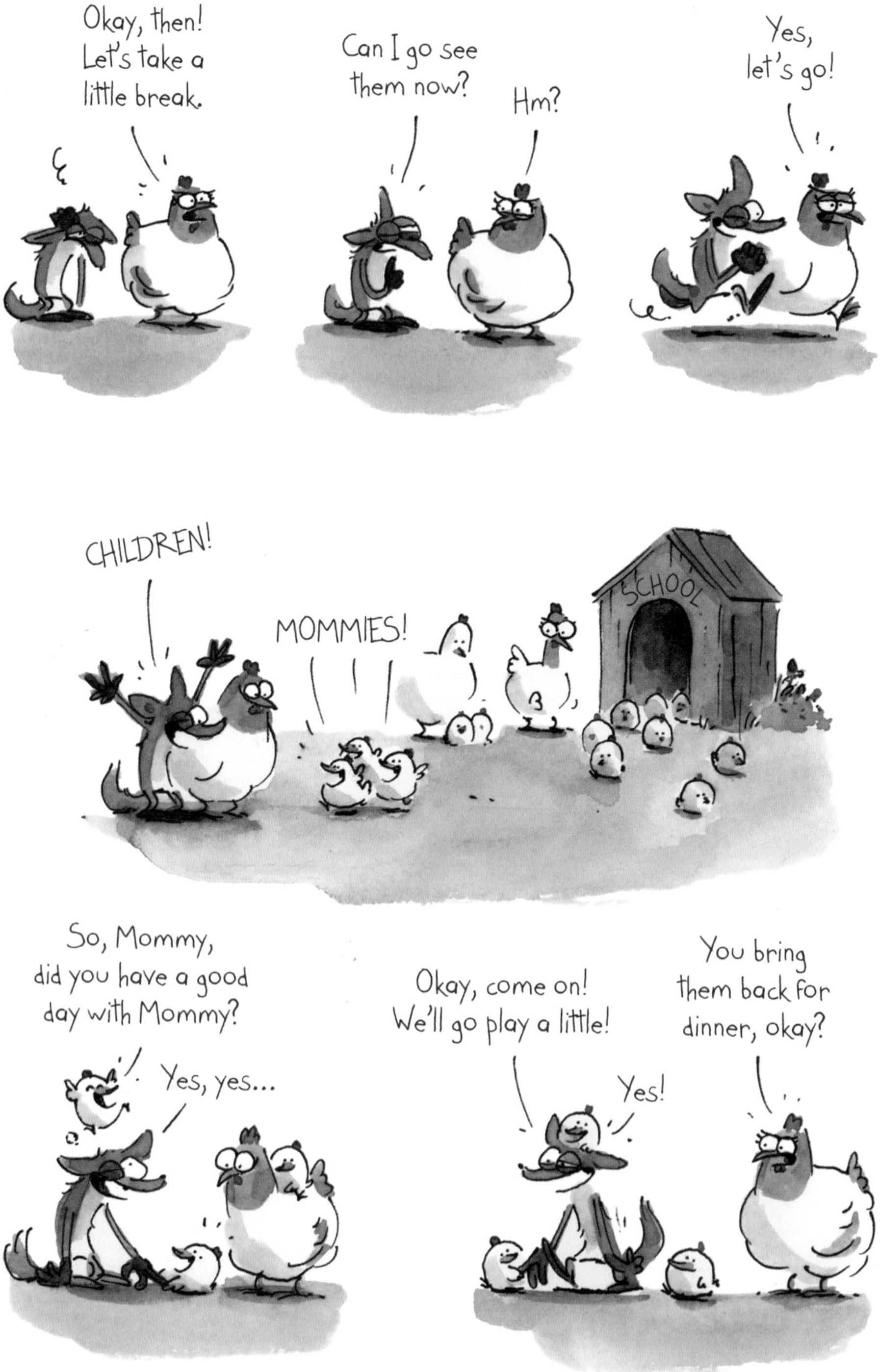
Okay, then! Let's take a little break.
Can I go see them now?
Hm?
Yes, let's go!
CHILDREN!
MOMMIES!
SCHOOL
So, Mommy, did you have a good day with Mommy?
Yes, yes...
Okay, come on! We'll go play a little!
Yes!
You bring them back for dinner, okay?

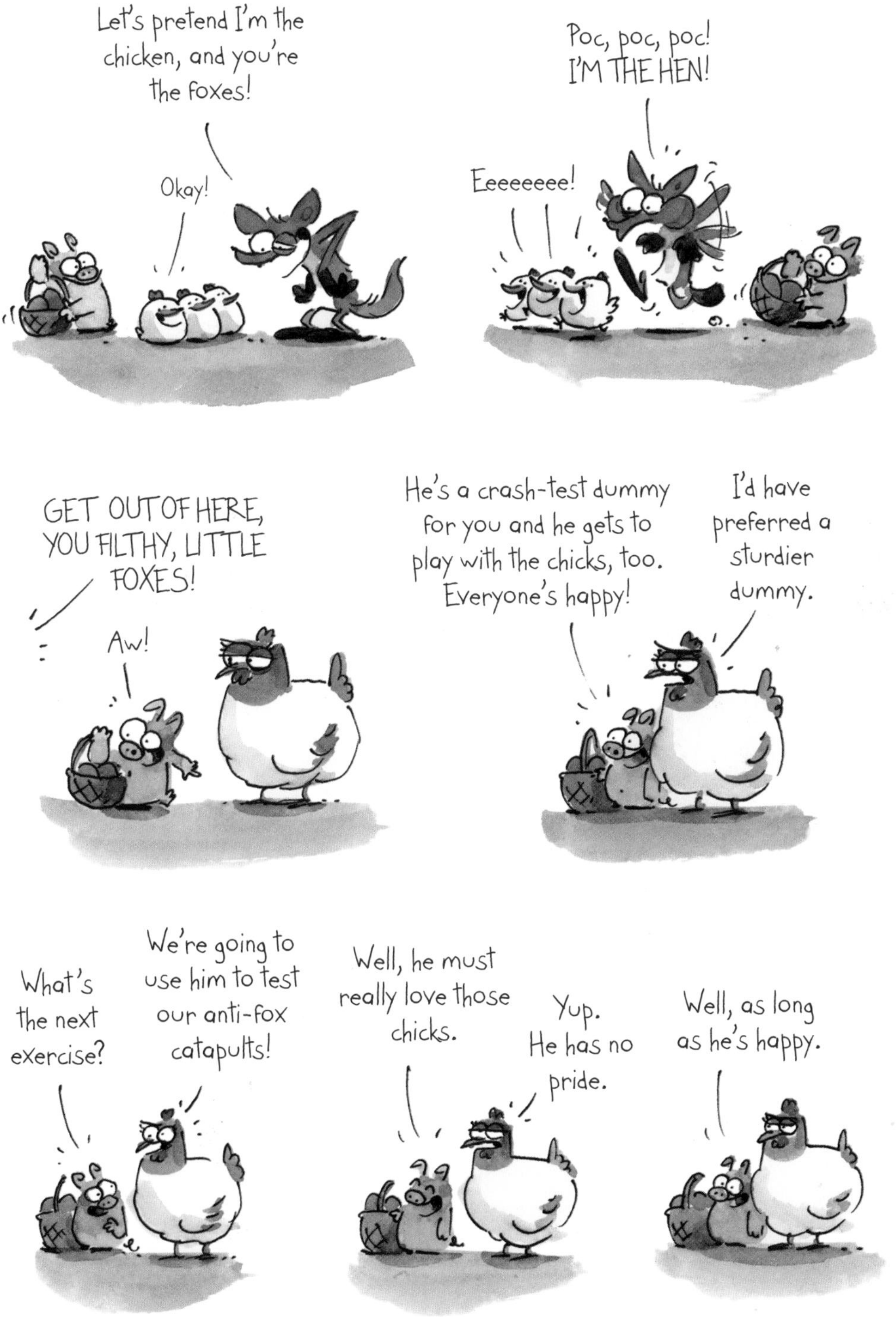
Let's pretend I'm the chicken, and you're the foxes!
Okay!
Poc, poc, poc! I'M THE HEN!
Eeeeeeee!
GET OUT OF HERE, YOU FILTHY, LITTLE FOXES!
Aw!
He's a crash-test dummy for you and he gets to play with the chicks, too. Everyone's happy!
I'd have preferred a sturdier dummy.
What's the next exercise?
We're going to use him to test our anti-fox catapults!
Well, he must really love those chicks.
Yup. He has no pride.
Well, as long as he's happy.

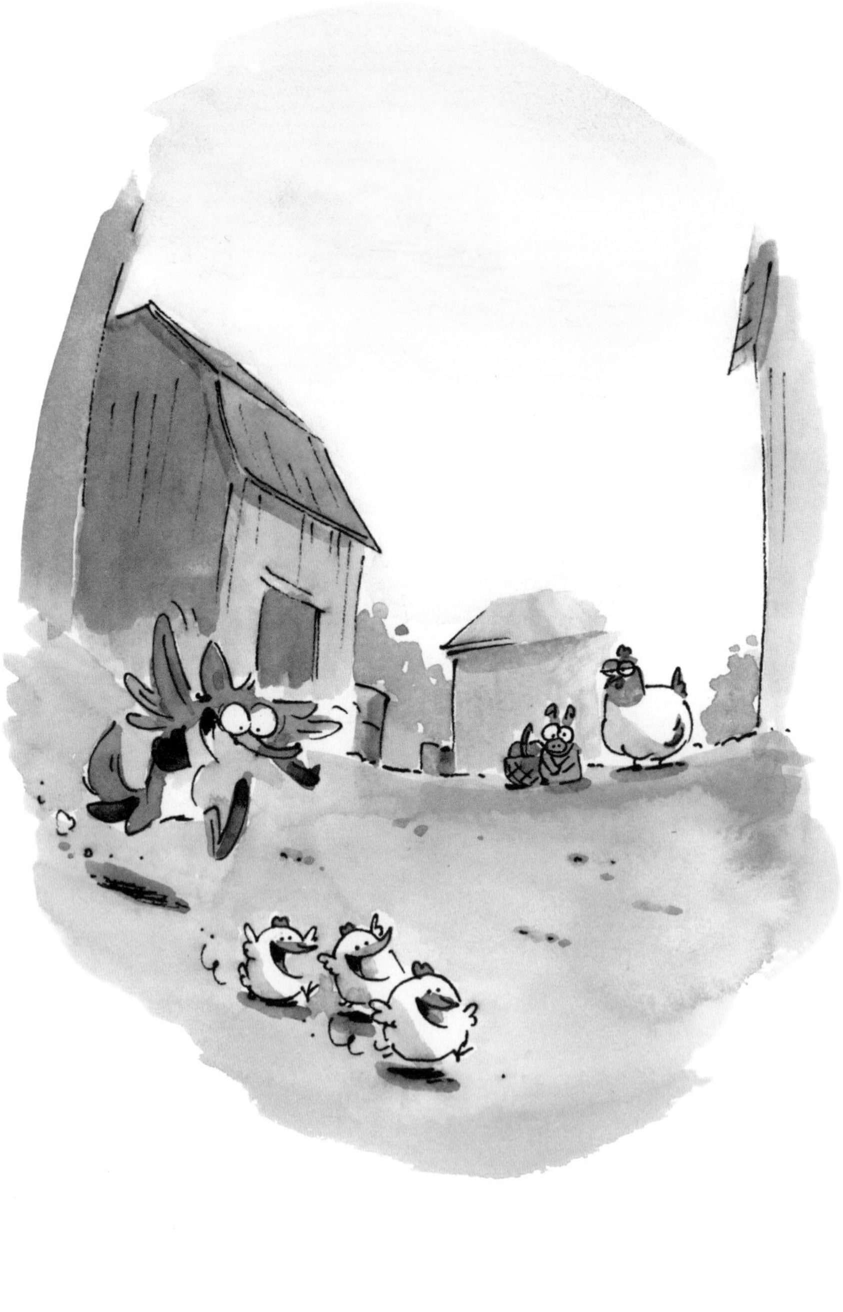

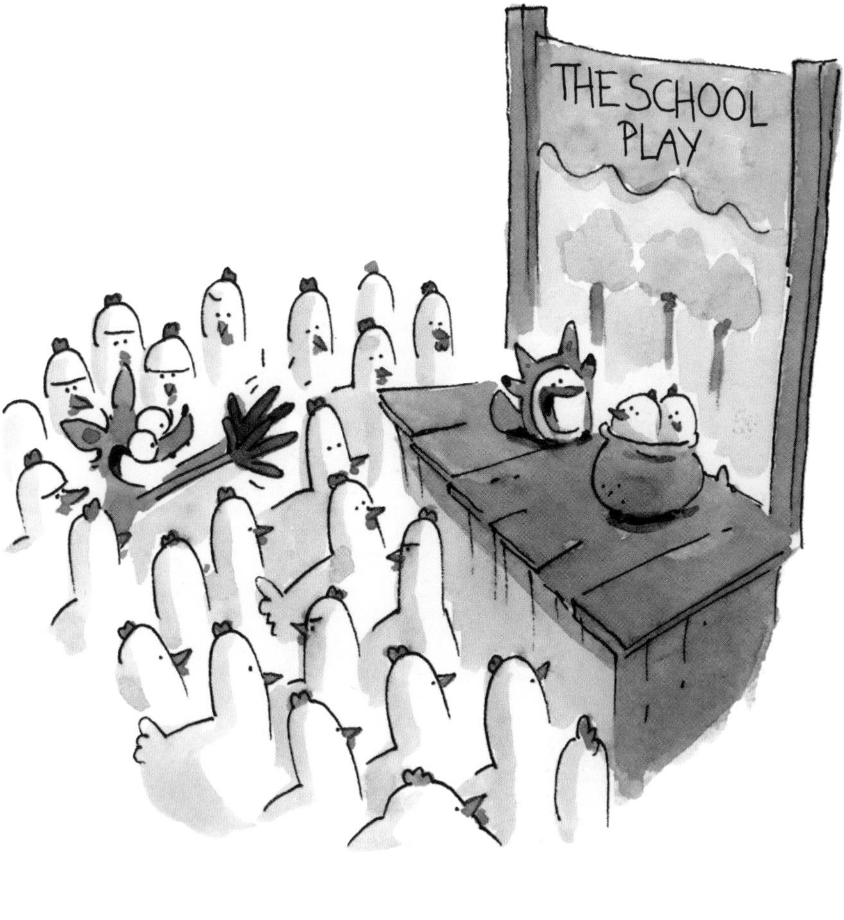
THE SCHOOL PLAY

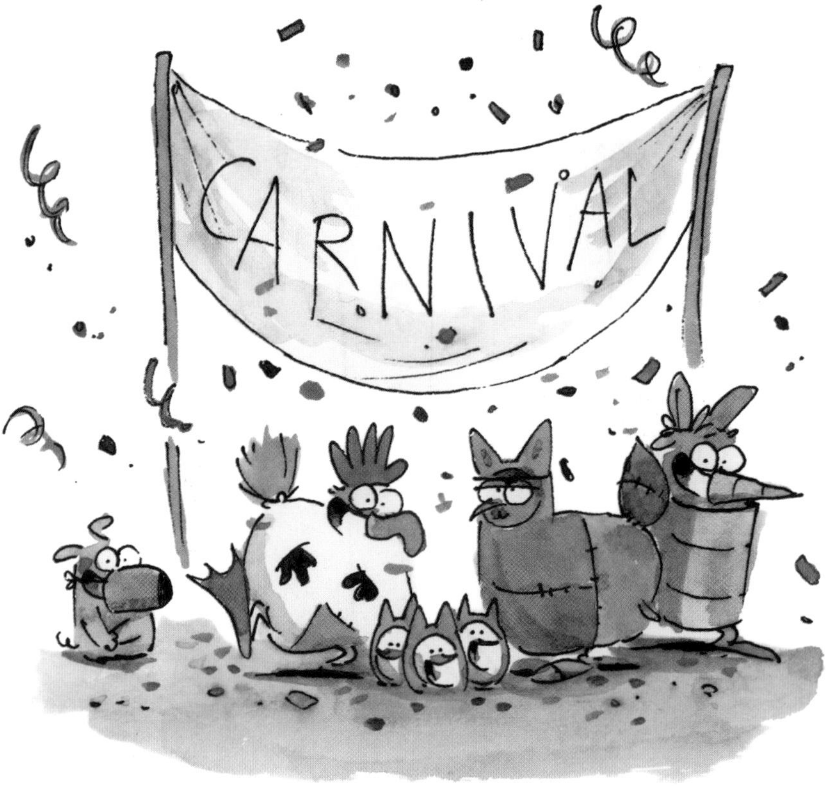
CARNIVAL

For support and invaluable help in my moments of doubt,
my thanks to Mai. Thanks to my family for their patience
and to Didier for his trust.